THE BODY
IN THE
GARDEN

THE BODY IN THE GARDEN

A LILY ADLER MYSTERY

Katharine Schellman

CROOKED
LANE

NEW YORK

Copyright © 2020 by Katharine Schellman Paljug

Published in the United States by Crooked Lane Books, an imprint of The Quick Brown Fox & Company LLC.

Crooked Lane Books and its logo are trademarks of The Quick Brown Fox & Company LLC.

Library of Congress Catalog-in-Publication data available upon request.

ISBN (hardcover): 978-1-64385-356-7
ISBN (ebook): 978-1-64385-357-4

Cover design by Nicole Lecht

Printed in the United States.

www.crookedlanebooks.com

Crooked Lane Books
34 West 27th St., 10th Floor
New York, NY 10001

First Edition: April 2020

10 9 8 7 6 5 4 3 2 1

*For everyone who had the
courage to start over.
And for Brian, who was there
every step of the way.*

CHAPTER 1

London, 1815

The empty windows and still curtains were a lie, of course.

Eyes watched from every nearby house as the carriage rolled to a stop in front of number thirteen, Half Moon Street—residents, some of them, ladies and gentlemen who merited those titles to varying degrees, or the servants who were expected to report what they saw.

The watchers narrowed their eyes as the carriage door opened and a woman descended.

The carriage was a shabby piece of equipment—obviously hired, with postboys grubby from hard riding—so they knew she did not have enough money to keep her own stables. But the woman herself was the opposite of shabby—about six and twenty, her coat and hat in the current fashion. And she had rented the house on Half Moon Street. If not the most expensive part of Mayfair, it was also not somewhere a woman frantically counting her pennies could live.

The postboys, if anyone had asked them, would have added that she tipped very well.

But when the curious watchers whispered their impressions to each other or shared their judgments over supper, there would be one thing that stood out: she was dressed in lilac and gray, the colors of mourning no longer in its first stages.

The woman held her hat against the April wind and eyed the house, keeping her expression carefully neutral. She had learned that lesson well in the last two years, and she had no intention of forgetting it now that she was back in London, where endless speculation could arise from the smallest smile or barest frown.

She was the sort of person who could weather speculation or the curiosity of the neighbors when they eventually came calling. But at the moment, all she wanted was a few more hours of solitude, time to wonder again why she had agreed to come here, to remind herself that she had nowhere else to go.

The woman took a deep breath, lifted her chin, and mounted the steps just as the butler opened the door. "I am Mrs. Lily Adler. I believe you are expecting me."

The butler bowed. "Mrs. Adler. Welcome home."

★　★　★

"The house came mostly furnished, ma'am, but a few things must still be purchased for the dining room. The drawing room is ready for visitors, though, and we've unpacked your books and linens and such."

Lily nodded, her hands clenched in her muff. She wasn't cold, but she didn't want the housekeeper to see the nervous way they were twisting. "I do not expect to receive many visitors, Mrs. Carstairs. I've not lived in London since before I married."

She knew she should say something else, something complimentary about the rooms or the furnishings, to the woman who would serve as both her housekeeper and cook. Mrs. Carstairs, light-skinned and plump, was the sort of woman whose motherly face and cozy manners invited friendliness, even from employers. But Lily was too exhausted to think of anything suitable, and though the house was beautifully done up, it did not feel like home. "Will you bring tea, please? I need to rest, but we will speak about management of the household later this evening."

"Yes, ma'am." The housekeeper hesitated. "I was terrible sorry to hear about your poor husband, Mrs. Adler. He was a good lad."

Lily had to take a deep breath before she could respond. It had been two years, but her chest still clenched almost too tightly to breathe every time she thought about Freddy. "Your sister was his nurse?"

"Nursed him and Master John—Sir John, I should say." Mrs. Carstairs shook her head. "Regular pair of scamps they was, pardon my saying so."

Lily's expression softened, though she could not bring herself to smile. "I think you could hardly help saying so, judging by the stories their mother has told me."

"Lord, yes. Near drove her distracted, and my sister too." The housekeeper cleared her throat. "I'll bring your tea up, Mrs. Adler, and speak with your maid to make sure all your things are brought in proper."

"Yes. Thank you."

The housekeeper closed the door, and Lily was left staring around the little sitting room, wondering what she was supposed to do with herself, alone, for an entire spring—and beyond, really, now that Freddy was gone and her carefully planned life had disappeared.

"First you will drink your tea." Lily laid off her hat and coat, glad there was no one around to hear. Talking to herself was an embarrassing habit she had developed in the last lonely year. "Then you will go see how Anna is getting along with unpacking. And then . . ."

Whatever other plans she might have made were interrupted by her new butler.

Mr. Carstairs was an imposingly large man, his brown skin so dark it looked almost black. Lily had not expected to have a butler in her new home, but Freddy's mother, Lady Adler, had insisted, and the husband and wife, together with her own maid Anna, were to make up her household—a small establishment, but respectable for a widow in her circumstances.

Carstairs had been, Lady Adler had confided, a boxer in his youth, which accounted for the size and muscle that made him unusual in his current profession. "But we do our best not to hold that against him," she added. "And he has a most quelling effect on visitors when he announces that one is not at home."

Now, as he handed Lily a crisp, white card, she wondered when exactly that quelling effect was to appear.

"I am not seeing anyone today, Carstairs," she said. The words came out more sternly than she intended, but she had made it clear when she arrived that she did not want visitors. Not yet.

"I did tell her ladyship that," Carstairs said gravely. "But she was most insistent."

"Her ladyship . . . ?" Lily trailed off as she looked at the name on the card.

"Shall I tell her ladyship again that you are not at home?" the butler asked.

"No!" Lily stood, her tiredness forgotten. "I shall go to her at once. And have Mrs. Carstairs bring tea to the drawing room, for two instead of one."

"Very good, ma'am."

Lily dashed downstairs without waiting for him to leave, not caring what her new staff might think. Bursting into the drawing room, she threw herself at her guest. "Serena!"

"Are you pleased to see me, then?" Lady Serena Walter asked, laughing as she returned the embrace.

"Always." Lily stepped back, trying to regain some sense of propriety as the housekeeper arrived to lay out the tea things. "Thank you, Mrs. Carstairs, I will ring if we need anything further. Will you sit, Serena? Or must you dash off at any moment?"

"Not any moment, no. Stand back and let me see you." Serena turned a protesting Lily in a circle. "You do look well, Lily. You might be the only woman who looks at all becoming in half-mourning. Lilac is such a difficult color."

"You were frivolous in school, Serena, and you are frivolous still," Lily said with mock-severity, her anxiety easing.

Serena only laughed. "Yes, and are you not relieved to find me unchanged?"

"More than I could ever say," Lily replied, meaning every word. Serena was clearly happy to see her; perhaps returning to London had been the right choice after all.

Lady Walter beamed at her friend. Between her sunny expression and her red hair, Serena always seemed to be beaming. She was the sort of woman usually described as a big, handsome girl, whom anyone could call clever without irony.

"But not," she had once said, "so beautiful or intelligent that I scare anyone off."

"Are you implying that I scare people?" Lily had demanded.

"Oh, not in looks. You will never be a beauty," Serena had replied with cheerful rudeness, and Lily, who knew she fell on the pretty side of average but no better, had not argued with her friend's assessment. "Though as tall as you are, you do look terribly regal when you come over all cool and disapproving. But no, your brains are what make you terrifying. You are dreadfully bright and never bother hiding it. We shall have to find you someone political to marry."

Lily's newfound cheer faded as she remembered Serena's almost prophetic words. Freddy had planned to become a member of Parliament, and Lily, always organized and methodical, had loved picturing the tidy path their lives would follow. Then he had fallen ill, and everything had changed.

"I cannot stay long," Serena was saying when Lily recalled herself to the present. "I am thrilled to see you, but—"

"But you must get back to the boys?" Glad to be distracted from her grim thoughts, Lily set about pouring the tea. "Do you still take yours with only milk?"

"You never forget anything, do you?" Serena asked as she took the cup Lily held out to her. "And yes, the boys returned home today after three weeks with their grandmama in Hampshire. It was mercifully peaceful without them underfoot!"

"Yes, I am sure you did not miss them at all," Lily said, knowing not to believe her friend's glib words. Serena might affect fashionable boredom with motherhood in public, but there was nothing she treasured more. And since she had lost two children—one son still-born, a daughter dead in infancy from a sudden fever—the two sons Serena had still living were the center of her world.

"Perhaps I missed them a little," Serena admitted with a smile.

"Well, before you dash home to them, you must first tell me how you knew I was in town. I've not yet sent around cards."

"Oh, I am quite devious. That little dresser of yours—Anna, was it? Such a nice girl—she is cousin to Jeremy, our second footman. She told him that you would arrive today, and he told my dresser, who told me."

"How impressive. Shall I soon hear of you taking up a position in the constabulary?"

"Lord, it would almost be worth it for the fits it would give Lord Walter's mother. The old bag kept the boys a week longer than expected. I was livid."

"Though I imagine Lord Walter was delighted to have you to himself?"

Serena laughed, blushing prettily. Her husband was several years her senior and doted on his charming young wife. "And that reminds me of one of my reasons for calling."

"More reason than just the joy of seeing me?" Lily teased. "Do tell."

Serena pulled a card from her muff. "The first is to deliver this and extract your *promise* that you will attend in spite of the short notice."

It was an invitation for a ball that very night. Lily stared at the elegant engraving, then shook her head. "I've not yet put off black gloves . . ."

"But you are out of full mourning. No one will disapprove, Lily, so long as you do not dance." Serena looked pleadingly at her friend. "Do say you will come? You cannot miss my first ball of the season."

Lily's hands clenched in her lap. She and Freddy had met in the middle of a cotillion when she was nineteen. They had both been dancing with other partners, but Freddy spent the rest of the set staring at her. Always impossibly romantic, he later said that was the moment he had fallen in love with her.

But Freddy was gone now, and as empty as life felt at the moment, she still had to find something to do with it—even if, for now, that something was only a ball. "Very well, Lady Walter, you have my promise. I will even arrive unfashionably early, so you shan't wonder if I have broken my word."

"Nonsense. You shall dine with us, *en famille*, and see how the boys have grown. I think you will scarcely recognize them."

"You are kind to offer—"

"It is pure self-preservation. Lord Walter's horrid cousin Bernard is visiting. If I have to listen to him explain the art of tying a cravat again, I may end up in Newgate for murder."

"Serena, you have often said that a well-tied cravat is the hall-mark of a gentleman."

"Yes, but Bernard's is not well tied, so it is dreadful to hear him go on about it." Serena's quip made Lily smile, but at the same time she felt a familiar prickle in her eyes. It was such a normal moment, and there had been so few of those in the last two years that she wasn't sure whether she wanted to laugh or cry. She tried to blink away the tears quickly, but Serena noticed, and her voice grew softer. "You came to London to get back to living your life. How can you do that if you stay cooped up and alone?"

"Yes, of course." Lily took a brisk breath, trying to pull herself together. "You are kind to be so patient with my moodiness."

"None of that." Serena laid a hand on Lily's arm. "We both know it is not moodiness. I've never known anyone so much in love as you and Freddy."

"You and Lord Walter—" Lily began.

"Are very fond of each other and rub along well together," Serena interrupted gently. "That is not the same thing. I know you miss him dreadfully, and you should. But I also know you, Lily, and you cannot shut yourself away forever."

"I know." Lily squeezed her friend's hand. "I am glad you came to see me, Serena."

"Of course you are. I'm delightful."

At that, Lily couldn't help smiling. "All right then, that was one. What is your other mysterious reason for stopping by?"

"We may have to wait . . ." Serena trailed off, her head cocked to the side. "Or perhaps not!" There were voices in the hall. "I think my surprise has just arrived."

Carstairs opened the door and bowed. He still looked unruffled, but Lily could hear an edge of uncertainty as he said, "There is a Captain Hartley to see you, madam. He says her ladyship instructed him to come by. Shall I say you are not at home?"

"Oh!" Lily stood, flustered. "No, show him in."

She barely had time to gather her thoughts before Captain John Hartley—Jack, she always thought of him, though of course she had never called him that herself—was bowing in the doorway. "Lady Walter." His eyes settled on Lily. "Mrs. Adler."

"Captain, what . . ." Lily turned to Serena and, not caring if it was rude, demanded, "You sly thing, however did you manage this?"

"I told you I am devious. Is it a nice surprise?"

"Yes." Lily held out her hands. "It is so good to see you, Captain. Had I known you were in London, I'd have written."

"It is good to see you as well, Mrs. Adler," Captain Hartley said. He took her hands, hesitated a moment, then gave them a quick squeeze before letting go. "And no matter, as Lady Walter has arranged things most efficiently." Serena laughed, delighted with the praise. "In any case, it would have been nearly impossible for a letter to reach me. I've only just returned to town."

"I guessed as much," Lily said. "How is your sister, Captain Hartley?"

"Good Lord." He stared at her. "Are you a mind reader, Mrs. Adler?"

Lily couldn't quite conceal the amused smile that lifted the corners of her eyes, though she tried not to look smug at his astonishment. "Nothing so dramatic."

"Then how the devil—" Jack broke off and grinned. "You know, I once told Freddy I thought you were rather a clever woman.

He laughed at me and said I only knew the half of it. So go ahead, Mrs. Adler. Tell me what gave it away."

Lily raised her brows, a smile pulling at the corners of her lips. "I keep track of the navy lists, you know, to keep an eye on you. We are engaged in France once more, so a ship like yours should be in the Channel or headed towards the Continent. Yet here you are in London, which means your frigate must be ashore. Repairs, I assume? In any case, your travel cannot have been military in nature. That leads one to suspect a family visit. Freddy mentioned that you have visited your relatives in the East Indies before, but that would have been far too long a voyage for wartime leave. Had you been in Hertfordshire with your parents, you would have called on the Adlers, which I know you did not since I have just come from them. From the lilt in your speech, I would say you have been in the north. And your sister, as I remember, lives with her husband and children in Derbyshire."

"Extraordinary." Jack shook his head admiringly. "I see Freddy was not exaggerating."

"She is rather marvelous, isn't she?" Serena said as she gathered up her furs. "And with that, I must show myself out. I shall see you both at seven o'clock?" With a final bright smile, she swept out of the room, leaving Jack looking bemused and Lily shaking her head. Serena loved a dramatic exit.

There was an awkward pause before Lily said, "I was not aware that you and Lady Walter were acquainted."

Jack grinned, an endearingly lopsided expression. "Just met her yesterday. Your friend cornered me on Bond Street, though how she found me is anyone's guess. Claimed an introduction and informed me that I would be attending her ball tonight. Refusal was clearly not an option."

"It never is. And I am glad of it." Lily sat, gesturing for him to do the same.

He did so hesitantly. "I was not sure you would be. Not after . . ."

"Captain, you were at sea when Freddy died. There was no possible way for you to be at the funeral." Lily's voice caught as she spoke, but she meant every word. Jack and Freddy had grown up together, inseparable until the day Jack left for the navy. And even then, they had stayed as close as brothers. She remembered dancing with him on her wedding day, the way he had teased her as comfortably as if they had grown up together too. That, she thought, was what happened when you loved someone like Freddy—you couldn't help caring for the people he loved as well.

"Terrible all the same, missing Freddy's final service."

"Wars have never been known for their convenience."

"No."

For a moment they were both quiet, the silence heavy but not awkward. Lily stared at the tea service, now grown cold. Nothing had seemed real the day Freddy was buried, and her eyes had been dry as she watched the gravediggers lower his coffin into the ground. Her father had complimented her on her composure. It had taken all her willpower not to slap him.

At length Jack cleared his throat. "I was surprised to hear you had come to London. What do you plan to do with yourself here?"

"I am not planning to look for a husband, if that is what you are wondering." Lily instantly regretted her sharp response, as Jack flushed. "Forgive me, Captain. The truth is . . . I do not know. The Adlers have been very kind. But without Freddy, there was nothing left for me in Hertfordshire. So I came to London, and now all I feel is . . ." She couldn't bring herself to say *lost*, but she felt it. "Freddy and I had plans, you know. What we wanted from our lives, what we would accomplish. Without him . . ." She met Jack's eyes, her expression filled as much with anger as with sorrow. "Tell me, Captain, what is a woman in my position supposed to do?"

"Marry again." It was not a suggestion but a statement of fact, accompanied by a sympathetic grimace. Clearly he did not like the thought of Lily marrying so soon after Freddy's death any more than she did.

"As every concerned busybody I have met in the past year has made very clear. But I've no wish to marry." She shrugged as well.

"So here I am, for a change of scenery at least, with no more idea what I am good for than I had in Hertfordshire. But I must find something." She looked away, her mouth twisting with cynical humor so she would not cry. "I had hoped for more time before wading into the murky waters of London society, but I suppose Serena's ball is as good a place as any to start."

"Which means I should take my leave, so I may return in a few short hours to escort you to dinner." Jack stood, and Lily was afraid she had said too much. But he took one of her hands. "You will find your way without him, Mrs. Adler. I've not had the chance to know you as well as I would like, but I knew Freddy. And he would never have fallen in love with a woman who needed him for her life to mean something."

Lily remained in the parlor after he left, staring around the house that was not her home, hoping very much that he was right.

Then her practical side reasserted itself, and she went upstairs to decide which of her gowns was least likely to get a scolding from Serena. "It is only a ball," she told herself sternly. "Nothing bad will happen."

CHAPTER 2

Secrets. Lily narrowed her eyes as she looked around the crowded ballroom. She could practically feel them in the air: the secrets, the gossip, and the scandal.

They were in the murmur of voices as couples floated across the dance floor, in the eyes of guests who looked each other up and down and turned to whisper to their neighbors. It was a glittering, beautiful, brittle world, one that took a certain amount of guile to navigate.

Lily took a deep breath. She'd had that skill once, and she had enjoyed it. Surely it was still there, ready to be used once more.

"A marvelous evening, is it not?" Serena materialized at Lily's side with startling ease, bearing two glasses of wine.

"A dreadful crush." Lily took one of the glasses and gulped a mouthful to steady her nerves. "You should be pleased."

"Baffling," a voice laughed behind them. "Why do ladies love a party where one cannot move without bumping into five other people?"

Knowing Jack was there made some of the tension in Lily's shoulders relax, and she smiled as she answered. "Because otherwise men like you would call it dull and abandon us for some scandalous gaming house."

"I have absolutely no acquaintance with the gaming houses in London," Jack said. He looked so affronted that Lily was about to apologize when he grinned and added, "Not been in town enough, you know."

Serena shook her head. "So here you remain, not doing your duty and dancing, I notice."

"On the contrary, Lady Walter." He bowed. "Will you honor me with a dance?"

"Captain Hartley, you are flirting." Serena tried to look severe. "You ought to know Mrs. Adler cannot abide flirts."

"But I was not flirting with Mrs. Adler," Jack protested. "Is that a refusal?"

"Go on." Lily took Serena's glass and handed it to a passing servant. "The two of you will make a handsome pair, and you know you shall enjoy that."

"I shall, shan't I?" Serena beamed. "Do try to stay out of trouble while I am gone, dear."

Lily murmured something that sounded like agreement as Serena swept away. Though she was not a shy person, there was something intimidating about the Walters' ball, and Lily felt more inclined to hug the walls than she ever had before in her life. If she watched the dancers too long, all she could think about was the last time she had been one of them, winding her way through a country dance with Freddy. The memory was so clear it made her catch her breath, and she closed her eyes against the pain until a familiar voice spoke at her elbow.

"Mrs. Adler." She opened her eyes to find Lord Walter watching her, his expression gentle as he bowed. "How goes your evening thus far?"

Lily raised her brows. "What can I say but 'splendidly' when my host is the one asking?"

"You could say 'a touch overwhelming, as these affairs tend to be, especially after several years' absence,'" the viscount said. Lily, caught off guard, felt her lips part in a surprised *oh*. "I told Lady Walter not to browbeat you into coming, but she has always had a mind of her own." Lord Walter's eyes rested on his wife, currently making her way down the dance floor, and he smiled fondly. "I saw you alone and thought I might help you become reacquainted with a few of the other guests. If you would like?"

Lily was touched. Lord Walter, as popular as his wife, with handsome wings of gray against his dark hair, had always been kind to her. "Whom do you suggest?" she asked.

"I believe there are several of your former schoolfellows here tonight," he said, looking around. "I think Lady Walter said you have kept in touch with some of them? Mrs. Harlowe and her husband are just across the room."

Lily turned to follow his glance, and her expression softened at the sight of the familiar face. Margaret Harlowe had been a dear friend since they were fifteen. The daughter of a respectable country gentleman, the great-niece of an earl, and expected to marry well, she had fallen in love with a sweet, round, red-faced peer's secretary. Margaret had abandoned her social aspirations to marry the man she loved, a choice not many women would have made. Her husband, Andrew, was active in furthering his patron's parliamentary concerns and likely to one day stand for a seat of his own. Lily had not seen either of them since the funeral, but Margaret had been a loyal correspondent and one of the voices urging Lily's return to London.

The Harlowes were speaking with Isobel Harper, another former pupil of Miss Tattersy's Seminary for Young Ladies. A few years ago, Lily would have been only too happy to avoid conversation with Miss Harper. Now, though, any familiar face was a welcome sight, and she gratefully took the arm Lord Walter held out to her. "I should love to join them." She glanced sideways at her host as they made their way across the floor. "It is good of you to accompany me, though I know you should be attending to your guests."

"You are my guest as well, Mrs. Adler." His smile was gentle. "And I intend to see you enjoying yourself at least a little before I must excuse myself. Though I would much prefer to stay. The conversation that awaits me does not promise to be the most stimulating of the night."

"The sacrifices we demand of our politicians," Lily said solemnly. "And we do not even bother to pay them for their trouble."

"A grievous oversight," Lord Walter agreed, mouth twitching with laughter. "Ah, here we are. Ladies, Harlowe, how do you do?"

"Lily!" Margaret Harlowe seized her friend's hands. "What on earth are you doing here?"

Mr. Harlowe's greetings were less effusive than his wife's, but equally warm. Even Miss Harper, whom Lily remembered as being cold and aloof, seemed sincere as she offered her own welcome. Settling in to talk with them—a conversation less intimate than the one she had shared with Serena earlier that day—Lily relaxed for the first time that night.

Lord Walter stayed with them a few minutes before offering his apologies. "Parliamentary duties call. My secretary insists that I use the evening to speak with one or two other members. If you will excuse me?"

He had only been gone a few moments when Serena returned, Jack still with her. "There you are, Lily! I wondered where you had got to in this crush. Margaret, Mr. Harlowe, so delighted you could be here. Isobel, I do love that shade of blue on you. Was that my husband I saw leaving just now? Did he see me coming and make a hasty retreat?" She laughed at her own joke. "Your friend acquits himself admirably on the dance floor, Lily, once he deigns to do so." Serena glanced at Jack and added in a loud whisper, "Though I was right, he is a shocking flirt. We must be careful introducing him."

"You invited him," Lily said dryly. Serena loved being flirted with. "Any responsibility for his shocking behavior belongs to you."

"I say, that is hardly kind," Jack protested. "Talking about a fellow when he is standing right here. That is what I call shocking."

"As is the fact that Lady Walter has neglected introductions," Margaret said with good humor. "Perhaps Lily will introduce us to her handsome friend?"

Lily saw Jack grin at the compliment and shook her head as she performed introductions, while Serena protested that she had been about to do that very thing.

Before much else could be said, a dandily dressed young man sauntered up, his cravat tied with elegant complexity and his hair mussed with stylish precision. He was dreadfully handsome, and Lily could tell with a single glance that he was fully aware of that fact. But she didn't recognize him until he planted a kiss on Miss Harper's cheek and greeted her with a careless, "Hello, sister." Reggie Harper, she remembered, was Isobel Harper's older brother. Lily thought she caught a scowl on Miss Harper's face and was sure for a moment that she was about to pull away. But a moment later she was smiling again, so quickly that Lily wondered if she had imagined the other expression. Reggie Harper bowed to Serena. "Lady Walter. A most splendid soiree you have thrown for us this evening."

"I am delighted that you think so, Mr. Harper," Serena said. "I should love to stay and talk, but I must steal Lily and Captain Hartley away for a moment. If you will excuse us?"

Lily was only too glad to let Serena lead her away. She did not like the way Mr. Harper was eyeing her up and down, or the tone of his voice as he asked, "Who was that woman with Lady Walter?" when she was not quite out of earshot.

"Lord, how warm it is in here!" Serena fanned herself briskly once they were away from the other group. "I need a sip of your wine, Lily. Now, where did Mrs. Meredith swan off to? I wanted to introduce you . . ."

"There was a real reason you pulled me away?" Lily raised a brow as she handed over her glass. "And here I thought you simply wished to avoid the Harpers. I was surprised to see you had invited them."

"Their uncle does so much work with the War Office that it would be impolitic not to," Serena said. "Miss Harper still keeps house for him, you know. He is here somewhere . . . I must remind Lord Walter to speak with him before the night is over."

"Their uncle is General Harper," Lily added, seeing Jack's confused expression. "Of whom I am sure you have heard."

"General Alfred Harper?" Jack looked impressed. "Of course I've heard of him. The man's a dashed hero."

"Well, the uncle may be heroic, but I have never particularly cared for the company of his niece or nephew," Lily said, fatigue making her words come out more sharply than she intended. She had almost forgotten how exhausting it was to be surrounded by so many strangers.

"Oh, Mr. Harper is harmless, for all his high opinion of himself," Serena said. "I will grant that Isobel spent too much time bragging about her dowry when we were in school, but she always was embarrassed that her mother's family was in trade, even if her father was a gentleman. In any case, you'll find her much improved ever since her . . ." Serena dropped her voice. "Misfortunes. Jilted," she added in a whisper to Jack. "Terrible scandal. Only a month before the wedding."

"And her family did not sue for breach of contract?" Jack asked.

"It turned out that she did not have any dowry at all," Lily said. "Suing would have reflected badly on them."

"Now, now, Mrs. Adler, you mustn't become one of those London gossips," Jack said.

"I was answering your question!" Lily frowned indignantly before she realized he was teasing. "Oh, go be useful and dance with one of Lady Walter's guests. Irritating man."

"As you command. Perhaps I shall even manage to dance with two guests. I have a strong sense of duty toward my hostess, you know." Jack grinned as he bowed to Serena, who sighed happily as Jack disappeared into the crush.

"How gallant navy men are," Serena observed. "Well, as Mrs. Meredith has disappeared, whom shall I introduce to you?" Lily, overheated and tired, did not want to make conversation with strangers. She was about to tell Serena so when her friend continued blithely on. "Oh, but I think this set is about to end, which means I can finally catch a moment of Miss Oswald's time. If you do not mind waiting while I spend a few minutes being political?"

Lily followed the direction of Serena's lifted chin and saw a young woman in the middle of the dance floor. In the sea of mostly pale

English faces, her dark skin and curly brown hair stood out. It was not unheard of, of course, for children of mixed heritage to make their way into the upper classes, but most of them were unable to enter London society unless they were like Jack, who looked as much like his English father as he did his Indian mother. "Who is she?"

"Miss Ofelia Oswald." Lady Walter dropped her voice confidentially. "No one knows much about her, except that she has no mother to speak of, and her father was a Devonshire Oswald. He went into trade in the West Indies—" She paused. "Where young Miss Oswald is *obviously* from."

"Do you know her well?" Lily watched Miss Oswald weave through the dance.

"Goodness, no. One can only imagine her to be quite vulgar. But Walter knows her father a little. She is staying the season with that dragon Mrs. Haverweight, who is some sort of aunt." Serena eyed the dancing couples with a hostess's critical eye. "Do you see the boy she is dancing with? That is Sir Edward Carroway, the new baronet. Who would expect to see a girl like that, whom no one in London ever heard of before three months ago, dancing with a baronet? But it seems she is fabulously wealthy. She goes absolutely everywhere, and of course no one wants to snub an Oswald. Which," Serena added, "is why Walter charged me to be sure to speak with her this evening. You never know when a connection might prove fruitful, and she has an uncle who is quite political."

As soon as the dance ended, Serena detached Miss Oswald from her bevy of admirers. The girl looked gratified to have been singled out by her hostess as Serena led her away from the dance floor, asking pleasantly about her evening and the interesting political uncle until they returned to where Lily was waiting. "Lily, this is Miss Oswald, who has taken London by storm. Miss Oswald, let me make you known to my dearest friend, Mrs. Adler."

"How do you do, Mrs. Adler?" Miss Oswald's curtsy was as elegant as her dancing. Lily thought her quite beautiful. Her brown hair, which needed no help to achieve the tight curls of current fashion, framed a face with a pert chin and wide mouth.

"Miss Oswald." Lily inclined her head politely. She was not so many years older than the girl, and those hopeful eyes had the look of someone on the hunt for a friend. "Lady Walter tells me you are new to London. I am recently arrived myself, though a journey from Hertfordshire is not nearly as exciting as one from the West Indies."

The girl smiled wryly. "The journey was quite an undertaking, to be sure, but the city itself does not feel so new as you might imagine. I have tried to convince Londoners that the West Indies are perfectly civilized, but they don't seem to believe me."

"You'll not find me in need of convincing," Lily said as Serena laughed. "In fact, you must tell me all about the Indies sometime, Miss Oswald. If it would not make you too homesick, of course. I imagine you must miss your family dreadfully."

"I do miss my father. But it is hard to be homesick in such an interesting place, and everyone has been so welcoming." Her smile took in Serena and the entire ballroom, but it looked a little forced. Lily could imagine that London, while welcoming her beautiful face and her fortune, had not treated her with absolute kindness. "I was delighted, Lady Walter, to receive your invitation for tonight."

After a few more pleasantries—and the sought-after confirmation that yes, her political uncle would be arriving in London soon—Miss Oswald excused herself, leaving behind her aunt's direction and a polite promise to talk about life in the West Indies with Lily "whenever Mrs. Adler might wish." When the girl was out of sight, Serena turned raised brows on her friend. "What did you think of her?"

"I thought her charming. Really, Serena, I cannot see why you would call her vulgar."

Serena shrugged, unabashed. "Well, one hears things. And I do think her manner is a little too eager for real style. But what can one expect of a girl raised in tropical latitudes?"

Lily raised her brows. "Were we any better when we were young?"

Lady Walter smiled as she laced her arm through her friend's. "You were. Lord, how I envied those icy nerves of yours when we were—oh, Lady Chartres! A moment, if you will. Excuse me, Lily, I shall be back as soon as I can but might not escape for some time. Try to mingle at least a little while I am gone?" Patting Lily's hand, Serena unlooped her arm and went to join a formidably gowned matron with a bevy of daughters in tow.

Lily hovered around the edge of the dance floor for a few minutes, uncomfortably aware of the curious glances directed her way. None of her school friends were in sight, and Jack was leading a pretty girl to the dance floor. Besides which, her feet hurt, her head was pounding from the noise and the late hour, and the air was stifling in the ballroom. Lily sighed and, giving up on following Serena's instructions, found a door and slipped outside.

CHAPTER 3

One benefit to being a widow, Lily reflected with bitter gratitude, was the liberty of movement. As Miss Pierce she had been carefully chaperoned, but as Mrs. Adler she was her own mistress. As long as she did nothing too scandalous, society would allow her to pursue her own course.

At that moment, all she wanted was a few minutes to be quiet and alone.

The doors from the ballroom opened onto a wide terrace. There were other guests outside, but they were far enough away that Lily could relax against the balustrade and stare into the gardens, her mind wandering.

It took her several minutes to realize what she was seeing.

Two people were standing at the edge of the garden. One was a man, the other a woman in a pale dress, but their faces were in shadow. Lily was too far away to hear voices—or perhaps they were speaking too quietly—but she could guess from the tense lines of their bodies that they were having a heated argument.

She leaned forward, unable to help herself. Judging by the well-placed slap that the woman below suddenly delivered to the man's face, the scene below was worth observing.

The man stumbled back a step. Immediately the woman stepped forward, the tension gone from her petite form as she reached for his face, urging him to turn toward her so she could inspect where she had struck him. The man shook his head and said something that made her drop her hands and step back, her fists clenching at her sides as she turned away. The movement took her into the dim light cast by the ballroom windows, and Lily held back a surprised gasp. The woman below was Miss Oswald.

"My dear Mrs. Adler."

The sudden voice behind Lily made her jump. The last thing she wanted was to be caught spying. Hoping that she didn't look too flustered, she turned to find Reggie Harper watching her.

Mr. Harper was tall, even compared to her own above-average height, and dressed to the height of fashion, with a brightly striped waistcoat, skintight pantaloons that showed off every muscle in his legs, and shirt points starched so high he looked as if he could scarcely turn his neck. As he saw her taking in his appearance, he bowed. "I apologize for startling you. You must think me a dreadful boor." There was an unpleasant edge to his smile.

"Pray think nothing of it, Mr. Harper." Lily hoped he would realize her interest in conversation was as vague as her tone. When he showed no sign of leaving, she added, "I am afraid I—"

"You must excuse my ill manners in approaching you like this," he interrupted. Lily, who disliked few things more than being interrupted, frowned, but he was too busy moving closer to her to notice. "But given my friendship with your late husband, I am sure you will forgive me."

Lily took a deliberate step away. "I did not know you and Freddy were acquainted."

"We were at Eton together, ma'am, and then Cambridge. Old friends, though we had fallen out of touch in recent years." His expression became a little rueful, the look so artificial that Lily felt her annoyance quickly turning into anger. "I had been seeing to family affairs and did not hear of his death until very recently." He sighed, one hand on his heart, the other rising to stroke the exposed line of her shoulder. "Such a terrible loss. You must feel it cruelly."

Lily forced herself to breathe deeply and evenly. It would not do to create a scene at Serena's ball. "It was very hard—" she began coldly.

"But life goes on." Mr. Harper interrupted her once more. "How wise of you, my dear." Suddenly, he was standing very close and clasping her hand. "For a woman such as yourself, life can become very interesting indeed." His free hand rose to her cheek.

"Release my hand, sir." Lily stepped back as far as she could, but he followed her swiftly, his fingers tight around hers.

"I should very much like, Mrs. Adler, to be granted the privilege of showing you exactly how interesting," he murmured.

Lily took a deep breath. "Tell me, sir, do you practice your half of these exchanges in front of a mirror?"

The question caught him off guard. "What?"

While he was at a loss for words, Lily took the opportunity to slip from his grasp and put several feet of distance between them. "I do not care to speak with you anymore, Mr. Harper. Kindly do not approach me again."

She turned to walk away, hoping he had the wits not to push his advances any further. He did not.

"My beauty, you cannot mean what you say!" Mr. Harper grabbed Lily's arm, pulling her to a halt.

Lily reacted without thinking, and he grunted in pain as her elbow struck the point just below his breastbone. Once she realized what she had done, she did it a second time.

Mr. Harper dropped her arm as he doubled over, gasping for air. Lily, her expression cold, considered boxing his ears for good measure. Instead she said, "Freddy went to Oxford."

He stared up at her with watery eyes, hands braced on his knees as he wheezed. "What?"

"My husband studied at Oxford, not Cambridge." Her voice was icy. "I suggest you depart for the evening and *never* approach me in such a manner again. Do I make myself clear?"

He winced as he used the balustrade to pull himself upright. "You are a damned harpy."

Lily began to regret her decision not to box his ears. "Just so, sir. And now would be an excellent time to leave, unless you wish to spend the next month explaining your broken nose."

For a moment he looked as if he was going to advance on her once more. But Lily lifted her chin and met his eyes, and something in her unruffled expression seemed to unnerve him. He settled for sneering at her before he strode away down the terrace.

Lily watched just long enough to see him out of sight, then let out a relieved breath and sagged back against the balustrade. She didn't actually know how to break a man's nose, but some further threat had been necessary. The thought made her laugh, a hysterical edge to the sound. There were always rumors that this widow or that was engaged in a dalliance once free from the restrictions of maidenhood and marriage, and they had always sounded rather scandalously delightful. But an unwelcome proposition was not at all pleasant.

She was shaking, she realized, her skin prickling and sweaty all over despite the cool air. Returning to the ballroom in such a state was out of the question, but a sudden flurry of laughter as a crowd of guests came out onto the terrace made her unwilling to stay there either. Needing a moment alone to gather her thoughts, Lily turned to the garden below.

The Walters, to Serena's chagrin, lived just north of Mayfair. The previous Lord Walter had wanted more property than generally came with a town house and had purchased space near Marylebone Park, which the architect John Nash was currently turning into a retreat for the Prince Regent. The Walters made up for their less-than-fashionable address with a London rarity: gardens that stretched behind their house, a delight of carefully pruned shrubbery and climbing flowers, hidden from the house by a tall boxwood hedge. It stretched nearly twice the length of the house beyond the terrace, and just as Lily had hoped, the heat and noise of the ballroom soon dropped away. Only moonlight illuminated the path, and she wandered through the shrubbery until the smell of horses and dung told her that she had arrived at the mews.

Lily shivered, the filmy sleeves of her gown no protection against the breeze, and brushed a stray curl from her cheek. She was not surprised to discover tears there as well. Freddy's mother had meant well when she suggested Lily move to town, but returning to London was not proving to be the immediate cure for grief she had predicted. "You need something to do, dear, something to distract you," Lady Adler had said kindly. "Perhaps some charity work?"

But Lily's grief still felt too fresh. She had waited three long years to marry Freddy, and his death had come after only two years of marriage. She had spent so long looking forward to living a life and starting a family together that she didn't know what to do with herself now that she was alone. Enjoying her widowhood was unthinkable.

Together, Lily, Freddy had promised her. *We shall do something that matters for the people of this country.* None of that was left for her now.

And as Reggie Harper had made clear, a woman in her position was considered useful for one thing only.

Lily took a deep breath, pushing such ugly thoughts out of her mind and trying to think practically. She had taken the house for the season, and unless she returned to Hertfordshire, there was no other place for her to live. She had friends in London. And even if she would have preferred staying outside to returning to the gossiping, flirting masses inside, the air was too chill for her to linger. It was time to put her society mask back on and return to the ball.

Making up her mind helped, even if it was only about what to do for the rest of the evening. Her tears were gone, and her breathing was calm. Giving her clothing and hair a quick pat to make sure they were tidy, Lily made her way back through the shrubbery.

That was when she heard voices.

The two men were speaking quietly, so she didn't hear anything until she was nearly on top of them. The urgent tone of the voices was clear, though. Without thinking, Lily paused behind a tangle of trees and leafless vines, not wanting to walk into the middle of an argument.

And then, because she couldn't help herself, she leaned forward to listen.

". . . cannot be serious," the first voice—deep, cultured, and angry—was saying. Lily thought it might be familiar, but the man spoke too quietly for her to be sure. "You insolent young . . ."

". . . am quite serious, sir. If I am not paid . . ."

". . . do not even know who you are!"

The second voice chuckled. "But I know who you are." That speaker was younger than the first, his voice lighter, with an accent she couldn't place. "And the information I have . . ."

There was another moment of low, tense conversation that Lily strained to hear, then, "Who wrote this?" the older voice demanded suddenly.

The voices dropped again, and the only thing she could pick out sounded like, ". . . ruined if you do not pay what I ask." A matter of unpaid vowels, Lily wondered, money lost and won at a gaming table?

At last the first voice rose enough to be heard more clearly. ". . . think anything you say would damage me? Publish your speculation. You are no one, and no one will believe you."

There was a rustle of footsteps, and Lily realized that the deep-voiced gentleman was turning to leave. A jolt of panic raced through her. If either man realized they had been overheard—or worse, caught her in the act of eavesdropping—she would be in very serious trouble. Lily began to back away, thankful for whichever efficient gardener had made sure the paths were clear of leaves and branches.

"I will not—!" The young voice burst out violently, and then just as swiftly was cut off.

In the sudden quiet, Lily clearly heard the click of a pistol's hammer being drawn back.

She had to get away. Feeling panicked, Lily told herself to run, but her legs felt frozen though her whole body shook.

"Easy, lad." The deep voice again. "No need for that."

The other voice replied but was again too low to hear. Lily didn't know which of them held the gun, and she didn't want to find out.

She was mere feet from two highly nervous men, one of them armed, and she had to get away. Bunching up her dress in her fists, she finally forced her trembling knees to bend and crept backward.

When she was out of earshot, Lily turned and ran until she reached the hedge. There she paused, breathing deeply, taking an extra moment to calm down before returning inside.

Gentlemen argued all the time, she told herself. But they wouldn't resort to violence in the middle of Serena's garden. If it was a matter of honor, they would meet to settle it privately. And if it was a matter of business, there was a court system to deal with such disputes.

This logical train of thought was making her feel better. Surely, her nerves on edge from the encounter with Mr. Harper, she had imagined the sound of a pistol being readied. What gentleman would bring a gun to an evening of pleasure? There was no reason to be scared—

The cracking report of a pistol echoed through the gardens.

Lily hiked up her dress and ran toward the house. Not stopping to think what someone on the terrace might see, she dashed up the steps.

She was looking back over her shoulder when she collided with someone tall, her momentum carrying them both back several steps before the other person steadied them both. Biting back a scream, Lily looked up, terrified that she might have run into one of the two men.

The light spilling out of the ballroom illuminated his face. "Mrs. Adler?" Jack didn't let go of her arms. "What's the matter? Are you well?"

"Perfectly well." She pushed herself away from him, her movements sharp and abrupt. The terrace was empty again, save for the two of them, but it wouldn't do to have someone come out and find her in his arms. "What are you doing here?"

He frowned. "Looking for you. Lady Walter said she saw you disappearing towards the terrace . . ." He trailed off, taking in her distress. "You're trembling."

"I said I am well." But he was right, she was still shaking. "I had a bit of a fright . . ." She wanted to believe she had imagined it all, but she had never been good at lying to herself. And if someone had been shot, he needed help, not for her to fall to pieces. Dragging in a long breath, she looked back toward the garden. "Not a fright. Something terrible happened."

He looked at her sharply. "Did someone . . . did you . . . ?"

"Nothing to do with me." Now that she had made up her mind, Lily was impatient to take action. "I was walking in the garden, and I heard . . . I think someone has been hurt." He grew very still, and Lily took that as a sign to continue. "I heard two men arguing, and one of them had a pistol. And just now I heard a gunshot."

His expression was unreadable as he studied her face; then he turned to look at the garden once again. "This just happened?" She nodded. "Did you see either of the men?"

Lily was about to answer when a quick, scuffling noise from the boxwoods made her turn sharply. "What was that?"

"What was what, Mrs. Adler?"

"I thought I heard footsteps . . . is someone there?"

The silence stretched until Jack said, his voice very patient, "Perhaps it was an animal?"

"It wasn't . . ." Lily frowned. "In any case, we mustn't delay. Whatever happened, someone may need help—"

"Did you see one of these men shoot the other?"

Lily scowled at the interruption. "No, I was already on my way back to the house."

"I did not hear anything."

Lily stared. It hadn't occurred to her that he would doubt her. "You think I imagined it."

"I did not say that. But it might not have been the sound of a gun—"

"Am I the sort of person who imagines things?" she interrupted, fists clenching with impatient anger. "Who makes up stories to get attention?"

He stared at her for what felt like a very long time. At last he shook his head. "No. Of course not. If you go back into the ballroom, I will look around—"

"*We* will look." She cut him off again. "You do not even know where to go." She lifted her chin. "I do not need to be coddled, Captain."

His expression might have been wry if it hadn't been so tense. "No, you do not, do you?" He glanced over her shoulder, eyeing the dark gardens once more. "Stay close behind me. If some jumpy fellow with a gun is nearby, I would rather you not be the one to surprise him."

The sense of danger, which had faded as they stood there talking, came creeping back. Lily shivered. "Very well. But we should hurry."

Side by side, they made their way between the hedges, Lily carefully retracing her steps. The sound and light from the ballroom faded once more, but bright moonlight illuminated the gardens.

Which was why, when they came into the clearing, it was only too easy to see the body on the ground.

CHAPTER 4

Jack stopped so suddenly that Lily walked into him. It didn't occur to either of them to apologize or move; they simply stared at the man lying on the ground in front of them.

Jack was the first one to recover, going quickly to the body and touching his wrist and neck. Lily didn't understand what he was doing until he said, "We'll not be needing a doctor." His voice seemed oddly loud in the silent garden.

Lily said nothing, only nodded and continued to stare, swallowing rapidly against the sick feeling in her stomach and throat. The body was a young man—the second voice, she decided slowly, feeling as though her mind was not working at normal speed. The one with the pretty accent. His clothing was well made but simple and unadorned; a merchant's clothing, perhaps, or something similar. His coat lay open, and she couldn't keep her eyes from going to the dark stain on the breast of his white shirt. In the moonlight it looked as black as his short, curly hair. There was something familiar about him, but she didn't know what it was. The realization annoyed her enough to make her focus; they couldn't count on the gardens remaining deserted forever, and standing around wondering if she was about to be sick helped no one.

She swallowed again and, taking a deep breath, crouched next to Jack.

He started to his feet, as surprised as if he had forgotten she was there. "What in God's name are you doing?"

"Looking for any clues, of course." Lily shivered and crossed her arms over her chest. "I think his was the second voice I heard. He wanted to be paid—the other voice was too old and deep for such a young man." She looked around, frowning. "No gun, though that is hardly surprising . . . Now, that is odd." Something white caught her eye, and she bent down to discover a dozen pieces of torn paper ground into the mud just a few paces away from the dead man. She fished out one of the pieces, but it was mangled beyond legibility. "No clear footprints on the ground either, and we've muddled them up ourselves, so there's no saying which direction the man who shot him went. But I only heard two voices." Tears blurred her vision as she studied the dead man's face. "This poor fellow—"

"Stop right now." The sharp tone of Jack's voice made her look up in surprise. "We are not going to stand around looking for clues. I am taking you home immediately. In case you've forgotten, there is a killer out here, and—"

"Don't be ridiculous, Captain. Anyone who shot a man in some-one else's garden is hardly going to wait around to shoot whoever happens to wander by." She turned back to the body. "The man who did this is long gone. What we need to do is have Lord Walter sum-mon one of the officers from Bow Street—"

She broke off with a yelp as Jack, grabbing one arm, hauled her to her feet. She yelped again when the petticoat of her dress snagged on the edge of a shrub, making her stumble. "Now look what you have done." She bent to twitch her skirt free and discovering a sizable bit of lace had been left behind. She yanked it free and shoved it in her reticule, glaring at the captain. "What is the matter with you? You were in the navy, for heaven's sake; you must have seen a dead body before."

"And have you as well? Is that why you are so damned calm about this?" Jack snapped, either not noticing or not caring that he was swearing at her. "You should be swooning or going into hysterics, not looking around for bloody clues."

"Would you prefer it if I did swoon or become hysterical?" Lily only barely remembered to keep her voice low. "Because I assure you, that would be my preference. I am staying *so damned calm* because anything else would not help the situation." Pursing her lips, she surveyed the clearing. "Now, what should we do? We cannot risk anyone else finding the body."

Jack glared at her. "I knew you were an unusual girl, but Freddy never mentioned that you were so—"

"A footman, perhaps," Lily interrupted, not interested in finding out what he might call her. "We should find one immediately and make sure he does not allow anyone else into the gardens. And then we should go straight to Lord Walter." She met Jack's eyes. "Do be some sort of helpful, please. You may berate me for being unfeminine later, but for now we have a dead body to deal with, and I do think that takes precedence."

Jack blew out an annoyed breath, but to her relief he nodded. "A footman's a good idea, and one of the Bow Street fellows." He held out his arm. "Try to look faint or ill. People will assume I am helping you to your carriage and hopefully will leave us alone until we find Lord Walter."

Taking his arm, Lily discovered she was glad of the support, and it didn't require much pretending to lean on him and let him help her from the grisly scene. Fortunately, they encountered a footman checking the candle sconces as soon as they gained the terrace. Seeing an apparently ill lady leaning on the arm of a gentleman, he came quickly to offer assistance.

"What is your name, young man?" Jack asked sternly.

"Jeremy, sir." The footman bowed.

"You are Anna's cousin," Lily broke in, noting the resemblance in their faces. "My dresser, Anna Swift."

"Mrs. Adler." Jeremy bowed again. "How may I be of service, ma'am?"

"We need to find Lord Walter," Jack said. "And, Jeremy, it is imperative that you prevent anyone from entering the gardens until he tells you otherwise. Can you do that?"

To Lily's surprise, Jeremy glanced at her before agreeing. At her nod, he bowed once more. "His lordship was in the card room last I saw him, sir. I'll make sure no one goes past the terrace while you find him."

"Good man." Jack clapped the footman on the shoulder, and Lily briefly saw the twinkle of several coins before they found their way into Jeremy's pocket.

"Thank you, Jeremy," she said, pausing, though it was clear Jack wanted to hurry.

He looked like he wanted to ask questions, but of course he knew better. He said only, "Anna speaks well of you, ma'am," before taking his position on the stairs.

★   ★   ★

Lily hoped the small parlor where she and Serena had sat after dinner was enough removed from the ballroom that they wouldn't be interrupted there. But though she and Jack managed to make their way through the ballroom without attracting attention, they were brought up short before they were halfway down the hall to the parlor.

"Mrs. Adler! Are you unwell?"

The woman's voice was quiet and concerned, and they turned to find Isobel Harper frowning at them.

"What are you doing here?" Lily asked without thinking.

Miss Harper's brows rose. "Looking for my uncle, the general. Do you need assistance?" She glanced askance at Captain Hartley.

Lily leaned more heavily on Jack's arm. "Thank you, Miss Harper, but please do not trouble yourself. I clumsily twisted my ankle out on the terrace, and the captain is helping me to my carriage."

"I should never describe someone with your grace as clumsy, Mrs. Adler." Miss Harper's eyes narrowed slightly.

Lily bit the inside of her cheek to stop herself from saying anything unwise. Miss Harper had never been known as a gossip, but even she would be suspicious of a lady and gentleman sneaking away from a ballroom. The last thing Lily needed was rumors following her. "The heat, you know. I stepped outside for a breath of air on the terrace, and—" She waved her hand vaguely, wondering how pained she should try to look. "It is nothing serious. May I make Captain Hartley known to you, Miss Harper? He was a childhood friend of my dear Freddy's and gallantly came to my rescue. Captain, Miss Harper."

"Charmed, madam." Jack somehow managed to bow smoothly from the chest up while keeping a supporting hand under Lily's arm. "I must apologize for my abruptness, but Mrs. Adler really should not be straining her ankle any further. But we should be most grateful for your assistance. Would you be so good as to seek out Lady Walter and send her to Mrs. Adler in the blue parlor?"

Somehow, whether it was his charming smile, his air of military command, or simply the practical nature of his request, Jack made quicker work of Miss Harper's watchful concern than Lily could have ever managed on her own. After Miss Harper left to fulfill her errand, he escorted Lily to the blue parlor, hesitating briefly over leaving her alone before promising to return with Lord Walter as quickly as possible.

Lily waited anxiously for them to return, pacing the room until she heard low voices arguing in the corridor. On edge and unwilling to sit around feeling vulnerable, she flung open the door, then stared in surprise.

Miss Oswald stood directly across from her, her back pressed against the wall as a man leaned toward her, his outstretched hand resting next to her head and blocking her escape. ". . . saw you sneak away . . ." he was murmuring.

"I was not sneaking anywhere," the girl protested, trying to edge away. She sounded scared. "Move aside, sir, or someone—" She caught sight of Lily and gasped, her eyes widening in sudden panic at being caught in such a position.

"What the devil—" The man turned, and his eyes narrowed. "You."

For the second time that night, Lily found herself staring down Reggie Harper, and this time she was furious. After all that had happened, to be confronted with such a man was the last straw. "I believe I suggested that you depart for the evening."

"I do not take orders from—"

"I suggested you depart," she repeated, not raising her voice, but her chilly tone made him fall silent. "It is no longer a suggestion, Mr. Harper. You will leave, at once, or you will regret it very deeply."

Mr. Harper glanced between the two women, clearly trying to decide whether to risk making a scene. But another look at Lily's furious expression made him hesitate, and at last he muttered, "*Frigid shrew*," under his breath and strode away.

Miss Oswald let out a breath and sagged against the wall.

"Did he hurt you?" Lily asked.

"No." The girl swallowed, still looking afraid. Lily did not blame her; if word got out that the young heiress had been alone with a man like Mr. Harper, her reputation would be ruined, even if she was only trying to fend off his advances. "I swear, Mrs. Adler, I was not—"

"I know." Lily cut her off. "He approached me in a similar manner earlier tonight." The girl's mouth quivered, and Lily would have moved to comfort her, but at that moment she heard voices coming down the hall and recalled why she was there in the first place. "Go splash some cool water on your face before you return. I will make sure no one hears any gossip."

"Thank you." The girl glanced in the direction of the voices, then scampered off down the hall, disappearing around the corner just as Jack and Lord Walter came into view.

Jack grimaced in apology as he saw Lily's tight expression. "My apologies. His lordship was not in the card room," he explained as they returned to the parlor and closed the door.

"Mrs. Adler, are you well?" Lord Walter's friendly face was wreathed in worry.

"Yes, I am. But . . ." Lily glanced around. "Is Serena coming? I sent for her as well."

"If you sent for her, I am sure she will arrive at any moment."

Lily frowned, but before she could say anything, Serena entered the room with a loud cry of, "Lily!" She seized her friend's hand, quivering with worry. "Isobel Harper said you injured yourself—"

"What has happened, Mrs. Adler?" Lord Walter's practical interruption didn't seem to upset his wife.

Lily was grateful; she didn't think she could deal with Serena's dramatics at the moment. She met his eyes and said, matching his calm tone as well as she could, "I am afraid there is a dead body in your garden."

There was a moment of stunned silence; then Serena and her husband began talking at once. It took several moments to quiet them down so Lily could explain what had happened.

"But, Lily, darling," Serena said, focusing on the one detail Lily had hoped her audience would overlook. "Why were you in the garden at all?" She glanced at her husband, and they both very deliberately did not look at Jack.

Lily had no desire to explain about Mr. Harper's advances. She would tell Serena in private, but not in front of the gentlemen. "Getting some air, of course."

"I sent one of your footman to make sure no one else wanders into the garden, but we should not leave him alone any longer than necessary," Jack said. He tugged at his cravat, looking as uncomfortable as Lily had yet seen him, and exchanged a glance with Lord Walter.

Whether she was saved further inquiry because they believed her, because of his lordship's discretion, or simply by the fact that she was a widow and entitled to do as she wished, Lily could not decide. Whatever the reason, Lord Walter merely nodded. "I will have another one of the lads join him, and someone will fetch one of the Bow Street fellows immediately."

"We cannot interrupt the party," Serena protested, bristling when Jack made a noise of protest. "I am not so flighty as that, thank you.

I meant we cannot let anyone know what has happened. We should have half our guests rushing for the door and the other half rushing for the gardens to get a look. It would be a dreadful mess."

"You are quite right, my love." Lord Walter touched his wife's shoulder gently, and she subsided, though she still scowled at Jack, who to his credit did look contrite. "The officer will come through the servants' door, and you shall do your best to keep things proceeding smoothly. All of London will find out tomorrow, but tonight we can maintain the fiction that nothing terrible has happened." He turned to Lily. "I am sure Mrs. Adler will assist you."

"I am sure Mrs. Adler will do no such thing." Serena looked thunderous. "For heaven's sake, she stumbled on a dead body not half an hour ago. How can you expect her to go dance a cotillion as if nothing happened?"

"I would hardly be dancing," Lily pointed out, but her friend was right. Despite her efforts to keep herself under control, the shock of her discovery was beginning to set it. She clasped her hands together to try to keep them from shaking, but by the sympathetic looks directed her way, she knew she hadn't succeeded.

"Besides which, you told Miss Harper that you twisted your ankle. You can hardly wander about after that," Serena pointed out. "No, you need a strong cup of tea and a good night's sleep. We all do, but the rest of us will have to wait a little longer."

"You are right once more, my love." Lord Walter bent to kiss the top of Serena's head. "I will see everything arranged as discreetly as possible. I do not like to wait any longer in case someone should get around Jeremy and find the unfortunate young man."

"I would be happy to escort Mrs. Adler home," Jack volunteered after Lord Walter had left, but Serena was already shaking her head.

"Lily will stay here tonight." She scowled as Lily tried to protest. "Think how dreadful you will feel if this is the first night you spend in your new home. No, I'll have someone fetch your maid and your clothes. We've plenty of rooms, and this way you shan't feel so alone."

"Well, I certainly am not going anywhere yet," Lily said, her voice sharp. Even though she knew Serena was right, she did not like having someone else making decisions for her. Her annoyance, at least, made her feel less overwhelmed. "None of us are, until the gentleman from Bow Street arrives."

"I am." Serena rose. "People will talk if I stay away any longer." She frowned at Jack, clearly still annoyed with him for scoffing. "You will stay with Lily?"

"Of course, ma'am."

Serena left the room as dramatically as she had entered, leaving Lily as close to smiling as she had been all evening. There were few London hostesses who would react to news of a dead body with such equanimity. Or, she thought fondly, such concern for their friends.

Jack, still standing near the door, cleared his throat. "Would they take it amiss if we rang for something to eat?" He looked embarrassed. "It seems dreadful under such circumstances, but I'm famished."

Lily wanted to laugh, but the sound caught in her throat. She hoped she wasn't becoming hysterical; the last thing she wanted was for Jack to gallantly insist that she take herself off to bed. "Well, if you are dreadful, then so am I." She nodded in the direction of the bell. "We may be waiting for a while, so see if you can persuade someone to bring us some sandwiches."

★　★　★

In the end, they were both glad they had sent for food. It took the officer from Bow Street nearly an hour to arrive, and after that, Serena reported indignantly, he insisted on being taken to the gardens right away, "even though there were guests on the terrace! Fortunately, we were able to let his men in the back gate so they could take away the body without anyone noticing." She shuddered. "The whole thing is dreadful. I am amazed I've not succumbed to hysterics."

As she swept back out of the small parlor to return to her duties as hostess, Jack stared after her. "She doesn't seem the sort who would succumb to much of anything."

"She's not," Lily murmured absently, her thoughts still with the poor young man, his body fetched from the gardens like a sack of potatoes. Jack noticed her shudder and moved to sit with her, and though she knew she should have protested his being so close, she was grateful.

It was another half an hour before Lord Walter showed the Bow Street constable, introduced as Mr. Simon Page, into the parlor. By that point it was nearly two o'clock in the morning and Lily was beginning to droop with fatigue. As soon as the constable was shown in, though, she sat up straighter, determined to be of use.

"Mr. Page has looked over the gardens, and his men have removed the . . ." Lord Walter cleared his throat, too much of a gentleman to mention a dead body in the presence of a lady, even if the lady had been the one to find it. "Everything seems to be well in hand, but he wanted to ask both of you a question or two. If you are feeling up to it, of course, Mrs. Adler."

"Certainly." Lily smoothed down her dress, which had grown rumpled from restless pacing. "It seems to me that hardly anything is in hand, unless Mr. Page has somehow managed to apprehend the killer already."

"No need to be worried; I'll only be asking a few questions to sort through the facts of the evening." Mr. Page was a very middling sort of man: about middle height, with middling brown hair that was beginning to show a middling amount of gray, and eyes of a middling brown color. But he spoke with an air of confidence that belied his average appearance, and his gaze was sharp as he looked them over. "I'm sure this is all very distressing for you, Mrs. Adler, so I won't trouble you for much longer. But let me know if you remember anything as we speak."

Lord Walter excused himself, claiming a need to return to his guests, and instructed Mr. Page to ring the bell if he needed anything else. Looking gratified at such cooperative treatment, the constable turned to Jack. "I understand you found the body, Captain Hartley?"

Jack nodded. "Along with Mrs. Adler."

The constable made several notes. "So the two of you were walking in the garden. And then you stumbled on the body of the young man?"

"No." Lily sat up straighter. "We did not stumble onto anything. I was walking in the gardens alone when I overheard two gentlemen arguing. It was obviously a private matter, so I started to return to the house. But when I heard the gunshot, I ran to find help—"

Mr. Page had stopped writing, and his brows rose as she spoke. "Mrs. Adler, I wonder if the shock of such a terrible discovery has upset you greatly."

His tone made Lily wary. "It was of course upsetting. Nonetheless, I remember the circumstances very clearly."

"Of course." Mr. Page nodded. "We'll return to all that in a moment, but first I'd like to ask Captain Hartley more about finding the body."

"Mrs. Adler was the one who led me there." Jack's stiff tone might have made Lily smile if she hadn't been so annoyed. Clearly, he did not like the constable's way of questioning either.

"And being a military man, I assume you checked the body to make sure the fellow was indeed dead?" Jack nodded stiffly, and Mr. Page made another note. Lily tried not to tap her foot impatiently. "And did you see anyone else about, or anything unusual?"

"Nothing that I particularly noticed." Jack glanced at Lily out of the corner of his eye. "There was no sign of whoever shot the poor fellow by the time we got there."

Mr. Page sighed. "That's usually the case with things like this. Fellow that no one knows, wandering around a place where he clearly doesn't belong. We'll do our best to figure out who he is, though even that may be unlikely." Mr. Page looked thoughtful as he closed his notebook. "Nasty business for Lord and Lady Walter."

"And I am sure you hope they will pay you handsomely to deal with it as quickly as possible." Jack didn't bother disguising the sarcasm in his voice, and Lily winced as Mr. Page's head shot up.

"I beg your pardon, Captain Hartley?" The constable's tone was icy.

Lily ground her teeth. The accusation was not unreasonable; while the fledgling police force at Bow Street was paid a salary to keep the officers from accepting bribes, many still did. But the fault was not entirely one-sided: most members of Lily's class were more than willing to use their money to turn an investigation in their favor or keep the law away from their families.

Regardless of its truth, Jack's comment had not helped the current situation. He and the Bow Street officer stared at each other with contempt, jaws clenched and nostrils flared. Trying to smooth things over, Lily spoke up before either man could say anything else inflammatory. "To return to the matter at hand, Mr. Page, I overheard the two gentlemen arguing. I could not say for certain what they were arguing about, but I heard—"

"Mrs. Adler." The constable stood so abruptly that she broke off. He was still scowling at Jack, and Lily had the feeling that his dismissive tone was directed at both of them—possibly at every scornful member of London's upper class. "I understand you've had quite a shock, and I sympathize. I can also see you want to help, and I appreciate that. But those of us who work with the law have a particular way of handling these matters. We like to stick to the facts."

"But—"

"I'm sure you'll feel better after a good night's sleep." He smiled coldly. "Try to forget about the whole business. It really isn't anything a lady of quality need concern herself with."

Stunned at the abrupt dismissal, Lily was at a loss for a reply, and Mr. Page seemed to take her silence for agreement. "Lord Walter has given me your direction, Captain, so I don't think I'll need to trouble you any further this evening. But if you think of anything else, you can find me tomorrow at the Marlborough Street Magistrates Court." He nodded to them both before heading toward the door. "Ma'am. Captain. I'll wish you a good evening."

"What a damned idiot!" Jack practically slammed the door after the constable, then grimaced as he remembered Lily's presence. "My apologies. But I think the situation warrants a bit of strong language."

"Why on earth did you say that to him?" Lily asked. Jack's anger made it easier for her to be calmer, though she couldn't keep the exasperation from her voice. "Now there is no chance that he will listen to us."

"Why—!" Jack stared at her. "How can you say such a thing after the way he spoke to you? He deserved a far worse insult. The bounder thought you were too much of a pea brain to have anything to contribute, when he should have been questioning you first and most!"

"It was infuriating." Lily pursed her lips. "Luckily, I have had practice dealing with that sort of attitude. After all, Captain, you said nearly the same thing when I first tried to tell you what had happened." Jack, who had been about to launch into another tirade in her defense, was left with his mouth hanging open. "Mr. Page, at least, has the excuse of not knowing better," Lily said. "We may not be deeply acquainted, but I would have expected you to have a more flattering opinion of me."

He had the decency to look embarrassed at that. "I did not think . . . That is, I did not mean . . ."

"I know." Lily stood. "But you still did. And now, if you will excuse me, Captain, the constable was right about one thing at least. I am very much in need of a good night's sleep."

"Mrs. Adler—" He broke off, clearly not sure how to reply.

Lily shook her head. "If you figure out what you wish to say, you may come by tomorrow to say it. I imagine I shall still be here. But for now, I really am exhausted." She gave him a slight bow, which he automatically returned. "Good night, Captain."

She was just closing the door behind her when she heard him say, quietly but distinctly, "Oh hell."

CHAPTER 5

"Well, it is all over London." Serena's voice was full of satisfaction.

She, Lord Walter, and Lily were seated in the breakfast room, and the butler, Reston, had just brought in the morning papers, freshly ironed. Serena was holding one of the London gossip sheets, a piece of toast forgotten in the other hand. "'The body of a murdered man, apparently of the working classes, found in the gardens of Lord and Lady W— during an evening soiree . . . No identification of the body has been made . . . No word yet from Lord and Lady W— on the matter, and This Author does not expect them to comment . . . One hopes the whole shocking affair will be tidily resolved . . .'" Serena threw down the paper with a gusty sigh. "As if another 'Lord and Lady W' hosted a ball in London last night!"

"You can hardly have expected it to stay out of the gossip columns, my love." Lord Walter's voice was mild, though there was a frown between his eyes as he read his own paper. "The *Times* has it as well; it seems murder trumps even this week's upset at the Newmarket races. Perhaps we should take a trip to the country until it blows over."

"In the middle of the season?" Serena looked horrified. "My love, have you lost your wits? We feature in one of the on-dits of the year! We will be invited simply *everywhere*. How can you think of missing such an opportunity?"

"Serena, you just said . . ."

Lily ignored them as they settled into a comfortable argument, if it could be called an argument when it was punctuated by Lord Walter's amiable comments of, "Whatever you wish, my love." It was a foregone conclusion that they would stay in London, but Serena would never relent until she could say she had convinced her husband. Lord Walter was still holding the *Times*, so Lily claimed the gossip sheet Serena had so dramatically cast aside. There wasn't much more to the article than Serena had read aloud, but Lily was surprised to find that it was accompanied by a sketch of the murdered man—"an *entirely* unknown person," as the piece described him.

"I will have to make a showing in the park this afternoon," Serena said, buttering another piece of toast. "Simply everyone will want to speak with me, and you should come too, Lily, as it was you who found him, though none of the papers have discovered that fact—"

"And we should keep it that way to save Mrs. Adler any embarrassment," Lord Walter put in gently.

"Oh, if you insist," Serena relented. "But I'll not be dissuaded from appearing entirely . . ."

Lily nodded absently, not really listening, still focused on the sketch of the murdered man. It was a good likeness, she thought, frowning as she examined the drawing. She still felt there was something very familiar about the man's face. No, familiar was the wrong word. She knew she had never spoken with him. But she was sure she recognized him.

Frustrated and feeling suddenly crowded in the small breakfast parlor, Lily stood abruptly. "Excuse me please, I need . . . excuse me." She needed to be somewhere quiet.

Not pausing to see the concerned looks that followed her out of the room, Lily headed toward the family book-room. She needed to be alone to think, to decide what to do. Shutting the door firmly behind her, she paced around, scanning the shelves without seeing them. Going to the Bow Street offices was the obvious choice, but after her experience the previous night, she didn't think anyone would listen to her.

Lily was so preoccupied that the sound of a clearing throat made her start.

"My apologies, Mrs. Adler," the Walters' butler, Reston, said with a bow. "A Captain Hartley is here to see you. Shall I say you are not at home?"

"Oh, no." She clenched her fists behind her back where the butler could not see them, then deliberately relaxed them, letting out her breath and schooling her expression at the same time. "No, I will see him. If you are sure he wanted me and not Lady Walter?"

"He asked for you specifically, ma'am."

"Then please show him in." Lily hesitated, then quickly added, "Reston?"

He turned back, bowing once more, waiting, but it took Lily a moment to work up the courage to ask, "Is Jeremy well this morning?"

"Jeremy?" The butler looked surprised.

"He was of great assistance in the . . . last night." Lily bit her lip, feeling awkward but determined to ask anyway. "I hope he was not too upset by the incident."

"He'll likely use the story to drink free at the public house for the next year," Reston said with a chuckle, then added, more somberly. "If you'll excuse me for saying so, Mrs. Adler."

"Of course. And did anyone—" Lily paused, reconsidering. She had been about to ask if any of the servants had recognized the murdered man, or had any inkling as to his identity. But it wasn't her place to ask, and surely the officer from Bow Street would have thought to question them? Shaking her head, Lily forced a smile. "Thank you, Reston, I did not mean to keep you from your duties. You may show Captain Hartley up."

"Mrs. Adler."

As the butler left, Lily again paced around the room, her mind returning to the matter of the murdered man's strangely familiar face. The memory of where she had seen him before hovered on the edge of her mind, and she nearly had it when a cold draft interrupted her thoughts.

The back terrace ran outside the room, and one of the doors had been left open a crack, though a curtain was drawn mostly over it. Shivering and drawing her shawl more tightly around her arms, Lily was about to close it when voices on the terrace caught her attention.

"All I ask is that the matter be dealt with efficiently." It was Lord Walter, almost too quiet to hear. "I believe three hundred should be plenty to arrange that."

"Of course, your lordship." She did not recognize the second voice, deep and genial. "I am more than happy to arrange things as you wish."

"Just see that you are discreet." A sharp edge entered Lord Walter's voice. "I have no interest in dealing with any sort of mess."

"I can assure you of that, sir."

The sharp click of bootheels told Lily that one of the two men was crossing the terrace. Unable to resist, she peered around the edge of the curtain. The man who walked past, with the broad build and red face of someone who thoroughly enjoyed both his wine and his sport, was not someone she recognized. He was heading toward the side door, and as he walked past, she could clearly see him tucking a thick stack of banknotes into his bright-blue coat.

Lily frowned as she drew back into the room. Why would Lord Walter need to be so secretive about paying a tradesman? Shaking her head at her folly—she was starting to see suspicious behavior in the most absurd places—she pulled the door shut and latched it tightly, putting the strange conversation from her thoughts. The puzzle of the murdered man's identity was harder to let go of, but she let it settle to the back of her mind; in her experience, that was the best way to remember the answer to a difficult question. Instead, she steeled herself instead for Jack's visit. She was fairly certain she knew why he had called.

When Reston showed him in, Jack looked more awkward than she would have thought possible. He bowed and asked after Lord and Lady Walter very politely, though one hand tapped nervously on his thigh and his face was flushed. Lily answered coolly, not feeling inclined to make what he had to say easier for him, though she was hard put not to smile at his discomfort.

"Look here, Mrs. Adler," he finally sighed. "I behaved terribly last night. You were utterly in the right."

Lily raised her brows. "About what, sir?"

He frowned, shifting from one foot to the other and looking like a boy caught stealing sweets from the kitchen. "You know about what."

"Yes, I do. But unless you know as well, your apology is not worth much, is it?"

He laughed abruptly. "You know, I've not known anyone quite like you before."

Lily was torn between amusement and annoyance. "I hear that with some frequency. I choose to take it as a compliment, though I suspect it is only intended that way about half the time. You were saying, Captain?"

To her surprise, he reached out to take her hand. His was very large and warm, with rough calluses on his palms. It had been a long time since a man had taken her hand with such easy familiarity, and she had, she realized, missed it. "You'll not make this easy on me, will you?" he said. Lily shook her head. "Very well. I apologize for my behavior when you came to me for help last night. You are obviously intelligent and level-headed and not prone to wild imaginings. I should not have doubted the truth of what you saw, and I am very sorry."

Lily couldn't keep her surprise from showing. "That was more thorough than I expected, Captain. Especially the flattery."

"I thought it was a helpful touch." Jack released her hand and stuck his own in the pockets of his morning trousers, grinning proudly. "Though I do mean every word. I know perfectly well that Freddy would never have married a woman who fell into hysterics for no reason, and I should not have treated you like one."

Lily smiled. "No, he certainly would not have."

"Am I forgiven, then?"

Lily swatted his shoulder. "Yes, you wretch. No need to make eyes at me to get back in my good graces. Just see that you do not do it again."

"You can be sure of that," Jack said, then added more seriously, "I am truly forgiven? There is not anything I can do to make amends for my behavior?"

"No, there is nothing . . ." Lily trailed off, a resolute expression coming into her face. "As a matter of fact, Captain, there is something that I need to do, for which I would appreciate your escort. Do you have a free hour or so today?"

"Immediately, if you desire."

CHAPTER 6

No one looking at her would have guessed, but Lily felt sick with nerves as she gazed up at the magistrate's office on Great Marlborough Street. Even without her frustrating encounter with Mr. Page, she would have felt out of place and presumptuous, given that she was going not to seek aid but to give information—information that, for all she knew, the magistrate's officers had already discovered. When she closed her eyes, she could practically see her father scowling.

But Lily also saw the young man, unknown and perhaps unmourned, lying cold in the basement of the Bow Street offices. She was doing the right thing. She knew it.

She took Jack's arm as she alighted from the carriage. "Shall we?"

He looked concerned. "If you are sure, Mrs. Adler."

"I am. No matter what that poor boy was doing there, he deserves justice."

"I meant, are you sure you wish me to take the lead?" Jack said, frowning. "It is your information, after all, and you have made it clear that you are not impressed with any sort of—"

Lily squeezed his arm, cutting him off. "I doubt I will get anywhere without your assistance, so I am content to make use of it." He still looked uncertain, so she added, "I promise to hold it against them, not you."

Jack sighed. "If you say so. But I've no desire to be on the business end of your glowering."

It might have made her smile if she hadn't been so nervous. "You shan't be." She thought about that, then added, "For this, at least. I am sure I shall find other reasons to glower at you in the future."

Jack snorted. "Certainly. Well, if you are ready . . ." He did a little glowering himself, then, staring at the stone facade looming before them.

Jack, Lily was realizing, did not approve of the new Bow Street Runners that had been attached to the magistrates' offices. Many among the upper classes and the military, both groups accustomed to handling their own affairs, felt the same.

Lily took a deep breath, determined not to let Jack's disapproval or her own nerves deter her. They had come for a purpose.

The young man at the porter's desk straightened as they came inside. "Morning, ma'am, sir," he said, managing to bow from his high perch without standing. "What can I do for ye?"

"And a good morning to you, lad." Jack's tone was both friendly and assured, and the porter sat up straighter in response. "Is this the office where Mr. Simon Page works?"

A wary look entered the Bow Street officer's eyes. "'Tis, sir."

Lily waited for more, foot tapping. When no further information was forthcoming, Jack asked, his voice taking on a more authoritative edge, "May we speak to him?"

"'Fraid not, sir." The porter shook his head. "Mr. Page is preparing to testify at th' Old Bailey. At a trial. Very important part of the process, that is," he added, in case they belonged to the group of people who still believed an accusation was as good as proof.

Lily let out an impatient huff of breath. "When will he be free?"

"'Fraid I dunno, ma'am."

"But we need—" Lily broke off as Jack laid a hand on her arm.

She could see a muscle beginning to twitch in his cheek, but he said calmly, "I can assure you, Constable, our business cannot wait.

We have important information concerning a case that Mr. Page is investigating."

Something about his quiet voice, or perhaps his military air, seemed to convince the porter. The young man's eyes grew wide, and he nodded, standing straighter as he hopped down from his perch. "Bide 'ere a moment; I'll go tell him. Who should I say . . . ?" He trailed off, clearly unsure of the protocol he should follow.

"Mrs. Adler and Captain John Hartley to see him, if you please," Jack said, betraying no hint of judgment at the man's unpolished manners. Though perhaps, Lily reflected, he did not feel any. In the navy, though his brother officers would have been gentlemen, he would have worked with men from a variety of classes, and his success as a captain would have depended on his ability to gain their trust and respect. Watching the ease with which Jack managed the young porter, Lily began to appreciate the air of command that lurked behind his comfortable manners.

They waited several minutes, Lily pacing back and forth in front of the desk while Jack settled into a chair and picked up a news sheet. At last the porter returned, motioning for them to follow him. "This way, if ye will."

He led them to a door with a small plaque on it: *Mr. Simon Page, Principal Officer.*

The office they were shown into was a surprise. Several tall windows let in the light, and there were shelves filled with what appeared to be books of law. It was rather like being in someone's underfurnished study, and Lily was impressed in spite of herself.

Mr. Page stood as they entered. He was just as average as Lily remembered him, from height to hair—all except his gaze, which was sharp enough to make her feel uneasy as it settled on her.

"Mrs. Adler, Captain Hartley." Mr. Page bowed in greeting. "To what do I owe the visit?"

Jack glanced at Lily; at her nod, he cleared his throat. "We wish to speak to you regarding last night's incident."

Mr. Page's jaw tightened. "If you are concerned for your safety, I can assure you, the Bow Street force has things in hand."

"No, that is not what concerns us." Lily tried not to speak sharply; he would be less likely to listen if she made him feel defensive. "I wanted another chance to tell you what I overheard concerning the murdered man."

"You wish to support the police in their work?" Mr. Page asked, one corner of his mouth lifting in an ironic smile. "How unusual. Unfortunately, Mrs. Adler, that incident is no longer under investigation."

Lily had expected to hear again that it was none of her business, or that she had imagined things, or something else equally dismissive. To be told that the case was laid aside entirely was so surprising that she was at a loss for words. They stared at each other, Mr. Page's expression as shuttered as her own, neither one betraying what they were thinking. "No longer . . . May I ask why?" she managed at last.

"Insufficient evidence." He paused a moment, then with evident reluctance added, "Our magistrates, Mr. Neve and Mr. Scott, have decided that pursuing the matter would tie up resources better put to work elsewhere."

"What do you mean, 'insufficient evidence'?" Lily demanded.

The constable shrugged, rudely casual. "The coroner's inquest was held early this morning. Jury ruled for *death by person or persons unknown*, predictably enough. But we can't identify the man, and without knowing who he is, we've no way to discover who did it."

"And that is the end of the matter?" Lily's hands clenched inside her muff.

Jack snorted. "Don't want to do any real work, I suppose? Bloody thief-takers," he muttered, arms crossing as he glared at the constable.

Mr. Page stiffened. "I am a principal officer of the Bow Street force, sir; I serve the law and obey my superiors, which I would have expected a military man to understand. If you have further concerns, you are welcome to take them up with a magistrate."

The two men scowled at each other, and Lily sighed. "Come along, Captain. If Mr. Page says there is nothing else to be done, then there is nothing else to be done."

They left the room in silence, Mr. Page glaring at their backs. Jack's expression was thunderous, and Lily's mood was not much better. She did not try to moderate her sarcastic tone. "You were wonderfully helpful back there, Captain."

"A man was murdered, Mrs. Adler, and they show no inclination to do a single thing about it. They can't identify the man?" Jack made a sound of disgust in the back of his throat. "What is the good of the taxes we pay for them if they do not do their job?"

"I know." Lily sighed. "But offending him was not going to get us anywhere. Why could you not manage him as you did the porter?"

"I don't know." Jack blew out a breath and ran one hand through his hair, a frustrated gesture Lily was beginning to recognize. "Something about that man sets me on edge."

Lily snorted. "Perhaps both of you are too accustomed to being the one giving orders."

She would have continued, but a figure down the hall caught her eye. A gentleman had just left one of the offices and was heading toward the front door. His broad-shouldered build and bright-blue coat looked familiar, but it wasn't until he paused to talk to the porter that she recognized him. She had seen him just over an hour before, leaving the Walters' home with three hundred pounds in his jacket.

Lily swallowed, feeling suddenly ill. "A moment, Captain." Lily approached the porter; when he looked up, she tried to smile, hoping she did not look as disturbed as she felt. "Could you tell me the name of the gentleman who left just now? In the blue coat?"

"Th' magistrate? That was Mr. Philip Neve." The porter looked confused by the question. "Him as runs the Great Marlborough Street office. Did ye need to speak with him?"

"No, I . . . thank you. That is . . . no." Not really sure what she was saying, Lily nodded to the porter just as Jack joined her. "Excuse me, Captain, I think I left something in Mr. Page's office. I shall return in a moment."

Leaving Jack looking confused behind her, Lily hurried back down the hall. She knocked sharply on Mr. Page's door but did not wait for a response before entering.

The principal officer started to his feet, then sighed when he saw who had burst in on him. "Mrs. Alder, this is a place of business. I realize you may not know what that is—"

Lily did not wait for him to finish. "What would you say if I told you that I know why this case was dropped? If it was because someone bribed your magistrate to prevent it from being investigated as it should be?"

Mr. Page's eyes had narrowed as she spoke, and his voice was cold as he replied. "I would say that I'm unsurprised. Your kind always thinks they can get away with anything because they have money."

"Then what do you plan to do about it?" Lily's heart was pounding. Surely he would realize that this could not be allowed, that someone had to find out what had happened?

"Do?" Mr. Page sat back down, no longer looking at her as he began to sort through the papers on his desk. "My job, Mrs. Adler, to the best of my ability. You can show yourself out."

Lily stared at him, unable to believe what she was hearing. But the constable did not look back up, and he did not reply when she said his name again. So at last she gave up, slamming the door shut behind her in an uncharacteristic display of temper.

When she returned to the lobby, Jack took one look at her face and hailed a hack carriage without asking any questions, staying silent until a driver had pulled up in front of them. "Shall I accompany you back to the Walters', Mrs. Adler?" he asked.

By that point, Lily had taken several deep breaths and managed to regain at least a semblance of her normal calm. "No, thank you. I am sure you have your own affairs to attend to today, and I will only be packing up my things to return to Half Moon Street."

Jack ran a hand through his hair. "We can try again tomorrow," he offered. "I shall even be polite next time. If we make ourselves enough of a nuisance, someone will listen eventually."

His offer took her by surprise. "You would do that?"

"Of course I would. Not as if I have much else to occupy my time while I'm stuck ashore," Jack said. He shrugged as if it did not matter, but his eyes were serious. "Say the word, Mrs. Adler, and I will do what you need. Freddy would box me soundly if I did anything else." He grinned, looking more like his usual self. "Have I done the unthinkable and shocked you into silence?"

"You are a dreadful man, Captain, I hope you know that," Lily said, but her expression softened as she added, "And you are also very kind."

"I like to be unexpected," Jack agreed. "So what will it be?"

Lily thought about Mr. Page's cold expression, the bitter way he had spoken of her class, and was about to tell Jack exactly what she thought of the infuriating principal officer. Then she thought about Philip Neve accepting a bribe worth more than his constables made in a year, about Lord Walter's cool insistence that there be "no mess" for him to deal with. Did Serena know what her husband had done? And if not, did Lily have a responsibility to tell her?

No, she decided quickly, her mind taking only seconds to jump through the possible consequences. She couldn't say anything without knowing why Lord Walter had made the bribe. If she could learn more, find out who the man was and why he had been killed, then she could figure out how Lord Walter was involved in the dreadful affair. But Bow Street had laid the case aside. *We can't identify the man* . . .

And suddenly Lily could. She remembered exactly where she had seen the murdered young man, and he had been very much alive at the time.

Lily drew in a sharp breath before she recalled where she was. Jack was still watching her, one eyebrow lifted. It had been no more than a few seconds since he had asked his question, but as far as Lily was concerned, everything had changed.

"I do not think we should press the matter. But you are very good to offer." Lily held out her hand. "Thank you for coming with me, and for your kindness."

"Mrs. Adler." Jack bowed over her hand, then helped her into the carriage. "I'm sure I shall see you again soon."

Lily watched him stroll off, then turned to the driver. "Take me to Audley Street, please. Number twenty-nine. And quickly."

CHAPTER 7

The footman who answered the door was rigidly dignified, staring at a point just above her head, his Adam's apple bobbing nervously. "Madam?"

Lily held out her card, silently amused when it took him a moment to notice; his gaze had been too high. "Would you inform Miss Oswald that Mrs. Adler has called to see her?"

The young man bowed her in. "If you would wait in the front parlor, madam," he said, opening the door to that room.

"Thank you." There was a fire in the room, and Lily settled gratefully in front of it. April was a brisk month in London. As she waited, staring absently around the room, she wondered if Miss Oswald would agree to see her. Under normal circumstances, of course, it would be odd for the girl to refuse. But as Lily had realized, the circumstances in which Miss Oswald had found herself were anything but normal.

A moment later, though, her question was answered as Miss Oswald came into the room. "Mrs. Adler, what a pleasure to see you again so soon." Lily rose, and the two women bowed politely. Miss Oswald smiled, but the expression looked forced, and her smile was uneasy as she invited Lily to sit down. The girl's eyes looked tired and red, as if she had been crying or not slept well, and her jaw was tight. "I am afraid my aunt is out at the moment."

"That is no matter, as it was you I wished to see."

"Then I am flattered that you should call so soon." Miss Oswald held a handkerchief in both hands, and she twisted and smoothed it repeatedly without seeming to notice what she was doing. "Is the draw of learning more of the West Indies so strong?"

For a moment Lily wondered if she ought to play along, but she quickly abandoned the idea. She needed information, and being direct was likely the best way to get it. "Not precisely, though I'd not be surprised if it were somehow related to the question I have for you."

Miss Oswald's shoulders tensed, and she met Lily's eyes quickly before looking away. "I'm afraid I do not understand."

"I am sure you do, though I understand your wish to deny it. It is an unfortunate situation, but you may as well have out with it now."

Miss Oswald stood abruptly. "I am terribly sorry, but if you will excuse me, I just remembered that my aunt asked me to—"

"I simply wish to ask some questions," Lily said, rising as well. She tried to sound soothing; it was not a tone of voice she often bothered with, but Miss Oswald looked as if she would bolt at any moment.

"I told you, I must—"

"I'll not be hurried out, Miss Oswald, so you may as well sit down."

"Mrs. Adler, I really am not—"

Lily interrupted as gently as she could. "You need to tell someone what you know of this business, so it might as well be me."

"Kn-know of what business?" Miss Oswald sank back onto the settee, but her shoulders were still rigid with tension.

Lily followed her own advice and sat back down as well. "You know perfectly well that I am speaking of the young man who was murdered yesterday," she said. "The young man about whom no one seems to know anything at all. Perhaps you can be comfortable with the idea of him dying anonymously, so far from home, but I did not expect you to be so heartless."

Eyes wide, Miss Oswald gasped, "Oh, Mrs. Adler!" before bursting into tears.

Lily wanted to sigh with impatience, but instead she fished out her handkerchief and handed it to the girl, who was reduced to hiccups in her effort to hold back her sobs. "You really should have spoken when you saw his face in the paper. But I suppose you were worried that someone would come banging down your door and call you a murderess?"

That made Miss Oswald sit bolt upright and glare at her. "I did not kill anyone!"

"Of course you did not," Lily said, glad to see the girl pulling herself together. "I'm not here to accuse you of anything. I simply wish to find out who the young man was and what he was doing in England. I assume he also came here from the West Indies?"

Miss Oswald nodded, looking miserable, and blew her nose loudly. "His name was Augustus Finch. He was my father's godson."

"And what was he doing in England so secretly?"

Miss Oswald looked even more miserable. "I am staying with my father's aunt so that I might find a husband, as I am sure you must have heard by now." There was a slight defensive note to her voice, for which Lily couldn't blame her. "His . . ." She took a deep breath. "My father's aim was that I find a wealthy Englishman to marry."

"The aim of many fathers," Lily said dryly. "Go on."

"Augustus followed me here, though I did not know it until yesterday. He . . . he wanted to ask for my father's permission to marry me, but . . ."

"No money?"

The girl nodded. "He was not poor, really, but he was never going to be anything more than a tradesman. Not quality, by any means." She laughed bitterly. "Not that most people consider me any better, but at least I've Papa's money and name to make up for it. Augustus did not have anything to recommend him as far as my father was concerned. And I—" she broke off.

"And you did not want to marry him?" Lily guessed.

Miss Oswald looked startled. "How did you know?"

"I know something of being in love and not being permitted to marry." It took some effort for Lily to keep her tone light. "You do not show many of the symptoms. Did he think more money would convince you?"

"He was certain we would suit if he could only get my father's blessing," Miss Oswald said, wiping her eyes with the handkerchief again and taking a deep breath before continuing. "He was a nice boy, most of the time, but so stubborn. We were not thrown together much until a few years ago, but he always had a wild streak. When I saw him last night—it was the first I knew he was in England at all!—he told me he had a plan to make himself rich. All he needed was a few more days and the right leverage."

Lily pursed her lips, holding back her own information a moment more. "And what do you think he meant by that?"

"I think . . ." Miss Oswald's voice dropped to a whisper. "I very much fear he intended to do something illegal."

"He did, I'm afraid." Lily took a deep breath. "He intended blackmail."

"What?" Miss Oswald leapt to her feet. "You knew him? You saw him?"

"I was the one who found the body."

"But . . ." The young woman twisted the handkerchief in her hands. "You mean to say he was at that party to blackmail someone *there*?"

"And it seems that someone was the person who killed him." Lily watched Miss Oswald closely as she asked, "Do you wish to go to Bow Street and tell them what you know? Who your friend was, and why he was in London?"

The young heiress hesitated before replying, "You may think me heartless, Mrs. Adler, and perhaps I am, but no. Without knowing who might have killed him . . . If I am the only person in London to know who he was, and he came to see me just before he died . . ."

"You are afraid they will take you up for his murder, having no one else to suspect." Lily nodded, inwardly relieved. If the magistrate had been bribed to let the mystery go unsolved, then he would be unlikely to listen to new information. And she had no desire to confront the unfeeling Mr. Page again, not until she knew what part Lord Walter had played in the whole business. "I agree—you cannot go to the authorities without knowing who else was involved, and why."

Miss Oswald let out a shaky breath. "It is quite the quandary, Mrs. Adler. If I stay silent, then Augustus's murderer goes free." She laughed humorlessly. "And if I speak up, I could hang for it, and his murderer will still go free. So perhaps not such a quandary after all."

"There is a third option," Lily said, her mind working quickly, hoping she could see another course of action. Before that moment, she hadn't wanted to think about what it meant that Lord Walter had bribed the magistrate. But though there were several conclusions she could draw—none of them good—there was only one clear path forward, and she had known that as soon as she left the magistrate's office. "Do you know where he was staying, Miss Oswald?"

"Where he was . . ." The girl looked wary. "What do you plan to do?"

"The only thing I can do. I shall find his murderer myself. Did Mr. Finch say where he was lodging?"

"He did."

"Excellent. His room is likely still undisturbed, since no one was able to identify him. I shall see what I can find there."

"I want to come with you."

Lily's eyebrows climbed in surprise. "Miss Oswald, you are trying to make a place for yourself in London society. I hardly think chasing a murderer is the wisest choice for you." Lily could have given herself the same advice, but she chose to ignore that fact.

"I shan't . . . I shan't tell you where Augustus was staying unless you agree to take me with you." Miss Oswald swallowed nervously as she spoke, but she raised her chin. "Unless you give me your word. There are hundreds of places where he could have been living. You could never narrow it down without my help."

Lily, who hadn't expected the girl to show so much backbone, was caught off guard. "Are you refusing to help me?"

"No, Mrs. Adler." Miss Oswald's voice trembled only a little. "I am, in fact, offering my help. It simply comes on certain terms."

Lily could not help it: in spite of the grim situation, in spite of her doubt that Miss Oswald had told her everything, in spite of her worry that she was getting in over her head, she was impressed. But she still shook her head. "Miss Oswald, it might be very difficult for you . . ." Lily hesitated. "He was your friend . . ."

"And that is why I must go. Please, Mrs. Adler." Miss Oswald swallowed again, blinking rapidly. "I had thought of going, to look through his things . . . I have to write to his mother, you see, and send her something of his, and how on earth I shall tell her . . . " More tears slipped down her cheeks, but she took a deep breath and ignored them. "I could not go by myself, of course. But perhaps I could be of some use to you, once we are there."

Lily wanted to say no. But Miss Oswald was right—it would be impossible to figure out where Mr. Finch had been staying. And given the desperate look in the young heiress's eye, Lily did not want to think what she might attempt on her own. Besides, keeping an eye on the girl might well be the safest course of action, particularly until she knew whether Miss Oswald was telling the whole truth about Augustus Finch. "Very well. Where do we begin our search?"

Miss Oswald wiped at her eyes with the back of her hand, then lifted her chin, determined once more. "The George Inn, on Borough High Street. In Southwark." She took a deep breath. "I am ready to go there immediately."

"Immediately is hardly an option," Lily said. "Unless you want all of London to be gossiping about you by sunset. We will go tomorrow afternoon."

Miss Oswald said something in reply, but Lily wasn't listening closely, her thoughts already racing ahead. She had no idea how to investigate a murder, but given what she knew, and did not know, of Lord Walter's involvement, she couldn't see another choice. Her stomach twisted at the idea that Lord Walter—kind, friendly Lord Walter, who was such a good husband to her friend, who had understood her so well—could be involved in a murder. She would not be comfortable around him or Serena until she knew what had happened.

"Mrs. Adler, what . . . how did you know to come here?" Miss Oswald asked.

"I saw you two in the garden last night," Lily answered absently, still preoccupied.

"You saw us . . . alone?"

"Yes. That was quite a slap you gave him." Lily eyed the girl in front of her, who looked horrified. "I wondered, of course, if you had killed him," she said bluntly, and Miss Oswald's eyes grew wide. "But as it would have made more sense to do it then, before you went back into the ballroom, I decided it was unlikely. Besides, I heard him trying to blackmail someone. Now, if you would be quiet for two minutes, I should be grateful."

Could it have been Lord Walter that Mr. Finch was blackmailing? Lily rose, pacing back and forth in front of the fireplace for several minutes, only a little aware of the way the girl's eyes followed her. That second voice had been lower, older, and somehow familiar, but maddeningly, she could not recall the exact sound. Shock, or perhaps fear, had driven it from her mind, and without a clear memory . . . But what secrets could Lord Walter have that were worth killing over? On the other hand, if he was not involved, why bribe the magistrate?

She looked up to find Miss Oswald staring at her with an expression somewhere between awe and confusion. "What is it?"

"You." Miss Oswald shook her head. "I can almost feel you thinking from all the way over here. Are you always so intense?"

"Are you always so direct?"

"Hardly ever. It is not exactly a trait that is encouraged in young ladies." Miss Oswald shrugged. "But I suspect that you prefer direct."

"You suspect correctly." Lily's lips quirked. "And to answer your question, yes, often. Now, for tomorrow, we shall have to tell your aunt I am taking you shopping. Do you think she will object?"

"Far from it," Miss Oswald answered with a little toss of her head. "Above all things, my aunt likes not having to chaperone me about."

Lily frowned. "I had not thought her so elderly as that. But perhaps she is unwell?"

"Neither old nor sick." Miss Oswald's voice was grim. "She does not care to have me living with her, or to have anything to do with me if she can possibly avoid it. Unfortunately for her, my father made it clear that my London season is one of those things she cannot avoid."

"Oh, I am sure that is not true," Lily said, and instantly hated herself for it. She recognized Miss Oswald's bitter tone; she had used it often enough growing up and had always despised the empty reassurances of well-meaning neighbors that her father surely cared for her a great deal. To be parroting such nonsense herself made her feel worse than foolish.

"She sponsors me, Mrs. Adler, because otherwise my father will cut off the very generous allowance that he provides, and she will have to admit to the world that her husband left her penniless when he died." Miss Oswald shrugged. "Pretending not to be embarrassed by me ranks above that, though I imagine just barely."

Lily nodded. Their circumstances were very different, of course, but they both knew how it felt to be unwanted. "I am sorry," she said simply.

Miss Oswald shrugged again. "When my father told his aunt that he was sending me to England under her care, she advised him instead to hide away all evidence of his *indiscretion* and return to England himself. She was kind enough to tell me so the first night I arrived in London. I am not naïve enough to believe her sponsorship indicates any affection."

"Were your parents unmarried, then? Or was the objection solely to your mother?" Lily asked. These were not polite questions, but the conversation had strayed far past the bounds of politeness already.

Miss Oswald looked away. "She was not of his class. But Papa always told me how dearly he loved my mother, and how he refused to marry another after she died." She hesitated, then said quietly, "It is kind of you to ask about my mother."

"Was it?" Lily's brows rose. "I thought it was abominably rude."

"But not cruelly meant. And after pretending so long that she did not exist, even rude questions are welcome," said Miss Oswald, and the forlorn expression on her face made Lily's stomach lurch in sympathy.

"Surely your father talked of her?"

Miss Oswald smiled sadly. "He told me she died when I was born, but beyond that, he did not much like to mention her. Easier, that way, for everyone to pretend I was like any other Englishman's daughter. Which I suppose I should be more grateful for, since it is the reason I am here, an heiress who never lacks for a partner on the dance floor, and with a father who raised me with his love."

"That is more than many girls can say of their fathers, though I imagine the rest of it is very hard." Lily did not press any further, though she noticed that Miss Oswald had not truly answered her question. If her father had been so reluctant to speak of it, most likely the girl herself did not know whether her parents had ever married. Either way, her father had raised her as if she was his legitimate offspring—and she wouldn't be the first natural child to inherit the wealth of a parent with no other heirs.

"It can be. But I don't really mind my aunt's disapproval." Miss Oswald shrugged. "Think how trying it would be to have a chaperone who watched my comings and goings."

"Much harder to sneak off, I imagine."

"Yes, the sneaking would be far more difficult." Miss Oswald's expression grew distant and, Lily noted sharply, a little sly.

But she did not ask about the odd comment, which she wasn't sure the girl even realized had been made loudly enough to be heard. Instead, she merely replied, "You are not quite the unassuming debutante that you seem, are you, Miss Oswald?"

"No." The girl smiled, her face open and guileless once more. "But I hope you shan't tell anyone."

"I am glad of it. If you were, I could not take you to a public inn in Southwark."

Miss Oswald was suddenly quivering with tension. "You promise you will take me?"

Lily was about to take offense at the suggestion that she would go back on her word, but a look at Miss Oswald's wide eyes and clenched jaw made her reconsider. Instead, she nodded. "I promise. Be ready at one o'clock tomorrow, and we shall see what we can discover."

★   ★   ★

As soon as Lily returned home, she settled at her writing desk.

In spite of blackmail, murder, bribery, and the possibility that her oldest friend's husband was involved in all three, Lily was not afraid— more, she had a plan in mind. She did not know how good a plan it was, but it didn't seem possible for her to make things much worse than they already were. The thought was comforting as she began her missive.

Captain Hartley, she wrote, then paused, wondering how to explain what she wanted. In the end, she decided, as usual, that blunt was best.

Would you be so good as to accompany me to the George Inn in South-wark tomorrow afternoon at one o'clock? I have a murder to solve.

★   ★   ★

Lily didn't have to wait long for an answer from Jack.

Worn out from the repeated shocks of the last twenty-four hours, she spent the evening in her small book-room. Situated in the back of the town house, it was separated from the front parlor by a narrow hallway and looked out over the postage stamp–sized garden. Filled with a collection of books that were mostly Freddy's, but to which she had begun adding as well, the room's best feature was its large fireplace. Outside, there was pouring rain and a chill wind; inside, everything was cozy. Wrapped in an oversized shawl and curled up in her favorite reading chair, a plate of tea and toast at her elbow, Lily dozed in front of the fire, trying to decide whether it was worth bothering Mrs. Carstairs for a real supper.

Her thoughts were interrupted by the jangle of the front bell and a commotion in the hall. Lily frowned, sitting up. Carstairs had strict orders to deny her to any visitors that evening, and she could hear him attempting to remonstrate with whoever had come calling.

"The devil she is not at home!"

Lily twisted just enough so that she was looking over the back of the chair as Jack stormed into the room, Carstairs still on his heels and protesting.

Lily fixed her visitor with a disapproving stare, then turned to Carstairs, whose displeasure she could feel even if his face was politely blank. "Please ask Mrs. Carstairs to send up sandwiches for two." Eyeing Jack's damp, disheveled appearance—had he walked from his lodgings?—she added, "And several towels." Lily turned back to her tea as the butler withdrew. "I do not want to see watermarks on any of my chairs, so you may not sit until the towels arrive."

"What the devil do you mean, you have a murder to solve?" Some of Jack's anger had subsided once he realized she wouldn't have him thrown him out, but he still looked outraged as he stood steaming in front of the fire. "If this is a joke, Mrs. Adler, it is a poor one."

"If it were a joke, I should say it was rather a successful one, as it prompted you to charge over here in the middle of a rainstorm." She eyed him over the rim of her teacup, brows raised. "Really, Captain, could you not have waited until morning? I would prefer not to set my neighbors gossiping about late-night visitors. Beside which, your coat looks thoroughly ruined."

"Navy men do not melt when they get damp, Mrs. Adler." Jack crossed his arms and glared at her. "Explain yourself."

Lily bristled at the demand, but of course he had a right to an explanation if she wanted his assistance. "I finally remembered why I recognized the man who was murdered. I saw him the night of the party, arguing in the gardens with a Miss Oswald, who is—"

"The Oswald heiress," Jack broke in. "I know something of her. From the West Indies?"

"Yes." Lily filled him in on the rest of the details. "Miss Oswald informed me that Mr. Finch was staying at the George Inn in

Southwark. And since two ladies cannot venture there unaccompanied . . ." She shrugged. "I should appreciate your escort."

They fell silent for a moment as Anna entered with a stack of fresh towels; the maid did not bother to hide her curious expression as she curtsied and left. Lily sighed. The last thing she needed was her servants knowing what she intended. It would be all over London within a day.

"Two ladies?" Jack's eyes narrowed once they were alone again.

"Miss Oswald wishes to come with me. She has even more interest than I do in discovering who killed her friend."

"In discovering who did it? Or hiding her own involvement? If you saw them together only a short while before he died—"

"After which I overheard Mr. Finch arguing with the man he was attempting to blackmail." Lily raised her brows. "I think it far more likely that murder was committed by the victim of blackmail than by the victim of a marriage proposal. But if she was involved—I admit there is that chance—would it not be better for me to keep her close, where I can watch her?"

"There is that." Jack scowled. "But if she is so interested in discovering who did this, why did she not take what she knows to the magistrate? For that matter, why haven't you?"

Lily sighed. "She cannot, for the exact reasons that caused you to suspect her. And I cannot, for an equally good reason." Quietly, she told him of Lord Walter's bribe, and the magistrate's subsequent disinterest in the murdered man's case. "Once I recognized the magistrate, I went back to speak to Mr. Page, and . . ." Lily scowled in frustration, then shrugged. "They have no interest in investigating the matter. But I have to know how Serena's husband is involved, and besides that . . . I have to do something, Jack." Lily used his given name without thinking. "Can you stand to see a murderer go free for lack of anyone to care?"

"Murderers go free all the time, Mrs. Adler." Having dried off at last, he sat in the chair next to hers, his eyes very earnest, his usual charming air abandoned. "If this is just for a lark, something to occupy you when there are no balls or parties to attend—"

Lily realized she was clenching her fists, nails biting into her palms, and it took several moments to force herself to relax.

Was she fooling herself, playing at a magistrate's work because she had nothing better to do? It was a struggle to push the thought aside. But . . . for the first time since Freddy's death, she had looked at a task in front of her and seen something that mattered, something no one else seemed to care about.

There was Mr. Finch to consider, lying cold and dead, and no matter what he had done, he did not deserve for his murderer to go free. And then there was Lord Walter—kind Lord Walter, who had always made her feel she had a place in his world—and Serena, whose husband might be involved in a murder. Didn't she owe it to her friend to find out the truth?

"Mrs. Adler?" Jack was watching her, lines of concern between his brows.

She thought of Reggie Harper's proposition to her at Serena's ball, his instant confidence that she would welcome his attention, his angry confusion at her rejection. Was that all she was good for now? To be one man's mistress until she could become another man's wife?

She refused to accept that.

"This matters, Jack." Trying to explain seemed inadequate; all she could do was hope he would understand. "It needs to be done. And I think I can do it."

Something of her resolution must have come through in her voice, because he stared at her for a long, considering moment. "I should lock you up instead of agreeing to anything so dangerous."

"I shan't be in danger if no one knows what I am doing," Lily pointed out. "If we do not find anything tomorrow, I promise I shall give it up. But I have to at least try."

"And if I do not agree?"

"Then I shall go without an escort," Lily said, with more confidence than she felt.

Her bravado seemed to work; Jack ran a restless hand through his hair before sitting back and nodding. "Then I shall do it, God help me." Casting a sideways glance at her, he added, with something more like his usual manner, "Impossible woman."

While Lily sighed in relief at his agreement, Jack glanced toward the door. "Now, where has that girl got to with the supper tray? That is the real reason I came dashing over here, you know. Not a bite to be had in my lodgings."

Lily snorted and pushed the tea tray toward him. "The dangers of bachelor living."

He grinned as he shoved a piece of toast into his mouth. "Something like that."

CHAPTER 8

The ride to the George Inn was a tense and silent one, Miss Oswald being occupied with fidgeting anxiously in her seat and glancing out the window, and Captain Hartley being occupied with scowling at Miss Oswald, whom he obviously still regarded with suspicion. Lily was grateful, because the silence meant that neither of her companions asked how she meant to gain access to poor Mr. Finch's room.

It seemed safe to assume that the proprietor would not simply allow strangers into a guest's rooms, no matter that the guest in question had not been seen for nearly two full days. She hoped she would come up with some idea once they got there—preferably more than one, in case the first did not work—but so far nothing had occurred to her.

She needn't have worried. As soon as they arrived, Jack directed their driver to pull the carriage around the back of the building and to wait with the two women while he went inside. "And you might want to pull your veils down, both of you," he added as he hopped out. "No sense letting everyone in here see your faces." He gave Lily a sideways look as he did so, still disapproving of the scheme. But he did not argue or try to talk her out of it, for which she was grateful.

"Are we going to do something illegal?" Miss Oswald asked, watching Jack disappear through the tradesman's door.

"Is it legal to enter a man's lodgings and search his things?" Lily asked, drawing the veil of her hat down as Jack had suggested.

"I very much doubt it."

"Then yes, we are."

"Oh." Miss Oswald looked uncertain, then shrugged. "Well, I suppose we haven't any other option." She pulled her own veil down as well.

In spite of her anxiety, Lily smiled. She was liking the girl more by the minute.

It didn't take long for Jack to return, the collar of his driving coat turned up as high as it would go and his hat shadowing his face. He spoke to the driver briefly, then opened the carriage door. "Inside, quickly."

Much as Lily disliked not knowing what was going on, there was a time to insist on information and a time to do what she was told. She motioned Miss Oswald to go ahead before following herself. Jack herded them into the back entrance of the hotel.

The hallway was not empty, which made Lily uneasy. But the servants went about their business, though a couple cast smirking glances in their direction. Behind her veil, Lily frowned, wondering what those looks meant, but she didn't have a chance to ask. Jack closed the door behind them, then jerked his head toward the stairs.

"Second floor," he ordered. Miss Oswald obeyed immediately, and Lily, after a moment's hesitation, did the same. Jack brought up the rear.

There was a nervous-looking maid waiting at the top of the stairs, and she cast an accusing look at Jack as he came up. "I dunno as I should," she whispered. "If these two are going wiv you—"

"As I said, we simply wish to wait for my friend." Jack smiled. "I assure you, the gentleman would not object, were he here to ask."

The maid still looked nervous, but a coin made its way from Jack's hand to hers, and in the end she shrugged and led the way down the corridor.

Her reaction cast a new light on the smirking looks they had received downstairs. Lily grabbed Jack's arm. "What did you tell her?"

she demanded. "Do you realize she thinks . . . the people downstairs think I am . . . and Miss Oswald is . . ." She couldn't bring herself to say it.

Jack's quiet chuckle did nothing to improve her irritation. "There is a reason I told you to put your veils down," he said, his voice maddeningly calm. "Try not to let it bother you, Mrs. Adler. If they think you are light-skirts, no one will wonder why a gentleman and two unknown women might want visit to another fellow's rooms."

He was right, of course, but Lily could not bring herself to say so. She was saved having to come up with a reply when the maid stopped in front of one of the doors. "This is it," she whispered, fishing through several keys before finding the correct one. She hesitated a moment, and Lily's stomach lurched with nerves. But Jack leaned in and whispered something that made the maid laugh and shove his shoulder. "Away wiv ye, flatterer," she said, shaking her head as she handed over the key. Jack winked at her, and there was enough light in the dim hall for Lily to see the shine of money changing hands once again before the girl scurried off down the hall.

Lily resisted the urge to roll her eyes. "Is there anyone that you can't manage to get your way with?" she demanded.

"My mother," Jack said wryly. "And my older sister. And you, apparently, since here we are." He unlocked the door and gestured for the two women to go ahead. "I hope it was not presumptuous of me to interfere with your plan to gain access to the room, Mrs. Adler." His tone was utterly sincere, but there was laughter lurking in the corners of his mouth.

"You know perfectly well I hadn't one," Lily said tartly as Jack locked the door behind them to keep anyone from intruding on their search. "You'll find I am a practical woman, Captain; I am perfectly capable of stepping back and letting others exercise their talents when those talents get me what I want." Ignoring Jack's amused snort, she surveyed the room.

It was comfortably, if cheaply, furnished, with a bed, writing desk, tallboy, and dressing table. There were a few possessions scattered across the table—brushes and shaving tackle, an extra cravat—and washing water in a pitcher next to an empty bowl. Clearly a servant had brought it that morning, not knowing that the room's occupant would not be returning.

"He did not bring much with him," Lily observed, opening the tallboy. A small part of her was horrified at the cavalier way she was rifling through a dead man's—a stranger's!—things, but she ignored such delicate concerns. There was no other way to learn what she needed to know. "A few clothes, a driving coat, an extra pair of boots." She glanced at Miss Oswald. "He wouldn't have had a servant with him?"

"No." The girl shook her head. She still stood by the door, hesitating, nervously fiddling with the buttons on her pelisse. "He never kept one."

"He did bring a number of books," Jack said from his corner of the room. "Or bought them once he was here." He looked up. "It seems your Mr. Finch was a fan of the inestimable Mrs. Radcliffe."

Miss Oswald smiled sadly and went to join him. "Augustus had a taste for novels. When we were younger he would loan them to me." Miss Oswald lifted several of the books, murmuring, "I should send them back to his mother."

Jack let out a low whistle. "He brought something else with him." He held out a slim object that glinted in the dim light. "Quite a pretty little pistol. Shame he didn't have it with him when he went to meet the object of his blackmail."

"He might have." Miss Oswald took the pistol from a startled Jack, looking it over in a calm, professional manner. "I learned to shoot with this pistol, or one like it."

"You shoot?" Jack's eyes narrowed.

"My father taught me," Miss Oswald murmured, still examining the pistol. "This was part of a set; my father gave them to Augustus for his twentieth birthday. If he brought one, he certainly brought both." She looked around. "Is there another?"

"Not that I found," Jack said. "Though there was space for another in the case."

"One of the gentlemen I overheard had a gun," Lily said, abandoning the uninteresting contents of the tallboy. "But if it was Mr. Finch's, how did it happen that he was the one shot?"

"They might have scuffled," Jack said thoughtfully. "If the other man got control of the weapon and was a competent marksman . . ."

His gaze lingered on Miss Oswald as he spoke. Lily was about to change the subject, but the girl spoke up first. "Why do you keep staring at me in such a manner, Captain?" she demanded, dropping the pistol down on the bedside table with a clatter. "I realize these are awkward circumstances under which to meet, but surely you can move past that if Mrs. Adler and I have."

Lily sighed. "He is not awkward, he is suspicious, I am afraid. He thinks it possible that you shot Mr. Finch."

Miss Oswald stepped back abruptly. "You cannot be serious."

"I know Mrs. Adler saw you arguing not long before he was shot." Jack crossed his arms and scowled at both women. "And you don't seem particularly distraught at your friend's death."

"Of course I am distraught! Why on earth do you think I'm here, trying to find out who killed him?"

"Calmly going through his things, traipsing about in Southwark?" Jack scoffed. "I would guess you even have plans for this evening. Not quite my idea of grief, I must say."

"What *right* have you—?" Miss Oswald's jaw and fists both clenched. "What makes you think you know anything about what I am feeling? Perhaps Augustus and I weren't close, perhaps I even disliked him this past year when he wouldn't leave off pursuing me, guilty though that makes me feel now. But that doesn't mean I *killed him*." Her voice rose sharply at the end; she took a deep breath, then said more quietly, "I did not kill him."

"We've discussed this already, and if we need to discuss it again, we shall," Lily broke in briskly. "But for now, lingering here to argue does not seem like a particularly good idea. Is there anything else noteworthy among his books?"

For a moment Miss Oswald and Jack left off glaring at each other to glare at her. Lily raised her brows and gave a pointed nod toward the door. Miss Oswald gave her eyes an angry swipe and stalked over to the desk, while Jack, with a sigh, bent to the books once more.

"A copy of *Brooke's Guide to the Peerage*," he said, hefting that heavy tome. "A London business directory, a map of the city . . ."

"All things he might have needed to pursue a course of blackmail against someone here," Lily said.

"Or to learn his way around," Jack pointed out. "It's not conclusive."

"Nothing helpful here either." Miss Oswald was sifting through the drawers of the desk.

To Lily's surprise, Jack grinned. "If you would step aside, ma'am, I might be able to find out what sort of letters your Mr. Finch was writing."

"There are no letters," Miss Oswald said, a note of irritation in her voice, though she did what he asked. "Just like Augustus not to leave anything helpful behind!"

"No letters," Jack murmured, not really listening as he bent to stare at the blotter at eye level. Squinting, he moved his head back and forth.

Lily, as soon as she understood what he was doing, could not help letting out a pleased laugh. "Is there anything there?" she asked, beginning to fish around in the drawers.

"There is." Jack still squinted sideways at the blotter. "But it is very faint."

"Then these should help," she said, handing him the sheet of writing paper and stump of pencil she had found.

Jack grinned as he took them. "You are a treasure, Mrs. Adler."

"What are you doing?" Miss Oswald demanded, peering around Lily's shoulder.

"A rubbing," Lily said as Jack placed the sheet of paper over the blotter and set to with the pencil. "It should—ah, there!" Lily smiled as the faint remains of handwriting, imprinted on the blotter, began to come clear under the sweep of pencil lead. "We should be able to see at least some of whatever he wrote last."

"As long as the fellow did not write too many letters," Jack muttered.

"That's very clever," Miss Oswald admitted grudgingly, giving Jack a sideways glance. "I should never have thought of such a trick."

"Freddy taught it to me," Lily said. "He used it to spy on his elder brother."

"And I," Jack said, finishing the rubbing with a flourish of the now-useless pencil, "taught it to him. Excellent way to discover what my sister was writing to her beaux."

"How beastly of you," Lily murmured, but she was no longer quite paying attention. Without waiting for permission, she plucked the paper from Jack's hands and examined it closely, ignoring the captain's sigh of resignation at having his carefully constructed clue taken from him. "Well, we may conclude from this that he was not a great writer, for there are the traces of only one letter here. And he did not have a heavy hand, because it's very faint." Frowning, she added, "That is, assuming that Mr. Finch was indeed the writer of the letter, and not the room's previous tenant."

"Let me see it," Miss Oswald said, holding out her hand. She stared at the paper, then thrust it abruptly back toward Lily with a gasp that sounded like a swallowed sob. "Yes, it is his writing. The stupid boy!" Taking a deep breath, she added, "There's not much to read, but lay it on the blotter, and we can look it over together. Perhaps one of you will be able to make it out."

Lily laid a gentle hand on the younger woman's arm. "Do you need one of us to take you home?"

"No," Miss Oswald said, her voice firm despite her trembling. "You may yet need me. How else would you have known it was

Augustus's handwriting on the letter? And I'll not have him"—she jerked her chin toward Jack—"say I am running away. No, I don't wish to leave. Lay out the letter, and let us take a look."

This sort of rubbing, Lily knew, depended on how firm a hand the writer used. Unfortunately, Mr. Finch was not a firm writer at all, for in places there was nothing to see. And his hand was such a scrawl that at first she could not make anything out at all. After a moment of frowning at it, though, she caught the trick of his writing and began to read.

> *Dear Sir,*
>
> *Though I am cur . . . tly unkn . . . n to you, I hope . . . ence of writing . . . I am sure th . . . when . . . learnt what I know, you will be most grtfl that I have approached . . . my information to more official channels.*
>
> *. . . which I . . . will be of grt int . . . est & mutual benefit . . . certain facts concer . . . the wa . . . ffort . . . activities on the Continent . . . favor of a meet . . . so that I may present my offer to you in person—As a sample of my knowledge . . . firm of Lac . . . est, & a certain clever method of communication involving . . .*
>
> *Pls be ass . . . provisions for . . . own well-being . . . not the only person in possession of these facts . . . deal directly . . . the manner I have suggested, rather than attempt . . . to complic . . . issue . . . greater trouble.*
>
> *I re . . . in,*
>
> *Yours &c . . .*

Lily sighed and straightened. "Well, that makes no sense. At least, not yet."

"Do you think—" Miss Oswald began, then broke off as a noise arose in the corridor and died down just as quickly.

"I think we oughtn't linger here," Jack said, rolling the paper up quickly and sticking it in his jacket pocket. "Mrs. Adler?"

"I agree," Lily said. Twitching her veil down, she added, "I should like to mull things over. Miss Oswald, did you want to return any of your friend's possessions to his family?"

The young heiress was already gathering up an armful of books and one or two handkerchiefs. "Do you think I could persuade the innkeeper to release the rest of his things to me?" she asked forlornly.

"We can send a servant to inquire in a day or two," Lily suggested gently. "Once it has become clear that their owner is not returning."

Miss Oswald nodded, her eyes red but her manner composed. "Then let us leave."

Jack cracked open the door and, after making certain there was no one there, ushered the girl into the hallway. Lily took a final glance around the room, frowning to herself. Something about the room had struck her as odd—something that was, perhaps, missing or out of place. But she did not have time to think it over; Jack was motioning her to follow, and Miss Oswald had already slipped down the stairs. Lily, shaking her head, put the thought from her mind and hurried to follow.

It was not until much later that she realized what she had noticed: Mr. Finch's pistol was no longer on the table.

★ ★ ★

It took Jack the better part of five minutes, and an additional six-pence, to sneak the two ladies out of the inn without anyone seeing them. But eventually they were ensconced once more in the carriage that had, fortunately, waited for them.

"Shall I tell him to take us to Half Moon Street?" Jack asked.

"No." Lily laid off her veil and settled back against the seat. "Bond Street, if you please. Or wherever you should like to be dropped off first, Captain."

"What?" The astonished word burst out of Miss Oswald.

Jack was no less surprised, though he controlled it better. "You intend a shopping trip, Mrs. Adler?"

"Of course." She frowned at them. "I told Miss Oswald's aunt that I was taking her shopping. Shopping we clearly must go, and I don't imagine you will wish to accompany us."

"The devil I will not," Jack said. "I'll not leave you to gallivant unaccompanied around London." His eyes flickered to Miss Oswald as he spoke. His suspicions, it seemed, had not been set aside.

Lily adjusted a button on one glove to hide her vexation. There was no point in arguing with him; it would only upset Miss Oswald further. Lily did not entirely blame him; she was sure Miss Oswald was still keeping secrets. But Jack was not helping the situation. "Very well, you may accompany us to buy new gloves."

Sticking his head out, Jack gave instructions to the driver, then settled back, arms crossed and a satisfied expression on his face.

"But this is absurd!" Miss Oswald said, voice raised before she remembered the driver and lowered it. "You said you wanted to mull things over."

"And I shall," Lily said firmly. "But however negligent a chaperone your aunt may be, she would hardly believe we spent an entire afternoon shopping and did not return with a single thing. Thus, gloves."

"Captain, surely you cannot agree!"

"I have recently made it my policy never to argue with Mrs. Adler," he said with an ironic smile. Lily resisted the urge to roll her eyes. She knew very well that not arguing did not mean agreeing. "It seems she is nearly always right, so argument will only make me look the fool." He cast his eyes at Lily and added, "Again."

"Hardly a fool," Lily said. "Merely wrong."

"Ah yes, a state of being which any gentleman greatly enjoys," he said dryly. "No, I'll not argue with her, Miss Oswald. And in any case, thinking things over often produces better insights than hours of discussion."

Pleased that he agreed with her on at least one thing, Lily let the matter drop and turned to watch their progress through London's crowded streets. It was slow going, but eventually the hired carriage rattled to a halt. "Here we are. Put off your thoughtful face, Miss Oswald; it will never do to look so serious for a shopping trip. I suggest at least two pairs of gloves, and perhaps a new hat as well."

"I thought you were joking about that bit." Jack suddenly looked horrified.

Lily raised an eyebrow at him. "I would never joke about gloves."

CHAPTER 9

Jack lasted through two new hats that Miss Oswald purchased on her father's account and a trip to the circulating library. But when the girl mentioned the dress waiting at the modiste for her to try on, he gave up and said he would return for them in half an hour.

Lily did not mind. As Miss Oswald disappeared into the back room for her fitting, she settled down on one of the shop's comfortable chaises. While waiting in the library, she had carefully copied out Augustus Finch's letter onto a new piece of paper; she pulled that out of her reticule now, angling her body so she could study it without any of the store's other patrons looking over her shoulder.

Dear Sir, the letter began, politely and maddeningly. Why did he not address the gentleman by name? It would have saved, Lily thought with grim amusement, a great deal of effort on her part. The object of Mr. Finch's blackmail must have been one of Serena's guests; otherwise, why choose the Walters' garden as a meeting place? But there had been two hundred people attending the soiree.

The ladies could be discounted—that *Dear Sir* was plain enough, and Lily had distinctly heard two male voices. But that left dozens of gentlemen to consider, and first among them was Lord Walter.

Lily frowned. Her friend's doting husband was the last person she would have suspected had she not witnessed him bribing the investigating magistrate. The members of London's upper class had been known to interfere with the new Bow Street police force simply to keep the constables away from their homes. But a bribe of three hundred pounds seemed too substantial to be due merely to dislike of the new police force, however conservative a man's opinions and politics. There had to be something more going on, something to make Lord Walter wary of having an investigation too near his family.

It should have been impossible for quiet, gentle John Walter to be a murderer. But blackmail could do strange things to a man.

She needed to know if he was involved, preferably that he was *not*, for Serena's sake and her own peace of mind. The best way to do that would be to prove that Augustus Finch's murderer was someone else.

Though I am cur . . . tly unkn . . . n to you . . . Currently unknown, Lily decided, which meant the man Mr. Finch was blackmailing had either never met him before or was a social superior and would not have taken note of him. Who then, had given the poor young man his information?

. . . which I . . . will be of grt int . . . est & mutual benefit . . . certain facts concer . . . the wa . . . ffort . . . activities on the Continent . . . favor of a meet . . . so that I may present my offer to you in person—As a sample of my knowledge . . . firm of Lac . . . est, & a certain clever method of communication involving . . .

Something there caught her attention, but Lily had to read through the scattered paragraph two more times before she realized what it was. *. . . . certain facts concer . . . the wa . . . ffort . . . activities on the Continent . . .*

War effort. There was nothing else that fit. Mr. Finch's *certain facts* must concern the war with France. It had been years since any Englishman's Continental activities were about anything else. Had Mr. Finch attempted to blackmail someone in Parliament? Or perhaps someone in the military?

The next part was the key. Mr. Finch had offered a sample of his knowledge. *. . . . firm of Lac . . . est, & a certain clever method of communication involving . . .* A law firm, or perhaps a financial firm? She did not know London businesses well enough to guess. It began with *Lac*, but that was all she had to go on.

Lily sighed in frustration. The writing had been too light, too scrawling. There was too much missing for her to determine any other details from the letter. "Mr. Finch," she muttered, "it is a sign of poor character to write in a hand so lacking in firmness." She considered, then added, "And also to blackmail someone."

"What was that, Lily?"

Lily started, quickly folding the paper over as she looked up. "Margaret!" She stood, hoping she didn't look too flustered, to give her friend a quick kiss on the cheek. "And Miss Harper, what brings the two of you here?"

"Margaret very kindly invited me out this afternoon. And when I saw you through the window, we thought we would stop in to say hello," Miss Harper said. Smiling solicitously, she added, "How is your ankle today?"

For a moment, Lily could only stare blankly. "My ankle?"

"The one you twisted." Miss Harper frowned.

Silently, Lily called herself ten kinds of stupid as she managed a weak smile. "Oh, much improved, I thank you. It was not serious."

"It was, perhaps, a fortunate injury," Miss Harper said. "To take you back inside at that moment."

"The poor man, you mean?" Lily asked, mentally scrambling for a way to divert the conversation.

"Of course!" Miss Harper's eyes grew wide. "Why, if you had been out on the terrace much longer, you might have come face-to-face with a murderer."

"Heavens, what a thought!" Margaret shuddered. "I hadn't realized you came so close to disaster, Lily."

"Then I suppose I must be grateful for my clumsiness." Lily hoped she sounded sufficiently unconcerned. "I should write our old deportment teacher and tell her."

Miss Harper looked as though she might have pursued the topic further, but Lily was saved by Margaret exclaiming, "Isobel, is that not the shade of silk you were inquiring about last week? You should pounce immediately; yellow always disappears so quickly in the spring."

As Miss Harper excused herself to examine the fabric, Margaret lowered her voice. "I am glad she is taking an interest in these things again. Poor dear, she never recovered after that army fellow jilted her. All because it turned out she had a smaller dowry than he expected! I am still amazed her uncle did not pursue action against the man."

"Perhaps General Harper did not approve the match in the first place." Lily glanced after Miss Harper's proper, upright form, feeling sympathetic. It had taken years for Lily's father to agree to her own marriage with Freddy. Had it been Freddy's elder brother, Lily suspected her father's pride would have been mollified much sooner, even though the Adlers' baronetcy was barely three generations old. But it had been the second son she had fallen in love with, and though Freddy's older brother had provided for him, George Pierce had refused to approve of a younger son of modest income joining his family. It was not until Lily had come into an inheritance left by her mother and had the means to marry without his approval that Mr. Pierce had reluctantly agreed to the match and settled a dowry on his daughter.

Poor Miss Harper, though, had never had that chance.

"Perhaps. She's not sought to leave her uncle's home since, not to my knowledge." Margaret dropped her voice even further. "In fact, Isobel barely came into society at all in the past four years. Then all of a sudden . . ." She lifted her brows suggestively. "A lady of seven and twenty may still find a husband, and what are old school friends for if not to help when it is needed?"

Lily sighed as Margaret gave her a sly glance. "Well, this lady is uninterested in matrimony," she said. "In case your mind was straying along those lines."

"Oh, you are no fun," Margaret laughed. "Will you join us for ices? Isobel suggested I ask you. I think she is trying to widen her circle of acquaintances, now that . . . well, you know."

Lily did know. Isobel Harper had been too self-satisfied and aloof for close friendships when they were in school. Back then, she would have looked down on a woman like Margaret, whose family connections were impeccable but whose husband was the younger son of a country squire, and who supported his family with a profession. But it seemed that sense of superiority had disappeared with the years and disappointments that followed. "That is very kind, but I'm afraid my time is spoken for this afternoon," Lily said as Miss Harper rejoined them. "I promised a friend I would stay to give my opinion on her new gown."

"You do have excellent taste," Margaret agreed. "And it looks as though you have some engrossing reading to keep you occupied while you wait," she added, glancing at the folded paper Lily still held.

"I hope there was nothing alarming in your letter," Miss Harper added. "Your expression was most serious as we came in."

"News from home," Lily lied, slipping the paper back into her reticule and hoping neither of them asked for details. News was entertainment, and not offering to share an amusing letter ran the risk of raising eyebrows. But she could not have anyone find out what she was up to, not even as close a friend as Margaret.

Luckily Margaret knew about Lily's strained relationship with her father. "Reason enough to look serious, I'm sure," she said sympathetically. "Did you sort out your silk, Isobel? Then let us be off. I am famished, and Gunter's has the most delightful little apple pastries . . ."

Lily watched them go, wondering if she was making a huge mistake. If anyone in her social circle found out what she was doing, the gossip would label her *eccentric*, *unwomanly*, and perhaps even *unstable* before two days had passed. That was how upper-class society in London worked, and Lily, for all she could be unconventional from time to time, had no desire to lose her place in society. Was it really worth risking so much?

"Mrs. Adler?" The voice made Lily start; lost in her thoughts, she had not noticed Miss Oswald rejoin her. The girl stood in front of her, fiddling with her gloves in an ineffective attempt to hide her agitation. "Have we stayed long enough? The mantua-maker kept asking about lace for the sleeves, and I've pretended to care as long as

I was able. But I cannot make myself think about clothes or shopping anymore."

Seeing Miss Oswald turned Lily's thoughts to Augustus Finch: a man—a boy, really—who had made a stupid decision in order to impress the girl he loved. A boy who was now lying dead, his murderer wandering free. He deserved justice, and she, it seemed, was the only person willing to find it for him.

And despite the obstacles in her path, she had made progress. Already she had learned not only the victim's name and where he had been staying, but what had brought him to London and led to his death.

No, she could not abandon her self-appointed task now, no matter the risks to her own reputation. Some things mattered more than the scandal they might cause.

"Mrs. Adler?" The young heiress was frowning at her.

Lily stood. "We need to find the captain. I've something to share with you both."

★　★　★

When they finally returned to number thirteen, Lily briskly ordered a fire made up in her parlor and asked Mrs. Carstairs to bring tea—and, with a glance at Jack, a measure of brandy.

"Miss Oswald, would you pour? I shall return in a moment. No, Captain, you wait here." Lily gestured him back when he would have followed her. "I shall call you if I need anything fetched from a high shelf. And do try to make friends with each other."

Jack sighed as Lily left the room, running a hand through his hair. "I swear, I am likely to wring her neck before this is done."

Miss Oswald looked indignant. "I think she's marvelous. I've never before met anyone so . . . so *charming* about ordering everyone around."

That made Jack laugh, though he didn't want to find Miss Oswald amusing. "I never would have thought to put it that way, but she is rather a force of nature."

"Were you a relation of her husband's, Captain Hartley?"

The question took him by surprise. "No, what makes you ask that?"

"You seem quite friendly, but I hadn't heard that Hartley was her family name. And you don't at all act like lovers."

"We don't act like . . ." Jack stared at her. "Good Lord, are you even supposed to know about such things at your age?"

"I beg your pardon," she said, though she didn't look contrite at all. "Once you accused me of murder, I assumed there was no need to worry about polite conversation."

"No wonder she likes you." Jack shook his head. "You're as bad as she is."

"I shall take that as a high compliment, given what I have seen of Mrs. Adler." Miss Oswald stood abruptly. Walking over to the fire, she said without looking at him, "She doesn't treat me differently, unlike so many here—and so many back home! Why is that?"

Jack shrugged uncomfortably, since the question touched close to home for him as well. "She likes clever people, I think, and the devil knows there are few enough of them in Mayfair. Somehow she pegged you as one. Perhaps that was enough for her."

"She is very different from most people here, then," the girl said. Her smile was unreadable as she fixed her eyes back on him. "And you, Captain Hartley?"

"I know something of being caught between worlds, Miss Oswald." His normally charming smile grew a little mocking.

Her brows rose. "I don't think any of your ancestors were slaves, Captain Hartley."

"No, madam. But a good half of them were Mughals." Miss Oswald's eyes widened, and he scowled, the old mixture of defensiveness and exasperation rising in him. It had been years since he had needed to explain his parentage to anyone. At his parents' home in Hertfordshire, the local population was so used to his mother that "the Indian lady" had ceased to be a topic of interest, and in London, he looked English enough that the question rarely came up. In the navy, his superior officers had raised a brow or two, and he knew some had written him off, but knowing the culture and language of the many Indian men who now sailed under the British flag had become more of an asset than a hindrance to his career. "You look shocked, but it has not been that uncommon. Colonel Kirkpatrick himself married an Indian wife, as did many men of the East India Company once upon a time."

"Your father had children with an Indian woman?" Her tone was still stunned.

"My father had children with his wife," Jack replied sharply. He had expected that she, at least, would be less surprised. "Who happens to be Indian."

"I did not mean . . . That is . . ." She looked away and fidgeted with her gloves, embarrassed. "You are fortunate to know your family and your parentage so clearly, Captain."

There was an awkward pause. In an effort to change what had become an intensely personal conversation, Jack cleared his throat and called out, "Mrs. Adler! You've not vanished, I hope?"

"Of course not," came the quick reply. There was a clatter on the other side of the door, and then Lily shouldered it open, carrying a large volume, which she dropped on the table with a flourish. "We shall need a London business directory shortly."

"Did you discover something? Was it in the letter?" Miss Oswald demanded, eyes wide. She clasped her trembling hands together. "Did you figure out what it said? Oh please—"

"Miss Oswald," Jack interrupted. If she had been one of his sailors, he would have given her a shake, but a firm tone worked just as well. "Perhaps you should sit down before you work yourself into a faint."

Miss Oswald glared at him. "I was merely asking a question, Captain."

"Then I suggest we pause for breath long enough to give Mrs. Adler a chance to answer." He gave Lily a slight bow. "You were saying, ma'am?"

Lily shook her head. "You two really must learn to get along if you wish me to keep you informed of my progress."

Miss Oswald turned to scowl at her too. "I feel no need to get along with someone who treats me like a silly girl."

"Then pull yourself together and prove him wrong," Lily said. Jack managed to hold in a snort of laughter. "If we've finished squabbling, shall I tell you both what I found?"

At that, Jack leaned forward eagerly. "You did discover something, then?"

"About the letter, yes." Lily shared her conclusions about the letter's contents. Miss Oswald insisted on seeing the copy of the letter and bent over it to study the patchy contents. Jack could see Lily watching the girl's shaking hands out of the corner of her eye; it seemed her high-strung swings between bravado and distress were worrying them both. To be fair to the girl, he thought grudgingly, that was perfectly normal behavior for someone who was grieving. And Miss Oswald, unable to publicly admit her relationship to the dead man, couldn't hide her messy emotions behind the social conventions of mourning.

"I have to admit that it is more like a conjecture than a discovery," Lily continued, breaking through Jack's thoughts. "But I believe it all fits together. Though as for activities on the Continent and something to do with the war . . ." She lifted her shoulders, then dropped them with a sigh. "There are dozens of possibilities."

"And with Bonaparte escaped from Elba and on the loose once more . . ." Miss Oswald shuddered. "A connection to nefarious activities on the Continent becomes even more dangerous. Stupid, stupid Augustus," she added, her jaw tight. "But what has me puzzled is how Augustus could have found out something worth blackmail." She looked from Lily to Jack, her brows drawn together in frustration. "I would have sworn he didn't know a single other person in London besides me, and I certainly didn't tell him anything. So who did?"

"Perhaps it concerned something between London and Nevis," Jack suggested, looking thoughtfully at Miss Oswald as he mentioned the island of her birth. He still thought it possible that Miss Oswald knew something about Finch's blackmail business; after all, what man would follow a woman who had thoroughly rejected him across the entire ocean? If the letter concerned a matter in the West Indies, then she might be hiding something after all. "It might have do with the war with America. The Treaty of Ghent was signed last year, of course, but treason remains treason, even after peace is declared."

Lily frowned. "It is a possibility . . . but the letter also mentioned the Continent. Perhaps whatever happened concerns *both*." She shook her head. "No, something is still missing. The letter mentioned another party that was involved, you recall. A firm of some kind. I suspect this firm is a London business. Hence the directory."

"I do not recall that part of it," Jack admitted. "Was there any hint of the name?"

"It began with *L-A-C*." Lily sighed. "But we have no clue as to the type of business. I do not suppose you have any ideas?

Jack shook his head, wishing he could be of more help. "I've not spend much time in London, which limits my knowledge of its business world."

"Then, we shall simply have to hope the directory provides some hint—" Lily broke off. "Miss Oswald, are you even attending?"

"No," came the agitated answer. The young heiress's eyes were fixed on a point in the distance. Her lips moved almost soundlessly, as if she was reciting something to herself.

"Do you think that—" Jack began, but she cut him off.

"Be quiet, sir. I am trying to remember."

"Remember what—" Lily began, but stopped abruptly upon receiving a very expressive scowl.

The young woman tugged on one of her dark curls without seeming to notice and murmured something over and over to herself. "Lace. Lace, lace, lace. Lace and . . . oh, drat it. Lace and . . ."

Lily gave Jack a perplexed glance, and he shrugged, crossing his arms and settling his back in his chair. They stayed that way for several moments, until Miss Oswald snapped her fingers, her face glowing with a triumphant smile. "I have it."

"Have what?"

"Well." The smile faded a little. "At least, I think I have it?"

"Have what?" Lily repeated impatiently.

"The name of the firm," Miss Oswald said as she held up the letter, tapping her finger against the relevant passage. "*Lacey and West*. It fits, do you see?"

Lily plucked the letter from the girl's fingers and read through it. "It could." She passed the paper to Jack, who nodded. "Who are they?"

"I'm afraid I haven't any idea." Miss Oswald sighed.

Lily stared at her. "I'm quite confused, Miss Oswald, and I assure you, that does not happen often."

The girl fidgeted with embarrassment. "I know it's not very helpful. But I remember the name from some of my father's correspondence. He never had any business with them, which is why I don't know more. But I know it's a firm in London, and they have to do with imports, or shipping, or something of that nature. And look." She scowled impatiently at Jack as she held out her hand for the letter, and he managed not to shake his head at the petulant expression as he handed it over. "See what is written. It starts *Lac*—, but there is not much space between that and the next word, which ends—*est*. *Lacey and West* works. I doubt we will find another firm in London whose name fits so neatly."

"It does make a good deal of sense," Jack said, nodding slowly.

Lily raised her eyebrows. "Do my ears deceive me? Do the two of you agree?"

Jack began to protest, but stopped, embarrassed, when he realized Miss Oswald was doing the same thing. It didn't seem to matter, though. Lily was already ignoring them to flip through the business directory. It did not take her long to find the relevant entry. "I have them. Lacey and West . . ." She paused. "Are shipping agents."

"Oh." Miss Oswald let out a long sigh. "Well, that makes perfect sense, I suppose."

"Excellent. Excellent. I was hoping you would say that." Lily dusted her palms off against each other. Her lips pursed, and she sounded put out as she admitted, "Unfortunately, I haven't any idea what a shipping agent is."

CHAPTER 10

Fortunately, thanks to her work with her father, Miss Oswald was well versed in the nuances of the shipping industry, and Lily was a quick study. She frowned at the listing for Lacey and West in the directory—owned solely by a Mr. Hyrum Lacey, the entry said, since the death of his partner, Mr. Charles West, six years before. "So they don't ship things themselves, merely contract with ship owners and handle their cargo and interests?" She looked at Jack. "What does that have to do with the war effort?"

"The War Office has worked with several shipping agents over the course of the war," he said. "They were responsible for arranging how and when goods were sent to the Continent when navy ships were unavailable. Food, boots, munitions—whatever the army needed."

"What sort of crime do you think Mr. Finch discovered, then? Smuggling?"

Jack shook his head as he poured himself another finger of brandy, then one for Lily, who took it with a nod of thanks. "Smugglers would need direct access to the ships, especially when they landed, to offload the goods. A shipping agency would not have that during wartime."

"What could they do, then?"

Miss Oswald answered promptly, clearly in her element now that the talk had turned to business. "Any number of things. If they owned their own ships, they could sink them en route to collect an insurance payout from the government, for example. But the most lucrative would be to falsify shipments or provide incorrect papers. A shipping agent could alter the docking manifests and the bills of shipment, so that what Whitehall thinks they have paid for is not what is actually shipped. Most likely so that they could be compensated for supplies they never bought, but it would also be possible to skim goods off the cargo and sell them a second time."

Lily raised a brow. "You seem remarkably enthusiastic about such a plan."

The girl looked embarrassed. "I've not had many opportunities to discuss business matters since I came to London. It seems I have missed it. And in any case . . ." She shook her head. "If that is what they did, I suppose I *am* impressed. It is a brilliant scheme."

Jack scowled at her. "It is a dastardly scheme, Miss Oswald. Men would have died without the equipment they needed."

"I did not say it was *good*. But you cannot deny it is clever. The whole business would be nearly impossible to prove."

Lily's stomach twisted as she took in the implications. "So they could be stealing from the soldiers who fought against Bonaparte, from the British government itself." She did not add that it was no surprise someone would kill to keep that secret.

"But we've no way of knowing for sure," Jack pointed out, a frown creasing the spot between his eyebrows as he stared into his glass.

"Someone knew," Lily said. "Someone had proof of what was going on, and it was sufficient for blackmail."

"Augustus." Miss Oswald was still holding the business directory, and her hands clenched around it as she spoke. "He knew what was happening. Otherwise . . ." She blinked back tears. "Otherwise he would not be dead."

"So he attempted to blackmail the shipping agent instead of reporting them?" Jack shook his head. "As I said, dastardly."

"No." Lily's calm voice made them both look up in surprise. She was staring at the fire, her eyes narrowed. "You forget, Mr. Finch was murdered during the Walters' gala. Why would he arrange such a meeting with a shipping agent?"

There was a pause; then Jack said quietly, "There is another player."

"In the very heart of Mayfair society," Lily said.

"Could it be a member of Parliament?" Miss Oswald said, shivering. "Or someone from the War Office itself? That would certainly be worth blackmail."

"Yes." Lily hesitated, then stood abruptly. She could feel Jack's eyes on her as she paced toward the fire, but he said nothing. She did not know whether to be grateful or not. Turning back, she squared her shoulders. "Miss Oswald, there is something you should know. The day after Mr. Finch's murder, I saw Lord Walter bribing the magistrate in charge of your friend's case. And when Captain Hartley and I visited the Marlborough Street Magistrates Court later that day, we discovered that the magistrate had suddenly ordered the investigation halted." Miss Oswald had gone silent and still, the fingers of one hand pressed against her lips. "There is indeed a chance that this other player is in Parliament," Lily continued, "because it may be Lord Walter himself."

"But . . ." Miss Oswald shook her head. "But he was so kind to me. And the husband of your friend! Surely you cannot . . ."

"I wish I did not." Lily turned back to stare into the fire. "But I'll not be blinded by my own wishes. If Lord Walter is involved in treason and murder, he must be found out."

"But how?" Jack demanded. "We could follow him, I suppose, and see what he does—"

"But we cannot be by his side every hour of the day." Miss Oswald frowned. "And who knows but he has stopped whatever Augustus was attempting to blackmail him for."

Lily shook her head and made a *tsk*ing noise, as if she were scolding children. "We find out by not limiting ourselves to only one method of inquiry. Think! We believe the murderer may be Lord Walter. We *know* the murderer was at the Walters' party that night.

And we also *know* that he worked with the shipping agents"—she thumped the directory—"so we look in both places at once. Where is the overlap between them? That is where we shall find our killer."

There was silence in the room for a moment; then Jack let out a low whistle. "You are right, ma'am. It's the only way forward. And a devilish good thing we found that letter, too, or we should have no way of figuring it out."

"But how do you propose we do that?" Miss Oswald asked, more practically. "Walk into the offices of Lacey and West and ask after their associates in Parliament and Whitehall?"

"I've not figured that part out yet," Lily admitted. "But I can pay them a visit tomorrow and, as they say, get the lay of the land."

"No," Jack said sharply.

"No?" Lily's eyebrows rose.

"Did you see the address?" he asked. "Henrietta Street, right across from Drury Lane. Can you imagine the attention you would attract if you visited an address in Covent Garden, waltzing through and asking questions? Give me a day," he continued when she started to protest. "Let me see what I can find. If nothing else, I can look around without standing out the way a lady will."

Lily did not like it, but he was right. That part of the city, away from the elegant homes and parks of Mayfair, was an area of business during the day and pleasure during the night. At no point was it a place where ladies of quality would walk unaccompanied. Reluctantly, she agreed.

It was not until Miss Oswald had bid them farewell and Jack was gathering his hat and gloves at the door that Lily caught his arm. "I want your word that whatever you discover you will share with me. Don't pretend you found nothing in an attempt to keep me safe, or to make me give this up for my own good."

"Do you think I would?" Jack protested, but there was enough shiftiness in his eyes that Lily knew she had hit close to the mark.

"I think you have been considering how likely you are to get away with it these last ten minutes. The answer to that, if you are curious, is not at all. You can attempt to pull the wool over my eyes, but I shall only continue on my own, without asking for your help again."

"You know, Freddy never mentioned that you were so stubborn," Jack said crossly.

"Really? I am astonished." Lily smiled, but she took a quick breath against the pain in her chest. "He pointed it out himself nearly every week."

Though she had spoken carelessly, Jack laid his hand over hers in silent apology. Lily wasn't sure whether to be gratified or annoyed that he saw through her so easily. But if he did, it was because he felt the same. That would be at least partly to blame for his overprotective behavior: grief for a friend who had been like a brother, and guilt that he had not been there at the end.

"On my honor," he said. "As soon as I learn anything, you will be the first to know."

She let out the breath she had been holding. "Then I wish you luck, Captain."

CHAPTER 11

At half past seven the next morning, Jack hailed a hackney carriage and made his way to Covent Garden.

It was a busy, if not entirely fashionable, part of town, full of shops, banks, and theaters. Fruit sellers hoping for a sale stood on every corner, while children begged for pennies, and London's growing middle class went about the business of trying to make their way into the upper class. At night, the streets would fill with London society, men and women dressed for pleasure, attending plays and rout parties, and the Cyprians—women who lived by their wits and their bodies—would come out to play. Only a short walk away stood the squalid, impoverished neighborhoods of St. Giles and the Seven Dials.

It was too early for most members of London's upper class to travel to Covent Garden, which suited Jack just fine. Turning his collar up and pulling his hat down, he slid into an alley just off Henrietta Street. It was a dingy, narrow passageway, but it offered a view of those coming and going from number eleven, the offices of Lacey and West, Shipping Agents.

Sighing at his folly—it was as bad as shipboard hours, and he could have been comfortable, at home, in bed—Jack settled down to watch and wait as the businesses of Covent Garden came alive.

By half past nine, he had slipped out to buy two questionable pasties from a street hawker, cheerfully cursed himself for not bringing anything to drink, lost feeling in one leg, pissed against the wall, and discovered a few things about the firm of Lacey and West.

There were no other doors into the building, though there was a cellar entrance around the back. Mr. Lacey, well dressed but pinch-faced and lacking any air of actual fashion, had arrived at eight o'clock on the dot. He hadn't left the building since, but there had been a number of other comings and goings, including a wily-looking porter who would probably be impossible to sneak past, two deliveries, and a messenger.

The messenger, a gangling figure who seemed to be an odd-jobs boy for the firm, was the one Jack found himself watching. He arrived with a parcel, stayed to sweep the front steps, and went out on two more errands, one for what looked like Mr. Lacey's morning meal.

Now, as Jack watched, he emerged once more, package under one arm, arguing with the white-haired porter. The boy held his own against the porter, scowling fiercely, and Jack grinned as the old man threw his hands up and retreated back into the office. Nodding in satisfaction, the boy pulled his cap down and hurried across the street, dodging between two carts while the drivers shouted at him. He passed by the alley without glancing left or right, intent on his errand. Swinging his cane and whistling, Jack sauntered onto Henrietta Street.

He didn't move so quickly that he drew attention but kept the boy in sight. It was not a short errand, he discovered. They passed St. Martin-in-the-Fields and went through Charing Cross before Jack realized what the boy's destination must be: Whitehall and the War Office Building.

Jack's step quickened, though he knew that if the messenger was actually admitted past the front gates, there was no way to follow. "You clever thing, Mrs. Adler," he murmured. She had been right— there was something going on.

The boy was stopped at the front gate, as Jack expected, and had a brief argument with the guard there. Jack hung back, leaning against the side of a building with his hat pulled down once more. At last the boy delivered his package, said something impertinent, dodged a cuff from the guard, and began to retrace his steps.

Jack choose his moment carefully, stepping into the boy's path with a grin. "In a hurry, lad?" he asked, his voice friendly.

The boy was thin, made up mostly of angles and feet with dark skin and curly hair cropped short. Jack guessed him to be around twelve or thirteen. His coat sleeves were too short and his shirt sleeves were too long, but he was clean and well turned out. "You're the gent as was follerin' me." The boy scowled. "What d'you want?"

The accusation caught Jack by surprise; it took him a moment to recover, and when he did, he laughed. "Observant fellow, I see. And I thought I had done so well."

The boy's scowl deepened. "Anyone grew up in the Dials knows when they're being follered. What d'you want?"

Hit by a sudden idea, Jack leaned forward and lowered his voice. "I am trying to find a murderer, and I think you may be able to help me."

The boy's eyes widened. "A murderer!" he breathed. Then his frown returned. "You ain't from Bow Street?"

"No indeed." Jack gave a small bow of the head. "Jack Hartley, captain of His Majesty's Navy. And quite famished at the moment," he added, realizing the truth of the statement as he said it. "Do you know a decent public house nearby?" He eyed the boy's thin frame and grinned. "My treat, if you help me."

The combination of mystery and food was too much for any boy to resist. "The George an' Pie is just 'round the corner, sir, if that suits?"

"Excellent." Jack resettled his hat and swung his cane expansively. "Lead the way, lad. What name do you go by?"

"Jem, sir."

"Lead the way, Jem. One should never discuss serious matters on an empty stomach."

"Yessir." In a few years, Jack thought, Jem's cheeky grin would be as roguish as his own. "That's what I always says m'self."

★ ★ ★

Years of navy service had taught Jack a thing or two about dealing with boys: he knew to start with food rather than questions, though he did drop a hint or two about the murder. Jem hung on to every word while devouring two servings of beef and carrots, plus a good amount of small ale, and within fifteen minutes he was eager to give whatever assistance he could. For his own part, Jack was surprised by how interesting the young fellow was. With a little prompting and a well-timed order of a treacle pudding, he soon had Jem telling his own story between sticky bites.

Jem had started his career, such as it was, as a climbing boy, cleaning out flues in the homes of the rich. "Awful," he said, shuddering. "Got stuck up a chimbley more than once, but the devil I worked for lit a fire underneath to get me out. Left half m'skin behind a time or two." Once he had grown too big for chimneys, he ran errands down by the docks, and had briefly considered a career in the navy. "Mum said my da were a navy man," he added with some pride. "Lascar, he were, one of them Indian sailors. But I couldn't join up; Mum were ill too often, she needed lookin' after." Once he had saved up enough from the docks, he purchased suitable clothes secondhand and convinced the porter at Lacey and West to hire him for odd jobs and delivering messages.

"Where is your mother now?" Jack asked.

Jem shrugged. "Still livin' in the Dials. When I save enough, we'll move to Covent Garden, maybe even Clerkenwell. Mum'll like that," he added, a little defensively.

"I am sure she will," Jack agreed, impressed by the boy's tenacity. But something uncomfortable had occurred to him as they talked. "Listen, lad, it might be better not to help me after all. I'd not want you to lose your position on account of me."

"D'you think Lacey is up to something cagey? He had something to do wiv this murder?"

"Something to do with it, yes." Jack hesitated again. "You delivered a message to the War Office. Is that something you do often?"

Jem nodded. "Lacey's got contracts wiv 'em, I think. He buys supplies here in England and arranges for 'em to be shipped to France and all, to the army."

Jack's jaw tightened. Miss Oswald's guess had been right, it seemed, which meant that something about Mr. Lacey's dealings with the War Office were not honest.

"Don't I gotta help you, sir?" Jem asked, eyes wide. "If Lacey's a villain, then what would I be if I didn't help?"

Jack still hesitated, but if he was to get the information Mrs. Adler needed—and keep her from waltzing into danger herself—he had to use the resources available. With a sigh he nodded his agreement, frowned Jem's delighted whoop into silence, and pulled a shilling from his pocket. "If you help me out," he cautioned, holding the coin where the boy's wide eyes could see it, "you do what I ask and no more. I'll not have you getting yourself in trouble on account of me, understand?"

"Yessir," Jem said, breathless with excitement. "What d'you want me to do?"

"I need a list," Jack said, setting the shilling down on the table and sliding it toward the boy. "A list of names that you know Mr. Lacey has worked with, either in Parliament or the War Office." He smiled at the eager face in front of him. "You are a clever lad, Jem. I am sure you can find what I need. But," he added sharply as the boy puffed up with pleasure at the praise. "Do not do *anything* else."

"D'you mean like the names of the gents what got him his contracts? What he writes to in the War Office? Or Parliament?"

Jack raised his brows. "Well . . . yes, that is exactly what I mean. Get me the information and bring it to me yourself. I lodge at the Albany, number five."

"Don't need to."

Jack paused, tankard halfway raised. "What do you mean?"

Jem shrugged. "Only two names as fit the bill."

"And you know those two names?"

"Yessir." The boy grinned. "I keeps me eye on things, I do. How else can I learn anything about business?"

Jack leaned forward. "What are the names?"

★ ★ ★

Twenty minutes later, long after Jem had scampered off with a promise to report anything else he learned and already anticipating a scolding from the porter, Jack was still staring across the room, eyes narrowed as he thought. With a sigh, he waved down the publican and ordered another pint, turning over the possibilities in his mind.

He couldn't help the way his thoughts turned to Mrs. Adler, wondering what she would make of Jem's information. He had agreed to help with her scheme to make up for his boorish behavior and keep her safe. He owed that much to Freddy, now that she planned to dash around London on her own. But the chase had become interesting in its own right, something he had not expected. And then there was Lily herself: dryly witty, carefully controlled, impressively intelligent. In his mind, she had always been the wife of his friend. But at some point, he realized, he had begun to think of her as a friend in her own right.

Jack settled back. And he had thought being stuck ashore would be dull.

CHAPTER 12

Lily was going over the week's menu with Mrs. Carstairs when the sharp, quick knocking began. It was a demanding, slightly frantic sound that echoed all the way up to the second floor. Frowning—and more than a little worried—Lily set aside her task and hurried downstairs.

Mr. Carstairs had just opened the front door, and Lily was greeted by the sight of Miss Oswald sweeping into the hall. "Mrs. Adler!"

"Miss Oswald." Lily dismissed Carstairs with a nod. "Whatever is the matter?"

The girl fidgeted with her gloves and glanced nervously after the servant. "Is there any word from the captain? I know it is early, but . . ."

Lily glanced around. "Did you come without a chaperone?"

"I sent my maid home with the carriage. Aunt Haverweight thinks I'm out visiting. Which I am, as you see. Is there any news?"

Lily shook her head. "It's not been even a day yet."

"Yes but—" The girl took a deep breath. "Of course. I know it is too soon to expect anything; it is just that—"

"It is just that you are impatient to discover what happened to your friend," Lily said gently. "I understand, of course. And believe me, I am just as eager for news as you are." She glanced toward the front door. "Since you are here, would you care to go for a stroll? It is a lovely day outside. And," she added wryly, "I fear you may wear a hole in my carpet if I keep you inside."

Miss Oswald glanced down at the floor, as if she had only just realized the agitated way she was pacing back and forth. Her brow wrinkled with embarrassment, and she sighed. "It would do me good, I suppose."

Lily called for Anna to bring her hat and gloves, then dismissed her maid, saying she and her guest were going to walk toward the park. Green Park, quieter and more pastoral than the popular promenade grounds of Hyde Park, was a mere step away from Half Moon Street, so none of the servants looked askance at their mistress's desire to walk there unaccompanied.

Lily expected Miss Oswald to return to discussing the murder as soon as they were out the door, but she was not given the chance. No sooner had they stepped into the street than a voice called out, "Mrs. Adler!"

Lily turned, unable to hide her surprise at finding Jack standing only steps away, one hand raised awkwardly toward his hat, frowning at her in confusion. His eyes went past her, and as he caught sight of Miss Oswald, his frown deepened. "What are you doing?"

"We are going for a walk towards Green Park." Lily frowned at him. "What are you doing on my doorstep?"

His expression turned grim. "I have news."

Lily wanted to ask Jack immediately what he had learned. But they were standing in the middle of the street, in the middle of the day, and no doubt would begin attracting attention soon. "Come inside, please."

Jack leaned over as she ushered them up the steps. "Cheer up, Mrs. Adler," he murmured. "It's not all bad news."

Carstairs was still in the hall when she opened the door and ushered her guests inside, but his only sign of surprise at her quick return was a slight raise of his eyebrows. "Mrs. Adler, welcome back. Will you and your guests require anything?"

"No, we will show ourselves into the parlor," Lily said, trying not to sound too impatient. She waited only for the parlor door to close before demanding, "Tell me. You may enjoy the suspense, Captain, but I assure you we do not."

"Very well." Jack took a seat and leaned back in his chair. "This morning I learned of Mr. Lacey's principal contacts in Whitehall and Parliament. Lord John Walter was indeed one of the names passed on to me. It seems he is the member of Parliament principally responsible for overseeing the money that pays for contracts through the War Office."

Miss Oswald let out a small gasp and sank onto a settee.

Lily stared. "I do not know how you define *bad news*, captain, but—"

"But his was not the only name given to me. The second one belongs to the man in Whitehall who *arranges* those contracts. He was the one responsible for giving Lacey the job. And it so happens that we know this man was at the Walters' ball that evening."

"Please say the other name is Reggie Harper." Lily smiled grimly. "I should dearly love to see him locked away for murder."

That made Jack pause. "Reggie Harper?"

Lily shook her head. "Pay me no mind. My dislike of him has nothing to do with this matter. The second name?"

"It is odd you said that, Mrs. Adler," Jack said slowly. "Because the second name is General Alfred Harper."

Lily dropped into a chair, mind working rapidly. "That . . . that could be . . ."

"Who is General Harper?" Miss Oswald asked, looking from Lily to Jack and frowning. "I do not know of him."

"Truly?" Lily was surprised. "I always thought him a very well-known figure." She considered, then added, "Though perhaps my perspective is biased, as I attended school with his niece, Miss Harper. She was there at the party as well. Do you remember, Captain?" At Jack's blank look, she added, "She was the one who fetched Serena."

"Ah, the jilted spinster?"

Lily smacked his shoulder. "There is no need to be unkind," she said. "If you were female, you would be quite the spinster by now, too."

"Luckily I had the fortune to be born a man." Jack grinned, earning himself another smack. "All right, I apologize, lay off abusing me."

"Will you two be serious?" Miss Oswald scowled fiercely at them both. "What should I know about the general?"

"He began his military career when he was quite young, fighting against the Colonies during their rebellion," Lily said. "And he achieved a good deal of distinction on the Continent. He and Miss Harper have settled in London since then. Her brother"—Lily scowled at the thought of Reggie Harper—"also lives with them from time to time." She cast Miss Oswald a sideways glance, not wanting to say too much in front of Jack. "I believe you had the misfortune of meeting Mr. Harper that evening."

"Mr. Harper? Oh. *Oh*." Miss Oswald's eyes narrowed, and she drew in a shaky breath before she regained control of herself. "Yes. I do remember him. He did not make a good impression."

"The nephew is a bit of a peacock," Jack agreed, not noticing or not commenting on the tension running between the two women. "But the old fellow was a war hero. And I seem to remember, Mrs. Adler, that when we encountered his niece, shortly after Mr. Finch was shot, she was looking for her uncle."

Lily sat up sharply. "Yes. I believe she was."

She was silent a moment, trying to remember her conversation with Miss Harper that night. Miss Oswald, though, had another question in mind.

"We only just decided to look into Lacey and West yesterday. How on earth did you find anything out so quickly?"

"Perhaps the good captain spent his night burgling the firm's offices?" Lily raised her brows at Jack, who was looking pleased with himself. "Dressed all in black, perhaps, and with a domino and mask to complete the disguise?"

Jack rolled his eyes. "Men of the navy do have many talents, but alas, I learned my information in a far more conventional fashion. I made the acquaintance of a . . . person who works for the firm. He gave me the information."

Lily ignored the slight pause in his speech. Though being kept in the dark irritated her, the source of his information was not immediately important. "Shame. I should dearly have loved to see you disguised and creeping about London."

"You read too many novels," he said severely.

The corners of Lily's eyes crinkled with humor. "I read just the right number of novels." A moment later, though, her expression grew thoughtful. "Two names for us to investigate."

"Investigate?" Miss Oswald repeated, her eyes wide. "How do you plan to do so?"

Lily considered the question, rising to pace around the room. "The first thing to discover is whether either of them had an opportunity to meet with Mr. Finch. There is a window where both of them had time to do so. You could not find Lord Walter in the card room, Captain, but that does not mean he was in the garden. And Miss Harper may have lost track of her uncle, but that does not mean he disappeared entirely. If we can account for the movements of one during that time—"

"Then he cannot have sneaked off to the garden, and certainly could not have had time to shoot Augustus." Miss Oswald finished the thought, her voice trembling. Lily watched, concerned but also thoughtful, as the girl took a deep breath, gathered her composure, and asked, "How do you plan to find that out? I don't suppose the captain has any more clever ideas for ferreting out information?"

Jack grinned. "I do as Mrs. Adler requires in all these matters."

Lily stopped in front of the fireplace, frowning as she thought things through. The truth was, she had very little idea where to begin. But she had confidence in her own mind—a next step was sure to present itself if she thought it over. Unfortunately, at that moment there was a polite knock on the parlor door and her butler entered.

"I beg your pardon for intruding, Mrs. Adler, but there has been an incident in the kitchen. It seems Mrs. Carstairs fell down the stairs, and her ankle may be injured. Do I have your permission to send for a doctor?"

"Damnation." The curse slipped out before she could stop herself. Ignoring her butler's raised brows—the only sign of surprise he ever seemed to permit himself—Lily nodded. "Yes, of course, do so at once."

"There is also . . ." Carstairs hesitated. "I wonder if you would speak to Mrs. Carstairs."

It was an odd request, and even odder coming from her inscrutable butler. But he would not ask without a reason, so Lily stood and nodded. "Of course, I shall come directly." She turned to her guests. "Captain, if you would see Miss Oswald safely back to her aunt's house, I would be grateful. I would take you myself, but . . ."

"There is no need, Mrs. Adler," said Miss Oswald with a poorly hidden grimace that made Lily want to smile. Jack was the sort of bachelor young ladies swooned over and mamas approved of, but Miss Oswald looked unhappily resigned to the prospect of his company. "I am sure Captain Hartley and I won't come to blows in the course of a brief carriage ride."

"As if I would come to blows with a lady, however long the ride might be." Jack looked affronted.

Miss Oswald rolled her eyes, and the childish expression made her look far younger than she generally did. "It was a figure of speech, sir. And in any case, you shouldn't be so quick to say so. My father taught me to box."

"Your father is a singularly liberal man," Jack muttered, gathering up his hat and walking stick.

Miss Oswald, in the middle of pulling on her gloves, paused. "Obviously so, or I should not be here at all."

"Be on your guard, both of you," Lily cautioned, interrupting their brewing argument. "If there is a murderer wandering the ballrooms of Mayfair, you can be certain he shall be on his."

★ ★ ★

Any confusion downstairs had been wrangled into submission by the time Lily entered the kitchens. Mrs. Carstairs sat polishing the silver with her foot propped up, Mr. Carstairs had gone for a doctor, and the remains of a porcelain teapot were gathered on the table.

"Mrs. Carstairs, what happened?"

"Oh, ma'am, I'm so dreadfully sorry for the bother." The plump woman made as if to rise, but Lily waved her back down before taking a seat herself. "I was so startled is all, and when I tripped, I lost my grip on the pot, which I know you will have to take out of my wages—"

"I am not worried about the china. I only wish to make sure you are well."

"Mr. Carstairs is making a lot of fuss over nothing, I declare. Insisting on a doctor, and getting you involved—"

"I would rather fuss over nothing than ignore something important," Lily said, kind but firm. "Tell me why he is worried."

Mrs. Carstairs sighed. "I was bringing up a fresh pot of tea, but when I was halfway up, I thought maybe I should be bringing you something to eat as well. I turned back for the scones, as I had just finished baking them, and . . ." In spite of her insistence that it was nothing, the housekeeper shuddered. "I thought I saw someone at the back door, Mrs. Adler, a terribly tall man peering in through the top window, with dark hair. Gave me a fair fright, it did, and I tripped and lost my balance." Mrs. Carstairs shook her head. "Being silly, I was, but no matter now. Dinner will be easy to finish up, and I'll be right as rain in no time."

"Do you think someone was trying to break in?" Lily eyed the door.

"Mrs. Adler, don't you go confusing real life with them novels." Mrs. Carstairs looked severe, and Lily nearly blushed, thinking of the copy of *The Sylph* on her nightstand. "I shouldn't worry about it. If I saw anyone, which I'm not certain I did, likely it was the rag-and-bone man come early, and him scared off by me shrieking like a banshee."

Lily would have pressed the issue, but at that moment Carstairs returned with the doctor in tow. Lily rose and held out her hand.

"Good afternoon, Doctor. I am Mrs. Adler. My housekeeper, Mrs. Carstairs, seems to have twisted her ankle falling down the stairs."

"Dr. Palmer," he replied, bowing over her hand before turning to his patient. "Let's take a look at you, my girl, and make sure nothing is broken."

As he knelt for his examination, Lily drew the butler aside. "Make sure she does actually follow his orders and rest her ankle. Anna can help with things in the kitchen as needed."

"Never fear, Mrs. Adler." The butler's white teeth flashed in a quick smile. "She thinks she can run circles around me, but I've learned a trick or two for managing the old girl these last twenty years." His smile faded as he glanced back at his wife. "Did she tell you what she saw?"

"She did." Lily frowned. "Though she insists she must have imagined it." Even if there had been someone at the door, there were any number of tradesmen who could have been stopping by. But a niggling voice in the back of her mind told her to be careful. "But . . . keep an eye on things. In case she did see someone, after all."

★　★　★

Jack and Miss Oswald managed to have a civil ride by exchanging only about twenty words before their hackney coach arrived at Audley Street. Once there, he handed her down and would have walked her up the steps to her aunt's house, but she dropped her hand from his instantly.

"Thank you for your kind escort, Captain," she said, stepping smoothly back. "I am sure we shall meet again soon." Her words, and the tone in which she delivered them, were perfectly polite and correct. But her posture, and the deliberate distance between then, said in no uncertain terms that she had no intention of letting him accompany her any farther.

Jack would have assumed that she didn't want her aunt or any of the neighbors seeing him and getting ideas—after all, the girl was already the subject of enough gossip. He gave her an amiable enough reply before swinging back up into the carriage to take his leave.

But something in her posture made him look back as the carriage pulled away, and it was suddenly clear to him that she had no intention of going into her aunt's house at all. She stood just off the street, head bent over as if peering into her reticule to look for something. No gently bred lady would linger on the street in such a manner.

For a moment be was tempted to call to the driver to halt. But caution took over. He wanted to know what she was going to do. So he waited until they had swung around the corner, before rapping on the roof of the coach. As soon as it stopped, he swung out, paid the driver, and hurried back to the corner of Audley Street, wondering if he was being ridiculous.

He was just in time to see Miss Oswald, walking slowly but deliberately, disappear around the corner of the street across from him.

The back of his neck prickling with suspicion, Jack followed.

When she was three blocks from her aunt's house, Miss Oswald hailed a passing chair and stepped into the box. Jack was too far away at that point to hear the direction she gave the chairmen, but they were near Hyde Park, and the streets were growing full as the evening promenade began. Jack was easily able to follow on foot through the slow-moving London traffic, keeping the girl's chair in sight as it turned south toward Hyde Park Corner.

At Chesterfield Gate, the chair halted, and Jack stepped back quickly, letting a passing knot of young dandies shield him from view as Miss Oswald stepped out. While in the chair, she had pulled her veil across her face and buttoned both her spencer and gloves as snugly as possible. Her clothing said without a doubt that she was a lady of quality, but if he hadn't been following her from the beginning, he wouldn't have recognized her at all. Jack pulled down the brim of his own hat as she glanced around, trying to turn his face away while still keeping an eye on her.

Even if he hadn't seen her sneak away from her aunt's house—for there was no possible way that she was permitted to wander the streets of London unaccompanied—her furtive behavior, and the way she was carefully concealing her identity, would have put him instantly on his guard. Something in the back of his mind had warned him to keep an eye on Miss Oswald ever since Mrs. Adler had revealed the girl's connection to the dead man. And it seemed his instinct had been correct.

It was easy for Jack to follow at a distance, keeping the strolling couples between them as Miss Oswald set off into the park, walking as briskly as she could without attracting attention. A few people glanced her way, or nodded to Jack as he passed, but they were too wrapped up in their own business and flirtations to pay anyone else much mind. At last, near the river, she slowed, and Jack ducked behind a shadowed stand of trees as a man approached. His face was mostly hidden by a tall collar and a hat pulled down low to shade his eyes, but Jack guessed by his loose-limbed way of moving, and the slight gangliness to his frame, that he was still young, perhaps just old enough to be out of university.

"Madam." The man bowed but looked nervously around, as if afraid someone would see them together, before offering his arm.

"Sir." Miss Oswald sent her own glance around the park, then, stepping close, took his arm.

"I did not know if you would make it." There was a slight tremor to the man's voice, and Jack saw Miss Oswald smile in response.

"I knew you would wait," she said, her voice almost too low for Jack to hear. His eyes narrowed as she continued, "Between my aunt and Mrs. Adler, I feel as though I am watched all the time. But . . . here I am." She lifted her shoulders in a graceful shrug. "And I have learned a few interesting things today. Should you like to hear about them?"

For a moment they came close to Jack's hiding place, and he heard her murmur, ". . . General Harper; do you know of him?" before they moved out of earshot again. Heads close together, they walked off, soon blending in with the other strolling couples.

Jack stayed where he was. There was no good way to continue shadowing them: they were heading into an open stretch of the park, where it would be far easier for one or the other to notice him. But the girl was hiding something, that was certain, and it seemed her mysterious gentleman was privy to all their secrets.

Frowning, Jack moved off in the other direction, then hailed a chair of his own.

He would need to tell Lily, of course. But she was fond of her new friend, and he had already misstepped with her once. This time, he needed to be absolutely sure before he said anything.

CHAPTER 13

Left to her own devices, Lily would have preferred to stay home that evening and mull over the new information she had gained. But mulling would have to wait. When Carstairs brought up the letters, she discovered a note from Serena. Lord Walter, it seemed, had left town unexpectedly—Lily frowned over that—and Serena was left without someone to accompany her to Lady Jersey's concert that evening.

And I insist, Dear Lily, the viscountess wrote, *that you join me. I know you will want to argue, but I have already told Lady Jersey that I will be bringing you, so you see you have no choice. We may even bring that charming Captain of yours along, if he does not mind sitting through a concert. Do not abandon me, Dear—you know I am depending on you!*

The concert was to feature a performance by Madame Catalani, the popular soprano who had fled France after Napoleon's return, and invitations were highly coveted. And then there was Lady Jersey herself: her opinions, repeated in every gossip sheet, could secure or destroy a person's reputation within the ranks of London society. Even taking into account her recent arrival in London and her black gloves, Lily knew that rejecting the invitation of such a prominent hostess would hurt not only her social standing but also her chances of discovering the murderer. Friendship with Serena had seen her admitted to the Walters' circle—a group composed of diplomats, government officials, and wealthy families, in which prominent members of society like Lady Jersey might cross paths with virtual nonentities like Lily herself. It was among this glittering, brittle society that Mr. Finch had been murdered, and there lay the clues to who his killer was.

So after a nap and a light dinner, Lily steeled herself for an evening out.

She fussed over her appearance more than usual that night, trying and discarding each of her evening gowns in turn. Sighing over her own nerves, Lily settled at the dressing table, still undecided, and addressed her maid. "Have you been practicing the new style *à la Meduse*?"

"I have, ma'am." Anna fetched the curling tongs, which had been heating by the fire. "Though why anyone named a lady's hairstyle after that Gorgon creature is beyond me."

Lily smiled. Anna had been appalled when she had learned what *à la Meduse* meant. "Greek and Roman style is all the crack these days. You'd not have me look out of fashion, would you?"

"No, ma'am. But it's clear to me it was a man had the naming of it," Anna said tartly. Going to the wardrobe, she added, "It will look a treat with your purple silk."

Lily ran an unsteady hand over the gown as her maid held it out to her. Made up in the latest style, with sheer sleeves and three flounces along the bottom, the gown—and most of her new wardrobe—had been a gift from Freddy's family. Lady Adler, Freddy's mother, had encouraged Lily to go to town "to begin living your life again, my dear," and, when Lily had protested that she had nothing fashionable to wear, had called in her personal dressmaker and commissioned no fewer than ten new dresses. She had even ordered two day dresses and an evening gown in colors for when Lily laid off her black gloves. Sir John, Freddy's brother, had taken it upon himself to find the cozy little town house on Half Moon Street and hire the staff.

Their kindness was overwhelming, and it made her feel terribly guilty. The income left to her after Freddy's death, combined with the marriage portion her father had reluctantly settled on them when he agreed to the match, had left Lily comfortably positioned. She could have maintained a town residence on her own if she had been economical, though perhaps not in Mayfair. She knew the Adlers expected her to remarry, and their gifts were intended to see her situated until she found another husband. But Lily could not imagine marrying again, and they could not supplement her lifestyle forever.

Still, she was in town now, with a beautiful new gown to wear. There was no use worrying about the rest of it that night.

She trailed her hand over the silk flounce on the petticoat, and it reminded her of a task she had forgotten until that moment. "I meant to tell you, the petticoat on the gray silk snagged the other night, and several inches of lace were torn off the flounce."

"I'll look at it tonight, Mrs. Adler." Anna laid aside the dress, then tested the heat of the curling tongs before beginning to set her mistress's hair.

"No need to rush; I shan't want to wear it for another week at least. And you'll need to change out the sash on it, and perhaps make over the neckline and sleeves as well." Seeing Anna make a face, Lily added, "I've no desire to be the subject of unpleasant gossip, which is exactly what would happen if I went out twice in a gown that looks exactly the same. And I can't imagine you would much care for that either."

"Of course not, Mrs. Adler," Anna said. "I know London folk are that persnickety. But that was one thing I did not miss in Hertfordshire."

"No, nor I," Lily said, fiddling with the pins on her dressing table and sighing.

Anna hesitated, then asked, "Are you feeling well tonight, ma'am?"

Lily grimaced at her reflection. "I feel the need to be well armored tonight, and that requires looking the part."

Anna made a motherly clucking sound, which made Lily smile in spite of herself. Anna was a few years her junior, but often fussed as if she were several decades older than her mistress. "Well, we'll make sure you dazzle them tonight, ma'am. Do you think London society has changed so much since you were last here?"

"No," Lily said. "I suspect it has not changed at all. Thus my apprehension." She thought about, but did not mention, the dead body she had come face-to-face with only days before—reason enough to make anyone wary of London parties.

Anna made another sympathetic sound and didn't ask anything further. Lily was grateful. Anna had been her maid since she was still Miss Pierce, and though she had been privy to many of her mistress's secrets from girlhood on, there were some things she was safer not knowing.

★　★　★

Just walking into Lord Jersey's house at number thirty-eight, Berkeley Square, that night was nearly enough to make the hours of fretting worthwhile. The platform at the head of the room was swathed in gold and silver cloth, and hundreds of candles cast a glow over the whole space. Already the hall was filled with elegantly dressed couples floating about, gossiping and flirting with all their might. The whole scene was breathtaking. Though Lily would never thrive on society the way Serena did, she sighed in pleasure, a sound echoed by her friend as they paused on the threshold of the room. Behind them, Jack let out a low whistle.

"And to think you planned to stay home tonight!" Serena beamed.

"Fortunately, I had you to force me out." Lily glanced around. "Heavens, Lord and Lady Jersey do not stint, do they?"

"Last month Mrs. Drummond-Burrell threw a masquerade in an Egyptian theme." Serena named one of Lady Jersey's social rivals in a loud whisper. "Very beautiful and *very* expensive. I expect our hostess did not want to be outdone, which is why she worked so hard to secure a private performance from Madame Catalani. Is that not so, your ladyship?" she added pertly as their hostess appeared out of the crush to greet them.

"Wait until you see the supper room, my dear; it is far and away superior to anything the Burrells managed." Lady Jersey touched cheeks with Serena—they were not social equals, but the Walter family was a wealthy one, and Serena had always been popular. "And these must be the friends you told me of?"

"Lady Jersey, may I present my dear friend Mrs. Adler, who has only recently arrived in town, and Captain Hartley, of His Majesty's Navy."

"Your ladyship." Lily and Jack both bowed.

Lady Jersey smiled. Though not a beautiful woman, she was elegant, loquacious, and above all, fashionable. "Mrs. Adler. I am pleased to make your acquaintance. Lady Walter tells me you have come from Hertfordshire?"

"I arrived in London just a week ago, your ladyship."

"And you, Captain?" Lady Jersey turned to Jack. "What brings you to London when our soldiers and sailors are well engaged in France once more?"

"Unfortunate timing, I am afraid, ma'am," Jack said. "My ship is being repaired."

"You must long to rejoin the fighting," Lady Jersey said.

"I confess I do," Jack said. "Though my poor mother was most relieved to hear that I am ashore for the moment, and I cannot be sad to have set her mind at ease."

"A most devoted son." Lady Jersey's eyes sparkled with humor.

"I do try." Jack adopted a noble expression that made their hostess laugh. "If you will be so good as to excuse me, ma'am, I see a former commander of mine and must pay my respects."

As he bowed himself away, Lady Jersey turned her sharp gaze on Lily once more. "Well, Mrs. Adler, I applaud your decision to leave Hertfordshire. There is so much more to keep one occupied in town." She cast a sly look at Serena and added, "All sorts of scandal and intrigue, even at the homes of the dullest people."

"Really, how can your ladyship say such a thing?" Serena exclaimed, looking torn between discomfort at the mention of the murder and delight at being the sudden center of attention as several heads turned in their direction. "I declare I've not slept a wink since it happened, and how Lord Walter could leave me alone so soon after the *incident* utterly confounds me. Why, good evening, Mr. Grant," she added, as a handsome man bowed to their group. "Did I promise you a dance last week and then leave early? I am sure I did, so you need not remind me that I am in your debt."

"I am sure you will manage to distract yourself from your distress tonight," Lily said dryly as Mr. Grant bent to whisper something to Serena, who then smacked him with her fan, looking happily scandalized. Lady Jersey laughed as she moved off to greet other guests, and Lily's heart lifted a little. Perhaps she had not completely lost the knack of London style after all.

"Come, darling." Serena looped her arm though Lily's. "We should stroll before the concert begins."

As Serena led them through the crowd, Lily asked, as carelessly as she could manage, "Why did Lord Walter have to leave town so suddenly?"

"Oh, something to do with taking Cousin Bernard home earlier than expected, though why the boy could not travel on his own, I've no idea." Serena laughed. "I'd no desire to press him on the matter, though, since it meant I was rid of Bernard at last, prosy bore that he is."

Lily frowned in thought, but was distracted from answering by the sight of a now-familiar figure; if they continued on their circuit, they would bump right into him. Trying not to make a face, she gave Serena's arm a firm tug. "Not that way, if you please." But she was a few seconds too late.

Reggie Harper caught sight of them and bowed, smiling as he eyed Lily. She returned his gaze, giving her chin the cold lift Serena had admired so often, and was rewarded as his smile faded into petulant confusion, then irritation. Scowling, Mr. Harper turned and shoved his way into the next room.

Serena had watched the silent exchange, frowning. "What was that?"

Lily's mouth firmed. "He knows I've no wish to speak with him. I was reminding him of that fact, as he seemed determined to forget it."

"Mr. Harper? I did not think you knew him well."

"I do not." Lily kept her voice low. "He approached me at your ball."

Serena raised her eyebrows. "He did not make a favorable impression?"

"He was . . ." Lily paused, searching for the right phrase. "Looking for a rather merrier widow than I turned out to be."

"Good heavens." Serena looked shocked. "I had heard whispers, but I never knew there was any truth in them."

"What sort of whispers?"

Serena dropped her voice. "*Everyone* found out about his affair with Mrs. Hammond-Smythe, and she left London immediately. The rumor is that her husband stopped supporting her. Well, what else can you expect when you are so clumsy as to have a liaison discovered? She claimed that when she ended things with him, Mr. Harper actually *sent her letters to her husband*—but surely no gentleman would ruin a lady simply because she refused him?"

"I can confidently say his manner is *not* gentlemanlike. If you knew such things, why on earth invite him to your ball?"

"Lord Walter needs to cultivate his uncle." Serena shrugged. "These things are all political, you know that. But—!" She turned to glare in the direction in which Mr. Harper had disappeared. "What a dreadful man. Should I ask Lord Walter to call him out? He would do it; he thinks of you quite as a sister. Though I am nearly angry enough to do it myself—and I am a good enough shot for that, you know!"

The mention of Lord Walter's regard for her caused a pang of guilt to twist Lily's stomach. "Thank you, but I managed to be sufficiently discouraging."

"How did you do it?"

Lily felt her face heating. "I threatened to break his nose if he touched me again."

Serena burst out laughing. Though the memory of Reggie Harper's oily smile, and the way his face had flushed with rage, made it impossible for her to laugh along, Lily found herself smiling as other guests turned to stare, and it was in that manner that Jack found them.

"Lady Walter. Mrs. Adler." He shook his head. "Hoydens, I see, no matter how much Mrs. Adler pretends otherwise."

"Be careful, sir." Serena fished out a useless lace handkerchief to dab at her eyes. "She is quite dangerous, you know."

His brows rose as he gave Lily a questioning look, which she returned blandly, but he said gravely, "I am aware." He bowed once more. "I believe the concert is about to begin. May I do you ladies the service of securing seats?"

"I fear it may be too crowded for us all to sit together," Lily said, looking around.

"The captain shall manage," Serena said breezily, looping her arm through her friend's. "I insist on being beside you, as I despise sitting through a concert with no one to talk to."

"You know, Serena, the point of a concert is to listen. I suspect the other guests came to hear Madame Catalani, not you."

"Nonsense. Half of them shall whisper through it as well. And even if they do not—" Serena dimpled. "Do you think anyone will tell me to hush?"

"I might."

"Then you will be speaking yourself and breaking your own rules."

As Jack handed them into seats, he bent to whisper in Lily's ear, "General Harper is here. During the interval, I shall take you over to him."

"How will you manage that?" she murmured as he handed her a program.

"By introducing you, very properly, to my former commander." He straightened and bowed. "Ladies. Enjoy the concert. I shall return at the interval."

He left to prop up the wall with the other gentlemen who had not secured seats—a situation which, Lily reflected with cynical humor, would thwart many plans for discreet, scandalous conversation under cover of the music. Lady Jersey stepped to the front of the room, glowing with pleasure as she raised her hands to quiet her guests.

"My dear friends, what a delight that you could all join me this evening. And what a delight to hear so accomplished an *artiste* perform! I am pleased to introduce—but of course she needs no introduction—the marvelous Madame Catalani."

The singer mounted the dais to truly appreciative applause. She was dramatically attired in deep-red satin and diamonds, her hair crowned with three dyed-to-match plumes that stayed impressively upright as she swept a deep curtsy to her audience. Taking a breath, Madame Catalani gestured to her accompanist, her eyes lifting heavenward, and a tragic expression settled over her face as she began to sing.

Lily sighed with pleasure. *This* was why she had returned to London. It felt wonderful to be surrounded by beauty once more, even if the piercing notes of the aria made her throat tighten. She was saved from an uncomfortable sweep of emotion when Serena poked her in the side. Lily turned to glare at her friend, who looked unrepentant as she leaned over to whisper.

"The program has the Italian, darling, but not a word of translation! Do tell me what this one is about."

Lily sighed, but could not help smiling. "Hand me the program." Her schoolgirl Italian was little better than her friend's, but she knew some French as well, and between the two she managed a translation. That satisfied Serena for a while, and Lily was free to look around.

Jack was standing along one wall, watching the soprano appreciatively. That surprised Lily—she had not expected him to be a lover of music. A moment later, though, he looked over and, catching her eye, tilted his head deliberately. Following the direction he indicated, Lily realized he was standing not far away from where General Alfred Harper sat. The general looked much as she remembered—tall and broad, with a distinctive military bearing, a red face, and impressive mustaches. His expression was so stern he almost seemed to glare at the soprano.

Lily suppressed a shiver, looking away as the first song ended and everyone applauded. Madame Catalani bowed, and the room fell silent—aside from the many whispers—as she began her next piece.

Predictably, Serena leaned close, fluttering the program. "A translation, if you please?"

Luckily, Lily knew the aria and did not need to attempt a translation from scratch. "She is saying—" She broke off, the back of her neck prickling.

"What is it?" Serena frowned.

Lily didn't answer as she glanced around the room, trying to discover what had set her on edge. It did not take long. Reggie Harper had chosen a seat across the aisle and several rows back from them. His gaze was fixed on her, not the stage. Anger rising, Lily stared back until he scowled and looked away.

"Lily?"

"A moment." Lily kept her unruffled gaze on Mr. Harper as he turned back, found her still watching him, and looked away again, an ugly flush rising over his features. Putting her chin in the air as if there was nothing in the world to concern her, Lily turned back to her friend. "Her lover has just left her destitute."

"How very shocking," Serena murmured, fanning herself with the program.

"And very Italian," Lily agreed, deliberately putting Mr. Harper from her mind.

★ ★ ★

They sat through three more songs after the first. When the audience grew restless and the whispers more pronounced, Lady Jersey announced a short interval and refreshment in the supper room. As the singer bowed to enthusiastic applause, Lily glanced around. It took only a moment for Jack to make his way back to them.

"If I may steal your friend away, Lady Walter, there is someone I wish to introduce to her. A former commander of mine, Admiral Folks."

"An admiral! You do collect navy men, Lily," Serena teased, already looking around the room for other friends. "Very well, you may abandon me for now, but Lily, do be sure to sit with me after the interval. I depend on your linguistic ability."

Lily's heart felt like it had sped up to twice its normal rate, but she smiled and assented as calmly as if she were promising to pick out lace. "Though you know my Italian is nearly as dreadful as yours, Serena," she warned.

Her friend waved her off with a dismissive, "Bosh, you've a better memory than anyone I know," before Serena caught the eye of the Mr. Grant she had been speaking to earlier and floated off through the crowd. That settled, Lily took Jack's arm and allowed him to lead her to the admiral, hoping she looked calmer than she felt.

Admiral Folks was a large, ruddy man in his late fifties, with the energy of someone half his age and the weathered look that came with spending a life aboard ship. Under any other circumstance, Lily would have enjoyed meeting him, as he was reported to be a very friendly man who, in spite of not particularly distinguished birth, was held in high esteem by the government and moved freely through the upper ranks of society. But beside the admiral stood General Harper, and Lily quivered with nervous excitement. Jack seemed to feel it, and he squeezed her arm reassuringly as they bowed.

"Captain Lascar!" Folks beamed with pleasure. "And with a beautiful woman on your arm, as always."

Lily raised an eyebrow, both at the implications of that *always* and at the nickname, but Jack chose to answer only one question. "My brother officers all call me that."

"Plenty of Lascars in the navy, but precious few of them made post captain, eh!" The admiral chuckled. "And what was it the Indian fellows began calling you in response?"

"Captain English." Jack grinned, though Lily noticed the lines of strain around his mouth. "Forever betwixt and between, I am."

"Done well for yourself in spite of all that." The admiral's tone turned affectionate. "I'm determined to see you make admiral yourself one day, you know, you're that good with the men. Just need a little more politicking to see your future secure. But we'll need to get you back out to sea for that to happen. Don't want to miss out on all the action! But I see what has occupied your time here ashore, lad. Do me the honor of introducing me to your charming friend, who must be wearied of my sailor's talk."

"Mrs. Adler, I have the pleasure to make known to you Admiral Folks, my patron and a very great friend. He knew me from boyhood and was the first captain I sailed under."

"A pleasure indeed, Admiral." Lily held out her hand, smiling with real warmth.

"Mrs. Adler." The admiral bowed over her head, then nodded to his companion. "Are you acquainted with General Harper?"

The general, who had been surveying the room with little interest in their conversation up to that point, turned back when he heard his name and bowed, his scowling expression subsiding into polite interest. "Mrs. Adler."

"Sir. You may not remember me, but I went to school with your niece some years ago, and our paths crossed once or twice then. I was Miss Pierce at the time."

"Pierce. Remember the name, yes."

Bracing herself, Lily turned to Jack and said, "You met Miss Harper at the Walters', do you recall, Captain?" Her tone stayed relaxed and casual, but she watched General Harper out of the corner of her eye as she spoke. "The general was the uncle she had misplaced."

"Eh, what's that?" the general asked, an edge to his voice that Lily did not miss. "What about the Walters?"

"Dashed terrible business with their party," Admiral Folks put in with cheerful black humor. "But makes for a good bit of gossip, which Lady Walter will surely manage to enjoy! This is Jack Hartley, Harper," he added. "One of the best captains we had."

"We ran into your niece, sir, when she was looking for you." Jack bowed. "She performed a very kind service for Mrs. Adler at the time."

"Ah yes, a good girl, Isobel." The general nodded, looking placated. "Always a helpful sort. I had to leave the party early, you know. No time to tell Isobel where I had gone."

"Harper has business at Whitehall from time to time." Folks smiled conspiratorially. "And they can be deuced cagey about interrupting an evening without warning!"

"Yes, well, no need to get into all of that." The general's jaw was stiff, and Lily had the impression he was fighting the urge to glare at his talkative friend.

"I hope it was nothing serious." Lily opened her eyes wide. Talk of war and Whitehall, the command center of Britain's military and spies, was enough to make anyone nervous now that Napoleon had escaped his island prison.

"No need to worry your lovely self, Mrs. Adler." Admiral Folks gave her arm a friendly pat. "Wellington will have the Frenchies routed in no time, mark my words."

"Amen to that, sir," Jack said, and the group fell silent a moment in heartfelt agreement.

The quiet was broken by the general, who excused himself. "See an old friend I must greet. Folks, I am sure we shall meet again soon." He seemed about to say something else to the admiral, but then his gaze fell on Lily once more, and he clenched his jaw shut. There was something unpleasant in his expression, and Lily had to fight to keep her own eyes wide and innocent as she met his. "Mrs. Adler, Captain. Pleasure." With an abrupt bow, he moved off.

Lily watched him leave, hiding a shudder. Their conversation had certainly made him uncomfortable, but which part, and why, was less certain. And, she admitted to herself, it had made her uncomfortable as well. There was enough there to continue suspecting him, and though she was determined not to be biased in her search, Lily thought him a much more likely candidate for murder than quiet, amiable Lord Walter.

Her thoughts were interrupted by Admiral Folks. "I think, Mrs. Adler, that you must be the wife of Jackie's boyhood friend I heard about so often." His voice grew serious for the first time. "My sympathies, ma'am, on the loss of your husband. From all Jackie said, he was as fine a fellow as they came."

"You are very kind, sir." Lily's voice caught only a little, and she smiled. "What brings you to London? Surely there must be ample occupation for men of the navy this spring?"

"Only too true, ma'am." He nodded gravely. "I come to report to the War Office, but my wife insists on seizing the opportunity to make me practice my manners." In a conspiratorial whisper, he added, "She says they grow unbearably coarse when I'm at sea."

"Perhaps that is her excuse, Admiral, to keep you by her side. It must be hard on a wife to be so much separated from her husband."

"Aye, you've the right of it there, Mrs. Adler." The admiral winked at her. "Louisa was often at sea with me when we were younger. But, now our children have little ones of their own, she keeps closer to home."

"You shall soon be resigning if you are not careful, sir," Jack said.

"Impertinent scamp, as always," Folks laughed. "Though I fear you're not far off the mark. Always gets her way, Louisa does," he added fondly.

They talked for several more minutes before Lily remarked that the concert would soon be restarting, and they parted amiably. She waited until they were out of earshot before saying quietly, "That was quick thinking, introducing me to your admiral so we might speak with the general. Though I would have appreciated the introduction even if it had not helped our investigation. He seems a very kind man."

"He is." Jack grinned. "When we're not at sea, at any rate. I shouldn't recommend putting his kindness to the test if you're ever on shipboard with him. Best man I ever sailed under, but he's the law on his ship and no mistake." He glanced at her out of the corner of his eye. Jack waited until they were out of earshot before saying in a low voice, "That was a clever way you managed to bring up the Walters' ball."

The corners of Lily's eyes crinkled up with pleased humor. "It was, wasn't it? And the general certainly did not like the turn of our conversation."

"Do you remember the voice of the man you overheard?"

Lily sighed. "Not well enough. There was nothing to make me think it could *not* have been the general. But when you over-hear a man whispering, and under such strange circumstances, it's hard to say for certain what he sounded like, especially several days later."

She sighed again, and Jack gave her arm a comforting squeeze as Lily returned to her seat. Serena was still absent, so Jack took her place for the moment. "We are making progress, Mrs. Adler. I have every faith you shall manage to unravel this tangle."

"With one of the best captains of the navy to help me?" Lily's lips quirked as Jack bowed in his seat, grinning. "Jackie, was it?"

Jack laughed. "He's the only one who still calls me that, at least since Freddy's death." Lily felt her throat tighten, but she didn't let it show on her face as he continued. "Makes me feel all of fourteen again, though I cannot really mind it, coming from him."

"Is that worse than Captain Lascar?"

Jack grimaced. "They called me that from the moment I got my first ship. It is mostly meant well, though."

"But still bothersome?" she asked quietly.

"It is . . ." Jack frowned. "It can be difficult to be reminded that you are different from your fellows, even if it is meant in fun. You always wonder if someone sets more stock by it than they let on."

"I can understand that," Lily said, nodding thoughtfully. "And do you truly wish to be back at sea, now that the war is in full force again? Being ashore must be dull in comparison."

Lily was genuinely curious. Jack had gone to sea when he was fourteen—a common age for sons of the gentry, though later than sailors from the lower classes, many of whom joined when they were boys no older than ten—but that meant more than half his life had been spent in the navy, in one conflict or another.

"The food is better here," he said, making her smile. "It *is* hard to be on land when I feel I am needed elsewhere. But my men are glad for the time with their families. And I would hardly call my time here dull." He grinned. "You have seen to that with your murder."

"Murder?" Serena caught the end of the conversation as she floated over on the arm of a handsome young man. "Good heavens, Lily, what are you talking about?"

"Opera." Lily held out the program. "The next selection is Italian as well, I fear."

Serena sighed as Madame Catalani took the stage once more. "Why can't they sing in English from time to time?"

CHAPTER 14

The next day, Lily was determined not to think about murder for at least twenty-four hours. Serena was hosting an "at-home" tea for all their schoolfellows who were in town—"I had not thought of it before, but there are quite a number of Miss Tattersy's young ladies in London these days! I shall even include Mary Forsythe, who is Mrs. Wilbur Green now; even if she did marry into rather a shabby family, I am sure she will be delighted to receive the invitation"—and Lily had agreed to arrive early to make sure everything was in readiness.

Not that her help was much needed. Lady Walter, in the midst of her new foray into the world of Tory politics, had become a capable hostess—and what she might miss, her housekeeper would not. Instead, Lily played a breathless game of hide-and-go-seek with John and Francis, who were five and three, respectively, and who possessed more energy than should have been possible in such small bodies. Toward the end of the game, Serena returned and watched fondly from the door of the family parlor.

"That is quite enough for today, my darlings; you will wear Mrs. Adler out." She gathered them to her with a laugh. "Mama has guests arriving, so you must go back to the nursery and play with nanny." This prompted a chorus of complaints, but Serena swiftly silenced them with the promise of a surprise waiting upstairs.

"What is their surprise?" Lily asked, dusting off her gown as John and Francis raced out of the room with excited yelps.

"Gingerbread," Serena said. "I know I spoil them, but I cannot help myself."

"They are such dears; no one could blame you for it."

Serena gave her friend a sympathetic look. "There is still time for you to have your own."

"Perhaps," Lily said thoughtfully. Without Freddy by her side, the thought of children had receded from her mind. At first she had mourned the loss. Now she was unsure she wanted that life at all. But she didn't know how to explain that to Serena, who was so happy in her own family. "For now, I quite enjoy yours. All of the fun and none of the responsibility." A loud crash echoed from upstairs. "You see?"

"Oh dear." Serena sighed as Francis's wail followed the crash. "If he's making that much noise, he's either perfectly fine or dying. I should go see which. Will you be all right by yourself for a few minutes?"

"Perfectly. Off with you."

Lily shooed her friend out and looked around the room for some way to occupy herself. There were plenty of books, and one of that morning's papers was thrown carelessly over the back of a chair. But she was drawn back to the open door, where, across the hall, she could see Lord Walter's study.

She wanted to let things alone for the day, but with Serena upstairs and the servants busy with their preparations, it was unlikely anyone would notice where she went for at least a few minutes. And if she was going to snoop, better to do it when Lord Walter was out of town. The opportunity was too good to let pass.

Before she could persuade herself out of it, Lily slipped out of the drawing room and into the study.

She eased the door shut behind her and surveyed the room. It was a beautiful, heavily masculine space, with crowded bookshelves taking up most of the walls and a large desk presiding at one end. In front of the fireplace, two chairs faced each other at a comfortable distance, a table with several decanters to one side. Most of the volumes, Lily could see as she glanced at the shelves, showed signs of wear—Lord Walter was not the sort of man to collect books for show.

With its owner gone from town, the whole room was dim and chill, the fire unlit and most of the curtains drawn. That was good, Lily thought. If no one was bothering with the fire or the drapes for a few days, she was less likely to be interrupted.

She intended to begin her search at the desk, but a stack of papers tucked under one of the chairs caught her eye. Whatever had been left there was likely what Lord Walter had been dealing with immediately before he left town. That was where she would look first.

Lily paged through the sheets carefully, preserving the order so that everything could be left as she had found it. The first letter was from Lord Walter's estate manager, detailing concerns about the roofs of several tenants' homes in light of the heavy spring rains. Perhaps that was what had taken him so abruptly from town? Lily couldn't fault him for that—and surely a man who took such care of his dependents couldn't be involved in anything worthy of blackmail?

That was wishful thinking, Lily knew, though she held on to the thought through several more pages of estate matters. But another letter, tucked between the pages of last autumn's agricultural yields, made her thoughts grim again.

> *Sir, my most humble apologies for the disturbance you have suffered—I can only beg your indulgence & state with conviction that it happened without my knowledge or my approval. I made clear to every constable under my purview that the case was to be dropped, exactly as we discussed. I can assure you that Mr. Page has been reprimanded & that I have made it clear to him what he risks should he approach you—or any of your servants or, Heaven forbid, Lady Walter—again.*
>
> *Yr. obedient &ct,*
> *Philip Neve, Presiding Magistrate*
> *Great Marlborough-street Magistrate Court.*

Lily, faced with the disheartening reminder of Lord Walter's bribe to the magistrate, had to read the letter through twice before the full meaning of it sunk in: Mr. Page, the Bow Street constable, had approached Lord Walter in what she had to assume was an attempt to continue investigating. He had been so unimpressed—so scornful—that day in his office when she had told him Mr. Neve had been bribed. But apparently he had listened enough, or cared enough, to try a second time.

Not that it amounted to much, it seemed. Lord Walter must have gone straight to Mr. Neve, who had promptly ended the whole thing once again. And if Bow Street persisted in taking no action, then solving the murder still fell to her. Jaw set with determination, Lily set Mr. Neve's letter aside and scanned the next paper.

> *G.C. & I thought it best you know before your meeting with Lord C.—he has expressed his reservations regarding various contracts you approved. You have G.C.'s backing—but Lord C. has a great deal of influence & no love for our politics, even in this time of war—though of course we all unite in abhorring the Bonapartist inclinations of S. Whitbread et al. Perhaps a reminder of that will encourage Lord C. to curb his disapproval regarding the contracts? Yrs, A. Harlowe.*

It was only half a page, the sort of thing dashed off by a man in a hurry, and Lily scowled at its lack of specific information. Andrew Harlowe, as secretary to a member of the House of Lords, was well known in political circles, and he and his employer often worked closely with George Canning—G.C., certainly—though Lily suspected Margaret's husband was becoming more Whiggish in his politics than the conservative Tory leader might approve of. *Lord C.* was likely Lord Castlereagh, the foreign secretary and Canning's rival. As foreign secretary, Lord Castlereagh did not have much reason to look into contracts concerning shipments to British soldiers, which Jack's informant at Lacey and West had said were Lord Walter's purview. So was Castlereagh's disapproval a simple matter of political jockeying? Or was Lord Walter involved in something more sinister that the minister has uncovered? Something worthy of blackmail?

Lily sat back on her heels, frowning in thought. From Miss Oswald's explanation of the options open to a shipping agent, and

Jack's additional military insight, it seemed clear that whatever treason their murderer was involved in, it was too small in scale to truly
disrupt the war effort. That was good for the conspirators—they were
less likely to get caught. It also meant the aim had to be profit rather
than politics. And there had never been any indication, after all, that
the Walters lacked for money.

Lily's thoughts felt lighter as she put Andrew Harlowe's letter
back among the other papers. It was not as thick a stack as it had first
appeared; underneath was a volume of *The Mysteries of Udolpho*, and
Lily couldn't help smiling, picturing the serious, conservative John
Walter indulging in an evening of sensational novel reading. She was
about to set the whole pile back when an edge of paper, peeking out
from between the book's pages, caught her eye.

She hesitated only briefly before letting the volume fall open, then
drew in an unhappy breath as she scanned the paper. It was undated
and ripped in half, but the content was clear enough—a gentleman's
vowels in the value of five hundred pounds, owed to a Mr. Benjamin
King, the sort of marker a man would give to a moneylender or in
promise of payment on a gambling debt. The bottom half, with the
signature of the man owing, was torn away. But across the top was
scrawled a note that the debt had been paid in full by Lord John Walter, signed by both parties.

Lily tucked the promissory note back in the book, feeling grim as
she replaced it, along with the rest of the papers, back under the chair
before rising and hurrying back toward the door. Her mind was racing,
but she didn't have time to think through the implications of what she
had read before she was distracted by the sound of voices on the other
side of the door. She hesitated, then pressed her ear against the wood.

". . . word that his lordship is expected back this evening." Lily
recognized the voice as belonging to Serena's housekeeper, standing
just on the other side of the door. "His study will need to be aired and
the fire laid as soon as her ladyship's guests . . ."

Lily didn't stay to hear anymore, glancing swiftly around the
room as she slid away from the door. Her eyes landed on a curtain

that was half pulled back, revealing a door she hoped would lead onto the terrace. Moving as silently as possible, she eased the door open and slipped outside.

She was just in time. She had barely shut the door and taken a deep breath before a voice called out to her.

"Lily!" It was Margaret Harlowe, just coming out onto the terrace, arm in arm with Isobel Harper. "Goodness, what are you doing snooping about?" Lily stared at her, unable to come up with a quick reply, and Margaret laughed. "Only my joke, dear. Did you come out to enjoy the fresh air after all that rain and mizzle? Sadly, there aren't many blooms to see in the gardens yet, but they are always worth looking at, don't you agree?"

"Serena's gardener is truly a maestro," Lily managed at last, still off-kilter and distracted by what she had read in Lord Walter's papers.

"Would that she could find as competent a nursemaid," Margaret said with a pitying look. She and her husband had two children as well, both girls, and employed a small army of servants to mind them. Margaret was a careful parent, and firm in her insistence that her daughters be well educated. But neither she nor Mr. Harlowe had any intention of curbing their social lives in service of their domestic concerns. "She is occupied with some minor catastrophe in the nursery, it seems. Again. Isobel said she had never seen the gardens. Shall we make it a party of three while we wait for the others?" She frowned at the sky. "Or do you think it will rain?"

"Perhaps you would show us around?" Miss Harper asked. Her voice was quiet and polite, but there was something too intense in her gaze, and it made Lily uncomfortable. Perhaps the other woman had grown awkward in her conversation in the last few years, she thought, trying to be generous. After all, Margaret had said Miss Harper hadn't been seen much since she was jilted and was now trying to be more friendly and approachable than she had been in their schoolgirl days. Lily could certainly understand feeling out of place—her return to London had left her feeling quite adrift herself, and unlike Isobel Harper, she had several close friendships, as well as her growing bond with Jack and Miss Oswald, to buffer her against discomfort. "Unless," Miss Harper continued, her quiet voice cutting into Lily's thoughts, "you would rather not. After coming so close to the . . ." She hesitated. "After the incident the other night, I could understand you wanting to stay far away from where it happened."

Margaret shuddered. "Goodness, I'd not thought of that."

Lily had to force a smile, suddenly uncomfortable with the turn of the conversation. "As far as I know, I left the terrace before anything untoward happened," she said, as lightly as possible. "I'm afraid I should have no idea if we were near where it happened or not." The first statement was not strictly a lie, but the second certainly was, and she hurried on, wanting to change the subject. "Besides which, I think Margaret is right; it looks as if the rain will be upon us again at any moment."

Margaret glanced at the sky and sighed. "What a bother. I had hoped the sunshine would last more than a few hours. No matter, though." She smiled as she turned their party back toward the house. "Did I tell you, Mr. Harlowe and I have begun the search for a governess? Kitty is nearly at that age, though how that happened, I simply cannot fathom . . ."

Lily followed the two of them inside. But she couldn't help glancing back at the gardens as they went, until she noticed Miss Harper looking at her curiously. Summoning a smile, Lily turned her eyes resolutely toward the house and joined in Margaret's chatter, trying to push thoughts of murder and political secrets from her mind.

★ ★ ★

The former students of Miss Tattersy's Seminary for Young Ladies had grown into a variety of situations—some of them young matrons, one companion to a wealthy aunt, others settled into a life of either content or resigned spinsterhood.

After the first murmurs of sympathy, no one showed any inclination to dwell on the subject of Freddy's death, for which Lily was grateful, though one newly married young woman avoided her company, as if widowhood might be catching. Lily held back both prickling tears and sharp words, choosing not to be offended, and settled instead into friendly conversation with Margaret and the former Mary Forsythe, who showed no embarrassment over her unfashionable marriage and spoke amusingly of her husband and three children.

All in all, it was a pleasant and entertaining afternoon, and Lily enjoyed none of it. Her thoughts kept returning to her discoveries in Lord Walter's study. Though she did not want to think it, things still looked grim for her friend's husband.

At last the clock chimed four, and the guests began to take their leave. Lily hung back a little, wanting to leave alone so she could finally think through what she had learned from Lord Walter's papers. Unfortunately, she said her goodbyes at the same time as Isobel Harper, who politely offered "to take Mrs. Adler in her carriage wherever she might need to go."

"How kind of you, Isobel!" Serena beamed with delight. "Of course I should have been happy to have our carriage brought around, but that is ever so much easier."

Lily, exhausted from making polite conversation when her mind was in such a grim turmoil, cursed silently and briefly considered refusing the offer. But declining would have seemed odd, so, with a smile and gritted teeth, she accepted a place in Miss Harper's vehicle.

"Where can I take you, Mrs. Adler?"

Lily, still distracted, gave her direction without attending. She let the groom assist her into the carriage as Miss Harper instructed her driver, "Half Moon Street, please, Arthur, and then to Mrs. West's house in Hans Town." The carriage seats were plushly padded, and Lily sank back onto hers with a sigh.

"Are you well, Mrs. Adler?" Miss Harper looked concerned.

Lily gave herself a quick mental shake. "Perfectly, thank you, only a little tired. I'm not yet accustomed to the busyness of town life."

"It must be a change from Hertfordshire." Miss Harper nodded sympathetically. "What are you finding to fill your time?"

"Oh, any number of things." Lily wondered what the quiet, proper Miss Harper would say if she knew the woman sitting across from her was investigating a murder. The thought nearly made her smile. To change the subject, she asked, "Did I hear you say you were visiting Hans Town?"

Miss Harper blushed. "You are thinking it an unfashionable neighborhood, perhaps? But my mother's cousin, who was my god-father, lived on Hans Place. He died several years ago, but my god-mother lives there still."

"How good of you to visit her. I'm sure your duties as mistress of your uncle's home keep you so busy that it is difficult to find the time."

She meant the comment sincerely and was surprised at the sharp look she received in response, as though Miss Harper suspected her of sarcasm. A moment later, though, Miss Harper smiled and said con-spiratorially, "My brother has mentioned your name several times in the last week, Mrs. Adler. I think he must have been quite taken with you the other night."

Lily's jaw clenched, but she settled for saying, as calmly as pos-sible, "I am surprised to hear it. We did not speak long."

"I'm sure you could make an impression during any length of con-versation, Mrs. Adler." There was something dry about Miss Harper's voice, and Lily wondered what, exactly, Mr. Harper had been saying. How much would a brother be willing to confide in his sister? As an only child, Lily had no basis for comparison, though she had never suspected Isobel and Reggie of being particularly close.

"You are kind to say so," Lily replied at last, hoping it was the right thing to say. Conversation in London society often went much deeper than what was spoken aloud, and the subtlety was more than she had energy for that afternoon.

She was grateful that the ride did not last much longer. When the carriage pulled to a halt in front of number thirteen, Lily thanked Miss Harper, allowed the groom to hand her down, and then paused, glancing around.

Ever since her unsettling discoveries, she had been on edge, and the feeling now grew stronger. Lily glanced around, trying not to feel nervous. Miss Harper's carriage was moving off. A young boy was scrubbing the muddy front stairs while Mrs. Carstairs kept an eagle eye on him through the open door. Two workmen cursed amiably as they repaired a window on the next house over. Everything was as it should be. There was no reason for the prickle between her shoulder blades, yet she could not shake it.

The boy was blocking the front door, so Lily changed course and turned toward the side of the house, where the narrow gap between buildings passed the side door and opened into the postage-stamp garden. Still preoccupied, she didn't notice the shadow that stuck out from beyond the wall.

Someone large struck her, knocking her to the ground.

Lily screamed, half from fright and half from a practical desire to summon help. Her attacker cursed eloquently, grabbing at her arms and trying to cover her mouth. She fought against him as well as she could, trying to hold off his hands, but he had the advantage of both size and being upright.

"'Ere now, get off 'er!"

"Get 'im, quick!"

Someone was grappling with her attacker, Lily realized, hauling him away from her. With a snarled curse, the man disappeared between the houses, the workmen from next door in pursuit.

"Ma'am, lady!" The boy had come running around the side of the house after the workmen and skidded to a halt, looking unsure what to do next.

Lily scrambled to her feet. "I'm fine," she said, trying to hide her shaking.

The boy gathered up Lily's hat and reticule, which had been knocked to the ground. "Are you hurt? Should I yell fer a constable?"

Lily was saved from having to reply by the return of the two panting workmen. "Lost 'im, I'm afraid, miss," the first said, clutching at a stitch in his side. "Cor, the blighter could run. You're not hurt, I 'ope?"

"I'm perfectly well, gentlemen, in no small part thanks to your timely rescue," Lily said, feeling more composed. "I don't suppose you were able to see the man's face?"

Both shook their heads. "Got away too fast. Tall fellow, though; ran like the devil."

"Dark hair," the other one added. "Pale, maybe? Couldn't get a good look at 'im neither."

"A loiterer, or some vagrant." Lily shook her head. "I must have caught him by surprise when I came around the edge of the building." Fishing in her reticule, she pulled out two shillings and handed them to the blushing workers. "For your aid, gentlemen, with my sincere thanks."

To her relief, they took both the hint and the coin and left, touching their hats and muttering that "it weren't nothing to help a lady what needed it."

Her staff by that point had come outside to see what the commotion was. Lily was left to the care of Mrs. Carstairs, who sent the boy scurrying back to his work, exclaimed over what the world was coming to when ladies were assaulted in the streets, and fussed in a manner that was both soothing and frustrating. The housekeeper insisted on a hot bath followed by tea in bed while she had Mr. Carstairs go over the whole house to make sure it was secured against any other "ruffians."

Lily, more shaken than she was willing to admit, managed to catch Anna's eye in time to ensure the tea was liberally dosed with brandy.

As she sipped it, tucked into bed with a warming pan at her feet, Lily shivered. Her attacker had been no vagrant. Likely he had not meant to attack her; she had surprised him when she came around the house instead of going in the front door. But he had not smelled of poverty or drink, and he had reacted too swiftly, his movements too controlled, calculated to incapacitate her as quickly as possible.

A tall, pale man with dark hair, lurking around her house. As descriptions went, it was almost uselessly vague. But it matched the man Mrs. Carstairs had seen at the kitchen door, the man whose presence had so startled her that she had fallen down the stairs.

Lily shivered again, forced to consider a possibility she had been trying to ignore. She hadn't imagined the sound of footsteps following her out of the Walters' garden the night Mr. Finch was killed. And if the murderer had overheard her asking Jack for help, he knew she was a danger to him.

Lily threw off her covers. Crossing to her writing desk, she slid open a drawer and stared at the pistol that lay inside. It had been part of a set once, bought by Freddy while he was at university. One had gone to Sir John, Freddy's older brother, but Lily, ever practical, had kept the other. Now, her heart racing but her hands steady, she loaded it and laid it back in the drawer.

Someone was after her. And she intended to be ready for him.

CHAPTER 15

It would have been easy, Lily reflected the next morning over tea, toast, and a halfhearted attempt to read *Cecilia*, to give up her self-appointed task. She could stay quietly at home or even leave London altogether. But a childhood of being bullied by her father had left her with an ingrained response to any attempt to intimidate her. It was irrational and defiant—and, she admitted to herself, this time it was dangerous—but the realization that someone was following her only left her more determined to continue.

Unfortunately, the next step was a ball thrown that night by a Mr. and Mrs. Chichester to present their daughter. The Walters had called for her in their carriage. Sitting with Serena would have been bad enough, given the state of her suspicions. But Lord Walter, as she had overheard, had returned suddenly the day before, and he was there as well. Smiling and conversing during the carriage ride, all the while wondering if he had been the one to attack her, was excruciating. Lily breathed a sigh of relief when, after greeting their host and hostess and complimenting Miss Chichester on the elegance of her dress and the style of her ball, Lord Walter excused himself to go in search of the card room.

Even that was short-lived relief. Lily watched him go, remembering the other times Lord Walter had disappeared into a game of cards and thinking of the debt owed and paid to the unknown Mr. King. She wondered how deeply Lord Walter would gamble that night.

"You have your battle face on," Serena whispered as they made their way toward a group of their acquaintance that included the Harlowes.

Lily stiffened. "I certainly do not."

Serena laughed. "What is battle face for you, my dear, is mildly bored on anyone else. But I know you." She nudged her friend. "Cheer up, Lily. It is a party, after all. You are supposed to enjoy yourself."

"I shall endeavor to do so, at your command." Lily's stomach twisted with guilt over the secret she was keeping from her friend, and she greeted the Harlowes effusively as an excuse to drop Serena's arm. "And here is Margaret, looking beautiful as ever!"

Margaret laughed as she leaned forward to kiss cheeks. "You are the best sort of friend to keep around." The other lady and gentlemen in the group made their bows. "Do you know, Lily, I had the pleasure of meeting your new friend the other afternoon."

"Do you mean Miss Oswald?"

"Indeed. I see why you like her so much. Though she is more forward in her manner than should be encouraged in young ladies."

"Perhaps because she was raised in such unorthodox circumstances," Mr. Harlowe put in. At Lily's slightly narrow-eyed look, he added, "I think any father raising a daughter on his own would be inclined to allow her greater liberty of manner than might otherwise be acceptable."

"Not necessarily," Margaret said, giving Lily a knowing look.

"I imagine it comes of being raised in the West Indies," one of the other ladies sniffed. "Such places are savage, and George Oswald is not the only man from a good family to fall into disrepute there."

Lily was about to offer a scathing retort when Serena laughed. "Nonsense, Mrs. Collins, the West Indies are quite civilized. Lord Walter used to have family property to visit there, and when he dined with the governor of Nevis, they always had three courses. And in any case, it hardly signifies. An heiress will always be forgiven for a too-easy manner that would be inexcusable in a girl of lesser fortune."

"I should be wary, Mrs. Collins, of saying a Devonshire Oswald has fallen into disrepute," Mr. Harlowe added, eyes twinkling. "The family is so well connected, you never know when one of their relations might overhear you."

Another gentleman chimed in. "Do you think the girl will make a match this season, given her . . . unusual background?"

"I cannot imagine the Oswalds would allow her to do anything else, though they may have their work cut out for them . . ."

Another time, Lily would have been quick to disapprove of such condescension and speak in Miss Oswald's defense. But her mind was playing Serena's words over and over, and she couldn't make herself focus on the conversation. Excusing herself, she hurried to the ladies' retiring room, her mind reeling.

It was one line of inquiry she had not yet pursued—how had Mr. Finch learned his information? According to Miss Oswald, he knew no one in London, which meant he must have met the victim of his blackmail in Nevis. That meant that the murderer, whoever he was, had spent time in the West Indies.

She hadn't known that Lord Walter had once owned property in Nevis.

At least this meant Serena knew nothing of her husband's involvement in the murder—if he was involved—or surely she would not volunteer that he had been to the West Indies? Unless she thought Bow Street's ignoring the matter meant there was no longer any danger . . .

Lily groaned, dropping her head into her hands. Nothing was coming clear, and much as she wanted to, she could not yet convince herself that her friend's husband was innocent. What was she to do next?

General Harper. She needed to learn more about General Harper—perhaps that held the key to proving Lord Walter's innocence. If he *was* innocent. Lily groaned again.

As if responding to her thoughts, a gentle voice asked, "Mrs. Adler? Are you unwell?"

Lily sat up with a start to find Isobel Harper watching her. Embarrassed, she quickly stood. "Perfectly well, I thank you."

"Shall I have a maid fetch something? A glass of water? A vinaigrette?"

"Oh no." Lily forced a smile. "I was only a little overwhelmed by the noise and heat." She gestured toward the door. "Shall we return to the ballroom?"

"Certainly, if you are ready." Miss Harper smiled obligingly. As they made their way out of the retiring room, she added, "You seem to make a habit of escaping from ballrooms."

"A habit?" Lily paused in the hallway, which was empty except for the two of them. "What do you mean?"

"At Lady Walter's ball you escaped to the terrace." Miss Harper laughed. "I almost think London does not agree with you!"

"It is rather a change of pace, especially after—" Lily broke off abruptly. She was sure she had heard footsteps following them down the hall. But as soon as they paused, the sound stopped. "Did you hear that?"

Miss Harper looked puzzled. "Hear what?"

"I thought there was . . ." Lily frowned, breaking off once more, but the only sound was the music and laughter from the ballroom. "Never mind. Next thing, I shall be taking fright at shadows under my bed." She managed a small laugh but still felt uneasy. Try as she might to tell herself she was imagining things, she knew that was not the case. "Tell, me, Miss Harper, who made your gown? It is the loveliest thing I've seen this season."

She had intended the question as a distraction but had underestimated either her former schoolfellow's perception or her concern. "Mrs. Adler, you look very pale."

"It was nothing." Lily shook her head but glanced down the hallway once more. "Only that . . . no, I apologize, I am being dreadfully silly."

"You look as if you have been dreadfully scared," Miss Harper said quietly. "Tell me what is the matter."

Lily hesitated, but the silent, dim hallway was still working on her mind. Before she could think about it too closely, she confessed, "I think someone has been following me the last few days. It sounds absurd, I know," she said quickly, feeling defensive. "But yesterday there was a man lurking outside my house. He knocked me down before running off."

"How dreadful." Miss Harper raised a hand to her heart as she looked around the deserted hallway. "Have you told anyone? Captain Hartley, perhaps?"

"Captain Hartley?" Lily's surprise was unfeigned. "Certainly not."

"But if you feel you are in danger . . ."

"I am sure it is nothing so dramatic as that." Lily began to wish she had kept her fears to herself. A plausible excuse for her worries suddenly occurring to her, she added, with a self-conscious laugh, "Perhaps that night at the Walters' is the reason for my being so jumpy, now I think on it."

"What about that night?" Miss Harper grew very still, and her voice quivered a little.

That quiver made Lily feel guilty; no doubt Isobel Harper, like most gently reared young ladies, preferred not to think of things like murder and death. But that only made her lie more believable. "That horrid business with the man in the garden." Affecting a shudder, Lily fanned herself, trying to infuse her voice with just the right amount of quaver. "Something so morbid, happening at a London soiree? I have been jumping at shadows ever since."

"Oh, indeed." Miss Harper sighed. "I feel the same. Such a terrible thing."

"But nothing to do with any of us." Lily snapped her fan shut. "Which I must endeavor to remember, rather than dwelling on it and upsetting my friends," she added gently, seeing that her companion looked pale. "Miss Harper, I am so sorry, I have distressed you greatly."

"And now we have switched roles, and you are concerned about me." Miss Harper's smile was forced as she endeavored to pinch some color back into her cheeks. "And I shall say, as you did, that I am perfectly well." She paused a moment, then added, "And I think you were right not to mention your worries to anyone else, Mrs. Adler, particularly not the good captain. Being the gallant navy gentleman, no doubt he would consider it his duty to sit up nights, guarding your door against intruders."

"Now there indeed is a terrifying thought." Lily did not need to feign horror at the idea of being so closely watched over.

Her tone made Miss Harper laugh softly. "You were always so impressively independent."

"Do you think it impressive?" An ironic smile lifted the corners of Lily's lips. "Not many do. My father despairs of me, and he assures me that my mother would as well, had she lived."

"Yes, impressive." Miss Harper's voice was firm and, Lily noted with surprise, even a little bitter. "It is something to be proud of. I hope you treasure it."

"I do not seem to be able to avoid it," Lily admitted. "You are feeling well again?"

"I am, thank you." Miss Harper's lips tilted up in a faint smile. "It seems we both find the idea of violence quite distressing."

"Then let us continue back to the ballroom and talk of something more pleasant," Lily said, glad to change the subject. "You still have not told me who made that marvelous gown."

★   ★   ★

By the time they returned to the ballroom, Miss Harper's concern had been sufficiently put to rest that she returned to her own party. Lily was relieved. She knew she was not imagining things, and trying to pretend nothing was wrong was giving her a headache. But her relief was short-lived: she rejoined Margaret and Serena just as Lord Walter arrived.

He bowed to the group, then smiled at his wife. "My dear." He dropped a dutiful kiss on Serena's cheek. The sweet gesture gave Lily a pang of guilt, and she turned away quickly. "Would you ladies care for supper? They have laid out a small repast in the next room." He bowed, holding out an arm to Lily. "If I may offer you my escort?"

Lily hesitated. But Lord Walter was waiting, and the Harlowes were watching. Lily summoned a smile and asked, "If you do not object to a fifth spoiling the balance of the party?"

"Oh, nonsense." Serena made a *pfft* noise. So Lily had no choice but to assent, and the group made their way out of the ballroom so the gentlemen could secure seats for supper.

It was, as Lord Walter had said, a small supper, laid out for guests to help themselves as the midnight hour drew near and they grew hungry. There were platters of warm lamb, cold chicken, and beef-steak wrapped in pastry. An array of silver tureens offered turtle soup, peas cooked with ham, asparagus in lemon sauce, and plain English mutton. For guests who were merely peckish, there was an array of nuts and cheeses, sweetmeats and five kinds of fruit, and both white and spice cakes. Footmen circulated, offering a selection of three different wines.

The gentlemen helped the ladies to fill their plates, and then all five joined the shifting sea of guests finding and leaving places at the table.

Mrs. Chichester had recently redecorated her supper room with a large, pastoral mural, and the beautiful scene drew admiring exclamations from guests as they passed through. Lord and Lady Walter— who shared an enthusiasm for painting—began discussing the relative merits of the piece, drawing the others into a lively conversation. The talk turned eventually to the construction of the Regent's new pleasure pavilion at Brighton, the sensation caused by Mr. Shelley's latest poem, and several bills before Parliament, the last of which made Lord Walter and Mr. Harlowe bluster loudly at each other. But when talk turned to the movements of the French, Serena was emphatic.

"Nothing of war, if you please, gentlemen. I am sick of the subject. Surely there is something else we may talk about?"

"Something like Miss Harper dancing twice tonight with Mr. Christopher Kettering?" Margaret suggested with a low laugh, tilting her head toward the doorway, where Miss Harper and her uncle had just entered.

"Twice?" Serena's eyes narrowed. "Do you know, I think my suspicions about Isobel may be correct. I had been wondering, with her going about so much this season."

"Wondering what?" Lily asked, distracted by watching the general. There was something sinister about his face, she thought—though perhaps that was only because she wanted him to be guilty so Lord Walter could be innocent.

"Wondering what—! Really, Lily, do not be so stupid." Serena lowered her voice. "Of course I am wondering if she is to be married."

"After all this time?" Margaret asked. "And I was determined to make a match for her—"

"Everyone says the Ketterings' land is dreadfully mortgaged," Mr. Harlowe said. "I should think the son needs to marry money—"

"They could be in love." Margaret smiled at her husband, who kissed her fingers.

"As if his family would care about that!" Serena shook her head. "Bluest blood and tightest arses in England, my father always said."

Margaret gasped with pleasurable shock at her friend's language. "Really, Serena!"

"Well, if it is true, her uncle will no doubt be pleased." Mr. Harlowe leaned forward. "Even his bottomless funds cannot find it easy to support two dependents."

"Especially when one of them needs so much supporting," Lord Walter said. "His whelp of a nephew is in the betting books at White's every other week, and he lost a small fortune at Newmarket."

"How do you know that?" Margaret asked.

"My cousin Bernard," Lord Walter sighed. "His taste in friends is almost as dreadful as his taste in cravats. He joined Mr. Harper's crowd of dandies at the Spring Meeting this year. Where, according to Bernard, Mr. Harper managed to pick the losing horse in every race."

"No wonder that boy chases every heiress in town," Serena laughed. "He cannot like constantly asking his uncle for money."

"And his uncle cannot like giving it to him, as he is quite the gambler himself," Mr. Harlowe put in, lowering his voice. "The man has a reputation for playing deep, and it seems his skill on the battlefield does not translate to the card table."

"Really?" Serena looked fascinated. "You know, I am not surprised to hear it. In fact, just last week . . ." She lowered her voice conspiratorially. Lily tried to concentrate on Serena's story, but something tickled at the back of her mind. It took her several minutes to figure out what it was: General Harper had been a younger son. And younger sons, traditionally, were not left with much in the way of income.

The elder Harper son, she knew, had not had a large fortune; that was why so little had been left to his children, why Reggie Harper wanted a rich wife, why Isobel Harper had been jilted by her betrothed. The general would have inherited even less, and though his military service would provide an income, it would hardly be unlimited, no matter how well invested. It was possible that, like many members of London's upper class, the general simply ran up debts he never intended to pay. But if that was not the case, it raised a very pertinent question: where did his money come from?

And had he turned to treason and war profiteering in order to replenish his accounts?

"Do you remember, Lily?" Serena's question called her back to the conversation.

"How could I forget?" she responded glibly, trying to rejoin the thread of conversation once more. But her thoughts kept returning to her suspicions, and to the shadowy figure that had been following her. Both her suspects were in attendance that night. Either of them could have followed her when she went to the retiring room. Either of them could still be her murderer.

The others were standing, she realized suddenly, preparing to leave the dining room, and she hurried to join them. As she did so, she caught sight of the last person she wanted to see. Reggie Harper had joined his uncle and sister, and he slouched at their table with

Checkout Receipt
Lawrenceburg Public
Library District

Title: Cajun Justice
Call Number:
Item ID: 35340636886961
Date Due: 12/29/2020

Title: The Body In The
Garden
Call Number:
Item ID: 35340636621418
Date Due: 12/29/2020

Renew online or
812-537-2775
www.lpld.lib.in.us

fashionable boredom. But his eyes were on her, and as he saw her notice him, he smiled slowly.

Lily felt her face grow hot with anger. How dared he continue to force himself on her notice. "Bastard."

She did not realize she had spoken out loud until her companions fell silent. "I beg your pardon?" Mr. Harlowe asked, one arm half raised to offer it to her.

Lily felt her face grow hot. "Not you. I beg your—" Mr. Harper was still watching her. Being around her friends as they happily shared kissed fingers and warm laughs with their husbands was suddenly too much to bear. "Excuse me, please." Not bothering to explain, Lily left abruptly, heading toward the ballroom. She would apologize later. Right now, she needed to get away.

★ ★ ★

When she saw Jack just making his way off the dance floor, she nearly sighed with relief as she caught his eye. Jack grinned, leaving his dance partner with her chaperone and making his way to Lily's side. When he drew close, however, his expression sobered. "You look distressed."

"Only annoyed with myself. I sometimes think I am no longer fit for polite society—or at least for making conversation without acting like a fool."

"You do well enough talking to me," Jack said, smiling again. "Or is that because Freddy told you all my unmanly childhood secrets?"

His teasing put her at ease in a way sympathy never could. "Oh, you are not polite society, Captain. I have it on excellent authority that you are a rogue."

"But a charming one, I hope?"

"Yes," Lily agreed with dry sarcasm. "It is a wonder the ladies did not swoon at your feet on the dance floor. In fact . . ." She narrowed her eyes. "You are dancing a great deal tonight. Are you courting, Captain?"

"Gad, no."

"Yet you do not meet my eyes when you say so. Why is that, I wonder?"

"Because . . ." Jack sighed. "If you must know, Mrs. Adler, I am watching your friend."

Judging by his shifty look, he could mean only one person. "Miss Oswald?"

"Yes." Jack glanced around. "She's keeping secrets from you."

Lily didn't argue with him, but simply said, "She is nineteen, Captain. Most nineteen-year-old girls keep secrets."

"Do most of them also sneak around, lie about where they are, and meet with strange gentlemen to discuss their friends' affairs?"

Lily was watching Miss Oswald weave very prettily through the figures of a country dance, but at Jack's words she turned abruptly to face him. "What do you mean?"

"The other day, when I escorted her home"—Jack lowered his voice—"I left her at the door, but she did not go inside, so I waited a few blocks away and watched her. She sneaked around the corner and out of sight of her aunt's house before hailing a chair."

Lily returned to her study of the dancers. "Did you see where she went?"

"Hyde Park."

"Walking in a park is hardly grounds for suspicion, especially with as pleasant weather as we have been having," Lily pointed out, but her voice was thoughtful rather than dismissive. "Her sneaking away from her aunt's house is odd, I grant you, but there could be a reason."

"Both she and the man she met hid their faces from view. I could not see who he was, and they were both so dashed twitchy that I feared they would recognize me if I ventured too close. But I did overhear her telling him something of the . . ." He cleared his throat. "The *business* you are about."

Lily's frown deepened. "That is peculiar," she said slowly.

"I know you've grown fond of her, but . . ." Jack looked uncomfortable. "You don't really know her. And if you intend to keep pursuing this business—"

"I do."

"Then you need to be careful."

Lily sighed. She had her own suspicions about what Miss Oswald was hiding, but she couldn't deny that what Jack had observed was odd. "I'll not be able to dissuade you from watching her, will I?"

"No." The reply was firm.

"Then you will do as you feel necessary, but I hope you'll not jump to any conclusions. Remember . . ." Lily hesitated, not wanting to put ideas in his head. "Remember, she has more at stake in this matter than either of us."

"So she says."

"Yes," Lily said, her eyes narrowing in consideration. "So she says."

She could feel Jack watching her. "You know something," he said. It was not a question.

"I think that she has not been entirely forthcoming with us," Lily admitted. "But what I suspect she is hiding is something which makes me trust her."

"Will you tell me what it is?"

"Not yet." Lily hesitated, then added, "I need you to trust me, just as I trust you to continue watching her without doing anything drastic."

She thought Jack might press the subject, but to her relief he let it drop, saying after a pause, "I saw you with Lord Walter earlier."

"Yes." Lily thought back through the supper conversation. "How much money should a general have when he leaves the army, assuming no family funds?"

Jack shrugged. "A good bit. Not unlimited funds, of course, but a decent amount. Why?"

Lily smiled grimly. "There is the critical word. Unlimited. What I have learned tonight is that General Harper is a very good suspect indeed."

"Then we are getting closer?"

"Bit by bit, Captain. And I shan't give up until I solve it."

"I know," he said, the confidence in his voice finally making her feel at ease again.

For several minutes they were silent, watching the dancers. Lily didn't realize how wistfully she was staring until Jack touched her arm. "What is it, Mrs. Adler?"

She looked away, embarrassed. "I miss dancing, I suppose. Freddy was hopeless at a country dance. He would get so distracted speaking with his partner that he lost track of the set." She sighed. "We had such fun waltzing, though. Not that we had many opportunities, but . . ." A small, sad smile briefly crossed her face. "We waltzed in London."

She could feel Jack's eyes on her, but she looked resolutely away until he surprised her by taking her arm and drawing her away from the dance floor. When she glanced up, he was smiling. "Come with me."

"Captain Hartley, it is hardly proper for me to leave the ballroom with you." Lily frowned and kept her voice low but didn't resist as he led her toward the hall.

"It's only improper if we make a fuss about it," he pointed out. "The rules have changed for you, so why not take advantage of that?"

"Take advantage how?" They were out of eyesight of the ballroom now, and Jack was opening doors a few inches at a time, listening at each one, and then moving on.

"You will see . . . Ah, here we are!"

The room he drew her into was a small library. Its tall windows were ajar, letting in a spill of light and faint strains of the music. The musicians were just striking up a waltz. Lily turned to Jack, unsure what he intended. He grinned at her and bowed. "Would you honor me with a dance, Mrs. Adler?" He offered his hand.

It was a sweet gesture. Even if it felt highly improper to sneak away from the ballroom, he was right—no one would raise a fuss. But still she hesitated. "You know very well that I'm still in black gloves, Captain. I cannot dance."

"You cannot let anyone *see* you dance. Surely you don't mean that I am just anyone?" His expression became more serious, and he took her hand but made no other move. "Dance if you want, Lily. Freddy would not like to see you so sad."

At last Lily nodded and let him draw her into a sweet, slow waltz. There wasn't much space to move, but they turned carefully around the room, neither one speaking, the sound of the music rising and falling with the breeze that blew through the window. Lily closed her eyes. Nothing else mattered in that moment but the notes of the waltz and the feel of someone's arms around her. It wasn't her husband, and she didn't try to imagine that it was, but Jack was right: Freddy had never liked to see her sad.

They spun to a gentle stop as the music ended, but he didn't drop his arms, and she didn't step away. They stood still for several moments, each thinking of the same person. Lily kept her eyes closed, but a few tears slid down her cheeks anyway. "Thank you, Jack," she whispered.

He was silent for a moment, then: "I miss him too," he whispered back. She felt his lips brush her forehead before he stepped away.

Lily heard the door close softly behind him. She didn't move, didn't open her eyes as, one more time, she let herself cry for her husband.

★ ★ ★

When she finally emerged into the hallway, Jack was watching the door with poorly hidden anxiety. "Are you all right?"

"I am." There was a lightness in her chest that Lily had not felt in the three very long years since Freddy had first fallen ill. "Thank you."

He surprised her by taking her hand and kissing her knuckles. "I am at your service, Mrs. Adler, and always shall be." A bit of his customary levity returned to his expression. "Though perhaps not to escort you back to the ballroom. Might not look quite the thing."

Lily's eyes crinkled up at the corners. "Who knows what dreadful gossip saw us leave together, after all," she agreed. She had to rise onto her toes just a little to kiss his cheek. "I am very glad to call you my friend, Jack."

His smile widened into a grin. "So am I, Lily. So am I."

CHAPTER 16

"Goodness, Serena, did you really need three new pairs of gloves?" Lily asked, fanning herself as she scanned the crowd that thronged the shopping thoroughfare of Bond Street.

"Oh, you needn't worry, Lily, they simply put it on account."

"You realize that means your husband must still pay for it later, do you not?"

"Which he is always happy to do, as you well know." Serena huffed in annoyance, resettling her packages. "In any case, Miss Oswald bought five pairs, and I've not heard you lecturing her."

Miss Oswald smiled pertly. She had indeed bought five pairs of gloves on their shopping trip, as well as ordering new lavender kid boots and a parasol. "Papa expects me to be well turned out."

"And it shan't hurt for the young men of London—and their mothers—to see you looking the part of an heiress." There was a glint in Serena's eye as she spoke. As she had been thrown into Miss Oswald's company more, she had revised her original opinion of the girl and declared her "the most charming creature I have ever met." Lily strongly suspected that was because Miss Oswald's love of shopping rivaled Lady Walter's own.

The three of them were spending the afternoon browsing the shops on Bond Street, though Lily was the only one who had not yet bought anything. Economy was one of the few valuable lessons her father had taught her, and after spending so much money to establish her household in London, she didn't want to make many new purchases. Instead, she tried to focus on Serena's cheerful gossip, but her mind turned again and again to the facts of the case. The outing with Serena was a good opportunity to seek out more information about her husband, and though Lily felt guilty, she was not dissuaded from pressing forward. She needed to solve the blasted thing, soon, before the trail got too cold, and a chance remark of Serena's might be the key. From time to time Miss Oswald caught her eye, and Lily knew the younger woman was thinking the same thing.

"Whyever did you purchase such an ugly bonnet, Serena?" Lily continued as they strolled in the direction of Gunter's Tea Shop for ices.

"Lily, do not be so unfashionable!" Lady Walter eyed the parcels her footman carried with proprietary pride. Jeremy, half hidden behind the stack of purchases, trailed behind the three women. "That leghorn style is all the crack this spring."

"It is the trimming I object to, not the style. That check ribbon is dreadful. Does Lord Walter ever complain about how expensive you are?"

"Oh, frequently," Serena said with a laugh. "But I always remind him that a mistress would be far more expensive, and she would not manage his calendar nearly so well." That prompted a giggle from Miss Oswald. "Oh, did I tell you?" Serena continued. "I discovered why Bernard was sent back to his father's house so abruptly. You remember that he went to the Spring Meeting at Newmarket?"

"Let me guess," Lily said dryly. "Cousin Bernard is a terrible judge of horseflesh."

Serena laughed. "He bet on every horse that Mr. Harper did, and every one of them lost! He went through his allowance and more, and the stupid boy decided to visit a moneylender to pay off the difference. Which of course meant he was still in debt, just to someone else. And then one of Mr. King's ruffians showed up at our door looking to collect on the debt!"

If Lily had been a fraction more clumsy, she would have tripped over her own feet in shock. "Mr. King?"

"The moneylender," Serena said, not noticing her friend's odd tone. "I had no idea at the time, of course, for Lord Walter didn't wish me to be upset by something like that. He paid off the debt himself, and then dragged Bernard home practically by the scruff of his neck!"

"Well, then as long as you stay away from moneylenders, I imagine you will be safe from his lordship complaining about your expenses," Miss Oswald said slyly, and the two women went into peals of laughter.

Lily smiled along with them, but her mind was racing. If the promissory note she had found in Lord Walter's study was Bernard's debt from the Spring Meeting, then she had no reason to think the Walters' finances were in trouble. And if that was the case, Lord Walter would not need to turn to turn to illegal activity to supplement his income.

But the general, as she had learned the night before, had two dependents, one of whom was very expensive indeed, and his own apparently extravagant gambling habit to support. He would need all the money he could get his hands on—and he had every connection necessary to engage in war profiteering, if he were unscrupulous enough to use them.

Her thoughts were interrupted as Serena caught sight of a familiar face. "Isobel! My dear Miss Harper, what a pleasure to see you."

"Lady Walter." Isobel Harper gestured for her maid to stop so she could greet the three women. "Mrs. Adler." She looked politely at Miss Oswald, and Lily hastened to make the introduction.

Miss Oswald, after murmuring a polite greeting, exchanged a speaking glance with Lily, while Serena launched immediately into talk of shopping.

"And is that a bit of blue silk I see peeping out of your parcel?" she asked, having finished showing off her own new bonnet and receiving the expected praise. "I have heard that blue is Mr. Christopher Kettering's favorite color."

"I believe it is the favorite color of many gentlemen," Miss Harper replied. She spoke calmly enough, but her cheeks flushed.

Serena's eyes gleamed, and she would have continued fishing for gossip had Miss Oswald not chimed in. "Only too true. When a woman says a color is her favorite, depend upon it, she has some reason for the preference. But when a man is asked his favorite color, he invariably says blue because he has never considered the subject at all."

"And which did you say was your favorite color, Miss Oswald, in that last shop?" Serena asked pointedly.

The girl smiled. "Blue. But a very particular shade! A blue the color of the water in the Caribbean. No one who has seen it can forget it."

"Indeed, it is a stunning hue," Miss Harper agreed.

"Why, Isobel, when have you been in the Caribbean?" Serena demanded. Lily, whose attention had wandered a little during the talk of colors, started.

"Oh, some five or six years ago at least." Miss Harper looked uncomfortable. "My uncle traveled there for some business, and I was . . . there was nothing keeping me in London at the time, so I went with him."

Six years ago Miss Harper had been jilted just before her marriage was to take place. Lily thought it no surprise that Miss Harper's uncle had wanted her to leave London for a time, or that she should dislike remembering the reason for her trip.

Knowing that was enough to make Lily hesitate. She did not want to make Miss Harper more uncomfortable, but if the general had been in the West Indies, there was a chance he had met Augustus Finch there. She had to know. "What a traveler you are, Miss Harper. I am quite envious! Which part of the Indies did you see?"

"Several islands, including Nevis, where I believe we had the pleasure of dining once with Miss Oswald's father at Government House. Mr. George Oswald?" The heiress, looking surprised, nodded. "I imagine that you were too young to dine in company at the time, but I remember your father being a most impressive gentleman." Miss Harper smiled a little pathetically. "I should have liked to travel more, but . . ."

"Now that your uncle has left the army, perhaps it is in your future." Lily adopted a bright tone to mask the intent of her question. "Do you think he will visit there again?"

Miss Harper shook her head, looking sad. "No, he has since sold his interests there."

Lily, unwilling to let the subject drop but not wanting to press, caught Miss Oswald's eye, and the girl cleared her throat. "Well, should you ever desire to visit Nevis again, Miss Harper, you must let me know. My father would be happy to make any introductions you require."

"I shall remember that," Miss Harper said, but whatever else she might have said was interrupted as a man emerging from the store-front of Mr. Hoby, bootmaker, bumped into her. After a moment of confusion and apologies, Miss Harper started as she recognized the man's face. "Mr. Lacey! What a surprise to see you."

"Miss Harper, a pleasure. I hope your uncle is well?"

"Lacey?" Lily was so shocked that she asked without thinking, "Of Lacey and West?"

Mr. Lacey looked surprised. He was a tall man, pale, with brown hair and a sharp nose. His clothes said upper-class businessman rather than gentleman, but he bowed to Lily with a good deal of confidence. "As you say, madam. I am gratified that we are so well known, for all we are a small endeavor." He smiled again, but his eyes had narrowed.

Lily cursed silently at her carelessness. "Oh, I had heard the name mentioned here and there." She tried not to look too interested. All expression was gone from Mr. Lacey's face, his look so carefully blank that it made Lily want to shiver. She was glad that their relative social standing prevented him from asking for her name.

"Well, we must be off," Serena broke in. Lily could tell by her tone that Lady Walter did not want to be seen conversing with the obviously middle-class Mr. Lacey. "Would you care to join us for an ice, Miss Harper?"

"Thank you, no, I must return home." Miss Harper, more polite than Serena, added, "I wish you a good day, Mr. Lacey."

"Miss Harper." He bowed to the group, but his eyes were fixed on Lily. "I wish you a pleasant day."

Miss Harper murmured her own farewell, and the ladies had begun to walk away when he called out after them.

"A moment, Miss Harper!" He stooped to the ground, and when he stood, there was something in his hand. "You seem to have dropped your glove."

"Ah, thank you, sir," Miss Harper said, looking a little flustered as he brought it to her. There should have been nothing odd in the gesture—it was both polite and proper—but something in Mr. Lacey's manner made Lily watch him closely. Which was why she saw him, under cover of returning Miss Harper's glove, slide just a little closer to her and slip a much-folded piece of paper into her reticule. Miss Harper, preoccupied with drawing her gloves on tightly, did not notice. Mr. Lacey lifted his hat to the women once more before striding off in the other direction.

Lily tried not to stare after him as he disappeared into the crowd on Bond Street. Looking back, she found Miss Oswald watching her, eyes wide. The girl nodded, ever so slightly, before turning away. She had seen it too.

"Goodness! What an odd man." Serena wrinkled her nose.

"He . . . yes, he is that," Miss Harper said.

"Did he say he knows your uncle?" Lily asked, as carelessly as she could manage.

"Yes, but not well," Miss Harper said quickly. "Why do you ask?"

"Oh, Mr. Adler left some shipping documents that I am at a loss to understand. I was wondering if I should seek professional help to sort through them."

"I don't . . . that is to say, I would advise against it, Mrs. Adler." Miss Harper's eyes darted back in the direction Mr. Lacey had gone.

"Good heavens, why not?" Lily feigned a look of puzzled disinterest. "If he's known to the general, he must be a respectable man."

"I am by no means confident in his respectability. My uncle knows him only by chance, and only . . . only to nod to in the street. If he had not bumped into me as he came out of Hoby's, I shouldn't have acknowledged him at all." Miss Harper shook her head. "I would stay away from him, Mrs. Adler. Surely your husband's lawyer can help to sort through his papers."

"Oh, very likely." Lily let the subject drop before her persistence made anyone curious.

"Miss Harper, are you well?" Serena asked, her face wreathed in concern. "You look pale. Allow me to take you home in my carriage; I insist. Ices will have to wait for another day."

Miss Harper was pale, Lily realized, paler than she had been when Mr. Lacey appeared. She tucked that bit of information away to examine later, along with everything else she had learned about the general. For the moment, she needed to focus on one thing: Mr. Lacey's note.

While Serena was kindly bullying Miss Harper into accepting an offer of assistance, Lily leaned close enough to Miss Oswald's ear to whisper, "See if you can make Miss Harper drop her bag, then keep her attention on you."

The young heiress did not bat an eyelash but simply moved closer to Miss Harper's side and began speaking of their shopping trip as Serena's footman signaled for her waiting carriage. He handed the viscountess in, then turned to offer Miss Harper his hand.

If Lily had not known better, she would have sworn Miss Oswald's fall was genuine. As the girl stepped out of the way, she stumbled, toppling into Jeremy the footman with a surprised "*Oh!*" He instinctively tried to catch her, dropping the armful of boxes he was still carrying. Parcels scattered everywhere, and Miss Oswald stumbled backward into Miss Harper, knocking into her arm so that she dropped her reticule and bandbox. The young heiress stammered in embarrassment and insisted on helping the footman gather up the packages, handing several to Miss Harper and the maid who accompanied her as she did so, while Serena called out in concern from the carriage door.

In the confusion, Lily quietly gathered up Miss Harper's things, keeping Jeremy between her and the other women as she fished in the reticule for Mr. Lacey's note.

It was not there.

The purse was not large, and he had dropped it in only minutes before. It should have been on top, easy to find and pull out, but there was no sign of it.

There was no time to look more thoroughly. Cursing silently, Lily bent and snatched up one of the fallen packages. She was just in time; as she stood, the footman moved out of the way, and Miss Harper called, "Oh, I see Mrs. Adler has them," as she held out a hand for her things.

Lily hoped she didn't look too frustrated as she handed them over. "And was this yours, Miss Oswald?" she asked, holding up the last parcel.

"One of mine," Serena said. "Jeremy, hand it up. Lily, are you coming?"

"I did promise Miss Oswald a visit to Gunter's. If you would still like to go?"

The girl took the hint immediately. "I would. Can we walk from here?"

As Miss Harper and her maid were handed into the carriage, and while Serena arranged for Miss Oswald's packages to be taken up so she could drop them off at Audley Street, the girl whispered, "Well?"

Lily motioned her to be quiet. They were still too public, so she kept her thoughts to herself and, ignoring Miss Oswald's impatient looks, talked inconsequentially of Hertfordshire and then about Nevis as they strolled through Berkeley Square. At last they were settled at a small, relatively private table in Gunter's Tea Shop, sipping wine and eating lemon ices.

"Do you have it?" Miss Oswald demanded.

Eyeing the other patrons around them, Lily shook her head. "I could not search the bag thoroughly, but it was not on top."

"I suppose it was jostled to the bottom in all the scuffle." Miss Oswald's pretty face was a picture of contrition. "I'm sorry; I could not think of a better way to make her drop her things."

Lily grimaced into her wineglass. "It is frustrating, but even without the note, we know more than we did before." She hesitated, then explained what she had discovered in Lord Walter's study, and how that fit in with Serena's story about Bernard's debt.

"So it seems as if Lord Walter does not have much reason to be working with Mr. Lacey, while the general has a great deal," said Miss Oswald, tapping her lips thoughtfully with one finger as she gazed past Lily. "And now we know the general has been to Nevis, and met my father, which means he would have had every opportunity to meet Augustus. He was much in my father's company a few years back," she explained, seeing Lily's inquiring look. "He assisted often with Papa's business before I was old enough to become involved."

"Was your Mr. Finch—"

"He was not mine," Miss Oswald interrupted quickly, looking distressed.

Lily pursed her lips thoughtfully at the retort but didn't press the matter. "Your friend, was all I meant. Was Mr. Finch the sort of man who would have been able to gain the general's confidence on such a short acquaintance? He would have been quite young at the time."

"He would have been the age I am now," Miss Oswald said, not meeting Lily's eyes as she circled one finger around the rim of her wineglass. There was a frown between her eyes. "Augustus was . . . he was the sort of person who could make friends with anyone, who could make you trust him. And I think he was always . . . a bit of a rascal. I think that was one reason Papa liked him so much. And why I did too, when I was younger." She cleared her throat abruptly. "In any case, he was amiable and a little unscrupulous. I could certainly see him teasing out the details of the scheme, even if the general wasn't aware that he had revealed anything."

"I see." Lily nodded thoughtfully. "We also now know there is some connection between the general and Mr. Lacey, and it is something underhanded, or they would not need to use his niece as an unwitting courier."

"At this point, it seems almost certain that they were the ones responsible for . . ." Miss Oswald swallowed, then continued firmly. "For Augustus. I've not met the general except in passing, but I think we may safely say there is something dangerous about Mr. Lacey."

"You had that impression as well?"

"It was impossible to miss. Miss Harper looked positively ill when you asked about him. If she is so uneasy about him . . ."

She fell silent as two other ladies walked past their table, chatting about a charitable society. Lily didn't mind the pause; remembering the cold gleam in Mr. Lacey's eye sent a shiver down her back. In spite of that, though, the tension between her shoulder blades was slowly relaxing. If General Harper was the murderer, then Serena's family was safe from suspicion.

There were other questions, though, that Miss Oswald's words about Mr. Finch had brought back to the front of Lily's mind. "You seem to make quite the study of others' characters," she said lightly.

"As you said once, Mrs. Adler, I am not quite the unassuming debutante that I seem." The young heiress raised her brows. "I imagine the same could have been said about you, once upon a time."

"I doubt anyone who knew me would have called me unassuming at any point in my life," Lily said with a small smile. "I was not so adept at playing the game as you are."

"It is a useful and dubious skill," Miss Oswald, her expression serious. As the charitable ladies made their departure at last, she leaned forward. "Mrs. Adler, whatever happens next, I want to thank you. For what you are trying to do for Augustus. And for . . . for me." The girl took a deep breath. "You talk about my home. You introduce me to your friends. You believe I have something of value to contribute to your investigation. And through it all, you never ask me to pretend to be anyone other than who I am."

"London society has never been known for letting women be their true selves," Lily said.

Miss Oswald's gaze grew distant. "No, being myself is not considered an asset in the hunt for a husband. As my Aunt Haverweight reminds me daily."

"But you are too wise to settle for anyone who does not know you and respect the person you are." Lily meant the statement kindly, and she was surprised when Miss Oswald looked up sharply, her expression suddenly wary. "Have I offended you?"

"No." The girl looked flustered. "No, of course not. I only hope you are right." She cleared her throat a little nervously. "Since you were not able to find Mr. Lacey's note, what do you suggest our next step be?"

Lily narrowed her eyes at the abrupt change in subject. Clearly, something she said had made Miss Oswald uncomfortable. But the girl was watching her, her expression open and earnest once more, so Lily did not press the matter. "We need to discover exactly what the general's connection is to the firm. You know more of business than I do; would they keep some kind of record?"

Miss Oswald stirred the melting remains of her ice, frowning. "Even if they communicated secretly, there would have to be something, especially if they were working with the War Office. After all, Captain Hartley was able to discover that the general was associated with them in the first place."

Lily nodded. "Then I think . . . I think we must find a way to pay a visit to Mr. Lacey's offices and see what we can discover there."

Miss Oswald's eyes were wide. "How do you plan to do that?"

Lily sighed, propping her chin in one hand. "I haven't the faintest idea. But give me time, and I will think of something. I always do."

CHAPTER 17

Lily stayed in bed late the next morning. She had kept to country hours since returning to London, rising well before noon. But a ladies' card party, followed by a very late supper, had kept Lily from seeing her bed until three o'clock in the morning. When, around seven, she was briefly roused by the sound of Anna laying the fire, she rolled over and pulled a pillow over her head, all thoughts of murder and intrigue banished by the allure of a few more hours' sleep.

At half past ten she woke again and, ringing for her maid, asked for breakfast on a tray. "And plenty of tea," she added, one arm over her eyes.

"Is your head all right, ma'am?" Anna rearranged the pillows so her mistress could sit more comfortably.

Lily sighed, though the sound came out more like a growl. "Mrs. Windermere delights in being just to the right side of fast and doing whatever shocking thing comes into her head. She brought out her husband's whiskey last night, and nothing would do for Serena but that we must share in every toast." Lily rubbed her head. "I admit it was fun at the time, but I am not convinced it was worth it. There was no gainsaying Serena, though."

"Her ladyship does have a most forceful personality," Anna agreed, twitching the curtains so the sun was not shining so directly into the room.

"Thank you, and yes, she does. Especially when it comes to Sally Windermere. Serena suspects she was one of Lord Walter's paramours, you know, before they were married. And she refuses to let the woman best her at anything." Lily moaned softly. "Or to best me, it would seem."

The corners of Anna's lips quivered, but she offered no comment on her employer's state other than to say, "I believe Mrs. Carstairs has a sort of concoction that is supposed to help these situations. My cousin Jeremy swears by it. Shall I ask her to make it up for you?"

"Will it taste foul?" Lily asked plaintively. Catching sight of Anna's smile, she sighed. "Never mind, of course it will taste foul. I shall try it anyway. Anything must be an improvement. I cannot imagine what gentlemen see to recommend this feeling!"

"You did say you had fun last night, ma'am. I think that's most of the draw."

"Not worth it," Lily said firmly. "Though the charades were the most amusing thing I have ever heard."

"Did they happen after the whiskey had been brought out?"

"Long after. So perhaps I do see the appeal after all." Lily frowned in mock-severity as Anna giggled. "None of your cheek now, Anna, but go and fetch my breakfast and whatever miracle brew Mrs. Carstairs can manage on such short notice. And have Carstairs send up the papers as well."

"*La Belle Assemblée* or the *Ladies' Journal*?"

"*La Belle Assemblée* and also the *Times*."

"The *Times*?" Anna looked surprised.

Lily understood. She had once stayed abreast of political issues to help further Freddy's career, but since his death she had not shown much interest in the events of the day. Anna was obviously hoping for some sort of explanation, but Lily only said firmly, "The *Times* as well, as soon as Carstairs has pressed the sheets."

"Of course, ma'am." Anna curtsied. "Just you close your eyes and rest that poor head, and I won't be a moment."

"Thank you, Anna." Lily took her maid's advice, but her mind was already beginning to work. Resting abed was all very well—especially after an encounter with Sally Windermere's whiskey—but she had a mystery to solve and a treacherous general to expose.

An hour later, what was left of eggs and tea forgotten on her breakfast tray, Lily was at her writing desk penning two short notes, feeling rather like a general herself. As soon as they were done, she rang for Anna.

"See that these are delivered to Miss Oswald and Captain Hartley immediately." Lily rose. "Whatever Mrs. Carstairs put in that terrible brew, it has done the trick. I shall give her an extra half day this quarter for her genius."

"You are looking very much better, ma'am," Anna commented as she took the letters. "And also very determined.'

"I am," Lily said, stretching her arms over her head. "I think I shall have quite a satisfactory day."

★ ★ ★

Her plans had to change only slightly. Miss Oswald returned a letter saying her aunt would not countenance her going out that afternoon, as it was possible Lady Worth, who possessed an unmarried son and mortgaged family property, might be calling that afternoon. Would Mrs. Adler and Captain Hartley call on her in Audley Street instead? She would be happy to try to sneak out otherwise—Lily frowned over that part of the letter, thinking of what Jack had told her at the Chichesters' ball— but it would be easier not to.

And so a little before three o'clock Lily arrived at Mrs. Haverweight's home on Audley Street with several pages of the *Times* tucked under her arm.

Miss Oswald was anxiously pacing the front hall when she arrived, and as soon as the footman opened the door, she pounced. Ignoring the frown directed her way by the butler whose job she had just usurped, Miss Oswald dragged Lily into the front parlor and shut the door.

"Where have you been?" she demanded.

Surprised enough to be amused rather than annoyed, Lily took her time removing her pelisse and hat. "One would think, Miss Oswald, that you were awaiting an actual beau from such behavior. You are not harboring a secret longing to become Mrs. Captain Hartley, are you?"

"Oh, how absurd!" For a moment Miss Oswald looked genuinely angry. "How you stay so calm when we are seeking a murderer is beyond me. If it had been your—" She broke off, taking a quick breath, before saying more quietly, "I wish I had your nerves, Mrs. Adler."

"Not showing is not the same as not feeling," Lily said calmly, though she watched the girl closely out of the corner of her eye as she took a seat. "What excuse did you give to your aunt?"

"I told her the truth."

"What?" Lily stared.

Miss Oswald could not seem to hide her pleased smile. "I wish you could see your own face, Mrs. Adler. It would serve you right, you know."

"You did not tell her the truth," Lily insisted.

"Well, no, not all of it. I told her I was worried about Mrs. Worth's call and suggested asking for your company." Miss Oswald shrugged. "Which is entirely true. If Mrs. Worth does call, I'll be quite glad for your company, nasty old bat that she is. Not that my aunt cares, beyond wishing to avoid any real responsibility. She will undoubtedly stay away as long as possible, so as long as no servants eavesdrop, we shall be quite private."

"Unless Lady Worth does call. Do you think her son means to court you? He doesn't seem a pleasant fellow."

"Oh, if he does, it will not matter for long." Miss Oswald started as soon as the words were out of her mouth. "I mean to say, I don't intend to encourage him. So it makes no difference to me if he does."

She spoke too quickly, and her eyes shifted away as she said it. Lily frowned, but there was not time to ask what the girl had really meant.

The butler, haughty with the dignity of his position and determined to show how things were correctly done, appeared at that moment, asking if Miss Oswald was at home to a Captain Hartley.

"Yes, show him in, and let me know immediately if any other visitors call."

Jack began with the typical pleasantries, but as soon as the door had closed, Lily interrupted, "Do you really want to ask about the weather, Captain?"

"Not in the slightest," Jack said. "The weather in London never changes; I cannot think how we all manage to say so much about it."

Lily resisted the urge to roll her eyes at him. "We had an interesting encounter yesterday . . . a chilling one, in fact, but it set us on a new track." She told him, as concisely as she could, about meeting Mr. Lacey the day before, while Miss Oswald perched on the edge of her seat, looking impatient.

Jack nodded. "So we know the general was in the West Indies. And in spite of what his niece believes, it seems safe to conclude that he and Lacey are in some kind of havey-cavey business together, which makes it likely that Harper is our man. That puts Lord Walter in the clear. You must be pleased, Mrs. Adler."

"I am relieved," Lily admitted. "But that's not the most interesting thing. Do you remember Mr. Finch's letter said something about *a certain clever form of communication*?"

Jack shrugged. "No, but I shall take your word for it that it did." Miss Oswald let out a soft "*Oh!*" of surprise, as if the matter had just come clear to her as well.

Lily paused long enough to give them a quick scowl. "How could you forget something as important as that?"

"Because we haven't your flawless memory, ma'am," Jack said, apparently impervious to embarrassment. "Which is why you are the captain in this matter, and we the lowly midshipmen."

"Well," Lily continued, not sure whether to be flattered or annoyed by his teasing. "I think we know what that clever form is." Leaning forward in her chair, she propped her elbows on the arms and steepled her fingers together. Her gaze was sharp as she spoke, as though she was seeing the encounter with Mr. Lacey playing out again in her mind. "Towards the end of the conversation, Mr. Lacey very discreetly slipped a folded note into Miss Harper's reticule. She was distracted at the time and had no idea."

"We tried to intercept it," Miss Oswald put in, grimacing. "But unfortunately there was not much opportunity. I am sorry," she added unhappily, turning to Mrs. Adler. "I should have thought of a better diversion."

"You did what you could; it was not an ideal situation." Lily spoke calmly, but two of her interlaced fingers tapped slowly against her lips as she thought. "If the general knew to expect a message, it would be easy for him to retrieve. Which means that Mr. Lacey must have bumped into Miss Harper on purpose. For all we know, he had been following her in an effort to find just such an opportunity."

Jack cursed softly. "The bounder. Using a lady for something so dastardly—!" He sighed. "Well, it makes sense. Too many letters sent between them would arouse suspicion. A chance meeting—bumping into the man's niece on Bond Street—would raise no eyebrows."

"Indeed. Now that we know Lacey is communicating clandestinely with the general—and how Mr. Finch could have been connected to them—we must move decisively." Lily stood and began to pace restlessly about the room. "The obvious next step is to look for something in the records at Lacey and West that will point to the general."

Jack had half risen, then settled back in his chair with a huff. He had given up standing every time she did, for which Lily was grateful. Pacing, she had discovered, was sometimes a crucial part of investigating, and it would have been distracting if he tried to be polite by pacing with her. "And how do you propose to see their records?" he asked.

"I would imagine they keep them in the office."

"Yes, but Mr. Lacey is not going to simply hand over the company books for anyone's inspection," Miss Oswald pointed out. "No businessman would under the best of circumstances. He certainly will not if there is anything nefarious going on. Particularly not when he knows he has a powerful patron working on his behalf."

"Which is why we shall have to be careful." Lily stopped pacing and smiled slyly. "Luckily, I know how to go about it."

Jack groaned and leaned his head back against the chair, covering his eyes with one hand. "Naturally, you have a plan. I can only hope it does not involve a midnight robbery or another equally illegal escapade."

"Nothing so dramatic as a robbery." Lily pursed her lips, then added, "Though it might be equally illegal. One of us shall have to gain access to the office and look through the books."

"And by one of us, I assume you refer to yourself?" Jack's voice was grim.

"Of course not." Lily sat down at last. "The best person to gain access is you."

"Me?" He sat up abruptly. "I've no more connection to the shipping business than you."

"But you do have the uniform of a navy captain." Still smiling, Lily laid out the newspaper she had brought, opened to the advertisements.

The firm of LACEY & WEST seeks a reputable SHIP'S CAPTAIN, preferably of NAVY or MERCHANT MARINE background. Please apply in person at no. 11 HENRIETTA STREET, LONDON, before the 24th of APRIL.

"You cannot use your own name, of course," she continued. "But it would be easy to give the name of another captain who perhaps made fewer captures during the war and is not so well lined in the pockets. One who, now he has been decommissioned, might look for work with a shipping agent. All you need is a few minutes alone to look around."

Jack and Miss Oswald both stared at her for several moments, as if they were turning over her plan and inspecting all the possible difficulties. At last he let out a small laugh, shaking his head. "It's brilliant."

"Thank you." Lily's lips kicked up at the corners. "I thought it was rather good myself."

"How will you ensure Mr. Lacey leaves the office long enough for Captain Hartley to inspect the books?" Miss Oswald asked, thinking practically.

"That is where you come in." Lily wished there were more than two people to appreciate her plan. "You are rather recognizable in London these days"— Miss Oswald snorted but did not disagree— "but that is to our advantage, because your father's business is equally well known. If you visit the office a few minutes after Captain Hartley, and ask to speak to Mr. Lacey, and indicate that your father is interested in working with a new shipping agent . . ."

"I imagine he would be willing to speak with me for as long as I wished," Miss Oswald agreed. "The family is terribly well connected; even two wars haven't been able to disrupt Papa's business. Any shipping agent in London would be happy to partner on a commission with him. But I could never keep him busy long enough for Captain Hartley to copy down every page of the accounts, and he cannot *take* their books. Someone would notice immediately."

"He shan't need to copy or take them," Lily said. "The captain has a contact at the firm, do you not? If we need records, we can arrange something through him. But I do not think we will need to *take* anything, really. This is more of . . ." She glanced at Jack. "What do you call it in the military? When you gather information?"

"Reconnaissance?"

"Exactly." Lily settled back into her chair, satisfied. "Reconnaissance. I am only sorry I cannot be there, too. But I think I put Mr. Lacey too much on his guard." She pursed her lips, considering. "I suppose there is some chance he will be wary of you, Miss Oswald, since you were with me. We shall have to hope that the lure of profit will be enough to tempt him."

"Enough to make him speak with me, at least." Miss Oswald looked at her gratefully. "How clever of you to spot that advertisement and think of how we might use it."

"I shall end up quite vain, between the two of you," Lily said, not wanting them to see how much the praise warmed her. "The only thing we need to make it convincing is a letter from your father to Mr. Lacey. Captain Hartley will need to write that so it is in a man's hand, though you will need to tell him what it ought to say."

"No need," Miss Oswald said, looking a little smug. "I can imitate my father's writing. Then if he and Mr. Lacey have crossed paths before, we needn't worry about him comparing the letters." Seeing the others staring at her, Lily with astonishment, Jack with disapproval, she added, "My father suffers at times from a palsy in his hands, and I learned to make a fair copy of his writing so that I could help with his correspondence. He was concerned that his business partners would object to instructions in a woman's hand." Her lips twitched into a smile at their shocked expressions. "Imitating handwriting is no more difficult than drawing a picture."

"I shall take your word for it," Lily murmured. "I was never accomplished at drawing."

"Well, I am quite good at it," Miss Oswald said, seeming resolute as she stood. "If you will excuse me for a moment, I shall compose the missive immediately."

As the girl disappeared into the next room, Lily turned to Jack. "Well, Captain, you should be pleased that I am keeping myself out of danger this time."

"I am pleased." His tone was far more serious than hers. "But I still think that girl is hiding something, and I mean to find out what it is."

"Most girls her age are." Lily refused to rise to his bait. "It is the first time in life that one really has secrets to keep. But very few of them have anything to do with murder."

"And if her secrets do?"

Lily lifted her chin. "Then we shall find that out as well."

Jack sighed but nodded, understanding that she did not wish to discuss the matter of Miss Oswald further. Instead, he slanted a glance at her and said, "You've made me curious to know what secrets you kept when you were Miss Oswald's age."

She could not help a small smile as she answered, "Perhaps, one day, I shall tell you."

Jack laughed and let the matter of Miss Oswald drop—just in time, as the young heiress returned, triumphantly bearing her forged letter. Lily knew, though, that Jack meant what he said. He didn't intend to let the matter go completely. She didn't really mind. She was fairly certain she knew one of Miss Oswald's secrets about Mr. Finch, and she intended to keep it from Jack. But there was something else going on with the girl, and Lily wanted to know what it was.

★ ★ ★

Jack took his leave before Lily did—she had noticed Miss Oswald's look of distraction as they were putting the finishing touches on their plans and lingered deliberately. "What is it?" she asked quietly as the door closed behind the navy captain.

Miss Oswald started, dropping the ends of the shawl she had been fussing with. "Nothing." At Lily's skeptical look, she sighed. "Uncertainty. Or regret. Or perhaps guilt. I am not sure what to call it, but it is not a pleasant sensation."

"You do not have to go tomorrow if it distresses you. I am sure Captain Hartley and I could—"

"Oh no!" Miss Oswald broke in. "That was not it at all. I assure you, my courage is more than up to the task. It was . . . Mrs. Adler, do you ever wish you had a mother?"

Lily's throat tightened at the unexpected question, her sadness for the mother she had never known tangling up with her grief for the husband she had lost. "I have spent nearly my whole life wishing that," she said quietly. "When I was small, I always thought if my mother had lived, perhaps my father would have loved me. And then everything would have been better."

"Sometimes I think if my mother had lived, I would have been a wiser person," Miss Oswald said, wandering to the window and staring out blindly, shivering as she pulled her shawl more tightly around her shoulders. "I make decisions so quickly, you know. In the moment, they seem like the only choice I could possibly make. And so often, once they are made, they cannot be undone." She looked back over her shoulder briefly, her smile sad. "Sometimes I talk to my mother, to ask her what I should do, or what I should have done. And I imagine what she would say in response. In some ways it is a comfort. But I know her life was so different from mine—differences I could never understand—so in other ways . . ."

"In other ways, it makes things worse," Lily said quietly. "Because it reminds you that you will never truly know what she would have said."

"Yes."

"Who has you feeling so guilty about your impulsive choices, Miss Oswald?"

The girl's shoulders tensed visibly. "Augustus. I regret his death so . . ." She let out a shuddering breath. "So very much. And I feel guilty, because if I were a better person, I would regret not loving him the way he loved me. But I did not love him, and I still cannot make myself regret it." She took another deep breath, then turned back to Lily. "Tomorrow, at least, I will do my part to prove the general and Mr. Lacey guilty of his murder." Her hands twisted in her shawl once more before she deliberately smoothed the fabric back out. "And perhaps then, I will be able to sleep easy once more."

Lily hesitated, then laid a gentle hand on the girl's arm. "Your mother would have loved you. She loved you for the brief time she knew you, and she would have continued loving you if she had lived. No matter what choices you made that you regret."

Miss Oswald smiled, placing her hand over Lily's. "Yours as well, Mrs. Adler. Your mother would have loved you too."

CHAPTER 18

Even though he had meant it when he called Lily's plan brilliant, Jack was still amazed by how smoothly things began.

He wore his uniform and affected a slight limp, introducing himself as Charles Henderson, formerly of the *Laconia*—a real person and a real ship, in case Mr. Lacey checked the navy lists—a decommissioned navy man looking for work after an injury took him from His Majesty's service. He had to wait a few minutes for Mr. Lacey to be free, which was just enough time for Jem to return from an errand and find a familiar face waiting in his employer's front office. The boy's jaw dropped, but only for a moment. An instant later he was all business and cheek, dropping a stack of letters on the porter's desk and asking loudly who "the toff in the fancy jacket" was.

The porter attempted a smack, which Jem dodged easily, and then Mr. Lacey was leading Jack upstairs to his private office. As he passed by, the boy dropped one lid in the barest wink, and Jack struggled not to laugh. As the office door closed behind him, though, he sobered. He had a task to complete, and there was a good chance the man in front of him was dangerous.

"We have generally handled only the business side of things—arrangements, as it were," Mr. Lacey explained. "But we've recently purchased two ships. Crews must be assembled anew for each voyage, but my partners and I wish to have captains that work for us exclusively."

"I should be happy to provide references, if you wish." Jack took the seat that Mr. Lacey indicated, setting down his hat and gloves.

"All in good time," the shipping agent replied, settling comfortably behind his desk. "Tell me about your work during the war. Did you see much action?"

"Not as much as I would have liked, or I'd not need to look for work." Jack laughed ruefully, and Mr. Lacey chuckled along with him. Many navy captains had made their fortunes capturing enemy ships; any officer who had not would be a little bitter. "But I saw my share. I mostly patrolled around Dover and across the channel to Normandy. Spent a bit of time sailing to the West Indies too."

"Excellent, excellent." Mr. Lacey made a few notes in his book, and Jack took the opportunity to look around. The shipping agent was clearly a meticulous man. The wall behind his desk was lined with files and ledgers, all carefully arranged. "Those are routes we—" He broke off at the sound of raised voices. "Excuse the noise; I'm not sure what . . ."

He was interrupted by a quick knock, and Jem poked his head in. "Beg pardon, Mr. Lacey, but there's a lady 'ere to see you."

Jack hid a smile. Act two in their drama was beginning.

Mr. Lacey frowned. "A lady?"

"Yessir. Says she's 'ere on behalf of 'er father's business."

Mr. Lacey's frown deepened. "Did the lady give her name?"

"Oswald, she says, from th' West Indies. Mr. Lacey, she . . . she's a black-skinned lady. A real lady!" Jem's voice echoed his wide-eyed delight.

"Good Lord." Mr. Lacey stood abruptly. "If Oswald has a commission he wants to partner on . . ." He remembered Jack suddenly and turned with an apologetic smile. "Captain Henderson, excuse me, I must see to this matter immediately."

"Of course," Jack replied pleasantly. "Wouldn't do to keep a lady waiting."

Jem lingered after Lacey had left, grinning when Jack held out a twopence. "And a second one if you tell me when he is about to come back."

"Wotcher up to, Captain? You gonna rob 'im?" the boy asked.

"Of course not!" Jack said, outraged, before he realized the boy's assumption was entirely justified.

Jem shrugged as he took the coin. "Wouldn't tell if y'did. But I'll letcha know when 'e comes back. Good hunting, sir."

Jack didn't waste any time; as soon as he was alone, he began to search.

His guess had been right; the office was carefully organized, and it wasn't difficult to find the records he needed. Mr. Lacey had several ledgers full of his government contracts, and it took Jack only a few more minutes of searching to find shipping logs for the same periods of time. Unfortunately, they all matched up—except for a few that were missing entirely.

"Damn," he muttered, turning back to the desk. Of course Lacey wouldn't keep incriminating records out in the open. But the actual manifests had to be somewhere—hidden, most likely. Where—

A quiet knock at the door nearly made him jump out of his skin, but it was immediately followed by a soft voice whispering, "Me, sir." Jem poked his head around the door.

Jack nodded at him but continued leafing through the books. "How long do I have?"

"The lady says to take you out the back way, sir. Now."

That made him look up. "What?"

The boy looked nervous, but he said firmly, "The lady says I must sneak you out the back so he don't see you."

"He has already seen me." Jack flipped through a few final pages. "Hiding now will not do much good."

"Not Lacey. The general. The lady said he mustn't see you."

Jack froze. "General?" he asked. "Big man, scowling sort of face, gray whiskers?"

"Yessir. We must hurry."

Jack cursed and began shoving the books back onto the shelves, hoping the order was correct. They had been so carefully organized . . .

There was a sound of footsteps coming up the stairs, and he cursed again. "Does that look about right?" He grimaced as he pushed a stack of ledgers back into place. "Never mind. Where do we go?"

Jem let out a small moan. "Too late. He'd see if you went out now." Eyes darting around the room, the boy gave Jack a little shove. "Into the closet, sir. He'll leave if you ain't 'ere, then I'll sneak you out the back. Go!" he hissed when Jack hesitated.

He would be trapped in the room with a man who might be a murderer, Jack realized. But there was nothing else for it. As Jem slipped out of the room, Jack squeezed into the narrow closet between precariously stacked boxes and papers. He pulled the door shut, then, thinking better of it, eased it open an inch so he could peer into the room.

"What the devil d'ye mean, gone?"

The general's voice filled the room as he opened the door, and Jack heard Jem explain that he had come to see if the navy man wanted a drink while he waited, only to discover that he had already left.

"Blasted nuisance, navy men. Waste of everyone's time. Very well, boy, very well. Go tell Lacey I shall wait here, and bring me a brandy."

"Yessir."

One eye pressed against the narrow gap, Jack watched as the general waited for the door to close. As soon as it had, he strode across the room, surprisingly quick for a man of his size. Jack winced. If it came to it, he was uncomfortably sure the older man could best him in a fight. He couldn't risk being discovered.

Distracted by his thoughts, it took Jack a moment to realize what the general was doing.

Harper had carried a gray ledger with him when he came in. Now he laid the book on the desk and quickly pulled down the same records Jack had so recently searched. He flipped through the books, a scowl of concentration on his face, and periodically stopped to compare them to various pages in his ledger. Twice he let out a short bark of triumphant laughter. "Got it, you old devil," he muttered once, grinning unpleasantly. Both times, he pulled a sheet from Lacey's log book and tucked it into his own ledger. "Shan't get the best of Alfred Harper." The general chuckled as he returned the log books and files to their shelves.

Trying to see which books the general had gone through—he thought it was the shipping manifests, but he could not quite make them out—Jack pressed forward against the gap in the door. The movement sent several precariously balanced papers sliding toward the floor with a soft *shush* that could be heard distinctly in the quiet room. He froze.

The general looked up. "Lacey? That you?" Closing the ledger with a sharp snap, he called out again, "Someone there?"

Jack held as still as possible. If he was discovered, there was no possible way to explain his presence. The general moved toward the closed door; then something made him pause. Jack craned his neck, trying to see what had caught the other man's eye, and his heart sank.

He had left his hat and gloves on the chair.

General Harper frowned at the out-of-place articles; then his head snapped up, a scowl on his face as he scanned the room once more. His eyes landed on the closet, and he took a step toward it. Jack tensed, ready to defend himself.

A loud knock on the door made them both jump. Luckily, any noise Jack made was covered by Jem's loud, cheerful voice saying, "Brought yer drink, sir. And Mr. Lacey says as it's convenient for him t' see you now."

"Convenient?" The general snatched the glass of brandy and threw it back in one angry motion. "Convenient, he says. As if I wait on his convenience! Out of my way, boy." Still grumbling, General Harper pushed past Jem and stormed out, the gray ledger under his arm.

Jack held still in his hiding place for several seconds that felt more like hours before Jem said, "You can come out now, sir; he's gone back down."

Jack came out of the closet and grinned cheerfully as he gathered up his hat and gloves, though inside he was still shaken. "Bit of a near thing there, eh?"

Jem grinned back, then craned his neck around to look out the door. "All bob now, sir. Time to scarper out the back."

At another time, Jack might have protested that he never *scarpered*. Given the circumstances, though, it seemed prudent to hold his objections and do as Jem said. With another quick check to make sure the hall was clear, the boy led the way down a back staircase to the basement of the building. This was dusty, dark, and clearly barely used. The ceiling hung low, making it impossible to stand fully upright, but Jem navigated his way through the piles of boxes at a crouch. Holding his breath against the dust and trying not to cough, Jack followed him to the back of the building, where Jem motioned him to help haul open the creaking cellar door. "This'll take you out behind Covent Garden. Go right and ye'll come to Bedford Street." At Jack's nod, Jem grinned and held out his hand. "I'll take yer tuppence now, sir."

Jack gave him threepence. It was only fair, after all. "If you ever need anything . . ."

"Shall let y'know, sir."

"And Jem?" The boy paused. "Make sure to dust yourself off before you show your face in the office again."

The office boy grinned. "And you, sir. Yer fancy coat looks a treat, it do," he added before disappearing back up the stairs.

Shaking his head, Jack took the boy's advice and patted the dust from his coat as soon as he was in the alleyway. Wishing he had a mirror, he resettled his hair and hat as best he could, then hailed the first chair he saw on Bedford Street. He needed to go home and change his coat. And then he needed a drink.

★　★　★

"You look as if you are about to explode," Jack whispered to Lily as he slid into the seat behind her.

Margaret Harlowe had sent a note around that afternoon—her husband had rented a box at the theater for the evening, and would Lily and her charming protégée join their party? Her cousins, a

Mr. and Miss Robertson, would be attending as well. If Lily said yes, Margaret added in the postscript, she would invite that dashing Captain Hartley along too.

Miss Oswald had received her aunt's grudging permission to attend, but unfortunately Mrs. Haverweight would not release her niece before the evening, and Jack was nowhere to be found all afternoon. By the time she arrived at the Harlowes' that night, Lily was convinced something had gone horribly wrong, until Margaret told her Jack had accepted the invitation for the theater but would not join them for dinner.

Miss Oswald had whispered to her just before they went in for dinner—the only opportunity they had for a private moment—that she thought everything had gone well. "The general!" she had managed to add, eyes wide, before they were interrupted. By the time dinner had ended, and the entire party set off in a fleet of carriages for Drury Lane Theatre, Lily was quivering with nerves, her cool facade as close as it ever came to crumbling.

The foyer was packed. Young dandies dressed in more color and pattern than tropical birds lined the walls, commenting on the ladies who passed and ogling them through quizzing glasses worn expressly for that purpose. Debutantes, gowned in demure, pale colors, fluttered with excitement as their chaperones steered them in the paths of any eligible gentlemen. One woman, overcome by the heat, swooned against her escort, a man Lily suspected was not her husband. Orange sellers called out their wares, and courtesans gowned with more extravagance than most ladies swept up the stairs on the arms of their chosen gentlemen.

As they made their way through the crowd, Miss Oswald's eyes were wide. Though she had more presence and poise than many young ladies making their London debuts, she was only nineteen years old and had grown up far from the noise and press of humanity that made up London. Lily couldn't blame her for staring; she only hoped her own expression was less overwhelmed. It had been a long time since she had attended the theater, too.

Eventually, after pausing to speak to other patrons and make introductions, Andrew Harlowe led them upstairs to their box. It was not the best seat in the house, but it commanded a good view of the stage and, more importantly, of the other boxes. Miss Robertson and her brother immediately set to gossiping, Mr. Robertson lifting up his quizzing glass to return the stares of those watching them while Miss Robertson commented that the gentlemen should have a hard time seeing the performance over the ladies' plumed turbans.

Their party numbered seven—it would be eight once Jack arrived—and the gentlemen helped the ladies to seat themselves where they would have the best view of the stage. Lily sat at the end of the row, with Miss Oswald next to her. The remaining gentleman, a Major Hastings, claimed the seat beside Miss Oswald, but the seat behind them was free.

When Jack finally arrived in the box—apologizing so charmingly for missing Mrs. Harlowe's dinner that Margaret blushed like a schoolgirl—it was all Lily could do to keep from jumping out of her seat. She contented herself with giving an extremely pointed look to the seat behind her own. He took both the hint and the seat, grinning broadly as he leaned forward to whisper his comment on her impatience.

Lily merely snapped open her fan to shield their conversation and demanded, "What happened?"

"Shame they always put the farce at the end of the program," Major Hastings said loudly to Miss Oswald. "Never much for the stuffy drama, myself, but I s'pose that is how they get you to stay through the whole thing."

"You are not a fan of Mr. Kean's work?" the girl asked, giving Lily and Jack a longing glance out of the corner of her eyes before returning her attention to the major. "I heard that he is mesmerizing."

"Oh, Kean's decent enough . . ."

Jack glanced at Miss Oswald to make sure the major was distracted before responding. "It was touch and go for a bit," he said in an undertone. "Did she tell you anything?"

"No." The quick movement of Lily's fan was the only outward hint of her impatience. "There was no chance, and why you could not send a note, as any decent person would—"

"Too busy drinking." Jack shrugged with the sort of careless good humor that made Lily realize *drinking* might be an understatement.

"Are you *foxed*?" she demanded.

He grinned. "Trifle bosky. Try not to scowl at me; I needed it after that run-in."

"What happened?"

The orchestra chose that moment to flourish to a stop, and under cover of the applause, Jack leaned forward to whisper in her ear, "I think we have him." The play began, and after that there was too much noise to continue. Lily sat still, to all appearances focused on *Othello*, while inside she quivered with eagerness. She thought about insisting that her two fellow investigators accompany her on a walk, but there would be too many people strolling in the hall to speak privately. So she was forced to wait until at last the curtain went down for the interval and Mrs. Harlowe rose to lead her guests out of the box.

Quick-thinking Miss Oswald—whether from her own desperation to find out what Jack had discovered or from a desire to escape Major Hastings—claimed a small headache as an excuse to sit out the promenade, and Lily immediately added that she would stay with her.

"But you and the others go on, Margaret," she insisted. "I am sure Captain Hartley can keep us company."

Major Hastings jumped in. "I should be pleased to do so as well."

Lily's jaw clenched at his polite, poorly timed offer, and at the belligerent look he cast toward Jack, who was lounging against the side of the box. "How kind, sir." Her voice betrayed none of her impatience. "And perhaps you would fetch us something to drink? I am sure Miss Oswald must be feeling the heat."

He gallantly agreed, sweeping a low and rather inelegant bow, before following the rest of the party out into the hall. Lily kept her polite face in place as the box's curtain fell behind the last of them, then turned to her companions. "Quickly now," she said, not letting her expression change in case the occupants of any other boxes were watching. "We have about five minutes before he returns."

Jack gestured unsteadily to Miss Oswald, who had pulled out her own fan and was deploying it vigorously to shield herself from prying eyes. "Ladies first."

She narrowed her eyes at him. "I am sure your part of the story is far more exciting, sir. Though I was delighted to meet your man on the inside." She turned to Lily. "Who is, in fact, a boy not much older than fourteen, and I cannot imagine what Captain Hartley was thinking to include a *child* in all this business."

"Captain Hartley was thinking that he joined the navy when he was fourteen and found it an excellent age to begin putting oneself in danger," Lily said dryly, bending her head in a pretense of reading the evening's program. "We can discuss whether or not that was sensible of him when we have more time. What did you mean by 'the general'?"

Miss Oswald's eyes grew wide. "The general himself arrived, Mrs. Adler, not more than five minutes after I walked in! And Mr. Lacey seemed terribly put out by his presence. He said that the general was only there because he had recently invested in the business, and tried to convince him to leave, but then the general insisted that he needed to meet the captain as well. I tried to distract them some, but . . ."

Lily felt herself grow pale. "Did they see you, Captain? Did the general recognize you? If I had any idea, I'd not have—"

"Calm down," he murmured. "Jem hid me in time."

Lily glanced at Miss Oswald. "Jem is the boy?"

"I assume so. I told him to sneak the captain out the back."

"Good lad, that one. Raised in the Dials." Jack nodded approvingly, wobbling a little before regaining his balance. "Quick head on his shoulders. Not enough time to sneak me out the back, but he hid me in the closet. And that, ladies, is how we got him."

"For God's sake, stop dancing around it and tell me what happened!" This time Lily did not bother to hide her glare behind her program, not caring what the residents of other boxes might think of their conversation.

Jack grinned. "They have more money than they should, to begin."

"How do you know?" Lily demanded.

"Lacey said the firm just bought two ships. Not common for a shipping agent, that."

"No," Miss Oswald put in confidently. "Ships are monstrously expensive, especially for such a small firm. They'd not have enough capital for ships in the normal line of things, unless the contracts from the War Office were shockingly grand."

Jack shook his head. "I saw the orders; they were large but not *that* large. But beyond that . . ." Jack leaned forward. "The general has a ledger of papers that is particularly intriguing." Quietly, he described what he had seen in Mr. Lacey's office, explaining about the missing shipping logs that corresponded with the government contracts. "I am sure he was taking them without Lacey's knowledge. He'd not sneak around like that, otherwise."

"He was holding it when he came in," Miss Oswald added. "The gray ledger, I mean. I saw it. And Lacey did not bat an eyelash at it, which means he must not know what it is."

Lily let out a shaky breath. "Thank God the general did not see you in there."

"Oh, he nearly did." Jack grimaced. "Left my gloves and hat out when I hid. Stupid of me. All worked out, but it was a near thing. Hence the drinking." He shrugged the matter off with a wry look. Though Lily suspected it had been more dangerous than he was willing to let on, she didn't press him. He had made it out safely, and that was what mattered. "But we have him, ma'am. The general is our man."

"He must be," Miss Oswald agreed. "But then, why was Lord Walter bribing the magistrate?"

"Keeping the constables away from his family." Lily sighed, feeling weak with relief to know, at last, that Serena's husband was not a murderer. "Just as wealthy men with political ambitions have always done. He must have been worried that a drawn-out investigation by Bow Street could reflect poorly on him and wanted to make it go away."

Jack nodded. "Not the most honorable thing, but nothing much out of the common line of things either. You must be glad to know—"

"A glass of wine, ladies?" Major Hastings's voice made all three of them start, and Lily noticed out of the corner of her eye that Jack nearly lost his balance before dropping quickly into a seat. A servant with a tray of glasses began handing them around. "I apologize for taking so long; what a crush it is out there!"

"I hope it was not too dreadful, sir," Lily murmured as she accepted her own drink, wishing the errand had taken him twice as long. Still, she could admit to herself that it was for the best. If their private conversation had lasted any longer, the gossips might have begun to pay attention. So she put her social face back on and nudged Miss Oswald to do the same. "Did you see anyone of note while you were gone?"

The major immediately began describing two politicians who had nearly come to blows during the promenade. Lily exchanged a glance with Jack and took a long drink of wine. Murder, unfortunately, would have to wait.

★ ★ ★

Worn out from her nervous day, Lily went straight to bed after the theater. But she couldn't sleep, still uneasy over the danger into which she had sent her friends. The fire had been banked and burned down, but the drapes hung open a little, letting a dim spill of moonlight into the room. She had become accustomed to the noise of London, but tonight there was an odd silence that left too much space for her mind to fill.

Sighing, Lily, threw off the covers. If she could not sleep, she would read. Surely a bit of *Evelina* or *The Italian* would prove distracting enough. Shrugging into her dressing gown, Lily padded on slippered feet toward the door, grateful for the unseasonable warmth that kept the floors from being too chilled.

Outside, no shouts from pedestrians heading home or clamor of passing carriages broke the stillness. Which was why she could hear, very distinctly, the creak of floorboards in the hall.

Lily paused, one hand on the doorknob, the back of her neck prickling. It could be one of her servants, of course. But none of them would have crept along so carefully, or paused just far enough away to be at the door of the other bedroom. Someone was checking to see which room was occupied. Someone wanted to know where she was sleeping.

Moving as quickly as she could while staying silent, Lily felt her way toward her writing desk. Holding her breath and straining to hear the footsteps as they resumed their careful progress, she eased open the bottom drawer and closed her hand around the pistol inside.

The footsteps paused outside her door, and the knob turned with a muffled click. Slowly, the door swung inward, opening toward Lily and blocking her from the intruder's view.

Whoever it was, he moved carefully. The curtains were still mostly drawn around the bed, leaving it shrouded and dark. The intruder inched forward. Lily held her breath, trying to make out something, any sort of distinguishing characteristic, but aside from the occasional shape of a breeches-clad leg, the figure was swathed in a dark driving coat that obscured any indication of size and shape. Lily was still trying to decide what to do when the man pulled something from under his coat.

The light from the windows glinted on the barrel of a pistol, and the sharp click of a hammer being pulled back echoed quietly through the room.

Lily screamed as the murderer fired at the place where her head should have been and, without stopping to think, swung up her own pistol and fired.

CHAPTER 19

The shot went wide—it had been years since she had fired Freddy's gun, and she had forgotten that it threw left—and the intruder jumped, his own pistol clattering to the floor. The shock ran up Lily's arm, but she didn't drop her gun. There was no time to reload, but she had the presence of mind to realize that the butt of a pistol could make a good weapon on its own.

There was no chance to use it, though. Before the echo of the shot had died away, the intruder was running, yanking the door open even farther as he dashed out. He moved too quickly for Lily, who had to stop to catch the door so it wouldn't hit her. Stumbling into the hall, she saw him throw himself down the main stairs, boots pounding now that he had abandoned silence in favor of speed. Yelling for her servants, she chased after him.

She gained the top of the steps in time to see the intruder collide with an unexpected figure. Anna had come running when she heard Lily's cry for help, and the two grappled until he pushed her down and ran for the passage between the parlor and book-room.

The side door, Lily realized. He had left it open for his escape. Not caring that she was still in her dressing gown or stopping to think what would happen if anyone saw her running out of her house in the middle of the night, Lily pelted after him.

She was too late. As she dashed toward the street, hands smacking the stone wall of the house to keep her upright as she rounded the corner, she heard the clatter of hooves. The burglar was swinging astride a horse left just two doors down. All that she could clearly see was the dark tail and white socks of the horse's hind legs as the rider galloped away.

Lily cursed and tugged the billowing halves of her dressing gown closed. For an angry, shaking moment, she stared down the street.

A sudden commotion behind her made her jump, and Lily turned just in time to see Carstairs run out the front door and vault his considerable person over the stair railing. He was resplendent in a red dressing gown, his entire body coiled for a fight as if he were still in the prime of his boxing days. He scowled down the street in the direction the burglar had gone, then turned to Lily. "Are you hurt, madam?" His respectful tone was so at odds with his behavior that Lily barely suppressed a nervous giggle.

"He had a horse," she said instead, then shivered. He had planned well, of course, because he was no ordinary burglar. But she refused to let herself dwell on that fact or to be shaken into panic and inaction. She had a household to calm down.

Mrs. Carstairs was waiting with Anna in the front hall when they went back inside, and both women turned to her, wanting to know what had happened. Lily thought she managed rather well. After she made sure Anna was unharmed—"Just shaken, Mrs. Adler, no harm done"—no one questioned her story that she had been on her way downstairs for a book when she found a burglar in the act of breaking in, or that there was no need to send for a constable because the bounder was long gone.

"He won't come back, in any case." Mrs. Carstairs sounded almost proud. "Wherever did you learn to shoot, ma'am?"

"My father," Lily replied absently; she had reloaded her pistol in a businesslike manner as soon as there was time, much to the surprise of her audience. Wanting to avoid any other questions, she sent Anna back to bed. Mrs. Carstairs, practical and soothing as always, went to make sure that the maid was able to settle in after her fright. All seemed calm at last, and Lily, drooping with sudden exhaustion, was about to dismiss Carstairs for the night and pour herself a stiff drink when a sudden pounding at the front door made all of them jump.

"What the devil . . ." Carstairs started toward the door, then hesitated. "Madam, perhaps . . . ?"

Lily ignored him, filled with something that could have been either fury or frustration. She cocked back the hammer on her pistol and yanked the door open herself, ready to give whoever was there an unexpected welcome.

It was hard to say who was more surprised, Lily or her late-night visitor. "Jack?" She lowered the pistol quickly. "What the devil are you doing here?"

They stared at each other for several stunned seconds, until Jack cleared his throat. "Were you going to shoot me?"

"I very well might have, you idiot man. I repeat, what the devil are you doing here?"

Jack cleared his throat again, glancing pointedly over Lily's shoulder to where her very curious butler was watching. Lily sighed. There would be gossip about this all over Mayfair if she was not careful.

"In or out, sir," she said sharply. "I'll not have you standing on my doorstep for anyone to see. I promise not to shoot." Jack had the decency to look embarrassed as he came inside. "Carstairs, please go over all the doors and windows in the house before you retire. I doubt our burglar will come back, but better to be thorough."

"Mrs. Adler, what—" Jack began, but she cut him off with a raised hand and continued to speak to Carstairs.

"Then have Anna make up a bed for herself in my dressing room. I will appreciate the company tonight, and I don't want her to be alone after her fright."

"Of course, madam." Carstairs looked relieved that his employer was providing herself with a chaperone.

"And Carstairs?" Lily waited until she had his full attention. "I am sure I needn't tell you how unwanted any sort of gossip about tonight would be. Above all things, I require discretion from those in my employ."

"Of course, Mrs. Adler." He bowed. "You may rely on me."

"I am sure." Lily favored him with a genuine smile, which faded as he left and she turned back to Jack.

Who was watching her with concern. "Are you all right?"

She sighed. "Book-room." When he protested, she glared at him. "I have no desire to continue standing in my front hallway, and I want a drink. So you will come with me, and you will explain yourself."

She stalked out of the hall without pausing to see if he would follow, but as she went to pour herself a whiskey, she heard Jack close the door behind him. She settled into a plush chair and crossed her arms without inviting him to sit. Jack shifted uneasily as she stared at him, and it was he who finally broke the silence.

"What happened here tonight? Don't say *nothing*, Lily; you had a pistol. And I know there was some sort of commotion—"

"And how do you know that?"

He ran a hand through his hair, not meeting her eyes. "I had your house watched." When Lily merely took a long drink, not saying anything, he continued anxiously. "I had to, Lily; you must see that."

"I must? I must see that you needed to invade my privacy, without my consent?" Her voice began to shake with fury. "How dare you?"

"It was for your safety. Do you have any idea how dangerous what you are doing is?"

"In fact I do." Lily moved her pistol from her lap to the table next to her, and the movement was enough to silence Jack. She began to suspect that he was arguing not because he thought he was right, but because he felt uncomfortably wrong. "And what did you intend to do? Politely ask an intruder to leave? Defend me with your walking stick? Cause so much gossip by showing up on my doorstep in the middle of the night that I'd have to leave London entirely?"

"You have to stop this. You've put yourself in far too much danger. If Freddy were here—"

"But Freddy's not here, is he? Freddy is dead." Lily ignored Jack's sharp intake of breath and barreled on, overwrought and angry and for once not caring who saw. "Freddy is dead, and he is not coming back, so this is my life now. I get to decide what to do with it, and I choose to do something that matters. What right have you to tell me otherwise?" He had no answer, and the silence stretched for several long moments before Lily sighed. "Who did you have do it?"

Jack started. "What?"

"Who is watching my home, Jack? I sincerely hope you were not sitting out there yourself."

"No, of course not. The boy from Lacy and West, Jem." Jack laughed shortly, running his hands through his hair again. "I was afraid something like this would happen, so he had instructions to fetch me if he saw anything suspicious."

"He ran all the way to the Albany that quickly?"

"St. James Street. I was at my club. Much closer."

"Ah." Lily let the silence stretch once more, then asked, "Did he see anything useful?"

Jack looked surprised at the question. "Just heard a commotion. Will you tell me what happened, Lily, or am I too much in disgrace?"

She considered that long enough to make him shift from foot to foot, but at last she gestured him to take a seat and pour himself a drink as she filled him in on the night's events. "I told the servants it must have been a common burglar, of course, and they seem to believe it."

"It wasn't," Jack said, and Lily shook her head.

"No, it wasn't." They were quiet for a moment; then she continued briskly, "I think the best thing would be to have your boy keep watching, as he seems to be good at it. But I want to be clear, Captain, that he is to report what he sees to me, not you."

"You intend to keep going."

It was not a question, but Lily raised an eyebrow. "I assumed I had made that clear."

"Freddy would never forgive me if anything happened to you."

"You keep saying that."

"I feel responsible—"

"But you aren't." Lily gritted her teeth in frustration, wanting him to understand. "I think about what Freddy would have wanted every day. Would he have approved? Or would he have wanted me to attend parties and teas and mind my own business? Perhaps. But when I close my eyes, I see Mr. Finch, cold and dead and lying in the dirt. I see a stack of money passed to the right hands that means his murderer goes free. I don't care what that poor boy did or tried to do, that is not right. So if I have the chance to do something about it, I won't turn my back on that." She lifted her chin. "I cannot."

Jack nodded slowly. "That was the reason Freddy wanted to go into Parliament. To do something that mattered."

"I know. And helping him do that would have been my work as well. It can't be, anymore. I still love Freddy dearly, Jack, but I get to live my life now, as I wish. It is the one consolation I have."

Before Jack could reply, they were interrupted by Mrs. Carstairs's discreet entrance. "Begging your pardon, ma'am. Carstairs has checked all the windows and locks, and Anna has a pallet made up in your dressing room. I wanted to see if you'll be needing anything else?"

"Thank you, Mrs. Carstairs. I knew I could count on you to see everything returned to normal." The housekeeper flushed with pleasure at the praise, which was genuinely meant, but Lily sighed after she left. "If you wanted to change my mind, Captain, a better tactic would have been to suggest that I not put my servants in danger. I'd not have been able to forgive myself if anything had happened to them tonight."

"I shall remember that for the future." Jack stood. "And I shall return to my own home, properly chastened, unless . . . do you feel safe for the rest of the night? Do you want me to stay?"

"Oh no." Lily raised her brows. "I am feeling moderately charitable towards you just now, so you should take your leave before I decide to be angry with you after all." She stood. "Did Lady Walter procure you an invitation to the Carroways' ball?"

"No need, I was already invited. Father knew the family."

"Then I will see you tomorrow evening, but right now it is still the middle of the night, and I am going back to bed."

"Of course." Jack bowed. "I wish you a good night."

"And Jack?" He paused in the doorway to look back, and Lily's face softened. "Get some sleep yourself. You look as if you need it."

He grinned, unable to hide his relief. "Good night, Lily."

★   ★   ★

After making sure the door was properly latched, Lily made her way upstairs, trembling now that all the danger was past. In spite of her bold front, she had been terrified the entire time. But there was one more thing to be done before she could return to bed.

It took a little bit of searching—and a little reassurance to Anna that she did not need any assistance—but at last Lily found the pistol that the burglar had dropped, kicked partially under her dressing table. She examined it slowly. The quality and workmanship said it had been custom made, clearly too expensive a weapon for a common burglar. And, on the underside of the barrel, she found what she was looking for: carefully inlaid initials that spelled out *AGF*. Mr. Finch's missing gun, which his killer had stolen after shooting him with it.

If the murderer wanted her dead, that meant she was getting close.

Lily shivered as she climbed into bed, and she lay awake for a long while, turning over possibilities in her mind.

CHAPTER 20

That night at the Carroways' ball, Lily decided there was nothing more ridiculous than trying to maintain a social life while solving a murder.

She was still irked with Jack for his high-handedness, nervous about being in her own home, and desperately trying to decide how to move forward. She was getting close but still needed proof. But no ideas presented themselves, and Lily was left with the unusual feeling that her mind was failing her, just as a murderer was closing in.

And yet, there she was, smiling her way down the receiving line. It was absurd, but there was nothing else to do. The Carroways were an old family, and though they were not members of the peerage themselves, they had enough social standing to make them influential. They were also popular, deeply integrated into London society, and, most importantly, Lady Carroway was niece to the Earl of Portland. There had been no good way to refuse their invitation.

The present baronet, Sir Edward Carroway, was only twenty-four and had succeeded to the title after his father's death from apoplexy some years before. Though he was of age, Sir Edward was a birthday away from achieving his full majority; as a result, the family was still very much under his mother's control, which seemed to suit the young baronet just fine.

The party that evening was for his sister, who would be presented at court within the week. After meeting Miss Carroway—eighteen years old and bubbling with delight—Lily thought it was no wonder that Sir Edward was content to let his mother run the family. Miss Carroway was the first of three sisters, and a young man of four and twenty could hardly be expected to take charge of launching three girls into society, however pretty and pleasant they might be.

So Lily went to the ball and chatted about London's fashion and scandals. It made her want to scream, though her face showed nothing but calm. The clock was just chiming eleven—with most of the night still to come—when Lily excused herself from her group, claiming that she was in need of refreshment.

"Allow me to accompany you, Mrs. Adler, and fetch whatever you might need," one gentlemen offered.

"No need." The voice at Lily's elbow nearly made her jump. Jack, just arrived, bowed politely. "I shall be happy to escort Mrs. Adler."

Lily, who had hoped to make a quick escape to the ladies' retiring room to steel herself for the hours still left, hid a sigh behind a neutral, social smile. "A gentleman with your grace, Mr. Trawson, should be on the dance floor, not squiring about a dull widow like me."

"Never dull, Mrs. Adler." Mr. Trawson bowed. "I shall hope for your company in a turn about the room at a later hour."

She offered him a more genuine smile. "A lovely idea, sir."

Jack was offering his arm, and it would certainly cause gossip if she refused to take it. So she did, managing to keep her neutral smile in place as she muttered for his ears alone, "That was rude, sir. Mr. Trawson has been most kind to me."

"I am certain he has been," Jack said dismissively. "I am just as capable of fetching you a glass of wine as he is."

"And I am perfectly capable of fetching it for myself, as you well know, so I must assume there is a reason behind your presumption."

Jack must have felt something of Lily's stiffness, because he cast her a puzzled look. "Are you truly upset? I know you hadn't any wish for Trawson's escort. No more," he added with a disarming smile, "than you had for mine."

They had stopped by a refreshment table, but neither made a move toward it. Lily's brows drew together before she remembered where she was. "You should know I don't care for being ordered about without being given a chance for refusal."

"Of course," he said, surprising her. "That wasn't well done. I offer my sincere apologies. If I promise never to do it again, will you stop scowling at me?"

Lily sniffed. "I do not scowl. It gives a lady wrinkles. But I will allow you to fetch me a glass of Madeira and tell me what was so important that you had to drag me away."

Jack's demeanor instantly changed, as if he had forgotten his errand until that moment. His back was stiff as he snagged two glasses of wine for them, and he looked around quickly to make sure there was no one nearby before saying, so quietly it was difficult to hear him, "There is something you need to know."

Lily felt suddenly cold, but she let nothing show on her face as she accepted the drink. "Have you discovered how to prove our suspicions? If so, I shall be rather put out. I had hoped to be the one to do so."

"This isn't a matter for joking, Lily."

His use of her given name in public, where anyone might overhear and wonder, told her how serious he was, and a shiver of apprehension slid down her spine. "What did you find?"

He had placed them in one of the alcoves that lined the ballroom, so that they stood some distance from the closest group of people. But Jack still lowered his voice. "You will not like this, but . . . Miss Oswald . . ."

"You saw something?"

"Yes. She disappears from ballrooms."

Lily took a sip of her wine, giving herself time to think before replying. "A lady may leave a ballroom without intending anything nefarious. Perhaps she tore a flounce and had to go mend it."

Jack shook his head, his expression stony. "I've watched her at two different galas. At each one, just before half eleven, she sneaked away from the main room."

Lily turned his story over in her mind. "At half eleven both times?"

"Yes. And after what happened last night . . ."

"Where did she go?"

"I've not followed her that far."

Lily's eyes narrowed as she watched the dancers, Miss Oswald among them. She had been certain for some time that the girl had not told the entire truth about Mr. Finch, and Lily, suspecting what that truth was, had not pressed. But she could think of nothing to account for what Jack had seen. And she remembered, quite suddenly, the evening of the Walters' party. Miss Oswald had sneaked away from the party twice that night: once to meet with Mr. Finch, and the other when Lily had found the girl alone with Reggie Harper. "What time is it now?"

"Twenty past eleven." He frowned. "I know you like her, Mrs. Adler, but you cannot deny that there is something odd going on."

"I do not."

"What do you think it could be?"

"I'm not certain." Lily lifted her chin, looking thoughtful. "But I intend to find out." Jack looked as though he wanted to say something else, but she turned to watch the dancers and only murmured, "Patience." Out of the corner of her eye she saw him shake his head but did not ask what the gesture meant. She had a feeling she knew already.

They were silent for several minutes, then joined the other guests in applauding as the music flourished to an end. Under cover of the noise, Lily looped her arm through Jack's and said quietly, "Let us stroll about the room and see if she does the same thing tonight."

He nodded and began to talk of inconsequential matters, his voice teasing and his charming grin deployed to full effect. Lily laughed at a quip of his, and they made their way across the ballroom, looking interested in nothing more than enjoying themselves.

Miss Oswald's partner delivered her back to her aunt, who had made a rare appearance that evening. But Mrs. Haverweight was busy in her own conversation, and as the strains of the next dance started, Miss Oswald quietly slipped away.

Jack gave Lily a pointed glance; she nodded, and they began to move more quickly, avoiding eye contact with those who might have stopped them. Lily's grip tightened on Jack's arm, pulling him behind the bulk of a well-dressed matron as Miss Oswald glanced over her shoulder. A moment later she slipped out of the ballroom.

Lily would have gone immediately after her, but Jack laid a restraining hand on her arm. "Wait a moment. I think the other side of that door is a hallway. She might look back and see us."

Lily nodded, nearly twitching with impatience as Jack finished up a story of a bet among his friends at Oxford. She laughed in all the right places, but her mind was fixed firmly on the doorway just a few steps beyond where they stood. After a minute, Jack nodded. With a quick glance around to make sure they, too, were unobserved, they followed Miss Oswald.

"Though being seen would not be as disastrous for us as for her," Jack whispered as they made their way down the dimly lit hallway. The few doors they passed were open and the rooms beyond empty. "Anyone who saw us would only assume we were having a liaison."

"I am certain a number of people already think that." Lily remembered to keep her voice low. "We spend far too much time in each other's company for London to refrain from gossip."

"Then I must be the object of a great deal of jealousy." He chuckled. "There are many gentlemen hoping to enjoy the charms of the lovely Widow Adler."

"You are absurd and more than a little vulgar," Lily said without rancor. Suddenly she laid a hand on his arm and breathed a quiet, "Look."

The doorway up ahead was closed, but a light shone underneath. Jack glanced at her, then silently pointed to himself and jerked his head toward the door, indicating that he would go first. Lily wanted to protest, but last night had made her cautious, so she nodded and stood back.

Moving with impressive silence, Jack slid toward the door and laid a hand on the knob. He held up one finger. Lily nodded, bracing herself as he held up a second. He lifted the third, then pushed the door open and burst into the room.

Lily followed immediately after him. She had time to see that the room was a small library, and that the light came from a large and very beautiful stand of candles on a table in the middle of the space, before her eyes fixed on Miss Oswald.

The young woman was alone in the room. She turned toward them with an expression of terror, taking three quick steps backward before recovering her composure and smiling brightly.

"Mrs. Adler, Captain Hartley. Were the noise and heat too much for you as well?"

Lily pursed her lips, but she could not help a small smile of admiration, though she tried to hide it. With a little more practice, the girl could have found herself onstage at Drury Lane. "You look surprised to see us, Miss Oswald. Were you expecting someone else?"

"Someone else?" Miss Oswald's eyes followed Jack nervously as he moved to place himself in front of the only other door in the room. She bit her lip, then attempted another smile. "What on earth do you mean?"

"Miss Oswald, you are too bright to think that will work on us." Lily swallowed the lump that wanted to rise in her throat. She had trusted the girl. She had considered her a friend. "Who have you been meeting?"

To her credit, Miss Oswald did not attempt another lie. After another quick, nervous glance at Jack, her eyes returned to Lily. "I cannot tell you. But you must trust me, Mrs. Adler, it truly is nothing you need worry over."

"No?" Jack did not snap, and he did not yell, but there was a threatening rumble under his quiet tone. "We trusted you. Mrs. Adler trusted you, and you know that is not something to take for granted.

And you have lied to us. Do not deny it." His voice rose as she tried to interrupt him. "You have lied to *Lily*, who has been nothing but a friend to you."

"For which I have the deepest gratitude," Miss Oswald said, speaking quickly as soon as she could get a word in. "But you must believe me—"

"Believe you?" Jack could have been on a ship once more, addressing a mutinous crew, as he took a step toward the girl. "Believe that you have been sneaking around, clandestinely meeting with mysterious men, for perfectly innocent reasons while we are trying to find a murderer? A murderer to whom we know you to have some connection?"

"Being connected to the man who was murdered is not the same thing as being connected to the murderer himself," Miss Oswald broke in, eyes blazing with anger. "Or do you forget, Captain, that Augustus was *my* friend, not yours?" Her hands were clenched into fists as she faced him. "Mrs. Adler knows—"

"It is Mrs. Adler I am thinking of, and the danger she has been in. I shan't risk another attempt—" Jack snapped his jaw closed abruptly, scowling.

But Miss Oswald was, as Lily had already noted, a very bright girl. "An attempt . . . on Mrs. Adler?" she demanded, looking ill but standing her ground. "Do you mean to say someone tried to harm Mrs. Adler? And you think it might have been *me* behind it?"

"Oh, stop it, both of you." Under less serious circumstances, Lily would have wanted to laugh, watching them confront each other. Jack stared down with all the fury of an officer of His Majesty's Navy, and Miss Oswald, for all that she was nearly a foot shorter, glared up at him just as belligerently. "Miss Oswald, you cannot pretend that he doesn't have a right to be suspicious, or that I don't have reason to watch the movements of those around me. So if you have an explanation, will you kindly offer it now?"

Miss Oswald struggled with a glare, but after a moment, she sighed, the stiffness going out of her backbone. "Ned," she called softly. "You had better come out."

The door behind Jack opened with a creak of poorly oiled hinges; the navy captain cursed and swung around to face whoever was entering, his posture tense and guarded. But both he and Lily were left staring in surprise as they found themselves facing Sir Edward Carroway.

"Good evening," he said. "Mrs. Adler, Captain Hartley. I trust you both are enjoying my mother's party?" He looked Jack up and down, his red hair and scattering of freckles standing out sharply against a face pale with anger. "I see we shall have to try harder to divert our guests next time, since you were so bored with our entertainments that you found time to accuse my affianced wife of murder and I know not what else."

Mind reeling, Lily latched on to the only thing she could. "Affianced?" she asked, and heard Jack's voice echo the same question.

Sir Edward had, with another glare for Jack, gone to Miss Oswald's side and taken her hand, looking her over as if to make sure she was unharmed. At Lily's question he turned back. "Miss Oswald has done me the great honor of agreeing to be my wife." His posture was still stiff, but a smile pulled at the corners of his mouth. He was obviously a man in love, and that, more than anything else, set Lily's mind at rest.

"Ofelia," she said reproachfully, using the girl's given name without thinking. "Why did you not tell me?"

"Oh, I wanted to, Mrs. Adler, believe me. But we promised each other we wouldn't say anything to *anyone*, and we truly could not. Not yet."

"A secret engagement?" Jack fixed Sir Edward with a stern glare. "That's hardly a decent way of doing things, man."

Sir Edward's dignity wavered a little at the rebuke, but he held his ground. "I can assure you, sir, it would not have been my choice had there been any other option. And I intend to rectify the situation and make our understanding public as soon as I am able."

"Your family?" Lily asked.

Sir Edward's nod was accompanied by a deep sigh, and he ran a hand through his unruly red hair, a gesture that made him look very boyish. "I come into my majority when I turn five and twenty. Until then, my mother and uncle hold the purse strings."

"And while marrying an heiress is all well and good, marrying one of questionable background—from foreign parts, no less—is not the done thing. It is all right, Neddy," Ofelia added as he cast a very pained look at her. "You know I do not blame you."

"Well, once you are Lady Carroway, they shall have to accept you and treat you with all the respect you deserve," he said, pressing a gentle kiss to her hand.

The gesture made Lily's eyes prickle; to shake the feeling off, she said briskly, "So it is Sir Edward that you have been meeting so secretly in the parks and ballrooms of London?" Ofelia looked embarrassed. "And I take it you have told him what we are about?"

Ofelia nodded. "Please don't be angry, Mrs. Adler. I could hardly keep something so important from him."

"Fellow can't much like his intended getting mixed up in murder." Sir Edward smiled down at Ofelia. "Wanted to object when she first told me about the whole business, but of course it was her father's godson. Couldn't help but admire her for wanting to help. Anyone might put themselves in danger for someone they love, but it's dashed brave of her to do it just because it's the right thing to do."

Ofelia cleared her throat awkwardly. "Well, there are other things to discuss at the moment than your high opinion of me, Neddy. Such as," she said with sudden vigor, turning to Lily, "this business of an attempt to harm you, Mrs. Adler. What happened? Why did you not tell me?"

"There's not been time," Lily said, trying to dismiss the topic. Remembering the sight of that figure standing over her bed, gun drawn, made her hands shake. "Truly, it was not nearly so grave as Captain Hartley would like to make out."

"It was every bit as grave as Captain Hartley would like to make out," Jack said, raising an eyebrow. "Mrs. Adler simply does not wish to talk about it. An armed man broke into her home with the clear intent of shooting her in her bed."

"Oh Mrs. Adler, how dreadful," Ofelia breathed, her eyes wide. "What on earth did you tell the *servants*?"

"Well, given that she woke the household when she shot at the bounder and left a bullet lodged in her bedroom wall, she had to tell them pretty nearly the truth," Jack said.

"You shoot?" Sir Edward looked impressed.

"Yes, I do." Lily wished they would let the subject drop. "As the captain now knows."

"Are we getting into that again?" Jack demanded.

"You are the one who brought it up, Captain, and the one who barged in last night—"

"Mrs. Adler, you are chasing a *murderer*. Something could have happened!"

"Something *did* happen," Lily said. "A man broke into my home, and I scared him off with a pistol, which I think constitutes taking care of myself quite handsomely."

She and Jack glared at each other, heedless of their small audience, both of whom watched the exchange with undisguised fascination. "I say, starting to think Mother was right about you two," Sir Edward said with cheerful nosiness.

Ofelia slapped his shoulder with her fan. "Ned, for heaven's sake, don't be so vulgar." With an apologetic glance at Lily, she explained, "Lady Carroway is—"

"An incorrigible gossip. Yes, I am well aware." Lily sighed, rubbing her temples. "Speaking of gossip, we should all return to the ballroom before the speculation grows utterly out of control. Miss Oswald and I shall go first, and you, gentlemen." Lily fixed them with a stern look. "You will wait several minutes before following. And do come from the direction of the card room if you can manage it."

"Think I know the way about m'own house, ma'am." Sir Edward looked affronted.

"I'm sure you do, Sir Edward. What I am less sure of is your attention to detail." Lily raised an eyebrow. "You should also fix your hair, unless you wish to invite more speculation as to how it got so mussed."

"Ah, yes." Sir Edward glanced at his reflection in the window and grinned. "Fair enough, ma'am. Ofelia was right about you. Not one to miss a trick, eh?"

"I hope not." Lily looped her arm through Ofelia's, ignoring the girl's giggle. "Gentlemen." They both bowed, Sir Edward with clearly restored good humor, Jack with a little more irony. "Will you still see me home after the ball, Captain?" Lily added, wanting to smooth things over. "I should like to talk."

For a moment, she thought he might still be too incensed to agree. But he inclined his head and said gravely, "It will be my pleasure, Mrs. Adler, as always."

And with that, she had to be content, at least for the time being.

★   ★   ★

As soon as the ladies had left, Sir Edward let out a sigh and dropped into a chair. "Rather like being told off by a wife and a governess, all in one go."

Jack did not have to ask to whom he was referring. "A bit," he agreed. "But she is a remarkable woman."

"Could see that easily enough," Sir Edward said. "And Ofelia's mad on her, talks Mrs. Adler without a halt every time I see her. Think she can do it?" he added, sitting up suddenly.

"Solve a murder?" Jack leaned against the table, crossing his arms thoughtfully. "If any woman in London could do it, she could."

"With a little help?"

Jack smiled. "With a little help. Which we all need from time to time." Unbending a little, he added, "Miss Oswald has been of great assistance. Mrs. Adler admires her."

"Dashed clever girl, you know. Got a better head for business than most men." He sighed. "Meant what I said earlier, but it's been hell, having her mixed up in all this." He held out his hand. "Thank you for keeping her safe, Hartley. Eased my mind greatly."

Jack gave the younger man a very assessing glance before taking the offered hand and shaking it. "Well, now you are in the thick of it, you can help me keep an eye on both of them. Full-time occupation, I assure you."

Sir Edward laughed. "Mrs. Adler would keep any man on his toes. Think she's counting the minutes before we return to make sure we time it well?"

Jack shook his head, unable to keep himself from smiling in the face of the other man's good humor. "Quite possibly."

"Well, in that case." Sir Edward pulled a key out of his waistcoat and crossed to the tantalus. "No harm in taking our time. What will you drink, Hartley?"

Jack chuckled. "I'm going to like you, Carroway."

Sir Edward smiled easily. "Most people do." He pulled out two glasses. "Brandy?"

★ ★ ★

"I cannot tell you how glad I am that you finally know everything." Ofelia seemed giddy with relief as they left the library. "Keeping our engagement a secret was exciting at first, of course, but after Augustus was killed, it was such a burden . . ."

Lily let her chatter, keeping her own conflicted feelings inside in order to be happy for her friend. But when they were nearly back at the ballroom, Ofelia added with breathless laughter, "And I knew you would not mind too much that I told Neddy what we were about."

That was more than Lily could let pass. "I very much mind the situation you have put me in, Ofelia," she said quietly.

"But . . ." The girl frowned. "But . . . Mrs. Adler, surely you don't mean to tell anyone about our engagement!"

"I do not. But you lied to us. To Captain Hartley. To me. You kept Sir Edward a secret from us, and perhaps you had that right. But you left us knowing that you were sneaking around, knowing that you were hiding something, with everything else that was going on."

"I promise, I did not mean to deceive you."

"Of course you meant to, or you would have told us about Sir Edward. And now you've shared heaven knows how much with a man we have no reason to trust."

Ofelia looked horrified. "But I assure you, you can trust Neddy! He thinks the whole thing a brilliant lark."

"In the first place, I very much doubt that," Lily said dryly. "I cannot imagine Sir Edward enjoys the idea of you chasing after a murderer. And in the second . . ." Her gaze became sharper. "I see no compelling reason to trust Sir Edward so completely when you clearly do not trust him yourself."

"Not trust—!" Ofelia was stunned into momentary silence. "Mrs. Adler, whatever do you mean? Of course I trust Neddy!"

"With my secrets, perhaps. But not with your own."

"With my own?" The girl laughed. "Mrs. Adler, how many engagements do you think I am hiding?"

Lily raised a brow. "Two."

Ofelia grew very still. "What do you mean?"

Lily glanced around. It wouldn't do to risk someone overhearing their conversation, so she ushered the girl through the nearest door, which opened into an empty sitting room. "Two engagements," she repeated, once the door was closed behind them. "The one with Sir Edward being the second."

"Mrs. Adler . . ."

"I imagine your engagement to Mr. Finch was not of long duration, of course. A month or two, perhaps?"

"A month." Ofelia's voice had grown hoarse. "How did . . . how did you know?"

Lily smiled a little sadly. "You weren't always successful at hiding your feelings about him. You were most insistent that you were not close, but you've been far more distressed over his death than a distant connection would warrant."

"He was my father's godson . . ."

"And the two of you would have been much thrown together as a result." Lily's voice softened. "I imagine it ended because of a quarrel?"

Ofelia nodded. "We didn't speak for several weeks, which was enough time for me to realize that I was not so in love as I had thought. We should never have suited. And I thought Augustus agreed, until . . ."

"Until he followed you to London?"

"He thought he could simply wait . . . You must promise to keep it a secret, Mrs. Adler." A look of sudden horror crossed Ofelia's face, and she demanded, "You've not told the captain?"

"Of course not." Lily shook her head. "Not that it has been easy. He was most insistent that you were hiding something about Mr. Finch, and I have had a devil of a time convincing him you weren't. Hopefully this business with Sir Edward will satisfy him at last."

"Thank God." Ofelia let out a heavy breath. "If anyone but you found out, my reputation would be ruined. *I* would be ruined. I cannot risk anyone knowing."

"So I gathered when it became clear that Sir Edward believes Mr. Finch was simply a distant connection."

"You don't understand." The girl's voice rose before she recalled where they were and dropped it again. "It was more than just the engagement—"

"I do understand," Lily said gently. "It is not surprising that in the moment, in the romance of a secret engagement, you would grow . . . intimate."

Ofelia's lips quivered. "I was seventeen," she whispered. "I thought I was in love."

"Of course you did." Lily nodded. "That is what happens when one is seventeen, and occasionally it is true."

"If you know all that, how can you suggest that I tell Ned the truth about Augustus?" Ofelia demanded. "It has been two years, you know; he would never know. Only if I told him. And what man would want to marry a woman who . . . I couldn't risk losing him,

Mrs. Adler." Her voice shook, and she had to blink back tears before she could add, "I love him."

"I wasn't suggesting that you tell him everything. It is certainly your choice if you want to keep such things a secret, and I can understand why you would." Lily's voice grew sharper. "But we were speaking of trust, you may recall. And if you cannot trust Sir Edward with your own secrets, then you cannot expect me to trust him with mine."

"Neddy would never betray my confidence or yours, Mrs. Adler," the girl said stiffly, turning toward the door as if she would storm off.

"I hope you are right," Lily said quietly. "For my sake and yours."

For several moments the girl said nothing, her back rigid, her hand on the doorknob. "Do you think I should tell him?"

"I think you should do what is best for you," Lily said. "But I hope that the man you have chosen is worthy of your full confidence."

"I couldn't risk losing him," Ofelia repeated, her voice quivering. For a moment it seemed like she would say something more, but she yanked open the door and hurried away.

Lily, sighing, followed her back to the ballroom.

★ ★ ★

Jack escorted Lily home that night, as he had promised, but though she had wanted to talk things out with him, he held up a hand to forestall her as soon as she began.

"Please," he said quietly as the carriage rocked along through the Mayfair streets. "I would rather we put it behind us. You will do things your way, and I shall do my best to keep you out of danger, and from time to time we shall butt heads over it."

"I don't like to leave it that way," she protested.

"And I don't like to leave you chasing around London after a war hero who has turned to murder. But that is what you keep asking me to do. We shall both have to make the best of it." He waited for her nod, then, with a deliberate smile, changed the subject. "What did you think of young Carroway?" They settled into a more comfortable talk, but Lily's mind was elsewhere, and after a few minutes Jack asked quietly, "What are you thinking of, Lily?"

"Our murderer," she said quietly. The immensity of what they were doing had suddenly struck her. "Nothing else fits, but . . . I went to school with his niece. I went to tea at his home once! To imagine him a murderer seems impossible."

"Lily . . ." Jack paused, selecting his words carefully. "The general was a soldier, of course, and soldiers must kill. But to kill a man in battle is very different from murdering in cold blood. Do you think he could have done it?"

An uncomfortable memory rose up in Lily's mind. It had been her last day at Miss Tattersy's seminary, and all the boarders were being fetched by parents and servants to take them home. Lily, her trunks already packed, had escaped from Serena's frantic preparations and gone to replace several borrowed books in the school's library. It was not a place where Miss Tattersy encouraged her pupils to spend much time, and Lily hoped to savor a few last hours of solitude before returning home.

She was wholly unprepared for the scene she walked in on. Isobel Harper, her face red with fury and streaked with tears, was shouting at her uncle, her words incomprehensible to Lily's stunned senses, as she shook a fistful of papers at him. Behind her, a terrified-looking maid cowered, her mistress's wraps over one arm, her eyes darting around the room as if looking for an escape route.

For Lily, who had spent her whole life dreading any such confrontation with her own father, that would have been awful enough. But what followed was worse. General Harper snatched the papers from his niece and ripped them violently in half. Isobel shrieked in fury, and her uncle raised his hand as if he would strike her. She didn't flinch, and at the last minute he turned and struck the maid across the face, hard enough to knock her down. Then, turning to Isobel, he said, very calmly, "Control yourself. And fetch your bonnet before we go. All the money spent on this place will be wasted if you end up with freckles." Isobel raised her own hand as though she would strike him herself, but lowered it abruptly, though she continued to glare at him, her face bright with rage. Both of them ignored the maid using the edge of the table to pull herself back to her feet.

No one had seen Lily. Shaking as if she were the one who had been struck, she retreated upstairs to help Serena finish packing. She had never mentioned the scene to anyone.

The whole memory came back at Jack's question and left her trembling once again. "I never knew him well. But from what I do know, yes, I would believe him capable of murder. And for Mr. Finch's sake, and Ofelia's, and now my own, we must find a way to prove it."

Even in her preoccupation, she saw Jack's eyes narrow. "What are you planning to do?"

"To get that ledger." A slow smile spread across Lily's face. "I think I know exactly how to go about it."

CHAPTER 21

"Lady Walter and Mrs. Adler to see you."

As she and Serena were shown into Miss Harper's sunny parlor, Lily was grateful for the rituals of London life. Despite her nervousness, it was easy to exchange greetings, to ask about one another's health and fall into chatter on innocuous subjects, to sip tea and accept the offer of a slice of cake. It was second nature to her, and no one watching would have guessed that her mind was not wholly occupied with Serena's discussion of the new mantua-maker on Bond Street who, it was rumored, produced the most lavishly naughty nightclothes in addition to stylish gowns.

"I saw Mrs. Crandoll emerging from there just the other day." Serena leaned forward. "When I asked what sort of dress she had bought, it took the dear lady positively a whole minute to come up with an answer!"

Lily laughed along, but she did not relax. It had taken no effort to persuade Serena that a visit to Isobel Harper would be a pleasant way to spend an hour or so. And the viscountess could be counted on to keep the conversation rolling, to make all feel natural with the latest gossip and cozy chatter. But Lily was searching for an opportunity, and she knew she would not have a second chance to take advantage of it.

"I know I shouldn't be speaking of such things." Serena looked as if she didn't mean a word, which, Lily knew, was exactly the case.

"But we have all known each other for years now. And I am sure, Miss Harper, that you will wish to know where to buy your own wedding clothes . . . and other things, of course."

"Lady Walter!" Miss Harper's protest was barely more than a croak; she cleared her throat quickly before continuing. "You know perfectly well that I am not engaged."

"Oh come now, Isobel," Serena said. "You've been seen at more balls and parties this season than in the last six years."

"One grows tired of staying at home." Miss Harper spoke defensively, flushing from her collarbone to her hairline.

"One does indeed," Serena agreed. "Especially if one has a certain Mr. Kettering whom one wishes to meet without anyone remarking on it. Though in that case, perhaps one should not dance with him twice in a single evening." Miss Harper's blush deepened, and Lily began to feel sorry for her. There were few things more intimidating than Serena when she was bent on winkling out some bit of gossip.

"It is only that . . ." Miss Harper hesitated, her hands twisting in the skirts of her morning dress, one lip caught between her teeth. Lily understood. The three of them had never been close, but clearly the poor woman was in desperate need of a confidante. And . . .

"Your uncle does not know of your understanding?" Lily guessed.

Miss Harper shook her head, looking guilty and excited at the same time. "Mr. Kettering has told his family, but—" She broke off.

"Oh my dear, you need someone to *talk* to!" Serena stood, lowering her voice. "Tell us absolutely everything that has been weighing on you. You can rely on our discretion."

"But perhaps not the discretion of all your servants," Lily put in, seizing the moment. "Shall we sit in the garden? We shan't be overheard by anyone there."

The sudden look of gratitude on Miss Harper's face made Lily want to squirm with guilt. But Miss Harper *did* need someone to confide in, and Serena, for all her gossipy ways, could be utterly discreet when the situation called for it. So Lily went along as their hostess led the way toward the small patch of garden behind the house.

Just as they came to the door, Lily hung back and cleared her throat apologetically. "I do beg your pardon, Miss Harper, but perhaps you could point me in the direction of a washroom?" She touched her hair delicately. "I think I have a few pins loose."

"Of course, Mrs. Adler." Isobel Harper seemed to hesitate for a moment, then gestured down the hall they had just walked along. "Under the stairs, next to my uncle's study. He had it put in last year so he would not be forever tromping up and down to his dressing room. I am sure he'll not mind you using it."

Lily nodded, silently amazed at her good luck. She had expected she would need to sneak back downstairs to search for the general's study; separate washrooms had become fashionable among the wealthy in the last few years, but very few households had installed them downstairs.

She paused just outside the washroom and glanced back over her shoulder. The other two women had already gone outside, and there were no servants in sight. Lily darted to the study door and tried the handle. She sighed with relief as the door swung open, and she slipped inside.

General Harper's study was smaller than she had expected, and she couldn't help comparing the ostentatiousness of the furniture—bought to be showy and imposing—to the quiet dignity of Lord Walter's study. There was no fire made up and no lamps lit, which left the room chilly and a little dim, so Lily twitched one curtain a little aside to provide more light before turning to take stock of her task.

The obvious place to start was the desk. For a moment Lily hesitated, wondering if that was too obvious. But she didn't have enough time to waste any of it standing there wondering, so she shook off her doubts and got to work immediately. There were several ledgers laid out on the desk. They contained the household accounts and—she shook her head disapprovingly—a record of Reggie Harper's personal expenses, which involved a great deal of money spent at the gaming tables. Lily put the ledgers back into place, making sure they were aligned with the blotter exactly as they had been before she touched them, and began searching the drawers.

She came up with nothing. The general's drawers were full of any number of papers and letters, along with a pistol in the bottom drawer, but no gray ledger. She couldn't afford to take much more time, or her friends would wonder where she was. Holding back a frustrated sigh, Lily stood, her eyes wandering around the room. There were bookshelves along one wall. What better place to hide a ledger than among other books?

Most of the volumes had titles embossed on the spines. Lily ignored those, scanning for books that were gray and slim enough to be the one she was looking for and pulling them out quickly to flip through the pages.

A book of maps. A walking guide to a village somewhere outside London. Sermons. More maps. Lily knew she was running out of time as she pulled out a fifth volume.

This one was different. Rather than being a printed book like the others, it was filled with papers, some carefully written, some stuck between other pages, all dense with numbers and lists. Lily was certain she had found the right one, but before she could look more closely at its contents, the sound of voices made her freeze.

"Is my uncle in his study?"

It was Reggie Harper, just outside the door. Lily's eyes darted around the room, trying to find a place to hide, but before she could decide what to do, the butler's voice answered.

"I'm afraid the general is out today, sir. There is every chance he will not be back until tomorrow afternoon."

"Bad luck, then," Reggie said cheerfully. "Well, not so bad for me; bounder's always breathing down my neck, you know, him and Isobel, confound the girl. Shall have to check back tomorrow or the day after . . ."

A third, deeper voice answered as footsteps moved away from the door, but Lily was too distracted by relief to pay much attention.

Hurrying across the room as silently as possible, she pressed her ear against the door and listened until the footsteps faded.

Even though she had not looked through the ledger as carefully as she wanted to, Lily needed to leave. Luckily the book was not large or thick, so she wiggled it down the low-cut front of her afternoon dress and under her stays. The edges dug uncomfortably into her skin, but the lacing of the short corset held the book in place. The fall of her dress did nothing to obscure the bottom edges, but she had worn a long coat that afternoon. She buttoned that up and said a quick prayer that the heavier fabric would disguise the odd shape now lurking under her bosom. Holding her reticule in front of her stomach to hide any still-visible outline, she hurried out into the corridor, trying to keep her breathing and her speed normal as she retraced her steps toward the garden door.

"Mrs. Adler. What a surprise to see you."

The voice stopped her in her tracks as she rounded the corner into the main hall. Lily managed to stifle a panicked gasp as she turned and found herself confronted by Reggie Harper and—her eyes flew wide before she could stop herself—Mr. Hyrum Lacey.

His had been the third voice, she realized too late. Mr. Harper had been taking the shipping agent to see his uncle.

It had been Mr. Lacey who spoke to her, and Lily, defensive and panicked but not wanting to show it, responded the first way that came to mind. "I beg your pardon, Mr. . . . ?"

"Hyrum Lacey, madam. You will recall we met the other day." Mr. Lacey's smile was distinctly unpleasant as he added, "You spoke so well of my shipping agency?"

Lily swallowed and nodded coldly, then quickly changed her mind and attempted a polite smile. "Ah yes, I do recall." She shrugged, feigning unconcern, though the motion made her all too aware of the ledger digging into her torso. "I have a difficult time remembering anything to do with business, I'm sure you understand."

"Isobel's the same way," Reggie Harper agreed with a laugh that was clearly meant to be friendly but left Lily's stomach turning with distaste. "Most females are, Lacey."

"Were you also looking for the general, ma'am?" Mr. Lacey glanced pointedly down the hallway, then back at Lily, and the coldness of his stare made her skin crawl. He had addressed her by her name, she realized with a sick lurch in her stomach. The name she very carefully hadn't given him when they had met on the street. The only way for him to know it was if the general had said something to him. And if they had been discussing her . . .

"No," she said abruptly, too desperate to be polite. "Mr. Harper, I was hoping to join your sister in the garden, but seem to have gotten lost as I left the washroom." Between the two men, she was not sure who unsettled her more, but Mr. Harper at least was not involved in treason and murder. "Perhaps you could show me the way?"

"I should be delighted. If you will excuse us, Lacey?" He offered his arm, and Lily had no choice but to take it. Her spine prickled as she turned her back on Mr. Lacey, and she was so focused on getting away from him that she didn't notice that Reggie Harper had pulled her too close until he leaned over and spoke. "You know, Mrs. Adler," he murmured, "You'd not feel the need to worry about business matters if you had a gentleman to . . . distract you."

Lily swallowed and tried to edge away from him. "I believe we have already had this discussion, sir. It did not end well for you."

"And yet here we are again—"

"And here is the door to the garden," she continued over him, her voice bright and brittle. "I must rejoin my friends." She pulled her arm very firmly from his and tried not to look too relieved when he let her go. She was a guest in his home, after all, and neither of them wanted to make a scene. "I thank you for your escort, Mr. Harper. And I continue to be uninterested in any offer you might have to make me."

Lily turned her back on him and walked toward the French doors. She could feel his eyes on her every step of the way, but she did not look back.

★ ★ ★

Lily thought she handled herself well through the rest of the visit, which consisted mostly of Serena pressing for more details, and Isobel Harper admitting only that she and Christopher Kettering had developed an understanding, with his father's approval. But once they had taken their leave—fortunately, without seeing Mr. Harper or Mr. Lacey again—Serena waited only until her carriage had pulled away from the steps before she demanded, "Lily, what on earth happened in there?"

"What makes you think anything happened?"

"Because your hands have been shaking these past thirty minutes."

"It's nothing—"

"It's not nothing," Serena interrupted, "so do not try to—" She broke off, eyes growing wide. "Oh, my dear Lily. You ran into Mr. Harper. Did he importune you again? That bastard."

"No. I mean, yes, but—since when do you curse?"

"Since someone upset my dearest friend. Tell me what happened."

"Truly, it was nothing. I met Mr. Harper in the hallway and had to give him another setdown. I shall be quite myself after I get home."

Serena narrowed her eyes. "You are a terrible liar."

"I am actually quite a good liar."

"Not to me. There has been something happening since you returned to London, and now you are dreadfully upset. You must tell me what is going on."

Lily hesitated. But Serena was her closest friend. And as she no longer suspected Lord Walter—she didn't even need to mention her suspicions, in fact—it would be a relief to unburden herself to someone not involved. "Well, in fact, it was not only Mr. Harper who had me overset." Lowering her voice in case the driver or grooms should be listening, she described her efforts to track down the murderer of the man in the Walters' garden, her suspicions of the general, and the role that Hyrum Lacey of Lacey and West, Shipping Agents, seemed to be playing. "And then who should I come face-to-face with in the Harpers' home but Lacey himself. And Serena, I am positive he knows I'm up to something. Or perhaps he is naturally suspicious of everyone, given his own crimes. But I have them now, I am certain of it," she concluded, a little breathless and surprised at her own eagerness to describe her work.

She had expected that Serena, with her love of intrigue and scandal, would be thrilled by such an exciting tale. Instead, her friend's expression had turned thunderous. "You mean to say you are actually *investigating* that wretched mess? For God's sake, what would possess you to do such a thing?"

It look Lily a stunned moment to come up with a response. "A man was murdered, Serena. I *heard* him murdered. I had to do something."

"No, you did not. You could have left it dashed well alone. Nobody knew him. Bow Street let the matter drop; why couldn't you?"

Her own ire growing, Lily snapped back, "Do you even know why the magistrate stopped looking into things?"

"Because my husband paid him to, of course."

Lily was left in stunned silence for the second time in as many minutes. "You knew?" she finally managed to ask.

"Of course I knew. I know everything that goes on in my home."

"And that didn't bother you at all?" Lily had always known that she and her friend were very different people. But to listen to Serena calmly state that she had known about Lord Walter's bribe was almost more than Lily could believe.

"I would rather it had not been necessary, of course. But what else could we do?"

"Allow the investigation to proceed, perhaps? Encourage the magistrate to find a murderer before he kills again? I cannot believe you would approve of such a thing."

"I would have done it myself if he had not."

"You cannot be serious," Lily insisted.

"I am." Serena's voice rose. "And I cannot believe you would go behind my back in such a manner, never mind that you would undertake such a foolish, dangerous—" The viscountess broke off with a deep breath. "We are nearly at your home, and this is an excellent time for you to take your leave."

"Serena—"

"I asked you to go, Lily."

Lily wanted to protest, to shake her friend and insist that she see things more clearly, with more compassion, to demand where Serena's sense of justice lay. But the carriage rolled to a stop at number thirteen, and the groom hopped down and swung open the door for her. Serena turned away, and Lily had no choice but to take his hand and step down.

At the foot of the stairs she turned, unable to let the matter lie. "It was the right thing to do, Serena."

Lady Walter glanced over her shoulder. "For you, perhaps." She gestured to the groom. "Close the door, Matthew."

Lily clenched her fists and pressed them against her abdomen, where the ledger was still tucked inside her stays, and watched as her friend's carriage rolled away. Then she turned, her face cool and blank, and went inside her home.

Serena would have to wait. Lily had work to do.

CHAPTER 22

Lily paced anxiously in her front hall, waiting for Jack to arrive. She had been pacing in the drawing room where none of her servants could see her odd behavior. But Ofelia was already in there, going through the general's ledger, and after the girl's second demand that Mrs. Adler "stop fidgeting and let me concentrate, if you please," Lily had resigned herself to watching out the window from the hall.

It was nearly time for tea when Jack arrived in a rush, explaining that he had been at his club and only just gotten her message when he returned home. "Are you well?" he demanded, looking Lily over from head to toe as soon as he had surrendered his hat to Carstairs. "No one has come by? No one suspicious?"

"Oh, for heaven's sake," Lily said, exasperated. "No, and I do not need to be reminded of that every time I see you. I would much prefer to forget the whole incident."

"Then why are you looking so frazzled?"

Lily frowned. "That is hardly a gentlemanly greeting." Catching sight of herself in the hall mirror, though, she grimaced and smoothed down her hair. "Come into the drawing room, and I will explain. Ofelia is already there."

The scene that greeted them would have been comical under other circumstances. Ofelia sat in the middle of the floor, her skirts puffing up around her like an awkward tulip, her hat, gloves, and wine all sitting forgotten beside her as she went through the general's papers. She scrambled to her feet when they entered, swiftly yanking down her petticoat and skirt to cover her ankles. "This is it," she said, breathless with excitement as she sorted the papers back into the ledger. "I am certain. Oh, Mrs. Adler, how clever of you to—oh!" Trying to avoid the wineglass on the floor, she knocked against a side table and nearly sent a vase of flowers flying.

Jack caught both the heiress and the flowers as Lily rescued the wineglass. He looked back and forth between the two women in confusion. "What the devil is going on?"

"Mrs. Adler did it." Ofelia trembled as she held out the ledger. "She did it!"

Jack took it, staring first at the book, then at Lily. "Is this—" He sat down abruptly, paging through the volume.

"General Harper's ledger." Lily couldn't help feeling smug at his dumbfounded expression. "I asked Ofelia to look it over, since she understands the paperwork better than I ever could. What did you decide, dear?"

"It's just as the captain suspected." Ofelia sat next to Jack and reached over his arm to flip through the pages, not paying any attention to his resigned sigh as he relinquished the ledger back to her before he had finished looking through it. "It was a shipping manifest you saw the general take, and look—"

"Where did you get it?" Jack interrupted.

"From the general's house, of course," Lily said. "So the shipping manifests—"

"His house?" Jack would not be distracted. "You went to his house and what? Simply asked for it?"

"Of course not; that would be ridiculous. I went for a visit with Lady Walter and sneaked it out of his study in my corset."

"You . . . what?"

"And now we need to determine whether it provides enough information for us to go to Bow Street." Lily paused, giving Jack a sideways glance. "Are you going to lecture me for doing something dangerous?"

"No," he said, shaking his head. "I am in awe of your boldness. And also appalled that you thought of that before I did. And perhaps a little tempted to wring your neck."

"That is quite a number of sensations to feel at once." Lily pursed her lips against a smile.

"It is rather an uncomfortable state of being, yes."

"You can sort out your feelings towards Mrs. Adler at a later time, Captain," Ofelia interrupted impatiently. "For now, can we decide what to do with the evidence she procured?"

"The shipping manifests," Jack agreed, looking suddenly flustered. "Everything seems to be in sets of two."

"Yes." Ofelia leaned over his shoulder and tapped the page. Lily watched, content to let them share their impressions without interruption. "The first is a contract and bill of order from the War Office."

"And each order contains a record of payment," Jack added as he turned the pages.

"And then there is a shipping manifest from Lacey and West for the same order," Ofelia added. "The *real* shipping manifest, not the ones Mr. Lacey provided them. Those are here"—she flipped further back in the book, her hands shaking with excitement as she turned the pages—"which I think are the documents you saw the general taking."

Jack whistled. "If the War Office saw these, they would know Lacey was cheating them."

"But that is what I don't understand," Lily put in. "Why would the general keep papers that prove his complicity?"

"Because they don't." Ofelia laid out the documents side by side. "These show that each shipment was not what the War Office ordered and paid for. There is no mention of General Harper at all."

"Blackmail?" Lily asked.

"Insurance at the very least," Jack agreed. "The general may have kept these documents in order to save his own skin, not thinking Mr. Lacey a trustworthy partner."

"In either case, it's enough to begin with," Lily said. "Enough to take to Bow Street."

"If Lacey does not want to hang for murder, he should point the finger at Harper, especially once he knows these documents are in the law's possession," Jack agreed.

"And Augustus shall have justice." Ofelia stood very quickly, turning away from them and swiping at her eyes with the back of her hand. "I owe him that. He was such a fool, but he meant no real harm. And he . . ." She sniffed, fishing for her handkerchief. "He would be alive were it not for me."

Lily couldn't think of anything to say. She hadn't realized that Ofelia blamed herself for Mr. Finch's death.

To her surprise, it was Jack who stepped in, taking the girl's hands. "You mustn't think that way, Miss Oswald. You made it quite plain that you were uninterested in his proposals. If he chose to follow you, to engage in some ill-gotten scheme to win your affection and your father's consent, that was his own choice." He lifted her chin with one finger. "His choice, Miss Oswald. Not yours. You are not to blame for this."

"And no matter what choices he made, his murderer should be brought to justice," Lily added. "So that is what we are going to do. For his sake and for yours, Ofelia."

Giving her eyes a final wipe, Ofelia nodded, her jaw firming. "Yes. We will."

Seeing that she was calmer, Jack stepped back, and Ofelia bent to gather up the papers and replaced them in the ledger. "To do that, we must decide what to do next," he said, gesturing at the ledger. "What do you propose, Mrs. Adler?"

They all stared at it for several moments, no one speaking. Part of Lily wanted to grab the book and run to the magistrate's office, brandishing it triumphantly. Part of her—the part that remembered the muzzle of a gun pointing at her bed—wanted to throw it in the Thames and be done with the whole business. But the practical part of her mind knew exactly what to do next.

"It cannot go to the offices on Great Marlborough Street," Lily said firmly. "Mr. Neve is the magistrate there, and he was the one who accepted Lord Walter's bribe. Even with new evidence, he might refuse to take up the investigation again."

"Bow Street, then." Jack nodded.

"We should take it to them immediately," Ofelia insisted.

Lily glanced at the clock and shook her head. "It's too late. Something of this import must be handed directly to a magistrate, not whichever fellow has been so unfortunate as to pull the late shift."

"In the morning, then?" Ofelia clutched the ledger to her chest, eyes wide and pleading.

"In the morning," Lily repeated, looking at Jack for confirmation.

The navy captain nodded, holding out his hands. "I shan't leave until I put it in the hands of a magistrate myself."

Ofelia swallowed as she handed over the ledger, then turned away, wiping at her eyes once more. Lily laid a hand on her shoulder. "It is hard to be so close, I know. But for now, we must let it be. And as that is the case, I think you should stay for tea."

They both stayed, Ofelia because she was not yet composed enough to go home and face her aunt, Jack because all he had to look forward to at home was the meager offering of a bachelor's kitchen. Lily had been amused to discover what a draw a hot meal was for an unmarried gentleman. It explained why they were such reliable attendees at society dinners.

Lily did her best to distract her two friends. They retreated to the book-room where, over cold meats and scones and a selection of fruits, they discussed society scandals, the latest exploits of the Dukes of Clarence and York, the possibility of travel to the continent— anything except the nearly solved case that had them all so on edge. It seemed to work. Ofelia laughed in shock at the princes' behavior, and Jack had several tantalizing bits of gossip to share that he had picked up over the last week. At one point, Lily fetched an atlas and began outlining the trip she and Freddy had planned to take, south through France and into the Iberian Peninsula, as soon as the war was done.

"You should still do it, Mrs. Adler," Ofelia insisted. "The war cannot last much longer."

"By myself?" Lily laughed. "Thank you for the vote of confidence, but I have never traveled farther from London than Bath. I don't think I could manage to navigate through the Continent on my own."

"Of course you could." Jack smiled. "If anyone gave you trouble, you'd simply turn that icy glare on them. You would leave a trail of terrified devotees in your wake."

"You make me sound dreadful," Lily protested. "I hope I am not terrifying!"

"Only when it does the most good," Jack said comfortably, and even Lily laughed at that.

Eventually, Ofelia stood. "I must go." A flush crept up her neck and ears. "A friend of my aunt's has offered us her box at the theater, and I shouldn't wish to be late."

Lily raised a brow. "Is Sir Edward attending the theater this evening?"

Ofelia ducked her head. "His family also has a box. And it is so easy to mingle during the promenade hour."

Jack laughed. "How much longer until he's his own man?"

"Two more months." Ofelia sighed. "It's very nearly unbearable."

"I'm sure you will manage," Lily said, squeezing her friend's hands as she led the younger woman to the door. She refrained from adding that at nineteen, any sort of wait for what you wanted was unbearable. She remembered far too clearly what it had been like to be forced to wait for Freddy. "Enjoy the performance this evening. Shall you see *As You Like It*? I hear Miss Foote is splendid . . ."

Once Ofelia was gone, Lily returned to the book-room, settling into her chair with her feet drawn up and casting a malevolent look at the ledger Jack had begun paging through once more. The expression made him laugh.

"Cheer up, Mrs. Adler; all that remains is details. The rest is solved. Between us, we must have some of the best brains in London."

"Do you mean the two of us, or are you including Miss Oswald?"

"Including her," Jack admitted, one side of his mouth kicking up in a grin. "I can admit when I'm wrong, you know, and there's more to her than I originally thought. Give her a few more years in the world, and she may might end up as clever as you are."

"Flatterer," Lily accused, but she smiled as she said it.

"That I am," he agreed cheerfully. "You would be amazed how far it gets you in life." He set the ledger aside, and without meaning to, they both settled back into their chairs, sighing in a nearly identical manner, which made Lily laugh and Jack grin wryly. "It seems we have been spending too much time in one another's company," he said.

Lily shook her head. "No such thing." Impulsively, she sat forward and reached out to take his hand. "Truly, I don't know what I would have done without you."

"On this case?" He raised an eyebrow. "I believe we covered that already."

"No, not on the case. In London. I felt so lost when I first came here, Jack. But you have been a good friend to me."

"Well, oddly enough, I discovered that I liked you." He grinned again. "Not that I should have expected anything else from someone Freddy fell in love with. I think you may be the most interesting woman in London."

"As long as there is a murder to solve," Lily said, but the mention of Freddy had made her catch her breath, though she did not pull her hand away.

Jack was watching her closely, and he saw. "You still miss him."

"Every day," Lily agreed. "Though it has been a little better, being so busy these last few weeks. Solving a murder is very distracting."

That made Jack chuckle. "And what will you do now?" he asked, absently running a finger along the back of the hand he still held.

A few weeks ago, such a gesture would have made her pull away, wrapping her grief around herself like an icy barrier. Now, comfortable in his presence and their unexpected friendship, Lily barely noticed. She shrugged. "I'm not sure. But I know I shall stay in London." Her look grew distant. "I have no desire to return to my father's home, and though Freddy's mother is all kindness . . ." She met Jack's eyes again. "I prefer being the mistress of my own home and my own affairs."

"You could always look for another murder to solve."

"Oh, don't tease." Lily pulled away, crossing her arms and scowling at him.

Jack smiled. "I wasn't." He stood. "I should be going, I think. Lady Bolton's card party is this evening, and she asked me to come balance the supper table."

"The benefits of being a bachelor with a well-turned leg and good conversation." Lily rose with him. "Rarely must you make shift to find your own meals."

"You forgot to mention my very dashing smile." Jack flashed that particular feature in her direction as they moved into the hall to collect his hat and gloves.

Lily laughed. "You are shameless, sir," she said as she held out the ledger.

"And you are a jewel among women, Mrs. Adler." He bowed as he took it. "I shall deliver this to Bow Street tomorrow."

"Jack." Lily's voice stopped him as he reached the door, and he turned back, waiting patiently. She hesitated, then met his eyes and asked, "Do you really think I could?"

He didn't need to ask what she meant. "I think you could do anything you wish, Lily. Anything at all." He settled his hat, offered a friendly salute, and sauntered down the steps, whistling.

CHAPTER 23

The next day, Lily hurried along Bond Street, unable to keep an expression of relief from her face. She moved so briskly that Anna, laden with parcels, had a hard time keeping up with her, and finally had to beg her mistress to slow down. "Whatever made you order so many hats, Mrs. Adler?" she asked as she rearranged her burdens.

Lily shook her head. "They are Lady Walter's. I offered yesterday to fetch them from the milliner for her, since she was going to be busy this morning."

"She couldn't ask her own dresser to fetch them?" Anna asked, a little crossly, for which Lily couldn't blame her.

"She just hired a new girl and did not trust her to look them over." The hats were now an excuse to see Serena and mend things after their fight, but she didn't tell Anna that. Lily eyed her maid, feeling guilty. "Would you like me to take one of them for you?"

"How positively democratic of you, Mrs. Adler."

The cold voice made both women look up sharply, and Lily took a step back before she could help herself. Standing in front of her, blocking her way forward, stood Mr. Lacey. He smiled, his expression as frosty as his voice. "A pleasure to see you again, ma'am. Do you remember me this time?"

He took a step closer, and Lily had to steel herself against retreating from him. They had left the shops and crowds behind to cut through the narrow passage that connected Bond and Bourdon Streets, but the area was hardly deserted. Surely she had no reason to fear him in the middle of Mayfair?

"Mr. Lacey." Lily smiled blandly. It was the smile that had become her best defense against curious gentlemen, and she wielded it with cold precision. "If you will excuse me, I must be going . . ."

She swallowed when he took another step closer. "I think, Mrs. Adler, that you've known who I am for some time now." He stepped closer again, clearly expecting his physical proximity to intimidate her. "As I know a few things about you, ma'am. That you are known to be friendly with a certain captain of the navy. And an heiress from the West Indies." Lily swallowed again, but her chin rose another defiant notch as he continued. "I'm not a stupid man, Mrs. Adler, but you may be a very foolish woman. You took things that are important to me. I want them back."

"You are mistaken, sir," Lily said, attempting to sound bored. She did not want him to know how much he scared her. "And you are in my way. Kindly step aside."

For a moment he looked so angry that she thought he might strike her, but immediately his smooth expression was back. Smiling mockingly, he swept her a bow and stood aside. "Just remember, you aren't a difficult woman to find."

Lily had stepped past him, but at his last words her temper rose. Before she had been scared. Now, his arrogant certainty that she would be too afraid to do anything but give him what he wanted only made her angry. So she did the last thing he would expect: she laughed. "Oh, Mr. Lacey, you are terribly amusing."

His stunned expression was exactly what she had hoped for. Looking away as if he were no longer of any interest to her, she beckoned to her maid. "Come along, Anna. The viscountess will be wondering where we are." Lily glanced back at Mr. Lacey, still glaring impotently at her, and smiled. "Do have a good day, sir."

She waited until she was on Bourdon Street proper and out of his sight before collapsing onto a bench, shaking all over. Anna, the awkwardness of her parcels forgotten, bent over her mistress. "Are you well, ma'am? Who was that dreadful man?"

Before Lily could answer, a small figure wiggled in between them and a rough voice demanded, "Miss is all right, ain't she?" Lily found herself confronted by a pair of bright eyes in a dirty face as a gangly boy peered up at her. "Old Lacey didn't do you no harm?"

"Get out of here, you urchin!" Anna ordered, about to give him a smack, but Lily held out a hand to stop her.

"Are you Jem?"

The boy nodded. "Cap'n said as I was to keep an eye on you."

"I hope you did not let Mr. Lacey see you, then," Lily said, looking him over. With his skinny frame and wrists jutting from his sleeves, he looked very young, and she did not like the idea of Jack involving him in such a dangerous task.

Jem grinned as Anna looked back and forth between them in confusion. "Not me, miss. Lacey don't look 'round when he walks. I been in more danger just walkin' from home t' work of a morning. He didn't hurt you, did he?"

"No, I am well. You get along now, and keep your head down while you keep your eyes open." Lily held out a penny, keeping it just out of the boy's reach as she ordered, "And remember you report anything that happens at my home to me, not the captain. Understand?"

"Yes'm." Jem scampered off as soon as he had the coin in hand. He disappeared from sight quickly enough, but Lily had no doubt he was still close by, keeping watch. She shook her head, impressed, and hoped Jack was paying the boy well for his help.

"Mrs. Adler, what is going on?" Anna asked, bewildered. "Why was that urchin following us?" Her voice grew indignant. "And what did that dreadful man mean by saying you stole something? How dare he accuse you of such a thing!"

"Well, he'd every right, considering that I had indeed. But I did not think he would know about it." Lily frowned, wondering how Mr. Lacey had known about the ledger if the general was keeping it secret. "This would be much easier if criminals were stupid."

Anna's eyes grew round. "Mrs. Adler, what are you mixed up in?"

"It doesn't signify, as it will be in the hands of Bow Street soon," Lily said, rising and brushing aside Anna's questions. Once the ledger was with a magistrate, it would not matter how Lacey had found out about it, after all. "Find us a hack, Anna. We need to get these things to Lady Walter, and I find I am no longer in the mood to walk."

★ ★ ★

It took less than half an hour for Lily's plans to fall apart.

When she asked to see Serena, the butler looked as uncomfortable as Lily had ever seen a butler look. "Will you be so good as to wait in the parlor while I see if Lady Walter is at home to visitors today?" he asked as Serena's dresser took the hatboxes from Anna and disappeared upstairs with them.

Lily nodded absently, her mind preoccupied, while Anna curtsied and left to visit with the other servants belowstairs. She and Serena had never before refused to be "at home" to each other, so she fully expected that Reston would return in a moment to show her to the viscountess's private parlor upstairs. After her confrontation with Mr. Lacey, her best friend's comforting, comfortable presence was exactly what she needed while she waited for news from Jack and Bow Street.

She was caught completely off guard when Reston returned, shaking his head. "I'm afraid Lady Walter is not at home today."

For a moment, Lily could not think of a correct reply. She and Serena frequently argued; there was no reason this time should have been any different. But apparently it was, and her friend did not want to see her.

"Shall I have your maid called back from the kitchen?" Reston asked.

Nodding to the butler, now feeling sick to her stomach for two reasons, Lily returned to the hall to wait for Anna.

When the maid reappeared, she was accompanied by her cousin, the footman Jeremy. Their heads were very close together, and as they drew closer, Jeremy's voice rose as he exclaimed, "Shot in his own study!"

A cold prickling made its way down Lily's spine. "Who has been shot, Jeremy?"

Both servants jumped guiltily. "Begging your pardon, Mrs. Adler." Anna glared at her cousin. "We wasn't gossiping, I promise. Jeremy was sharing some news, is all."

"What is the news?"

"I've just come from the market, ma'am." Jeremy glanced down the hall to where Reston was visible in the drawing room and lowered his voice. "Greatest shock the news was, Mrs. Adler; you don't expect to hear the like in Mayfair—"

"Jeremy, stop your babbling and get on with it," Anna snapped. She glanced sideways at her employer. "Begging your pardon, Mrs. Adler."

Lily nodded. There was no reason to think his news had anything to do with her, and yet . . . "I need you to tell me who was shot."

"It's a general, Mrs. Adler. General Alfred Harper." Jeremy took a deep breath. "His niece found him in his study this morning, shot in the chest. He's been murdered."

Lily had always prided herself on the strength of her constitution. She rarely fell ill and certainly never fainted. So when her vision began to blur, she had no idea what was happening. Dizzy, she clutched at Anna's arm for support. "I believe I need to sit down."

★ ★ ★

Jeremy helped her to a chair before he dashed off, calling for help. As soon as they were alone, Lily grabbed Anna and ordered her to find Jem, who she knew would still be lurking outside. "Tell the boy to find Captain Hartley and say, 'The general is dead; we need to know what happened; do not go to Bow Street.'" Anna looked confused, but she repeated the message dutifully and slipped outside.

It was done just in time. As soon as Anna was gone, the housekeeper arrived, saying deferentially that Lady Walter was not well enough to come downstairs and had sent her to see to Mrs. Adler. That made Lily's racing thoughts pause—either Serena was far angrier than she had thought, or she was genuinely ill. Both possibilities left Lily worried, but the news of the general's murder did not leave enough time for her to think the matter through yet. It was several minutes before Lily could assure the servants that she was well enough to go home by herself, but when she agreed to accept the offer of Serena's carriage, they relented. Lily was handed in, Anna climbing up beside her and whispering that Jem was doing as Mrs. Adler had bid.

Lily waited until she was several blocks away before giving the driver a new direction.

Ten minutes later, Lily left Anna to wait in the carriage and knocked on the Harpers' front door with no idea what she was going to do next.

The young footman who answered her knock seemed equally unprepared to deal with the situation. He stared at her, confused, for a long moment. "I don't think the family is receiving right now," he said at last, eyes wide and flustered as he glanced around the street. "I'll tell them— I'll let my mistress know you called, Miss— Mrs.—" He stumbled over his words, swallowing and casting about for someone to help him.

"Lily!" Miss Harper's voice cut through the footman's uncertainty, and Lily took immediate advantage of the opportunity to brush past him. "You heard?"

"I could not believe it when I did; I had to come straightaway. Oh, Isobel, how dreadful! What can I do?"

It was what a friend would ask, and part of Lily's mind was appalled that her question was not more genuine. But even as she spoke, she took stock of the house, eyeing the frantic, hushed movement of servants and noting the way Miss Harper's voice trembled.

"I cannot even begin to . . ." Miss Harper trailed off helplessly, and she took a deep breath. "Reggie is home, thank God, and handling things as best he can. But what can one . . . it is too terrible. They have sent for a Runner from Bow Street, of course, but what on earth are we to say? None of us knows what happened, and . . ." She trailed off, pressing the back of her hand to her mouth and shaking all over.

"First you must sit down. You've had a terrible shock." Lily glanced over her shoulder to summon the footman with an impatient look. Springing into action, he helped her guide Miss Harper into the morning room, which a glance around told her also doubled as a small study. Once his mistress was settled, he seemed at a loss once more, hovering until Lily sent him off for a glass of Madeira wine.

"Can you tell me what happened?" Lily asked as gently as possible once they were alone. "Talking might help you calm down before the Runners get here."

"There is not much to say." Miss Harper twisted her handkerchief. "I came down this morning, as I usually do. Reggie was still abed—he never wakes before eleven and usually not until noon. I saw the door to Uncle Alfred's study—" She broke off with a gasp. Lily stood immediately, looking for something to help. There was a silver vinaigrette bottle on the writing desk nearby, which she held under Miss Harper's nose. The sharp smell of the salts cleared the other woman's head, and she managed to rally and continue. "The door to Uncle Alfred's study was open. He never likes to have anyone in there but himself, barely even lets the servants clean it, so I went to see if one of them had gone in. And I found . . ." She shook her head, pressing the handkerchief to her mouth.

"You found your uncle?" Lily asked gently as she went to replace the smelling salts on the desk. As she did so, her eyes lingered over the letters scattered there, half a dozen of them addressed to Isobel Harper, the postage franked by Sir Andrew Kettering, Christopher Kettering's father. Another stack of letters, tucked behind the first, made her frown. The hand looked masculine, but far more scrawling than young Mr. Kettering's firm style. Another one was only half written; one of the Harper siblings must have been interrupted in the middle of their correspondence and had pulled a blank sheet up to cover most of the letter's contents.

"He was slumped over his desk, and the door to the garden was open." Miss Harper's quavering voice recalled Lily to what she was doing, and she sat down once more. "Mrs. Adler, you cannot begin to imagine . . . Reggie thinks a burglar must have surprised my uncle and shot him in a panic. How could such a terrible thing happen?"

"Makes a chap wonder what we pay those Bow Street fellows for if criminals still wander around, shooting gentlemen in their own homes," Reggie Harper sauntered in as he spoke and bowed, his eyes on Lily. He smiled in a manner that was far too flirtatious for someone whose uncle had just been killed. "Mrs. Adler. A pleasure to see you once more."

Miss Harper swayed. "Did you see Daniel in the hall, Reggie? He was supposed to fetch me a glass of Madeira." She shuddered. "Will you hand me the vinaigrette again, please? I know it must be my imagination, but I almost think I can still smell the gunpowder . . ."

"I am sure he's on his way," Mr. Harper said, carelessly tossing his sister the bottle, which she fumbled to catch. "Never known you to be squeamish about guns before, Iz."

"My previous experience with them has not involved the murder of my uncle," Miss Harper answered faintly, closing her eyes and breathing deeply as she swayed back against her chair.

"Lord, no, I suppose not. Lucky we weren't all murdered in our beds," Mr. Harper said with a grim laugh. "And how are you today, Mrs. Adler?"

"Dreadfully shocked." Lily didn't try to keep the chill from her voice. "You have my deepest sympathies, Mr. Harper."

"Awfully good of you to say so, Mrs. Adler." Mr. Harper was not bothered by her unspoken admonition. Lily had the feeling he spent most of his life not hearing any censure directed his way. "Of course we are terribly upset, are we not, Iz?" He gave his sister's shoulder a lazy pat. "Uncle Alfred was a miserly, grumpy old fellow, and neither of us much liked him, but that doesn't give anyone the right to go shooting him. Especially not in his own home. Damned indecent, that."

"To say the least." Lily's eyes narrowed. Luckily, at that moment, Daniel the footman returned with a decanter of wine and several glasses, preventing her from saying anything further. Instead, she studied the siblings as Mr. Harper poured out the wine, handing a glass first to Miss Harper, who looked faint once again, before offering one to Lily. She had never thought the Harper family had any strong family sentiment, though death usually prompted more fond feeling, or at least a pretense of it. But Mr. Harper was clearly not a grieving nephew. Whether Miss Harper was genuinely distressed or simply in shock from her discovery, Lily did not know.

Before Mr. Harper could say anything else insensitive, Daniel returned again, begging their pardon for his interruption. "But the gentlemen from Bow Street are here to see you, Mr. Harper, Miss Harper. Shall I show them in?"

"More than one?" Mr. Harper scowled. "I suppose that is some consolation for Uncle, in spite of being dead. At least they are taking the business seriously, though no doubt we shall have to pay handsomely to see any results."

Miss Harper lowered her eyes and said nothing, though Lily saw the other woman's hands tremble as she lifted her glass. Feeling uncomfortable, Lily looked away, her eyes lingering again on the letters strewn across the desk. The sight made her frown, though she could not have said why.

"Show them the body first, Daniel, while we finish our wine," Mr. Harper continued. "It's laid out in the kitchen. Then bring the fellows here."

Ready to take advantage of the distraction the Bow Street officers provided, Lily stood, setting down her wine. "If you will excuse me, I should take my leave. I shouldn't wish to intrude now that I know Miss Harper is well looked after."

"Damned decent of you to come by." Mr. Harper stood and bowed.

Miss Harper did not stand, but she lifted her eyes. "Thank you for your concern."

"Of course." Lily tried not to shift uncomfortably, all too aware of her ulterior motives. "If you need anything more, you will send for me?"

"We will," Mr. Harper said with another bow, not giving his sister a chance to answer. "I hope you'll not think me rude for not seeing you to the door, Mrs. Adler, but I don't like to leave my sister at such a time."

Considering that his sister had been quite alone when she first arrived, Lily thought it more likely that Mr. Harper did not like to leave his wine. But she had no intention of insisting on his escort.

The hallway was empty, as she had hoped, the servants no doubt shadowing the Bow Street gentlemen to see what they would say about the general's body. The news must have spread all over London by now, Lily thought as she hurried down the hall. It made her angry to think that the death of someone like General Harper could garner so much attention, while the murder of a man like Mr. Finch sank into murky oblivion. Her anger made her bold, and she slipped without hesitating into the general's study, closing the door silently behind her.

★   ★   ★

It felt much as it had the last time she had been there, and Lily shivered at the memory of Mr. Lacey standing just outside the door. If she had known then how dangerous he was . . . She pushed the thought aside and set to work surveying the room. The curtains were drawn, but there was no telling when someone would come in. There would be time for fear later, once she was home and safe. For now, she had to hurry.

The room was a gruesome scene. Red-brown splatters pooled on the blotter and the floor around the desk. The chair was pushed back and the rug scuffed, presumably from where the servants had moved the body. But Lily noted with interest that the desk itself was remarkably organized. The general's pens and papers were laid out neatly, as if he had just finished tidying up for the night when he was shot.

If he had been caught by surprise by the appearance of a burglar, surely there would have been some signs of a struggle? Lily frowned. At the very least he would have been startled, leaving behind shifted papers or some spilled ink. Or he could have reached for a weapon . . .

Moving as silently as she could, which still sounded unnaturally loud, she knelt behind the desk to look. The pistol that had been in the bottom drawer was gone.

Lily dusted off her hands on her dress as she stood, satisfied. The case against Mr. Lacey looked bleak indeed. And if he had killed the general, he had surely killed Mr. Finch as well.

She was feeling pleased with her deductions when she was suddenly made aware of another person in the room by a very irate male voice hissing, "What the devil are you doing?"

Lily only just had the presence of mind not to shriek in surprise. Standing in front of the closed study door, arms crossed, was Mr. Simon Page. The Bow Street officer, it seemed, was much more experienced in the art of stealth than she.

As usual, Lily took refuge in cold politeness. She lifted her chin and said, with as much poise as if she had been found in her own library instead of the study of a dead man, "Mr. Page. What a surprise to see you again."

"Mrs. Adler." His greeting was not a warm one, though Lily was impressed by the way he managed not to scowl at her. Most men, in her experience, were not so restrained when confronted with a woman trespassing on their territory. But then, most men were not officers of the law. He crossed his arms and regarded her as coolly as she was looking at him. "What are you doing here?"

"Miss Harper is a friend." She met his gaze calmly, reconsidering, then pulled a handkerchief from her reticule and dabbed at her eyes. "Such a tragedy for her to endure."

"A tragedy." Mr. Page's mouth twisted. "Why is it, Mrs. Adler, that I find you on the scene of a second tragedy so soon after the first?"

"As I said, the Harpers are friends, and I knew the general—"

"I take it, then"—Mr. Page's sarcastic tone made her forget her sorrowing posture and glare at him—"that if I mentioned to Mr. and Miss Harper that you were poking around their uncle's study, they would be unsurprised?"

She was caught, of course, and they both knew it, but she still tried to carry the moment off. "I am sure they would understand the need for solitary reflection after such a terrible—"

"Bollocks." Mr. Page plowed on without giving her room to speak. "You think I don't know why you're here? You may fancy you have a right to intrude wherever you like, Mrs. Adler, but you've no knowledge of anything involved in the pursuit of truth and justice. So I suggest you take yourself home and leave this work to those who know what they're about."

"Who know what they are about?" Lily drew herself up, well aware of how disconcerted most men felt when confronted with a tall woman and happy to use that fact to her advantage. She had thought, when she read the letter in Lord Walter's study, that Mr. Page had some sense of decency that had prompted him to continue his investigation against Mr. Neve's orders. But there was no sign of that strength of character now. "Then do please tell me exactly what you are about, Mr. Page. Have you discovered who murdered the young man found in my friend's garden? Have you even learned who he is or what he was doing—"

"As I told you before, that case is no longer being investigated. And if it were, that still would not excuse—"

"His name was Augustus Finch." If he could interrupt her, she felt no need to behave politely either. "He came to London from the West Indies and stayed at the George Inn in Southwark. He intended to persuade a girl to marry him, but to do that he first needed money, so he was attempting to blackmail—"

"Enough!" Mr. Page's glare was so fierce that Lily nearly took a step back. "I don't know what you hope to gain with such a display, but—"

"I should have thought it obvious that I am sharing the information you would have discovered yourself if you had bothered to do your job!"

"I am doing my job, Mrs. Adler. I'm investigating the murder of General Alfred Harper, which investigation, I point out, you are currently hampering. I'm not investigating that other man's murder because it isn't my job to do so."

"You are not investigating that poor man's murder because your employer was paid not to care!" Lily snapped. They stared at each other, both breathing heavily. Lily shook with anger, and her fingers were clumsy as she stuffed her handkerchief back into her reticule, preparing to leave.

The utter coldness of Mr. Page's voice made her stop. "I'm not investigating that murder because I was ordered not to by a king's magistrate, at the risk of my continued employment. And I, like any man who works for a living, must sometimes swallow my pride and abandon my own inclinations if I don't wish to see my children go hungry. We don't all have the benefit of leisure time and a large widow's portion."

Lily turned away very quickly, and the constable seemed to feel that he had gone too far, because he cleared his throat awkwardly before lapsing into silence. When she felt more calm, Lily took a deep breath. "I am not doing this because I am a bored young widow with too much time and money."

There was a long silence. "Then why are you?"

Lily turned back, her own arms crossed so that they mirrored each other in belligerence, but her voice was quiet as she asked, "Why did you try to continue investigating after I told you the magistrate had taken a bribe?"

He couldn't hide his surprise. "How did you know that?"

"One learns things. Why did you, Mr. Page?"

He regarded her steadily, his expression unreadable, before answering, "Because a man was murdered."

"Just so, sir," Lily agreed. "Because a man was murdered."

"People are murdered every day," he said. It was an echo of what Jack had once said to her, but this time Lily could see behind the cynicism of the words.

"As you have better reason than I to know. And no one can do something about all of them." She lifted her chin. "But we can do something this time."

Mr. Page muttered something that Lily thought sounded like, "Going to regret this," then let out a long breath. "Very well. Then I'll make a bargain with you." Something that was almost a smile lightened his grim face. "You stop looking down your nose at me like I'm a bumbling, know-nothing peasant. And I stop thinking of you as a bored, self-righteous featherbrain. You don't get in my way here, and I let you poke around and see what you can find. And maybe I can help you out with your murder as well."

"But I believe they are connected!"

"Prove it, then." He raised a challenging eyebrow. "I don't care what you think, Mrs. Adler, unless you can prove it."

Lily bristled at his rude words, until she realized he was actually paying her a compliment. He was speaking to her the way he would to another man, to someone whose intellect he respected. A slow smile spread across her face. Mr. Page frowned, looking wary, until she held out her hand. Mystified, he took it, and looked surprised when she shook it firmly. "Very well, Mr. Page. If I may make an observation to begin?" His wary look didn't fade, but he nodded. "General Harper used to keep a pistol in the bottom drawer of his desk."

"And you know that how?"

Lily raised her brows but did not answer. Mr. Page grumbled, but he went to check anyway. She watched calmly, no longer feeling the urge to bolt for the door. She still didn't like him, but she was sure he wouldn't reveal her presence to the Harpers.

"It's not there anymore," he said, after a moment. "Nor under the desk, or anywhere about."

"Exactly." Lily snapped her fingers. "Mr. Harper and his sister think their uncle was shot by a burglar, but if there were an intruder, he would have defended himself. So either he did not try to, or the pistol was already gone when he reached for it. Do you see?" she demanded when Mr. Page remained silent. "The general knew the man who killed him."

"Of course I see that." The snap was gone from his voice. "I'm surprised you did."

"You did not think me clever enough?"

"It's not something most people would see." Mr. Page's scowl was puzzled this time. "I had come to the same conclusion, in fact."

"Why?" Lily asked, not expecting him to share his thoughts with her.

To her surprise, he did. "The way he was shot. You can get an idea of how far away the shooter was. The general was shot by someone only a couple feet away."

"About the distance of a desk?" Lily glanced at the piece of furniture in question.

Mr. Page followed her gaze. "Possibly."

"Then whoever shot him was allowed to come very close." Lily shivered. "It must have been someone he knew quite well. He either trusted his murderer very much, or he was sure that he had enough control over the man that he posed no threat."

"A miscalculation on his part," Mr. Page said. "Mrs. Adler, I think you have an idea. Are you going to share it?" At that moment, a jumble of voices in the hallway recalled them to their location. Lily glanced toward the door, and Mr. Page sighed, looking in the same direction. "You're not supposed to be here."

She made a face. "No, unfortunately. Which means I should probably not stay any longer. But . . ." She pulled a card and a stump of pencil out of her reticule and scribbled her direction. "Can you come by this evening?"

Mr. Page took the card and tucked it into the pocket of his blue coat. "I'll be there at five o'clock. I assume you'll be going out later?"

"Yes, doing the sort of things frivolous young widows with large portions tend to do," Lily said, but there was far less acid in her tone than there would have been half an hour before. Mr. Page had the decency to flush.

The noise in the hall grew louder for a moment, and they could both hear Mr. Harper's voice raised as he called for more wine. Mr. Page grimaced. "I hope you're going to tell me that bounder killed his uncle for the money."

"He did have a great number of debts, but it seems the general paid them without complaint." Lily's voice grew thoughtful. "Though he is unconcerned by his uncle's death. Perhaps you should watch . . ." Mr. Page's eyebrows climbed toward his hairline, and this time it was Lily who blushed. "I apologize, sir. You've no need of me telling you how to do your work."

"No, but I'll be glad of any insights you have," he said, relenting a little. "As I said, this is your world, Mrs. Adler, and its citizens do their best to keep me out of it." Lily tried to think of a polite reply to such an uncomfortably true statement, but the Bow Street officer didn't seem to need one; he was already peering out the door. "The way's clear. I'll make sure they stay in the other room long enough for you to get out the front door." Looking far more of a gentleman than Lily expected, Mr. Page bowed. "Until five o'clock tonight."

Lily waited for him to enter the parlor, then slipped out the front door to where Serena's coachman was waiting around the corner as she had instructed. She allowed herself to be handed in, telling the relieved driver that he could take her home at last.

She did not notice the movement of the curtains at an upstairs window, or the shadowed face that watched her finally drive away.

CHAPTER 24

As soon as she was home, Lily penned two quick notes, informing her friends as much as she dared of the day's discoveries.

It is time, she wrote, *to lay this business to rest—now that I have the ear of Bow Street, I believe the end shall be achieved swiftly & Mr. Finch's murderer at last brought to justice.*

And then there was nothing to do but wait. It was half past two in the afternoon, hours still to go until the evening's drama would unfold. Lily busied herself with catching up on correspondence, with discussing the week's menus, with a volume of Miss Burney's *Cecilia*, all in a useless attempt to keep her mind occupied.

As she waited, she found herself nervously watching the passage to the side door, the one her mysterious burglar—the burglar she was now sure had been Mr. Lacey—had fled through. Twice, she nearly summoned Anna to sit with her, and twice she made herself take deep breaths and settle back down. It was broad daylight, and there was no possible way the shipping agent knew what she had planned.

Still, she wished Mr. Page had offered to come earlier. Waiting had become her least favorite activity—especially, she thought as the hall clock chimed five, when the people she was waiting for were not punctual.

When the bell finally rang at five past five, Lily was at the front door only three steps behind Carstairs, quivering with nervous energy. Anyone who did not know her would have been hard-pressed to see it, but Jack noticed, and he frowned as he handed over his hat and gloves, the ledger tucked tightly under his arm.

He didn't say anything, though, until they were settled into the drawing room. "Tell me."

"The general is dead."

"I know." Jack ran a hand through his hair. "Jem brought your message. The family is trying to keep it quiet, but word is spreading. What does that mean for all our theories?"

"It means we have been looking at the wrong man." Lily described her day, beginning with her confrontation with Mr. Lacey—Jack's eyes narrowed, but he said nothing—and ending with the odd understanding she and Mr. Page had reached. "He agreed to speak with us this evening, which is why I wanted you and Ofelia here. I shall be glad when this whole business is done."

"I don't wonder at it." Jack's jaw was tight as he rose to pace around the room. "And you swear you are all right? Lacey did nothing more than talk? I dislike you being here alone when he knows you took the ledger." Jack frowned. "Though, come to that, how did he know about it in the first place? The general was clearly not taking those papers with permission."

"Perhaps he meant the papers themselves?" Lily mused. "If he saw they were missing after you and Ofelia . . ." She shivered. "He said he knew about my connection to you both."

"Either way, I cannot like it. Whatever he thinks you have, he might come after you."

"He shan't have the chance." Lily's voice was firm. "After tonight, both ledger and mystery will be in Mr. Page's hands. And Hyrum Lacey, I hope, will be in Newgate on charges of murder." In spite of herself, she shivered. "I cannot begin to describe how I felt when I heard news of the general's death and realized I had been talking to the man that killed him. I nearly fainted on the steps of the Walters' house."

"You nearly fainted?" Miss Oswald had arrived and overheard the last words of their conversation. She laughed. "You? Mrs. Adler, I am shocked. I thought you were made of stronger stuff than that."

"You shan't laugh when I tell you why," Lily said. Ofelia sobered as Lily related her confrontation with Mr. Lacey and the news of the general's murder. "When Lacey cornered me, I could stand my ground because I was sure he hadn't the backbone to actually harm me. We knew he was a criminal, but we were so sure it was the general who was the violent one. But now . . ."

"You think it was Lacey, then, who killed Finch?" Jack asked.

"It must have been," Ofelia said. She had taken a seat while Lily paced and talked, and now her hands shook in her lap, though she was clearly trying to stay calm. "The general knew there was no need to take Augustus seriously, because once he went inside . . ." She shivered. "They could have planned, when they received Augustus's threat, that Mr. Lacey would be there as well, just in case. And when the general left, he . . ." she swallowed. "He finished the job."

"So what happens now?" Jack was watching them over steepled fingers. "Please do not say you intend to confront the man."

Lily shook her head emphatically. "If I never have to go near him again, I will be content. No, Mr. Page has agreed to hear us out this evening. Once he knows what we have discovered, he should have enough to arrest Lacey. And since he is the only one tied to both Mr. Finch and the general—since he stood to lose so much from Mr. Finch's threat of blackmail—"

"No jury will hesitate to convict him for murder as well as treason." Jack shook his head admiringly. "I cannot believe you did it, Mrs. Adler."

Lily shook her head. "We did it. I should have been lost without the two of you."

"I doubt that, Mrs. Adler," Ofelia said. "It might have taken you a little longer—"

"And Lord knows how you would have managed that business at Lacey and West by yourself," Jack added.

"But you would have solved it." Ofelia still looked shaken, but she nodded firmly. "You'd not have accepted anything less."

"Well, I am glad I did not have to do it alone," Lily said.

A knock at the front door stopped her from saying more, and in the silence they could hear the rumble of a male voice. There was a short pause, then footsteps that sounded very loud, before Carstairs swung open the drawing room door.

"Mr. Simon Page of Bow Street to see you, madam."

Lily and her friends stood. "Thank you, Carstairs," she said, glad that she sounded calmer than she felt. "If you would please pour for the gentlemen before you go. Mr. Page, would you care for something to drink?"

"Mrs. Adler." The principal officer bowed very correctly. "Whiskey, thank you, if you have it."

"She always does." Jack's tone was stiff, but he nodded politely enough to the other man, apparently ready to extend him the benefit of the doubt at last. Lily was grateful, since Mr. Page had already demonstrated his willingness to do the same for them. Jack glanced back at the butler. "The same for me, Carstairs, thank you."

They all sat while the butler handed around drinks. Ofelia's expression was strained as she watched Mr. Page; Lily, worried about the girl, gestured for Carstairs to pour her a glass of sherry before he withdrew.

Mr. Page, by contrast, looked far more at ease in an upper-class drawing room than Lily would have expected. He did not slouch or lounge in his chair, but sat upright and comfortable. It was confidence in his profession, she decided. He believed in his work and, by extension, his right to be there. Her estimation of him grew.

Mr. Page sipped his drink, grimaced with appreciation, and lifted his glass to her. "My thanks, Mrs. Adler. But I hope you don't think to distract me."

She was about to protest when she noticed the glimmer of humor in his expression; he was teasing her. For a moment that left her even more flustered than her indignation had, though she did not show it. "Merely attempting to make a difficult revelation a little more palatable."

The constable set aside his glass and leaned forward. "So you hinted at the Harpers' residence, ma'am. And I assume these two friends of yours"—his gaze took in Jack's watchful posture without changing, though he looked surprised by Ofelia's presence—"have something to say to the matter?"

"Captain Hartley you know already. And this is Miss Oswald—"

Mr. Page's chin jerked in surprise. "Oswald?" he interrupted.

Lily paused. "Miss Ofelia Oswald. The two of you are not acquainted?"

"No, no." The Bow Street officer cleared his throat. "My apologies for interrupting, ma'am. Please continue."

Lily exchanged a look with Ofelia, who looked equally confused, and cleared her throat. "Miss Oswald has lately come from the West Indies—as did the murdered gentleman who was found in Lord and Lady Walter's gardens two weeks ago." Lily grimaced. It was still strange to have words like *murdered gentleman* leave her mouth so easily.

Mr. Page's voice was gentle as he addressed Ofelia. "Your sweetheart, was he?"

"No." She lifted her chin. "My affections are elsewhere engaged. And that was the trouble." With admirable brevity, she explained how Augustus Finch had followed her to London without her knowledge before confronting her at the Walters' ball.

"And how did you become aware of his presence that night?" Mr. Page pulled out a small memorandum book to make notes.

"I saw him through a window," Ofelia said at last. "Of course, I knew he was not supposed to be there. I oughtn't have gone out to speak with him, but I did not want him hanging about and ending up arrested for trespassing. Or . . ." She hesitated, then added, "Or saying anything about me that might be misconstrued if anyone had discovered him."

"And what did you talk about when you went out to the garden?" Mr. Page's pencil paused as he waited.

Ofelia hesitated again, and Lily leaned forward in her chair. Somehow, she had never thought to ask what Ofelia and Mr. Finch had discussed that night in the garden, and the realization surprised her.

Ofelia looked down at her hands. "He asked me to marry him. Again. I told him not to be absurd, that he knew I did not care for him in that way. I told him I had to return before someone noticed my absence, that he needed to leave before someone saw him lurking about. And then . . ."

"And then?" Lily prompted when the girl trailed off.

Ofelia scowled. "I tried to leave. He grabbed my arm to stop me and said all I cared for was catching a rich husband. And I slapped him."

Mr. Page let out a surprised laugh. "Beg pardon. I shouldn't laugh, I know, poor fellow being dead and all. And I can see you're distressed, so I apologize. But good for you, girl."

"I did not think it so well done when I saw a sketch of his face in the paper the next morning," Ofelia said quietly.

"No, I imagine not." Mr. Page nodded. "Is that how you left things? With a quarrel?"

His voice had sharpened again, and Lily felt a twinge of unease. But Ofelia shook her head. "No, thank heavens. We both apologized, and . . . then I left. I left him there, and I shall never forgive myself for it."

"It was not your fault," Lily said.

"And he didn't tell you what he intended to do with the rest of his night?" Mr. Page asked. When Ofelia shook her head, he turned to Lily. "I suppose, Mrs. Adler, this is where your story comes in. Repeat it for me, if you will." There was a hint of a smile on his face. "This time I promise not to interrupt."

"How generous," Lily murmured, unable to resist. Jack snorted. She laid out the facts of her involvement, beginning with the blackmail attempt she had overheard and continuing on through the investigating of her suspects, one by one. Mr. Page began by taking notes but eventually laid down his pencil and simply listened.

When she got to arranging for Jack to apply for work at Lacey and West, though, Mr. Page held up a hand. "I should like to hear this part from Captain Hartley, if you will, Captain?"

"Certainly." Jack leaned back in his chair, grinning, and Lily fought the urge to roll her eyes. The navy captain told his part of the tale with a sailor's flair for drama, making it sound far more harrowing than he had when trying to reassure her after the fact—though she suspected no more harrowing than the actual scrape had been.

"I'll admit this is all fascinating," Mr. Page said once Jack was done. "And it makes a damned good—beg pardon—a dashed good story. But you have yet to offer me proof, Mrs. Adler. And that is what the law requires."

"When it chooses to require it," Ofelia murmured. Mr. Page scowled, and Lily jumped in.

"Then you will be pleased, sir, that we do have some proof to offer. Captain?"

His expression more serious now, Jack handed Mr. Page the gray ledger. It was such an unassuming thing, Lily thought as she watched Mr. Page look through it. But so much rested on the information it contained.

Lily cleared her throat and continued. "Captain Hartley was going to bring that to a magistrate at Bow Street today. But when I heard of General Harper's murder, I knew the situation had changed. And after . . ."

"After I caught you sneaking around their house, you knew you had to see me in person to convince me you were right?" Mr. Page finished dryly.

"Something like that. And now you have seen our evidence, is there anything else you wish to know?"

"I wish to know how you came by these documents." Mr. Page shook his head. "But it's easy enough to say it was found in the general's library." He looked up at last. "I assume that was where it was found?"

"Quite possibly," Lily agreed, the corners of her eyes crinkling with humor.

Mr. Page shook his head again, but this time he was smiling grimly. "Well, Mrs. Adler. I'll admit to being impressed, both by what you've discovered and by your willingness to involve yourself in such a messy business."

Lily could not help the edge to her voice. "A man was killed, sir. Someone needed to care." With an apologetic glance at Ofelia, whose jaw was clenched very tightly, she amended her statement. "Someone who was in a position to do something about it needed to care."

"Aye, you've the right of it there." Mr. Page rubbed his chin thoughtfully, eyeing her, before apparently making up his mind. "Very well then, ma'am, you've made what I have to do a good deal easier, and in exchange I'll share with you what I've learned myself."

Lily's eyes widened in surprise. "I thought you said you could not investigate without putting your job in jeopardy."

"And it was true enough," Mr. Page agreed, though the tips of his ears had grown red with what she was shocked to realize was embarrassment. "But now I've been tasked with solving the murder of General Alfred Harper, and as you keep insisting, the two deaths are related. Besides which, such a masterful dressing down as you gave, ma'am, is enough to shame even the most cautious man into action." That made Jack laugh, and the two men exchanged a wry glance that was, for the first time, full of genuine understanding. "Your young friend was correct," Mr. Page continued, with a nod toward Ofelia. "The law is supposed to be concerned with truth and justice above all, but it does not always choose to be. And that's not right."

Lily leaned forward. "How could you have discovered something so quickly?"

"I believe it is his job to do so," Jack said quietly, a hint of laughter in his voice.

Mr. Page's expression could almost be called a smirk. "I spent my afternoon paying a visit to the George Inn in Southwark," he said, pulling a packet of papers from his jacket. "And I found a few things of interest."

"The George Inn?" Lily asked. "How on earth did you know to look there?"

The Bow Street officer raised an eyebrow at her. "'His name was Augustus Finch, and he was staying at the George Inn in Southwark.' Those were your words, were they not, ma'am?"

"Yes, but . . ." Lily paused, flustered. "I'd no idea you were even listening to me."

"I wasn't really," Mr. Page said with a grin. "But I still remembered it."

"What on earth could you have found?" Ofelia asked, leaning forward. "I would swear we combed every inch of that room."

"I'm sure you did, but these weren't in his room," Mr. Page said. "He had left them in the innkeeper's safe. Paid a pretty sum for the privilege, I'd hazard, but they were happy to hand them over when I said the fellow'd been murdered. Folks don't want any of that sort of nastiness attaching to their place of business." He looked pleased by their surprise. "There are some benefits to being an officer of the law, you know."

"There would have to be, to make anyone choose it as a profession," said Jack, but his voice lacked any malice.

The constable grinned at him. "Makes up for all the sour expressions from your folk."

"I'm sure it is charming to see you two getting along so well, but what was it you found, sir?" Ofelia broke in, her hands clutching impatiently at the fabric of her dress.

"Well, miss, though I didn't know it until just a moment ago, what I found is a letter for you." He held out a neatly folded missive, still sealed, with *Miss Ofelia Oswald, 29 North Audley-street London* scrawled across the front. Lily frowned at the direction—no, she realized suddenly, at the handwriting. The rubbing Jack had taken of Mr. Finch's letter to the general had given her a sense of the poor boy's hand, but seeing his writing in its original form reminded her of something. But, for the life of her, she couldn't quite remember what.

"For me?" Ofelia's quavering voice recalled Lily from her thoughts; the girl was reaching toward the letter with a trembling hand. "What does it say?"

"I had planned to call on you at Audley Street tomorrow and ask you to tell me," Mr. Page said, his voice gentle as he handed the missive over. "I'd no thought of finding you here." He gave Lily a wry glance. "Though, given Mrs. Adler's tenacity, perhaps I should have. Will you tell us what it says?"

The young heiress nodded as she slit open the blot of wax and unfolded the letter. She was shaking all over but was so drawn into herself that Lily did not feel she had the right to offer comfort just at the moment. Ofelia, she remembered with a stab of sympathy, had loved Augustus Finch once—and here he was, writing to her from very nearly beyond the grave.

Ofelia cleared her throat and read the letter aloud. "*General Alfred Harper, of Park Street, London, has conspired with Mr. Hyrum Lacey, of the shipping firm Lacey and West, to steal from the British Government in a time of war. The general has used his rank and position within the War Office to grant contracts of shipment to Lacey and West, with the private understanding that the goods paid for are not to be fully stocked or delivered. Between them, they split the profits from the bills of sale. If you—*" She cleared her throat again, and her voice trembled as she continued. "*If you are reading this, one of them has killed me for this knowledge.*" Ofelia's voice dropped to a whisper. "*I love you, Augustus.*" She turned to Lily, tears slipping down her cheeks. "Why would he do this?"

"Oh, my dear." Lily held out her arms and let the girl bury her face against her shoulder, sobbing. "He meant what he said in his letter. If something happened to him, he made sure he wouldn't be the only person in possession of the facts."

"I imagine he thought that if he failed to return from his mission of blackmail, the innkeeper would eventually clear out his papers and send the letter on." Mr. Page's voice was grim. "Who knows, he might have even intended to see them brought to justice, regardless of whether they paid him or not."

"Questionable morality, that," Jack said, but he said it quietly, which Lily was grateful for, so that Ofelia did not hear it over her tears.

It only took a moment more for the girl to gather herself together, though she still hiccupped with emotion as she pulled out her hand-kerchief and wiped her eyes. "I apologize; I was overcome," she said quietly. "Mr. Page . . ." She hesitated; then her jaw firmed and she held out the letter. "Will you see that this is returned to me, after it has served its use as evidence?"

"Of course, ma'am," he said, and his brisk tone made them all sit up straighter, even Ofelia. "Between this letter and the ledger Mrs. Adler *acquired*"—his lips twitched with something that was almost a smile—"I think the matter is sewn up pretty tightly."

"I am pleased to hear it," Lily said, still watching Ofelia out of the corner of her eye. "But I would be more pleased to know that you intend to do something about it."

"Oh, I'll do something about it, sure enough." Mr. Page's expression was grim as he stood. "I asked Mr. Harper if his uncle had any visitors last night. Apparently the general was expecting someone to come by about business and had his niece tell the servants not to wait up. Mr. Harper said that was when he thought the burglar was able to sneak in. I'll admit, I first suspected the nephew—I thought he was spinning quite the story. But Miss Harper confirmed it. And Mr. Harper, I discovered this afternoon, was gambling at his club until six in the morning. Dozens of people saw him. But now I'd say we have a damned good—beg pardon—a good idea who the general was meeting."

"What happens next?" Ofelia asked, twisting her handkerchief tightly between her hands.

"I give this evidence to a magistrate," said Mr. Page gently. "And with evidence to tie Lacey to Finch's murder as well as the general's, we set about getting justice for your friend. He'll be arrested before morning, assuming he's not fled."

"He has not," Jack said. At their surprised looks, he shrugged. "Told Jem to keep watch as soon as he brought news of the general's murder. He would have sent word if Lacey tried to leave London. No need to look so surprised," he added, grinning. "I have been known as a competent strategist from time to time."

"Aye, aye, Captain," Lily murmured, smiling.

"I hope you'll call your watcher off once Lacey's in custody," Mr. Page said. "And Mrs. Adler?" He fixed her with a stern look. "You've done a remarkable job, but you mustn't put yourself in danger any further. This man has killed twice now. You'll leave the rest of this matter to Bow Street."

"Hear, hear," Jack agreed.

Lily nodded. "I would never dream of interfering, Mr. Page."

He nodded in return before tossing back the rest of his whiskey, but he caught her eye and held it as he set down the glass, and there was a sharpness in his gaze that made her pay attention.

"Ofelia, if the captain pours you something stronger than sherry, will you drink it?" she asked. The girl nodded, still looking shaken, and Lily stood. "I am going to show Mr. Page out."

"Much obliged," he said, bowing as he held open the door for her.

Lily waited until they were at the front door. "Is it the other papers?"

He snorted. "You're a quick study, ma'am."

Lily took the closely written sheets of paper that he held out to her. "Letters?"

Mr. Page nodded. "I don't think there's much in them, but I thought you ought to have a look. You know the rules of your world better than I do. What can you tell me of them?"

"A description of a house party, which seems innocent enough, but there is no signature at the bottom." Lily glanced at the constable. "You did not want Miss Oswald to see these."

"No. Did she write them?" Mr. Page asked bluntly.

"They are not in her hand," Lily replied, shaking her head. She frowned as she turned to the next sheet. "The style is quite distinctive, but . . ."

"But odd," Mr. Page agreed as she trailed off. "If you pressed me, I don't think I could say for sure if it was written by a man or a woman."

"Given the lack of signature, if the writer is a woman, I would say she is either quite young or quite married. Otherwise she'd have less need to hide her identity. If it is a man . . ." Lily found herself trailing off once more as she glanced at the final page. The others she had merely skimmed, but this one began in the middle of a sentence at the top of the paper, and her eyes grew wide as she read it.

> . . . *beg you will say nothing of this matter to anyone else. You know me well enough by now—& we have always been so much in sympathy with each other—that you will understand why there is no one else to whom I may confide such a thing—but nor can I keep it to myself any longer. It is dreadful to contemplate and yet, at the same time, I almost find myself admiring the mind that could devise such a clever scheme. Practical as you are, I can almost believe you would feel the same!*

Lily looked up. "You think this was how Mr. Finch got his information."

"It is a possibility." Mr. Page spoke cautiously, but there was a gleam of certainty in his eye that was unmistakable.

"And the rest of the letter is missing." Lily frowned. "If it was his proof, why would Mr. Finch not have put the whole letter aside for safekeeping?"

"You saw the body, Mrs. Adler. Do you recall seeing anything on the ground beside it?"

Lily stared at him, trying to picture that awful night. Her mind had been racing with horror and panic, but she had forced herself to stay calm as she looked around and saw . . . "Paper. Scraps of paper, ripped up and trod into the mud." Another memory intruded, one that she hadn't stopped to think about before. "I think I heard the man who was being blackmailed ask, 'Who wrote this?'"

"Did you?" Mr. Page nodded in satisfaction. "Then I would hazard that Mr. Finch brought the incriminating letter as proof of his seriousness, and the murderer, rather than risk it falling into someone else's hands, simply destroyed it then and there."

"A careless way to destroy something," Lily pointed out.

"But effective for someone in a panic with no time to spare."

Lily nodded, but her mind was already moving past that detail. "But then who wrote the letters?" she asked. "I had assumed Mr. Finch learned of the scheme when the general visited Nevis. But it seems someone else knew."

Mr. Page frowned as he took the papers back. "A puzzle, that. You said it was not your friend, but she might have some idea who else Mr. Finch knew in London."

Lily nodded, glancing back at the parlor door. "I shall keep my ears open, but I won't press her just yet. The poor thing has gone through enough these past weeks." She gave Mr. Page a quick glance. "They were engaged once."

He nodded. "I suspected something like that. In which case, she may not know anything. If these were written by a woman . . ."

"He would hardly tell her that," Lily said quietly.

"Just so." The constable scowled at the letters, then tucked them into his coat with a sigh. "Well, whoever the writer was may not matter once we have Lacey. I won't keep you from your friends any longer, or they'll begin to wonder what we're talking about out here."

"They likely already are," Lily said, holding out her hand. "Thank you for hearing me out, Mr. Page. I am sincerely glad that you came to yell at me in the general's study."

"Mrs. Adler." He took her hand and bowed over it, smiling wryly. "I am, too. And I hope that after this, you will be able to spend your evenings doing only the sorts of things frivolous young widows do."

Lily watched the door close behind him, a thoughtful expression on her face. "But that sounds so very dull," she murmured to herself as she went to rejoin her friends.

★　★　★

The letter from Mr. Page came the next morning.

Lacey is arrested, it read. *He will remain at Newgate in whatever comfort his ill-gotten gains can purchase & will be brought to the Assizes after an inquest into the general's death.*

It should have made her relieved. But Lily, with nothing more to do, felt restless.

In an effort to distract herself, she called on Serena, but the butler told her at the door that Lady Walter was indisposed and seeing no one that day. He unbent enough to assure her that the viscountess was, in fact, unwell, and he had been instructed to admit no one.

Though Lily was glad to know Serena was not turning her away specifically, she still felt out of sorts with their quarrel unresolved. Returning home, she began and abandoned three letters, let a pot of tea grow cold, badgered Anna about new sleeves for one of her dresses, and finally found herself cataloging the books in Freddy's library for lack of anything else to keep her attention. She was wondering if she should get rid of the two volumes of James Fordyce's *Sermons to Young Women* when Carstairs came in to ask if she was at home to visitors.

Glad of the distraction, Lily immediately replied in the affirmative, only to find herself handed Isobel Harper's card. Her stomach lurched, but she dusted off her hands, gave her hair a quick pat, and went into the drawing room.

"Miss Harper! What brings you here?"

Miss Harper looked pale. "I needed . . . I had to see someone, Mrs. Adler, and I felt sure that you would understand. Mr. Page of Bow Street came to see us this morning." She glanced at Lily. "I believe you know Mr. Page?"

"He came to investigate that dreadful affair at Lord and Lady Walter's." Lily hesitated, wondering how much it was safe to say, before adding, "He seemed a competent man. I trust he had some news for you and your brother?"

"Ah." Miss Harper's face was unreadable, and she lifted her handkerchief to dab at her eyes, further obscuring her expression. "It was as good as such news can be. It seems—" Her voice caught. "It seems they have made an arrest in the matter of my uncle's murder."

Lily hoped her expression gave nothing away as she said, "What a relief that must have been. Please, sit down and tell me what happened. If you wish to, of course."

Miss Harper sat, but her gaze beneath her lashes was unexpectedly sharp. "I shan't be coy, Mrs. Adler, and I beg you will not be either. From what Mr. Page let fall, I gather that the murderer's arrest was not solely the result of Bow Street's efforts."

It took Lily a moment to decide how to respond. "I am sure that the Bow Street gentlemen did everything they could to find the man who killed your uncle."

"But they generally do not move so quickly, especially for as little incentive as my brother offered them." Miss Harper's voice grew sharper. "Nor do they generally spend several minutes in conference with ladies of quality who have paid me a visit of condolence but delayed leaving the house when they said they would." Lily's eyes widened, and Miss Harper looked down. "My dresser saw you leave and told me of it. I can hardly be anything but grateful, Mrs. Adler. Will you not tell me how you came to be such a benefactor to my family?"

"You've a shrewd mind, Miss Harper," Lily said, stalling while deciding how to respond.

Miss Harper smiled sadly, inclining her head to acknowledge the compliment. "It was one of the few traits my uncle and I shared. If you do not wish to tell me, I understand. But . . . my brother and I owe you more than we can repay. I should at least like to know the extent of your efforts on our behalf."

Lily hesitated, feeling both uncomfortable and flattered. In that moment, as Miss Harper raised the handkerchief to dab at her cheeks once more, Lily caught the watchful expression in the other woman's eyes. Miss Harper's tense posture, Lily realized, had nothing to do with either gratitude or grief.

Lily's jaw firmed. "You asked me not to be coy, Miss Harper, so I shall be blunt instead. You are not here to express your gratitude."

The handkerchief dropped abruptly. "I—I beg your pardon?"

"No." Lily raised a brow. "You are here to learn what I know of your uncle's business and how likely I am to reveal that information."

Miss Harper's hands trembled. "My uncle's business?"

"Not the army, of course, but the affairs of a more secretive nature that he engaged in with Mr. Hyrum Lacey." Lily paused. "I trust it was Mr. Lacey they arrested?"

"It was." Miss Harper's voice was faint.

"And did he confess?"

"No. Not to murder, nor to—" Miss Harper broke off, eyes narrowing. "Nor to the business he engaged in with my uncle."

"The treasonous mishandling of English goods, to the detriment of the war effort?"

Lily said the statement so baldly that Isobel flinched, the motion knocking her reticule from her lap and spilling its contents. Flustered, she bent to gather her purse and letters; Lily retrieved the silver vinaigrette that had tumbled under her own seat.

"What were we saying?" Miss Harper asked faintly as they resumed their seats.

Lily kept her voice more gentle this time. "We were discussing treason, Miss Harper. I don't wonder that you flinch at it."

Miss Harper's nod was jerky. "Just so. Apparently Mr. Lacey refuses to say anything, but the police have their evidence. The inquest is this afternoon, and likely the case will go to trial."

Lily sighed. "It will be a dreadful business for your family, and I am sorry for it. But justice will prevail, and we can hope the scandal blows over quickly."

"It is just that which concerns me. You seem to know a great deal about my family's affairs, Mrs. Adler, and you must understand how that racks my nerves."

"If I were interested in scandal, I should have shouted the rumors at the next rout party, not gone to the Runners."

Miss Harper blushed. "I do not doubt your goodness, Mrs. Adler, but in such a matter, you must understand—"

"That you have a great deal to lose." Lily sighed. "I know. And hope you will believe me when I promise that I've no intention of saying anything publicly. Not unless it is required of me at the trial, which I hope to God it will not be." She made a face. "I should hate to be part of such a spectacle."

"As should any lady," Miss Harper agreed. "A clever mind likes an audience, but to speak at a public trial—!" She shuddered. "I hope it will not come to that for either of us."

"Your uncle's actions will come out in the trial, though. They must. Otherwise no jury will believe that Mr. Lacey had a cause for willful murder."

"I know. But the next session of the assizes is not for six months, and that is enough—"

She broke off abruptly, but Lily recalled Miss Harper's first failed engagement and understood. "That is enough time for your engagement to Mr. Kettering to be formally announced. You'll not be able to marry, of course, until your year of mourning for your uncle has passed. But if the formal announcement is made, Mr. Kettering will not be able to cry off when the news comes out."

Miss Harper looked away, but she nodded all the same. "Do you think me heartlessly mercenary, Mrs. Adler?"

"No." Lily pitied the other woman. "I have never known what it is like to be penniless, nor to be dependent on a man who has done such terrible things. I cannot fault a woman who wishes to escape that fate."

"So you know everything, then." Miss Harper's sigh was shaky enough to make her whole body tremble. "The war, the money . . . But you will say nothing?"

"I will say nothing. Life with your uncle has been filled with enough suffering, Isobel, and there is more yet to come when Mr. Lacey's trial begins. I do not have it in me to add to it."

Miss Harper said nothing, merely nodded and gathered herself together, standing. Lily, her heart aching with sympathy, stood also and showed her out.

But sympathy did not stop her mind from working, and there was something in Miss Harper's performance that made her frown—for a performance it had been, at least at the beginning, when Miss Harper had wanted to find out how much Lily knew.

Lily rang for a servant, pacing the room thoughtfully until Anna appeared. "Excellent, you are just who I wanted to speak with," she said without preamble when the maid appeared. "Would you say your cousin Jeremy knows most of the gossip about Mayfair families?"

It took Anna a moment to get over her surprise; clearly, the question was not one she had been expecting. "Jeremy, ma'am?" she asked. "In the general way of speaking, if he doesn't know it, no one does."

"Excellent." Lily stopped pacing, but her thumbs still tapped together thoughtfully. "When will you see him next?"

"At services on Sunday."

Lily nodded. "I need you to ask your cousin what he knows of the Kettering family."

"Are you curious about anything in particular?"

"Their finances. And about the elder son, Christopher." Lily fixed Anna with a pointed look. "And I hope I do not need to tell you to be discreet about asking."

"Of course not, ma'am." Anna started to say something else, hesitated, bit her lip, and finally said, very carefully, "I've never known you to take much interest in gossip, ma'am."

"Only when I need to. And this time I think it might be important."

Anna's brows drew together. "Mrs. Adler, are you mixed up in something . . . unwise?"

Lily laughed shortly. "Most likely, Anna. But not the sort of unwise you're thinking of."

"I'm thinking, Mrs. Adler, that you've been acting odd of late. And there was that burglar who broke in here—with a pistol; I saw you searching for it that night—and you meeting secretly with the captain and that Miss Oswald. And that awful shopkeeper who said you stole something from him, and that man from Bow Street last evening . . ." Anna stopped abruptly, looking concerned that she had said too much. "I don't mean to be impertinent, ma'am. Only I'm worried."

Lily pursed her lips. "I've never been able to sneak much by you, have I, Anna?"

That made the maid grin. "No, ma'am. Not for years."

"Well then. What would you say if I asked whether you thought I could solve a murder?"

Anna's eyes grew wide. "I would say . . ." She swallowed. "I would say, ma'am, that if any lady of quality could, it's you."

Lily smiled faintly. "I hope that is true, Anna. And I hope I am simply overthinking things. But to be sure, I need to find out what Jeremy knows of the Ketterings. Can you do that?"

"Yes, ma'am."

"Excellent." Lily's smile grew. "I shall even throw in an extra half day for you next month. But remember," she cautioned. "Discretion."

The maid curtsied. "Yes, Mrs. Adler. Always."

CHAPTER 25

Though she did not want to mix in company, Lily was even less inclined to sit at home, where she knew she would feel as though someone were watching her. The Walters were holding a small evening party, and Margaret Harlowe and her husband, blissfully unaware of both murder and mystery, had offered to call for Lily in their carriage. It would do, she decided, for a distraction, and would hopefully be a chance put things back to normal between her and Serena.

Lily stretched as she emerged from her bath, trying to shake away the tension between her shoulders. "The gray silk tonight, Anna." Wrapping the robe that Anna held out around herself, she went to her dressing table and began to brush out her hair. "But only if you had time to mend the tear in the petticoat. Otherwise, the lavender-and-gold will do."

"There's nothing wrong with the gray silk, ma'am. I looked and looked for that tear, but the petticoat was right as rain, far as I could see. Nothing ripped at all."

Lily paused, hairbrush still half raised. "I found at least three inches of lace torn off."

"I don't mean to argue, ma'am, but you can see for yourself." Anna held out the gown. "There's nothing wrong with the petticoat."

She was right. Lily stared, puzzled by her mistake and wondering why an undamaged petticoat left such a sinking feeling in her stomach. It meant something, but she couldn't quite . . .

Lily sat up abruptly. "Anna, do you remember which reticule I carried that night?"

"The night of the Walters' ball?" Anna didn't ask why she wanted to know; she was far too used to the quick jumps Lily's mind made. "The silver-and-black one, ma'am."

"Fetch it for me. See if there is anything inside."

Lily continued brushing her hair as her maid rummaged in the wardrobe. She didn't want to draw any conclusions until—

"Well, if that isn't the prettiest thing!"

Lily set down her brush and turned from the mirror. "What is it?"

"Fancy that, ma'am." Anna held the piece of lace Lily had found next to the dead man's body, a curious expression on her face. "It's quite fine, but it didn't come from your gown. Someone else must have suffered a tear. Lord, I don't envy trying to mend that rip!"

"No, I am glad it was not my gown after all." Lily fingered the delicate ruffle.

"Is everything all right, Mrs. Adler? That bit of trim isn't important, is it?"

"No." Lily frowned. Something was making her uneasy. "I cannot think why it would be . . ." She stared at the fabric in her hand, trying to catch the idea fluttering at the corner of her mind, but was interrupted by the chiming of the clock from downstairs. "Goodness, is that the time?" The Harlowes would be calling for her soon, and she still needed to dress. Lily tucked the matter of the lace in the back of her mind to examine when she had more time.

She had just finished dressing, and Anna was setting the final ribbon in her hair, when Carstairs cleared his throat from the doorway. "Beg pardon, Mrs. Adler, but there are visitors here to see you."

Lily turned in surprise. "Carstairs, you know perfectly well I am expected at the Walters' at half eight."

"Lady Walter sends her apologies." He held out a folded card with Serena's monogram on it. "The viscountess is unable to entertain this evening and begs her guests' forgiveness for the late notice. And I thought that you would wish to see the two gentlemen."

"Two gentlemen?" Lily frowned over her friend's note. Serena was normally so energetic, but this was several bouts of ill health within a single week.

"Yes, ma'am. Captain Hartley and the gentleman from Bow Street."

"Oh! I shall see them immediately." Lily hurried downstairs, concern about Serena set aside. Jack and Mr. Page would not have called unless they had news, especially not together. Judging by the grim expressions that greeted her in the drawing room, it was not good. Too impatient for polite inquiries, Lily asked bluntly, "What happened?"

"Mrs. Adler, are you at liberty for the next two hours?" Mr. Page, normally so stoic, was twisting his hat between his hands.

Lily frowned at him, then at Jack. "I am, as a matter of fact. My plans for the evening were just a moment ago canceled. Why?"

Mr. Page hesitated, so Jack spoke up. "Mr. Page needs you to come to Newgate with him. He has asked me to provide my escort as well, as it is not a safe destination."

"To the prison." It was the last thing she expected. "What could I possibly do there?"

"Lacey has asked to see you."

Lily shivered, remembering Mr. Lacey's cruel expression as he cornered her on the street. "Did he say why?"

Mr. Page and Jack exchanged an unhappy look before the constable spoke. "You won't be surprised to hear that Lacey denies any involvement in General Harper's death. He says he *does* have information to share—but only with you."

A sick, nervous feeling settled in the pit of Lily's stomach. But both men were looking at her with such a mixture of worry and hopefulness that she could not bring herself to say no. Instead, she took a deep breath and lifted her chin. "Of course I shall come. If you will give me a moment to fetch a cloak?"

"You should wear one with a hood, and a veil as well." Jack's agitation made Lily feel a little better about her own nerves. "It would not do for anyone to see your face as we arrive."

By the time they climbed into the waiting carriage—one without markings of any kind, which Mr. Page said Bow Street kept for the use of its officers—Lily was swathed from head to foot and totally unrecognizable. The thought gave her some comfort as they rattled through the twilight to Newgate Prison.

The carriage lamps cast a dim glow inside the carriage as they rode, enough to illuminate the expressions on the two men's faces. Mr. Page looked every inch an officer of the law determined to do his duty, however unpleasant. Jack looked thoroughly dismayed and wasn't bothering to hide it at all.

"You look as if you have a toothache," Lily said, nudging him with her elbow in an attempt to lighten the grim mood, which was weighing on her already tightly wound nerves. "I thought military men were supposed to be fond of charging in, ready for action at a moment's notice and so forth."

"Perhaps you are thinking of the army," Jack said with enough dignity to make Lily smile in spite of herself. "But in the navy, one does not make it so far as captain without learning when is the time to charge and when is the time to proceed with caution."

"And what time would you say this is, Captain?" Mr. Page asked.

Jack glanced at Lily. "Most certainly time for caution. I'd not trust Lacey as far as I could throw him."

The Bow Street officer grunted in agreement. It was strange, Lily thought, to watch them getting along after the undisguised animosity of their previous meetings. Both were men of action, accustomed to taking charge of whatever situation they found themselves in. And both, she reflected ruefully, had a great deal of pride. That had been obvious as much in their dealings with her as with each other. When they had set that aside, however, they had clearly discovered a great deal in common with one another—and, Lily realized with no little pride of her own, with her as well.

The thought bolstered her nerves as they entered the gates of the prison and alighted, though Lily was still content to stay hidden behind her veil and let Mr. Page handle the guard who came to meet them. She had never understood the men and women who visited the prison for entertainment. A feeling of misery hung in the air, and the smell of too many unwashed bodies crowded too close together made her feel faint. She could not feel sorry for men like Mr. Lacey—those imprisoned and awaiting trial for serious crimes. But many of the prisoners, she knew, were guilty of no more than small theft or petty fraud, and too many of them were no more than children. The thought made her shudder, and she was glad of the support when Jack offered her his arm.

As Mr. Page approached a surly-looking man in something that might once have been a uniform before it became covered in food stains and muck, Jack bent to murmur in her ear, "Lacey had money enough for the State Side; Mr. Page will negotiate a visit. Hopefully they will not charge too highly for the privilege."

They did not have to wait long; either the turnkey was accommodating or Mr. Page had brought plenty of money. Within a few minutes he was guiding them through the ugly stone corridors, away from most of the noise, to the twelve private rooms of the State Side that those with money could purchase to keep themselves separate from the incarcerated masses. With a surly glance, the guard stopped at the door and informed them, "Only one visitor a'time."

The two gentlemen exchanged uneasy glances and attempted to argue, but the guard was adamant. Lily took a deep breath. It was time to rally. "Then I shall go in alone, gentlemen, since it was I that Mr. Lacey wished to see."

Predictably, they protested, but in the end they had to concede that she was right. "We'll be right out here, and you call for us if anything seems amiss," Mr. Page said, glowering at the unconcerned turnkey.

"I shall be perfectly well," Lily said, as much to reassure herself as her escorts. "Hopefully he will say his piece quickly and be done."

"Prisoner is shackled," the guard offered with surprising helpfulness. "Stay t' this side o' the room. Won't be able t' touch ye. Bang twice on th' door when ye want t' be let out." Lily nodded and thanked him, and the guard, apparently having used up his supply of words for the day, grunted in response and unlocked the cell.

Lily took a deep breath and went through, trying to ignore the anxious faces of her companions. The door shut with a dull crash, and the key turned in the lock once more.

The cell was long, narrow, and very dark; only the barest gleam of light struggled through the barred window. Close to her was a table with two candles, one flickering through its last moments, the other unlit. At the other end of the dim space was a narrow bed, and it was there that Mr. Lacey sat, waiting for her. Lily wondered if he had heard them arguing, for he said nothing. She took another deep breath, determined to get the business over with. "I have come, sir. What did you wish to tell me?"

He did not reply, merely waited with his head tipped to one side, still watching her. Lily shivered and, guessing what he wanted, laid back her hood and veil. "There. Now you can see my face, and you know it well enough. But it seems only fair that I should see yours. I dislike this darkness."

Ignoring Mr. Lacey's unsettling stare, Lily lit the larger candle, and its comforting glow filled the cell. Feeling more in command of the situation, she settled the candle where she wanted it, pulled out the single chair, and sat at the table. Only then did she turn back to Mr. Lacey, who had watched her in silence the whole time.

She stumbled to her feet and screamed.

Instantly there was a commotion on the other side of the door, men's voices yelling, a loud thump, the sound of keys and argument. Lily heard none of it. After the first shock wore off, she was silent, staring at the figure on the bed. Mr. Lacey's head listed to one side, his eyes wide and unseeing, the bloody hole in his chest staining the white linen of his shirt.

"Lily!"

"Mrs. Adler!"

Two heavy male bodies nearly crashed into her as the door finally swung open, and she felt Jack's hands pull her toward him. Lily shook her head and, surprised by the calm tone of her voice, said, "He is dead. I am sorry I screamed; I was very startled."

"What?" Neither of them had yet looked toward the far end of the room; they did now, and one of them cursed. Jack's grip tightened on her arms, and for a moment Lily had the distinct impression that he wanted to drag her from the room. But he let her go a moment later, while Mr. Page yelled for assistance.

The guard provided no help at all, saying that he had only just come on duty and insisting that they leave so he could summon the warden. Ignoring him, Mr. Page leaned over the body.

"Pistol shot," he pronounced decisively. "Whoever did it got very close."

"Just like General Harper." Lily came to peer over his shoulder.

For a moment Mr. Page looked surprised that she would come so near the body; then he nodded. "Very much the same." He turned to the guard once more. "How could anyone let a visitor in with a weapon?"

"Wouldn't 'ave." The man looked nervous. "You need t' leave. Warden must be fetched."

"But they would be allowed to bring food." Lily had caught sight of a basket under the table. "Friends and family may bring food." Ignoring the dirtiness of the floor, she crouched down and dragged the basket toward the flickering candlelight. In it were two loaves of bread, several carrots and turnips, and a jug of something that smelled vile even with the stopper in it. Lily set them all aside, and even the turnkey fell silent to watch her search. At the bottom of the basket she found what she was looking for: a slim, elegant pistol, wrapped in a man's coat that had a hole burnt through its layers. She pulled it out, and Mr. Page let out a low whistle.

The guard shook his head. "No one woulda been allowed in wiv that."

"Hence the food," Lily pointed out. "And, I imagine, a large bribe to prevent the basket being searched too thoroughly."

"But why leave it here?" Jack crouched down next to her.

"Nowhere to conceal it." Lily held out a hand so he could help her to her feet. "The guard would have been suspicious if the food were not left behind. So there was no choice but to leave the pistol as well."

"The coat would have muffled the shot somewhat, but not over-much," Jack said, glancing at Mr. Lacey. "Anyone in the corridor would have heard it."

The Bow Street officer nodded, his expression grim as he dusted off his hands and stood. "So several bribes, most likely."

"Is there any way to discover who was on duty earlier?" Lily asked.

He grimaced. "I can ask. But there aren't always records of such things, and if more than one guard was bribed . . . well, none of them will be much inclined to talk. It isn't as if the police have authority over a prison." He took the bundle from her and turned the pistol over, then abruptly moved closer to the candle to inspect it. Lily and Jack exchanged a puzzled glance as Mr. Page held out the weapon. "Do you recognize it, Mrs. Adler?"

"In fact I do." Lily could not keep the surprise from her voice as she pointed to the crest stamped on the underside of the barrel. "I last saw it in a drawer of General Harper's desk. And it was not there after he was shot."

Mr. Page nodded, his face grim. "Well, we know what Mr. Lacey wanted to tell you."

Lily shivered. "There is a third conspirator in this business. And whoever it is, he has silenced the two men who could name him."

★ ★ ★

Even though she had been the one to discover Hyrum Lacey's body, Lily found herself set aside and sent back home while Jack went with Mr. Page to give evidence to a Bow Street magistrate. She understood why, but it irked her to be out of the action, without any way of knowing what was being done. Worse, it left her feeling vulnerable once more. With Mr. Lacey behind bars, she had felt free from the memory of that figure standing over her bed, pistol drawn and ready to fire. But with Lacey himself murdered, how could she feel safe?

A restless night left her with the continued sense that she was missing something important. It was not until she had spent half an hour pacing around her sitting room that Lily remembered the scrap of lace on her dressing table.

She spent several minutes turning it over in her hand. If there had been a lady in the garden that night, someone other than her . . . Clenching the lace in her fist, Lily went to her writing desk, intending to send a note to Mr. Page.

Or perhaps it was nothing. Lily set aside her pen, frowning. The person who had attacked her outside her home had certainly been male, perhaps someone else from Lacey and West, or a man from the general's army days. There was nothing definite to say a woman was involved. The bit of trim could have been torn from one of Serena's dresses days before the party. It might have nothing to do with Mr. Finch's death at all.

That, at least, she could learn without much trouble and with the added benefit of a little morning exercise. Ringing for Anna and her pelisse, Lily set out toward the Walters' town house.

Only to find, when she arrived, that the household was in a frenzy of packing, the servants dashing up and down the stairs and a number of trunks already stacked and waiting. The poor butler, when he met her in the hall, looked as harried as she had ever seen him— though for him that meant merely the addition of a few tight lines around his mouth and an air of resignation added to his normally stoic expression.

"Oh dear." Lily eyed the controlled chaos behind him. "I don't suppose Lady Walter has a moment to spare?"

Reston bowed. "She asks that you come up to her rooms, Mrs. Adler, if you would be so good. I'm afraid that the downstairs parlors—" The lines around his mouth tightened a little more, and his sigh was one of deep forbearance. "As you see, we are in a bit of disarray."

"Of course." Anna already having gone to the kitchens to wait, Lily followed Reston up to the second floor. There she found Serena still in bed, propped up amid an ocean of pillows, wearing a peevish expression.

"Lily, is this not the most vexing thing in the world?" the viscountess exclaimed as soon as she caught sight of her friend. "That dreadful man"—she spared a glare for Reston—"would not even allow me downstairs to sit with you! Lord Walter insists I remain here, and of course none of the staff will disobey, no matter how I protest. It is too ridiculous!" She frowned thunderously at the butler, who bowed and withdrew, seemingly unperturbed by his mistress's ire.

"Serena, what happened?" Lily perched on the edge of the bed. "Are you unwell?"

Serena sighed gustily. "I have told them all I feel *perfectly* well, but you know Lord Walter."

Serena's absence of the last few days, her husband's protective hovering and reluctance to be away, suddenly fell into place. If Lily had not been so distracted the past weeks, she might have put the pieces together sooner. "Serena, you are not increasing again?"

Her friend blushed. "Yes, I am."

If Serena was pregnant, of course Lord Walter would want to avoid anything that would cause her distress. And for a man as conservative as he was, accustomed to the privileges of the peerage, that would mean keeping any scandal as far from his family as possible. His bribe to the magistrate suddenly made far more sense, though Lily still could not agree with it.

Serena had continued talking. "And then I made the mistake of telling Lord Walter that I had pains a few days ago. Nothing severe, as I tried to tell him, but of course he sent for Dr. Abernathy. Who suggested, *most* boorishly, that I be taken out of London and kept in the country until the babe arrives. An early confinement; can you believe it? I shall miss the rest of the season. Lord Walter, the beast, shall come back as often as he likes, of course, but me? Oh no, I shall be imprisoned in that wretched dungeon! And I shall miss Mrs. Winston's party next Thursday, which is a dreadful shame. She knows all the best gossip, besides being friends with some very scandalous gentlemen . . ."

Lily could not help smiling at Serena's description of Lord Walter's Surrey property—a delightful estate surrounded by acres of rolling parkland and well-tended gardens—as a dungeon. "If the doctor thinks it best, Serena, you must do as he says. You've a great deal of energy and overtire yourself too often. If you'll not attend to your own health, then your husband and your friends must do so for you."

"Oh, you are far too practical." Serena grumbled. "I shall do as they say, but only on the condition that you will visit for at least a month this summer. If I am to be imprisoned, I insist on having entertaining company."

"I promise." Lily raised her brows. "Does that mean we are no longer quarreling?"

Serena glanced at the door to make sure it was closed. "You know I never hold a grudge, Lily. And I admit that your intentions were good, though you seem to have an absurdly low opinion of mine."

"Well." Lily knew she should have let the matter rest, but she couldn't seem to help herself. "I understand why Lord Walter thought the bribe was necessary, though I still think it wrong. But you were perfectly comfortable flouting the law and allowing a murderer to go free. You would have made the bribe yourself! Can you really be surprised that I disapprove?"

"Of course I was surprised." And she really was, Lily realized. Serena was not angry anymore, but she was clearly baffled. "Even without my condition, there was every chance of a scandal arising if Bow Street continued their investigation. I would never let that happen to my family, and since we were able to prevent it, why not?"

"Just because you can do something does not mean you should," Lily said quietly. "The whole point of the new police force is to ensure that everyone is treated equally."

"Well, we all know that is not going to happen anytime soon," Serena said dismissively. "Yes, I see you looking outraged. You can stand on principle as much as you like, but I shall look after my family with whatever means are at my disposal. Would you not have done anything you could to keep Freddy safe and well?"

"That is not the same thing at all," Lily insisted.

Serena shrugged. "Perhaps not in the details. But women's lives are precarious, Lily; you know that as well as anyone. Even once we think we are secure and provided for, it all can be taken away from us. What if I had married a cruel man who left me and decided I could never see my children again? He would have every legal right to do so. What if you had no money when Freddy died? You would have had no choice but to return to that heartless shell of a man who calls himself your father. The world gives us precious few choices, Lily. We make what we can of them, but I cannot think of a single woman who would not do whatever was necessary to protect what she built for herself." Serena raised a brow. "Can you?"

Lily, about to respond, froze as her friend spoke, her eyes growing wide and her mind working rapidly. "Serena . . ."

She had been assuming Augustus Finch had been murdered by the victim of his blackmail. But what if that was not the case at all? What if he had been killed, not by the men he had tried to black-mail, but by someone who was threatened by his mere presence in London? But then, who was the man who had been lurking outside her home—the man following her—the burglar who was not a bur-glar after all?

Lily pressed the heels of her hands against her eyelids. There were too many secrets to sift through, too many people hiding something.

"Lily? What on earth is the matter? Are you ill?"

Lily had almost forgotten about the scrap of lace in her reticule, but now she pulled it out. "Is this from one of your gowns?"

Serena took the piece of cloth, her expression concerned. "Lily, what—?"

"Did you tear that lace off one of your frocks when you were in the rose walk?"

"Not this time of year." Serena turned the lace over in her hand. "I find rosebushes depressing without blooms." Her expression grew suddenly sharp. "You found it in my rose walk? When?"

"The night of your party."

"The night of the murder." Serena, for all her affected frippery, was not slow to grasp the implications. "I suppose it is too much of a coincidence to imagine that *another* secretive conference took place in just that spot." She scowled. "If I find that this Mr. Lacey of Lacey and West was in *my* gardens uninvited—"

"Really, Serena, I hardly think his lack of invitation was the most repellent—" Lily broke off abruptly. "Say that again."

"What?"

"Say what you just said again."

"I hadn't a chance to say anything at all, dear; you interrupted me before I made my point, which was—"

"You said Mr. Lacey of Lacey and West."

Serena frowned. "Was that not his name? Or Tacey or something like that?"

"It was Lacey. Of Lacey and West." Lily stood abruptly. "I have to go. I am not sorry for expecting the best of you, Serena, but I am sorry for our quarrel. And for interrupting you just now. Both times." She leaned forward to press a quick kiss against her friend's cheek. "Have a safe journey. You will write to me when you get to Surrey?"

"I will. Lily?"

Lily paused with her hand on the door. "Yes?"

Serena's eyes were wide. "Be careful."

★ ★ ★

Lily was glad she had Anna with her as she made her way home—her mind was so preoccupied with all she had to think over that she could barely attend to the matter of finding a coach or telling the driver where to go. But as soon as she walked through the door at Half Moon Street, Carstairs was waiting with news that shook her out of her distraction: there was a boy in the kitchens asking to speak with her.

"I'd have sent the urchin on his way with a swift kick, I assure you, ma'am, but Mrs. Carstairs insisted that I allow him to wait for you." He scowled. "She said he mentioned Captain Hartley's name."

"You did perfectly right in allowing him to stay." Lily stripped off her gloves and handed them over. "I thank you for it. Now, show me to the boy."

Mr. Carstairs insisted upon coming along, claiming there was no knowing what sort of swindle the boy would try, and Anna made no attempt to hide her curiosity. Lily sighed and allowed them to follow.

However Carstairs felt, it seemed his wife could not resist feeding any child put before her; Lily found Jem sitting in the kitchen devouring a plate of biscuits and a tall glass of milk. He jumped to his feet when he saw her. "Missus Adler." He surprised her with an awkward bow. "You said as I was to report t' you."

"Exactly right." Lily sat down and gestured for him to do the same. Behind her, Carstairs cleared his throat disapprovingly, but she ignored him. "And when we have finished, I shall see to it that Mrs. Carstairs gives you a proper supper before you go on your way."

That won her a smile. "A real lady, you are."

"What news do you have for me, Jem?" His expression became secretive, and he glanced nervously at the assembled servants. Lily tapped a finger under his chin to bring his attention back to her. "They live here as well and have a right to know if anyone threatens their home. Your news?"

"Y' got a scary way of lookin' at a chap, missus. I been here since Lacey got took and there weren't no work at the office. And I thought as you should know, missus, there's still a man watchin' your house." He jerked his head toward the door. "He stands on the other side o' the street, like, in the shadows. Hours at a time, allus at night. Right creepy, it is."

Lily silenced the nervous murmur that went through her servants with an upraised hand. "You are sure it is a man? Could it be a woman wearing a man's clothes?"

"Oh no, missus. Fellow had to do his business at some point, didn't he?" Jem shrugged. "Right up against the wall, plain as day. It's a man for sure."

A chill made its way down her back, but Lily kept her expression calm as she continued her questions. No, the man was not always there, but he had been watching for the past three nights and had arrived just after eight o'clock each time. Yes, he had come near the house once, but mostly he stayed across the street. No, he had never tried to enter through any of the doors. No, Jem had never seen the man's face.

The boy answered each question with a thoughtful confidence that made her trust what he told her. When he was done, Lily nodded to Mrs. Carstairs, who set herself to the task of feeding Jem while Lily went upstairs to her sitting room, lost in thought. She did not realize she was not alone until she heard a throat being cleared behind her.

Mr. Carstairs and Anna had followed her, and they both looked worried. "Mrs. Adler," the butler asked. "You believe the boy?"

"Completely. The man he saw has, I think, been watching this house for some time."

"Then what are we to do?"

"He shall be dealt with, never fear. Please tell Mrs. Carstairs that I will be dining at home tonight after all." The butler looked confused, but her calm manner seemed to reassure him, and he went to do as she asked.

Anna remained in the room; Lily turned to her. "Did you speak to your cousin yet?"

"I did, ma'am." Anna's eyes were wide. "He knew . . . somewhat of the Ketterings, though he wouldn't swear to any of it as true, there always being so many rumors flying about."

"And what are those rumors?"

"Seems there's speculation that all their property is mortgaged to pay the family debts. Mr. Christopher Kettering isn't said to be spendthrift, but his father and mother are known for . . ."

When Anna hesitated, Lily guessed, "Outrunning the tradesmen's bills to keep up appearances?"

"Yes, ma'am." The maid hesitated again, then asked, "Were you wanting to know about him before you sent your letter?"

"My letter?" The question caught Lily off guard. "What letter?"

Anna gestured at her mistress's writing desk. "I found it under a table in the drawing room, but I didn't like to send it on without your instruction."

There was indeed a letter addressed to Mr. Christopher Kettering there, as Lily discovered when she went to her desk. She immediately recalled Miss Harper's visit, the startled way she had upset her reticule and sent its contents flying, the distracted way they had gathered them up while they continued talking. It was unsealed, and the contents were innocent enough—she read it with only a moment of quickly dismissed guilt—but the letter itself sent Lily's mind racing.

Letters. The letter copied from the blotter in the George Inn, a faded representation of Mr. Finch's scrawling, careless hand. His belongings scattered around the room . . . and the pistol, Lily remembered suddenly, the pistol that had been missing when they left.

Mr. Finch's unsigned letters, from someone who knew of the business that tied together Parliament, the War Office, and a shipping firm engaged in treason. The stack of letters on Miss Harper's desk, not all of them franked by Christopher Kettering's father. Ofelia's shocking letter from Mr. Finch, delivered after his death. Ofelia, who had decided to keep her first engagement a secret rather than risk losing the man she loved.

Mr. Harper, cornering Ofelia in the hallway outside the Walters' ballroom, only moments after he had driven Lily into the garden where Mr. Finch was shot, not long after Ofelia herself had left those gardens. Mr. Harper, eyeing Lily over his wine, unconcerned by his distraught sister in the wake of the general's death.

Serena, ready to do whatever was necessary to defend against even a hint of scandal. *The world gives us precious few choices, Lily. We make what we can of them, but I cannot think of a single woman who would not do whatever was necessary to protect what she built for herself. Can you?*

And Mr. Lacey, of the shipping firm Lacey and West.

Lily spoke slowly, turning over the possibilities in her mind. "Tell me, Anna, could a woman shoot a man she cared for?"

"There was one as did just that in Clerkenwell last month, ma'am." The question clearly made Anna uneasy. "Her beau wanted her to run away with him, but she was married already, and her husband rich enough to give her pin money every week and new gloves whenever she wanted. She wouldn't leave him, and the beau threatened to tell the husband that she'd cuckolded him. She shot him to keep the secret, but it came out anyway." Anna shivered. "If that will be all, ma'am, I'll go see if Mrs. Carstairs needs any help with supper."

Lily was left alone at last. Her mind sorting through everything she had learned that day, she was very still for ten minutes. Then, moving to her writing desk, she penned two notes, careful which details were included in each. When those were done, she summoned Jem from the kitchen, handing him the two letters for delivery with careful instructions. Jem, grinning broadly, saluted and scampered off.

Lily wished she could feel as cheerful as he looked. But one way or another, she reflected, it would all be over soon.

She had a murderer to catch.

CHAPTER 26

Jack arrived at Half Moon Street at a quarter to eight o'clock. Jem caught him at the end of the street, materializing out of the shadows to whisper that Missus Adler had given two of her servants the night off; only the butler remained.

"Do you know why?" Jack murmured back, not turning to face the boy.

Jem's surprise was obvious. "I'd-a thought you'd know, Cap'n," he said.

Jack frowned. "Stay close, and keep watch." The boy gave him a quick salute before melting back into the shadows.

The butler showed Jack into the parlor, where Lily was waiting with drinks. She kept to general conversation as they sat, but Jack did not miss the slight tremble of her hands, or the way she kept glancing at the windows. Finally, impatient to know what was wrong and why she had summoned him, he set his glass down with a *thunk* and leaned forward.

"Out with it. I know there is something the matter."

Lily nodded in agreement. "I needed to wait until eight o'clock."

"Why?"

She stood. "Snuff that branch of candles to your left."

Mystified, Jack did as he was told; Lily put out the ones on the other side of the room until only one flame and the dim light that came through the open dining room door remained. She was left mostly in shadow, but Jack could hear her take a deep breath before she crossed to the window and pulled back the edge of the heavy curtain. "Someone is watching my house. According to your urchin, he has been there for the past two nights." Her voice shook a little as she turned toward him. "Would you look?"

He obeyed, taking the curtain from her hand and standing to one side of the window so he could not be seen from the outside. He wanted to believe she was imagining things, but he had learned better than that: Lily Adler did not imagine what was not there. So he was unsurprised to see a shrouded figure lurking in the shadows opposite them, watching the house. Jack swore. "There is no good reason for a man to lurk in Mayfair like that."

"No," Lily agreed quietly. "There is not."

Lacey's missing conspirator. Jack's jaw clenched. It had to be. "Do you want me to go after him?"

Lily's expression was unreadable in the dim light. "Yes," she said. "That was what I was hoping for."

"Good." Jack lifted the edge of the curtain again and eyed the street. Struck by a sudden thought, he added, "Is that pistol of yours nearby?"

Lily's hesitation was so brief, he almost missed it. "No, I sent it to the gunsmith to have the hammer repaired. Should you not hurry?" She lifted an edge of the curtain once more to peer out at the street. "He may leave if you wait too long."

Jack frowned over the absence of the pistol but did not press the issue. "Not to worry. Jem's out there. With his help, it should be a quick thing to catch the bounder." He eyed her warily. "You will stay inside, I hope, and not rush into danger after me?"

She smiled in a way that, had he not been distracted, would have struck him as odd. "I give you my word I'll not leave the house."

"Good." Jack rolled out his shoulders and gave her a quick nod. "Lock the front door behind me."

★　★　★

Jack swung his cane, idly whistling as he sauntered down the front steps, looking like nothing more than a society gentleman heading out to his evening engagements. As he passed the spot where the silent watcher waited, the man's head turned to follow him for a moment, then turned back to Lily's house.

Jack watched out of the corner of his eye. The lurker was clearly not a patient man; Jack had gone only a few houses down when the man made his move, slinking out of the shadows and heading toward number thirteen.

Jack abandoned stealth, shouting for Jem as he ran toward the black-cloaked figure. He could see the boy bolting down the street, suddenly looking less like a gangly urchin and more like a fighter. The man paused in the middle of the street, realizing his mistake as two angry figures barreled toward him. He turned and fled.

With another shout for Jem, Jack chased after him. He didn't stop to think about what might happen if anyone saw them tearing through the streets of Mayfair. He only knew that he had to keep the unknown man from threatening Lily ever again.

Freddy would never forgive him if he failed.

★   ★   ★

Lily watched out the window as Jack and his shadow disappeared in pursuit of the watcher. Still standing to one side, out of the light, she kept watching until she saw another figure peek out from the alley next to her home, then vanish back into the shadows.

Lily smiled, took a deep breath, and let the curtain fall back into place. A murderer would be calling on her soon.

★   ★   ★

It took longer than Jack expected to run his quarry to ground, but the twisting path the man took meant that none of them could move particularly fast. The watcher was about to dodge into an alley off Sackville Street when Jack launched himself into a flying tackle and caught the man around the waist, both of them tumbling to the ground.

He was vaguely aware of Jem, unable to help in such close quarters, standing ready to stop the unknown man if he tried to flee again, but Jack was occupied with two wildly flailing fists, one of which caught him in the stomach. Bellowing, he swung a right hook of his own squarely into the other man's jaw. The stranger dropped instantly.

Slowly, wincing as he straightened and shaking out his numb fist, Jack climbed to his feet, aided by a friendly hand from the boy.

"Hell of a facer, Cap'n." Jem was beaming. "All right? Looked like he caught you a good 'un hisself."

Too out of breath to answer, Jack nodded. When he had recovered enough, they bent together to heave the unknown man over onto his back. There was just enough light spilling into the alley to make out his face.

"Harper?" Jack stared at the figure sprawled on the cobblestones. Reggie Harper groaned as he opened his eyes to narrow slits, then threw an arm over his face to block the light. "What the devil have you to do with any of this?"

"He ain't wrapped up in your murder business?" Jem frowned. "Wiv his uncle?"

"Murder?" Harper groaned again. "What the hell are you— Gad, my head. What the hell is wrong with you, Hartley?"

"Wrong with me?" Jack grabbed Harper by the coat, hauling him to his feet and shoving him against a wall as the other man stumbled, protesting feebly. "Jem, is this the man that has been lurking outside Mrs. Adler's home?"

"Looks like him, Cap'n."

"Adler? Lily Adler?" Harper licked his lips, looking panicked. "You have it all wrong, Hartley. She and I have an arrangement."

"Liar." Jack's grip tightened, twisting the fabric around Harper's neck until the other man coughed and tried to pull away.

"You didn't think you were the only one bedding her, did you?" His attempt at a sneer was ruined as he winced, one hand clutching his bruised jaw. "Each night after you leave, she opens that little side door for me—" He broke off, gasping, as Jack tightened his grip again.

"Well, that ain't true," Jem said scornfully. "Can't the blighter come up wiv a better lie than that?"

"Apparently not." Jack leaned in until his face was only inches away from the other man's. "You had best start telling me the truth, Harper. Bow Street cleared you of your uncle's murder, but I know someone broke into Mrs. Adler's house. Did Lacey put you up to this before he died? Were you the one who killed him?"

"Lacey? That peasant?" Harper scowled. "What the devil are you on about?"

Jack held out one hand. "Jem, do you have a knife with you?"

"Always, sir."

"Easy, easy!" For the first time, Harper looked genuinely panicked. "No need for any of that, Hartley. We can be civilized."

"Then tell me what you were doing outside Mrs. Adler's house. Were you planning to try to shoot her again?"

"Shoot her? I told you, I was—" Harper's eyes grew wide as Jem handed over his knife, and he scrambled against the wall, trying to get away. "All right, all right! I've not been bedding her, are you happy? She'd not have me, the bitch; I was just going to make her see sense . . ."

Jack suddenly remembered the gossip he had heard about Reggie Harper, the way Lily had scowled when she mentioned his name. *He did not make a favorable impression*, Miss Oswald had replied, both women looking disgusted.

Harper wasn't a murderer, Jack realized. He was a predator, bent on frightening and manipulating women into bedding him.

His grip relaxed, and Harper pulled away instantly. "Glad you can see sense. And I can assure you she is not worth all this fuss. Women like that are practically begging—"

Jack smashed his fist into the man's face, and Harper dropped like a stone.

He and Jem stared at the unconscious figure, both of them disgusted. "He didn't have nothing to do wiv the murder at all," the boy said. "Well, I s'pose Missus Adler's instructions make a lot more sense now."

Jack felt suddenly chilled. "Her instructions?"

Jem nodded. "When she had me deliver her letters, she said as you would be catching the man who was watching her house, and I was s'posed to have some of my mates ready to take care of him. Said to make sure as no one hurt the blighter, though. I wondered why she didn't want me to call them Bow Street fellows." The boy frowned down at Harper's prone body and used his toe to nudge the man farther into a puddle of filthy water. "Seems as she just wanted him served a nasty turn."

"She knew it would be Harper, then," Jack said slowly, his hands slowly clenching into fists. "And that he wasn't involved in the murder at all."

"But then whoever killed old Lacey is still—" Jem was about to dash back toward Half Moon Street when Jack caught his arm. "Cap'n, we have to go back!"

"Wait." Jack's tone was grim. Lily had sent him after the man on purpose. And if that was the case . . . "We need a plan. Are your mates nearby?"

Jem nodded. "Should've followed us." He let out a shrill whistle, and a moment later three wary-looking urchins of various ages materialized out of the gloom.

Jack looked them over, thinking rapidly. "All right, boys. Whatever he has on him is fair game, but no injuries." With grim humor, he added, "I imagine his clothes would fetch a good price all on their own." The three boys glanced at each other, grinning, before setting to work.

"What about Missus Adler?" Jem demanded, his wiry body coiled as if ready for a fight.

"If I give you an address and my card, can you fetch a man to Half Moon Street? He's quality, so you will need to be persuasive." At the boy's eager nod, Jack gave his instruction, and Jem took off at a run.

A moment later, Jem's three mates followed, melting into the shadows, leaving behind the completely stripped body of Reggie Harper, pale and defenseless in the dim light, except for the visible bruise growing on his jaw. The night watch would pick him up soon enough, and that, at least, was grimly satisfying.

Jack wavered for a moment, wanting to go back to Half Moon Street and make sure Lily was safe. But he had to trust that she could take care of herself. With a muffled curse, he set off back toward Mayfair.

★　★　★

Lily moved across the hall into the well-lit drawing room. She would have preferred to sequester herself somewhere else—the book-room or her upstairs sitting room would have felt cozier and safer—but the drawing room had a clear view of the street and, more importantly, was next to the passage that led to the side door. So that was where she had to remain.

After letting herself be seen at the front window, alone and unguarded, Lily felt a pang of fear. There was every chance she had just made a terrible choice. And even if she was proved right, Jack might never forgive her for the way she had tricked him. But she couldn't think of another way.

She took a deep breath, quickly checked that the door to the outside was unlocked, and settled down with an open book in her lap. She was sure her pounding heart was loud enough to be heard halfway down the street, but she did her best to ignore it, staring at the book without reading and counting seconds to distract herself from her shaking hands.

It had been less than five minutes when the soft click of the latch reached her ears. A shadow flickered past the door to the hall, and a woman slipped inside after it. The candlelight glinted off the knife in her hand.

Lily watched out of the corner of her eye, waiting until the door closed before lifting her head. "Good evening, dear."

CHAPTER 27

Isobel Harper started, and the knife she carried wavered ever so slightly. But she recovered and inclined her head as if in polite greeting. "Mrs. Adler. I am surprised to find you still awake."

"It has been a rather eventful evening." Lily's voice was as pleasant as she could manage while a woman she had known since her schoolgirl days pointed a knife toward her heart. "I imagine they will have caught your brother by now; he did not look to be a swift runner." Lily sighed, using the quick rise and fall of her shoulders to hide the movement of her hand slipping further under the book in her lap.

"Reggie." Miss Harper's lip curled, the sneer so at odds with her usual demure expression that it made her look like a different person. "He never could stand to be turned down by a woman. I realized you were his latest obsession when I drove you home from Lady Walter's and saw him lurking outside your house. And then the very next evening you told me someone had been following you! Amusing, really, how distressed you were. Reggie's a despicable fool, but he could not have been a more helpful distraction if he had been trying."

"You have been fortunate in the number of distractions you managed to hide behind." Lily shook her head. "I am not proud of how long it took me to discover your role in the events of the last few weeks."

"For some time I was sure you already had." Miss Harper's voice had steadied. "But even when I realized you'd not seen me that night,

I knew it was only a matter of time before you put the pieces together. Bow Street gave up quickly, but not you. If it helps, Lily, you have my admiration. And I truly wish this were not necessary." She took a firmer grip on her knife and stepped forward. "But I cannot have you exposing me."

"I never much liked you, Isobel, but I would never have imagined you growing into a murderer."

Miss Harper shrugged. "It is rather amazing, the things one will do to secure a happy life. And the sensational novels are correct in one thing. It does become easier. Augustus's death was . . ." She paused, shaking her head. "I liked him very much, and even fancied myself quite fond of him for a few months there. He was quite charming, and he had a practical mind. Almost as practical as my own. His death was unfortunate." Her voice was as calm as a hostess regretting that there was no milk for the tea, and it sent a chill down Lily's spine. "But not my uncle's. The stupid man spent his life taking credit for the work of others, first during the war, and then when *I* devised a way—" She broke off as her voice began to rise with fury. Taking a breath, she smiled and said, calm once again, "My uncle's death was a pleasure."

"What about Mr. Lacey?"

"Lacey?" Miss Harper laughed, her face twisted with the scorn that Lily remembered so well from their school days. "Who will miss a man like that?"

"And I?"

"A sad necessity. I do apologize, but one does what one must. Unfortunately, I had to leave my pistol in Newgate, and I imagine being stabbed to death is most unpleasant. I shall do my best to make it quick, and I can offer you this comfort: since I know you are too proud to have told anyone before you were absolutely certain it was I, you will fortunately be the last."

"Not quite the last, Miss Harper."

Miss Harper started, looking before she could stop herself to where Ofelia Oswald watched her from the passageway. As soon as she was distracted, Lily was on her feet, the pistol she had held concealed in her lap pointed steadily at her assailant.

Miss Harper froze.

"I shot at you once, Isobel," Lily said. "You know I shan't hesitate to do it again, and there is not a court in the land that would convict me of anything but defending my home against an intruder." Lily cocked the hammer on her pistol, and the click echoed through the room.

Isobel Harper trembled, but she still managed to look calm. "I doubt that, Lily. You did not know it was me before, and even someone as cold as you could not shoot a woman you have known since girlhood."

"Fortunately, I have not known you nearly so long." There was a second click, and over Isobel's shoulder Lily saw Ofelia raise a pistol of her own. The candlelight glinted off a spot on the barrel, and Lily knew that if she examined it closely she would find the initials *AJF* inlaid in the wood—Mr. Finch's second pistol, which Ofelia had taken from his room at the George.

"All I know of you," Ofelia continued, her voice shaking with emotion, "is that you murdered a man I have cared for since childhood. Believe me when I say it will be my pleasure to shoot you."

"Ofelia, no," Lily said urgently, suddenly cold with dread. When she had instructed Ofelia to wait for Miss Harper, and to be armed, she had intended that, between them, they could subdue the woman until Jack returned and a constable was fetched. She had not counted on the girl taking matters into her own hands. "This was not the plan. Put it down."

"She killed Augustus." The girl was shaking, her eyes bright with anger and tears. "She *killed* him—"

Miss Harper made her move in a sudden lunge. Ofelia screamed in panic as Isobel grabbed the pistol, trying to wrestle it from her. The gun clattered to the floor as they grappled, Isobel swinging her knife wildly toward the girl's unprotected face and throat.

Lily raised her arm and fired.

The report echoed deafeningly through the small room. Though Lily had fired directly into the ceiling, both Isobel and Ofelia flinched, falling apart as they tried to see who had been shot. The momentary distraction was enough. Lily threw her now-empty pistol aside and lunged to grab Ofelia's. Isobel Harper moved at the same time, but Lily was quicker; she kicked out, her foot connecting solidly with Isobel's shoulder. The other woman rolled away, grunting in pain as Lily stumbled to her feet, pistol clutched in her hand.

And then there were shouts all around them, bellows echoing from both the side passage and the front hall, people running into the room. Someone was calling Ofelia's name—Sir Edward Carroway, Lily saw with confusion, running in from the hall and seizing her, checking for injuries—and someone was grappling with Isobel Harper, wrestling the knife from her hands. Someone grabbed Lily's shoulder and pulled her around; without thinking, she brought the gun up and found herself pointing it at Jack, who backed away very quickly.

And then there was silence, almost as deafening as the confusion had been, broken only by the sound of muffled sobs as Ofelia cried into Sir Edward's shoulder. Two men—one of them was Simon Page, Lily realized with a start—held Isobel Harper's arms behind her back. Miss Harper was very pale and breathing heavily, her gaze darting around the room as the truth of the situation slowly dawned on her. She was caught.

Breathing as heavily as Isobel, Lily turned back to Jack, her stunned mind latching on to one question. "Where did you come from?"

"The magistrate's office." He was panting too. "Luckily, Mr. Page was on duty and took me seriously when I said you were about to have a visit from a murderer. Are you hurt?" He was looking her over from head to toe. "We heard a gunshot."

"I fired into the ceiling." Lily hoped it didn't sound like a stupid thing to have done. She looked up at the hole in the ceiling, shaking. "I shall need to have that replastered."

"Never mind the damn ceiling. What happened? Why was—" Jack broke off, at a loss for words, and made a sweeping gesture that took in the entire room, from Miss Harper to Ofelia, still tucked in the protective circle of Sir Edward's arm. "What happened?"

"Mrs. Adler told me her plan to lure the real murderer out." Ofelia spoke too fast, her voice shaking. "If she saw you chasing after another man, Captain, Miss Harper would think the house unprotected. Who was he?"

"Her brother, apparently. Not part of this business." Sir Edward had not let go of his intended, and she turned to look at him for the first time.

"What are you doing here, Neddy?"

"Making sure you are safe, of course. Hartley's boy fetched me."

"But what . . ." Jack trailed off, his gaze returning to Miss Harper. "I realized too late that you were planning something, and I knew you must be using yourself as bait. But I did not expect her."

"I did." Lily took a deep breath. "Miss Harper is our mysterious third conspirator."

"She killed Lacey?" Mr. Page demanded.

"She killed all three of them." Lily laid aside the pistol, her voice growing more steady. "Mr. Finch, Mr. Lacey, and of course, her uncle."

"Her own uncle," the second Runner repeated, disbelieving. "Why?"

"For money, in the end, though that makes it sound simpler than it was," Lily said sadly, her eyes on Miss Harper's furious face. "It started with your father's will, did it not? Of course he expected that his own brother would take excellent care of his daughter. So the money went to your uncle for your care and upkeep, without you seeing a penny, and it was to go to your husband after you married. I expect your father set you up to receive an allowance from the interest after you wed, but until then you were at your uncle's mercy."

"He gambled it away." Isobel's voice rose angrily. "The stupid man—horses! And cards. And whores, I have no doubt. Him and

Reggie, useless, both of them. I'd no idea it was gone until—" She broke off, shaking. "You do not understand. I did not . . . I do not need to explain myself to you."

"No need," Lily said. "I believe I can manage. You became engaged to a charming army coronet, and when the marriage settlements were drawn up, you discovered that there was almost no money left. He jilted you publicly—a humiliating experience, I have no doubt—and ruined your chances of making another match by putting it about that you were a practically a pauper. You were forced to remain dependent on the uncle you hated."

"He was a weak fool," Isobel snapped, unable to stay completely silent.

"But how could she have known about—?" Mr. Page frowned in confusion.

"About the general's scheme with Mr. Lacey to profit off the war?" Lily shook her head. "Because it was not the general's scheme after all." Miss Harper glared, but there was a look like pride in her eyes. "As Miss Harper said, he was a stupid man. They had to all work together—she needed her uncle's government contacts, after all, and the shipping agency of Lacey and West—but the idea behind it was all hers. You gave me the key to it, Isobel, without meaning to, though I did not realize it until today. You told me you were going to visit your aunt in Hans Town. Your aunt, Mrs. West, who is a widow."

"Lacey and West." Jack shook his head. "We knew he was dead, so we never concerned ourselves with him."

"And with that connection, she was able to pull the scheme together. When I saw Mr. Lacey drop that note in your reticule, Miss Harper, I assumed he was using you to pass messages to your uncle without your knowledge. But, in fact, he was passing it to you. And once we uncovered the scheme, she killed both Lacey and her uncle so they could not reveal her involvement." Miss Harper said nothing, but her gaze moved around the room to each of the Bow Street officers, and there was panic growing in her eyes.

"But then how did the Finch fellow become involved?" Simon Page asked.

"Isobel told him." Lily turned to Ofelia. The younger woman was shaking visibly, still in the protective circle of Sir Edward's arm, but her eyes were hard and angry. "You wondered how he could have known about something that was happening in London. But Miss Harper told us she had been to the West Indies with her uncle some years before. She and Mr. Finch struck up an acquaintance and had corresponded ever since."

"The unsigned letters were hers?" Mr. Page demanded.

"She dropped a letter in my home when she came to see whether I suspected her. When my maid found it, I recognized the hand. And then I remembered seeing two piles of letters on Miss Harper's writing desk the day the general died. One franked by Mr. Kettering's father, the other in a hand I finally realized was Mr. Finch's. It took realizing her connection to Mr. West, though, to put together the pieces together." Lily raised her eyebrows at Miss Harper. "It was most unwise to keep Mr. Finch's letters after you killed him, Isobel."

"Augustus never told me he corresponded with an English lady," Ofelia said quietly.

Lily laid a comforting hand on the younger woman's shoulder, but her attention was still fixed on Isobel Harper. "The letter that you showed me, Mr. Page, was when Isobel told him about the whole business, though doubtless she said it was all her uncle's doing."

"Do you not see how absurd this is?" Miss Harper interrupted, speaking too quickly as she looked from one stony face to another. "If I were responsible for my uncle's scheme, as you insist, why would I tell this Mr. Finch about it?"

"A clever mind likes an audience." Lily's voice was cold as she repeated Miss Harper's words. "Is that not what you said, Isobel? You were so proud of your cleverness that you had to tell someone. Augustus Finch was safely away in the West Indies, where he could never interfere. Except that he did. His presence in London threatened to expose your family to scandal. And the Ketterings were so close to announcing your betrothal to Christopher. You would have been out of your uncle's house, finally, living the life you felt he had stolen from you." She turned to her flabbergasted audience. "Which is why, when she overheard Mr. Finch attempting to blackmail the general, Miss Harper panicked and shot him."

"You killed him." Ofelia's cheeks were wet with tears, and the fury in her voice made Lily glad that the girl no longer held a gun. "You killed him just so you could have money—!"

"I did not mean to!" Isobel said, her voice desperate. "Augustus— he came to see me—I'd no idea he was in London! Then I saw him that night through the window—I went out to the garden to find him . . ." She sagged against the arms that held her, as if she no longer had the energy to protest her innocence.

"You followed him out to the garden?" Lily prompted her when no one else seemed inclined to speak.

Isobel nodded. "I overheard Mr. Finch threaten to expose my uncle . . ." She looked from one stony face to another. "I'd not meant to hurt him, but I could not . . . I could not bear the thought of being stuck in the general's house any longer. You have to understand, my uncle was not going to pay him!" Isobel's voice was becoming frantic. "He laughed at Augustus, and told him to go ahead. He could only ever, *ever* think of himself. His name might protect him, but what would become of me? I would be ruined a second time. No husband, no reputation, *nothing!*" She was breathing heavily, her eyes wide and frantic. "Christopher would never want to marry me then, and I would have been stuck with my uncle forever. Forever! After what he did to me—you must see I had no other choice. I had to kill them." Her eyes traveled over their faces, pleading for understanding. "How could I risk losing everything, again? You've no idea what that is like."

"You had your life planned out when you were younger," Lily said quietly. "And then, through no fault of your own, it was taken from you. I understand how that feels. I know how—" She broke off, and when she spoke again, her voice was cold. "But you were not owed that life, Isobel. None of us are. And none of that— *none* of it—justifies what you have done."

Isobel laughed bitterly. "If I had gone after my uncle from the beginning, no one would have been the wiser. But it never occurred to me that I could until—"

"Until after you shot Augustus Finch," Lily said. "And having killed already, when we were getting too close to the truth, it seemed the obvious course of action a second time as well."

"But Lacey visited that night." Simon Page frowned. "The general sent all the servants away to keep the meeting secret."

"No." Lily shook her head, eyes still fixed on Isobel Harper. "Mr. Harper told you that the general asked his niece to dismiss the servants for the night. Which she did, but I doubt it was at her uncle's request. She removed any witnesses, and then she shot him. The story of a secret meeting pointed the finger squarely at Lacey if anyone came poking around. It was easy for her to pretend to discover him the next morning. No one questions a lady in hysterics too closely."

"And I suppose she visited Lacey in prison and shot him as well?" Jack asked.

Lily nodded. "He wanted to tell us something that night. And he was the only one left who could reveal her role in the scheme."

"Except for you," Ofelia said, her eyes never leaving her friend's murderer.

Lily inclined her head. "Except, as it turns out, for me."

There was silence in the room for a long moment; then Isobel Harper lifted her chin as regally as if she were in a ballroom. "I should like to leave now, if you would be so kind, gentlemen."

No one protested.

CHAPTER 28

The weeks passed in a blur. The inquest into the deaths of General Harper and Hyrum Lacey, and the reopened interest in the death of one Augustus Finch, sent shock waves through Mayfair society. There were rumors about Lily's involvement, and for a time she felt something almost like notoriety. But nothing definite was known, and the principle result was that she received twice as many invitations from hostesses who were hoping she would be a scandalous addition to their parties. In that hope, they were disappointed, but the rumors continued.

It all came back to secrets. There were so many of them in the air, Lily commented wryly to Ofelia one evening, that they practically held up the walls of London's town houses. The girl, who fortunately had managed to escape such rumors, merely laughed. She did that more now that Augustus's killer was awaiting trial for his murder.

Not wanting more public attention, Lily had asked Jack to testify at the inquest on her behalf. He had agreed, but she had not seen him since. After spending nearly every day in his company for weeks, she found herself missing the navy captain. If he had called, she would have apologized for keeping him in the dark about Isobel until the last possible moment. But he sent no word, and Lily was angry with him for avoiding her.

"He'll come around," Mr. Page told her sympathetically. They were meeting in his office on Great Marlborough Street. The same wide-eyed porter from her first visit had taken notes as Lily described her confrontation with Isobel Harper, then left to go report to Mr. Neve, the magistrate, who—Lily was dismayed to discover—was as much in charge of things as ever, with no questions asked as to why he had dropped the case. Lily wondered if that, too, was due to Lord Walter's influence. If Mr. Page was frustrated by this fact, he never said, though Lily thought she saw him scowl at the magistrate's private office as he escorted her to the front door. "He didn't like you putting yourself in danger."

"Or intentionally deceiving him," Lily said, unable to keep the glum note from her voice.

"Or that," the Bow Street Runner agreed. "You could have told me what you were planning, you know."

"I worried that if too many people were involved, Isobel would suspect a trap. And we had no real proof—even her letters to Mr. Finch proved nothing definite. She had to be caught in the middle of things."

"Still, always better to have a second plan in case something goes awry."

"I shall remember that for next time."

Mr. Page raised his eyebrows as he collected his coat from the porter. "Do you intend there to be a next time, Mrs. Adler? I'd think you would be glad to put things like murder behind you and have your life return to normal."

"Oh, of course. I am sure that is precisely what I need." Lily smiled weakly, wondering what exactly normal meant for her anymore. But she couldn't say such a personal thing to Mr. Page, so instead she asked, "Is your work finished for the day?"

"Yes, homeward I go."

"To your wife and children?" Lily's smile was more genuine this time as Anna, who had been waiting for her mistress, joined them.

"Oh no, I've never been married." Mr. Page grinned at her suddenly blank expression as he held open the door for her. "I've shocked you, ma'am. The children are my nephew and niece, but my sister and I have raised them since our brother and his wife were taken from us by an inflammation of the lungs."

Lily swallowed, feeling suddenly exposed as they stood on the steps of the magistrate's office, though no one on the street was paying them any attention. "My condolences."

"Thank you. It was seven years ago, but still . . ."

"Yes."

Something in Lily's quiet reply made the constable look at her sharply. "Your husband went the same way?" he asked. When Lily nodded, he said gently, "And my condolences to you, ma'am. It's a nasty business, that."

"It was." Not wanting to dwell on such an uncomfortable subject, Lily cleared her throat and said, more cheerfully, "I heard that the night watch stumbled upon a most shocking person in Piccadilly the morning after Miss Harper's arrest."

"Ah yes, the gentleman wandering around stark naked and completely unwilling to explain how he had ended up in such a state." Mr. Page cast her a sideways glance. "How surprising that young Mr. Harper should find himself in such a scrape on the very night of his family's disgrace. It seems a great many people witnessed his shameful walk to the watch house. And then, of course, his family was in such disarray that it was some time before a friend could be found to secure his release."

"How terrible for him to be humiliated in such a manner, on top of all the trouble he will face now his family has been exposed so criminally." Lily kept her voice carefully neutral. "And of course his financial prospects are quite ruined—who knows how he will support himself?"

"You needn't try to sound innocent," Mr. Page said dryly, but he couldn't hide his grin. The friendly expression made his otherwise unremarkable face seem almost handsome. "Captain Hartley told me how the whole business came about. Remind me never to cross you, ma'am." As he hailed a carriage for her—it wouldn't do to walk from Soho, even with her maid in attendance—the constable gave her an encouraging smile. "And don't fret too much about the captain," he advised. "It's hard on a man to discover a woman doesn't need his help."

"It didn't seem to bother you," Lily pointed out, taking his hand as she mounted the carriage step.

For a moment she thought his fingers would linger on hers, but he stepped back so abruptly that Lily was sure she was imagining things. "I have the advantage of being authorized to make an arrest. So you did need my help in the end, didn't you?" Mr. Page asked, his expression suddenly unreadable as Anna mounted the steps. When the maid was settled, he bowed politely. "Good day, Mrs. Adler."

If Jack was still upset with her, Lily was relieved to discover Serena was not. The viscountess, as she had promised, had written as soon as she was settled in Surrey. Her letter, once she was through describing the very shocking marriage of a neighbor's only daughter and her own delight at Reggie Harper's disgrace, reflected the thoughtful mind that was so often hidden beneath her frivolous facade.

> I cannot pretend to be easy with what you have done—both for the danger in which you placed yourself and for the manner in which you went about it. To be frank, knowing that my life & my family were under such scrutiny—I do not imagine that we were spared your examination, given the circumstances surrounding the unfortunate man's death—is repellent to me. I understand that your motives were honourable, and I cannot argue with your wish to see justice prevail, nor your success in doing so (Isobel Harper a murderess! never have I been more shocked & appalled)—tho I know myself well enough to say I would feel differently had any whisper of scandal touched my family as a result.
>
> Still, I cannot help but reflect on what you said to me in our final interview. I maintain that if a privilege is available which may

protect my family—in which body I include, of course, my husband & by extension his reputation & career—it is both logical and reasonable that I shall make use of it. Protecting what I love is not a crime. And yet, what you said was also true—it is not always right that we do, simply because we can. (Any woman, faced as we so often are with the power of men, who may do much at our expense, whether it is right or not, must admit the truth of your belief.) You leave me (as you always do when we quarrel, my dear friend) in a state of agitated mind and confused conscience—& I hope, in this case at least, that you will ask for no more concession on my part. If I am leaving you alone to wrestle with the moral good of the world, it is at least a task to which you are eminently more suited than I, and I have no doubt that you will succeed in making this world the better for your presence and you demands—howsoever they may inconvenience me!

With best love, &c., and always your affect. friend,

S.W.

By the bye, have you bewitched my footman? L.W. writes that he has overheard Jeremy talking about "Anna's Mrs. Adler" no less than five times last week. I hope you are not planning to steal him from me. I should never find another young man with such splendid calves . . .

True spring finally came to London, and Lily spent as much time as she could out of doors. She had just returned from a walk in Hyde Park with Margaret Harlowe—who insisted on knowing the truth behind the rumors—when Carstairs, meeting her in the front hall, cleared his throat and announced that Miss Oswald was waiting to see her, along with "a most distinguished visitor."

"That will be a nice distraction. Who is it?" Lily asked as she laid off her hat and gloves.

Her eyes widened in surprise as she read the card Carstairs held out to her. *Sir Edward Carroway*, the crisp white pasteboard declared in elegant engraving.

"I've taken the liberty of showing them into the parlor," the butler added.

A suspicion bloomed in Lily's mind. If Ofelia and Sir Edward were publicly paying visits together, that could mean only one of two things about their secret betrothal. Sweeping into the parlor, she found them waiting for her by the fireplace, heads close together and wide smiles on their faces. "And what are the two of you whispering about so secretly?"

They started apart, looking momentarily guilty, before breaking once more into matching smiles. "Mrs. Adler!" Ofelia's dark curls bounced around her face as she laughed a little nervously. "Ten to one you have already guessed what we came to tell you. The announcement will appear in the *Times* tomorrow, but I wanted to tell you in person." She held out an envelope.

It was a formal invitation, Lily discovered when she had opened it, to the wedding of Miss Ofelia Oswald and Sir Edward Carroway, to be held on the fifth of June.

Lily laughed in relief. "Thank heavens. It was either this or you had come to tell me Sir Edward persuaded you into a Scottish elopement, and you were already married."

"Thought about it." Sir Edward grinned. "Too scandalous, though."

Ofelia laughed again. "Well, this will perhaps be equally scandalous, considering who you are marrying."

"But what about your father?" Lily asked. "You are only nineteen, after all. Surely he needs to approve the match before you begin planning a wedding. Besides which, even someone so in love as your Ned would never marry without the marriage settlements being signed, would you, Sir Edward?"

"Oh, Papa's man of business has taken care of all of that," Ofelia said carelessly. "I wrote my father as soon as Ned offered for me, and

I had a response at the beginning of the week, giving his permission and instructing Mr. Clancy how to draw up the settlements. As soon as that was taken care of, Ned went to Lady Carroway and put the notice in the *Times*."

"Your father gave his permission by post?" Lily shook her head disbelievingly. "Without having met the young man? And with no word from your aunt?"

Ofelia smiled. "Do not look so shocked, Mrs. Adler. Papa always trusts my judgment. It is one of the benefits of being very nearly his business partner for the last four years."

Lily thought of her own cold, distant father a little sadly. "Then you are very fortunate, in both your parent and your choice of husband. I wish you joy, Ofelia, and you Sir Edward, with all my heart."

"Should call me Ned, you know." The young baronet had not stopped smiling through the entire conversation. "Caught a murderer with my wife, after all. Makes you as good as a sister. Or a cousin." He frowned in thought. "Second cousin, perhaps?"

"What he means to say," Ofelia put in with loving exasperation, "is thank you. From both of us."

"And I am glad to know that you are doing things properly at last," Lily added. "No more of this sneaking around and hiding." Her voice was teasing, but she caught Ofelia's eye as she spoke, and the girl smiled, understanding.

"I very nearly asked Neddy to get us a special license so we could marry, just the two of us. But I want a big wedding." Ofelia smiled slyly. "If the Carroways want my money, then Sir Edward must wed me publicly, with five hundred people in attendance, a cake at the wedding breakfast, and my aunt Haverweight a guest of honor just to spite her."

Ned gazed back at her adoringly. "My mother wants your money," he said, voice gruff as he pulled her into his arms. "All I want is you."

Averting her eyes—they seemed to have forgotten for the moment that they were not in their own home, but some allowances had to be made—Lily expected to feel the familiar tightness in her chest as she thought of Freddy. But to her surprise, it had eased.

For a moment she was angry with herself. Shouldn't she miss him still? Shouldn't she miss him always?

But she did. It was still there, but quieter, a sad memory instead of a broken heart. Her glance slid to her friends, then back out the window. She had begun to create a life for herself here in London, a life that was all her own. A life that mattered. Freddy would have admired her for that, she knew. He would have been happy for her.

The young couple was recalled to their surroundings—and Lily was saved having to remind them that she was still in the room—by Carstairs' well-timed appearance, a calling card in his hand. "Captain Hartley wishes to see you, Mrs. Adler."

"Oh dear." The words escaped before Lily could stop herself.

"Have you spoken to him since . . . ?" Ofelia trailed off as Lily shook her head. "Oh dear, indeed." Collecting her wraps briskly, she herded Sir Edward efficiently toward the door. "Come along, Ned. We do not want to make things worse."

Lily scowled at her friend. "Coward."

"Practical," Ofelia countered, but she hesitated on the threshold. "You go on, Ned. I am sure the captain will be happy to hear our news, and I need a moment alone with Mrs. Adler."

The young baronet looked at them curiously, but to his credit, he merely bowed. "Shall wait in the hall."

"What is it?" Lily frowned in concern.

"I thought about what you said," Ofelia said quietly. "About trusting Neddy. And . . ." She let her breath out in a rush. "I told him."

Lily was shocked. "About Augustus?"

The girl nodded. "Yes. I told him before we announced our engagement to his family so he could cry off if he wanted." She took a deep breath. "I remembered what you said. And I did not want to be married to someone who needed me to pretend to be someone I am not."

"And here you are."

Ofelia's smile was like a sunrise. "Here I am. I knew that Neddy loved me, but this is . . ."

"To be fully known and fully loved is a wonderful thing," Lily said quietly. "I am glad you have that chance."

Impulsively, Ofelia threw her arms around her friend. "I would not have, had it not been for you, Mrs. Adler. Thank you. For everything."

"Well," said Lily wryly. "Perhaps not for involving you in the investigation of a murder."

"Even for that. Though I think Ned would rather I not make a habit of it." Ofelia's expression grew curious. "May I ask you one question?"

"By all means."

"I thought about it, and you had every right to distrust Ned. I had told him everything, after all. And you did not know him at all, and he had been at the Walters' that night . . . How did you know he was not involved? That he had not . . ." Ofelia shuddered. "Oh, say, found out about Augustus somehow and shot him in a jealous rage?"

"I suppose he could have," Lily said. "But as you said, you had told him everything. Given that, he would have had no reason to harm the general, who was his perfect scapegoat."

"True." Ofelia smiled. "And he and the captain certainly timed their arrival well that last night." Her expression grew sober, and she glanced at the door. "Speaking of . . ."

"Speaking of," Lily agreed. "I suppose I have to deal with him eventually."

"I wish you luck with that." Ofelia shook her head. "Whatever happens, you've a right to be proud of yourself. Don't forget that."

"I shan't," Lily murmured as Ofelia took her leave, but she was already focused on the coming confrontation. By the time Carstairs showed Jack into the parlor, she was perfectly composed—at least on the outside.

"Captain Hartley, madam." The butler bowed. "I'll take your boy to the kitchen, sir."

Lily and Jack eyed each other as the butler discreetly withdrew.

"Your boy?" Lily asked, stalling.

Jack nodded stiffly. "Jem needed a new job, since his last employer got himself shot."

"That was good of you." She meant it—the gesture was exactly the sort of kindness she would have expected of Jack.

"Least I could do."

There was a long, awkward lull. Lily lifted her chin. Jack cleared his throat. Neither wanted to break the silence. But Lily decided, with an inward sigh, that there were some duties a hostess could not escape. And it was probably better to get it over with.

"You are angry with me."

For a moment, Jack looked as though he would explode, but his voice remained quiet. "You are damn right, I am angry."

"I hope you will tell me why."

"Why!" This time he didn't bother keeping his voice down. "Why the devil do you think? You asked that slip of a girl to help you, but not me. You sent me off on a wild-goose chase, knowing full well it meant leaving you in danger!"

"I sent you off on a wild-goose chase so I could catch a murderer." Lily took a shaky breath, trying to gather herself into some semblance of calm. She did owe him an explanation. "It had to be Ofelia staying behind, not you. I knew Miss Harper would not show herself unless she saw you—Jem also, but especially you—tearing off after someone who, as far as she knew, we thought was the one trying to harm me."

"You could have told me." His voice was tight with anger. "I'd have circled back without her seeing and been there to protect you. You should have told me!"

"You'd not have gone if I had, and then I would not have been able to catch her!"

"I know!"

The outburst surprised both of them into silence. For a moment they stared at each other, each breathing heavily, before Lily asked, "You what?"

"I said, I know." Jack raked a hand through his hair. "You were right then, and you are right now. That was what I wanted to tell you."

"It was?" Lily had amassed a mental list of counterarguments for whatever he might throw at her. But his admission caught her completely off guard.

"I had planned to come here and tell you that I understood and you were right." Jack laughed shortly. "But apparently I was still more angry than I realized. So there you are, Lily. I do not like it, but you were right. I'd not have gone. And do you know why?"

"Because you think you owe it to Freddy to look out for me."

"No. Because I owe it to you."

"What?" The conversation was not going at all how she had expected.

"You may be a brilliant woman, Mrs. Adler, but you are not invulnerable. So while you are bashing about, being more clever than everyone else, you need someone—you need a friend—to keep an eye out. After all, what would have happened if I'd not turned up with Mr. Page? Could you have shot Miss Harper?"

"No," Lily admitted. "And there is a very good chance Ofelia would have, however I might have tried to prevent it."

"And you would have had another murder on your hands, only this time you would have been trying to take the blame for it to save your friend."

"Captain—"

"Are we friends, Lily?"

To her annoyance, she blushed. "I have thought that we are."

"Then let us agree to act as friends do. I will listen when you tell me what you need and give you my help when you ask for it. And in return, you will allow me to be at least a little protective, when I think you may need it."

"And when else will I need it, Jack?"

"Oh, from time to time." He looked pleased as he pulled a parcel from his pocket and held it out to her. "After all, if I know you, you have already decided that you want to do it."

"Do what?" Lily took the package, frowning in confusion. "What is this?"

"A peace offering, of sorts. Open it."

Lily unwrapped the parcel to find a stack of crisp, white cards. She was about to protest that she already had her own when she read the engraving. Her lips parted in surprise. "Jack . . ."

"What do you think, Lily?"

She shook her head in disbelief. "I had thought . . . but it really . . . that is . . . do you think I can?" The note in her voice could almost have been called shyness.

"Of course I think so," he said. "You will take London by storm, I've no doubt."

Lily laughed a little breathlessly. "I rather hope not." She tapped the top card. "I would prefer to be more discreet. I could not advertise, of course, but the secret would get around. They always do, in London."

"You like them, then." It was not really a question, but he still looked uncertain.

"I love them. Shall I be called an *adventuress*, do you think?"

"Would that be so terrible?"

Lily considered the idea. "Perhaps not. Curiosity alone would certainly secure me any number of invitations in the next season."

"Freddy would be proud of you."

"Yes," Lily agreed, turning the cards over in her hand. "I rather think he would be." She looked up at her friend and smiled, a broad, genuine smile so different from her usual guarded expression that it completely transformed her face. "But more importantly, Jack, I will be proud of me. And I have begun to suspect that matters even more."

She looked down at the cards in her hand, a neat, crisp stack of white pasteboard, and she could not help smiling in satisfaction as she read them once more.

A Lady of Quality
Enquire by Letter
General Post Office, Old Cavendish-street, London
Discreet Inquiries, Confidential Investigations
& Mysteries Solved

AUTHOR'S NOTE

Writing historical fiction is a tricky combination of searching out the facts and creating the world that serves the story you're telling, no matter what the historical record says. I've done my best to balance both sides of that equation. Critical readers, however, may appreciate knowing a few places where I have and have not tweaked the details.

The Bow Street Runners were a real police force in Georgian England and one of the first professional police forces of the eighteenth and nineteenth centuries. They were founded in 1749 by Henry Fielding, a London magistrate, and attached to the magistrate's office at Nos. 3 and 4, Bow Street. Before this, law enforcement was primarily in the hands of individuals, including local magistrates, who were usually wealthy or prominent local citizens. Anyone who had been the victim of a crime could make an arrest, which would then be handed over to a constable or night watchman. Members of the upper class were likely to handle "justice" on their own, accusing or convicting members of the lower classes without proof and protecting members of their family who had committed crimes in order to avoid scandal. It was also possible for anyone with money to hire private thief-takers to seek out criminals. Thief-takers were often criminals themselves, and whose interests they served usually depended on who paid them the most.

The Bow Street force was intended to change all this, and its members were paid a salary from government funds in order to limit the likelihood that they would accept bribes. (They also disliked the term *runners* and generally referred to themselves as constables or principle officers.) However, many of the original runners were former thief-takers, which led to a sometimes-unsavory reputation for the force that was not always undeserved. Their intrusion into the world of the upper classes was also deeply resented by those who saw themselves as the constables' social superiors. By the time Lily's story begins, the Runners would have been a well-known but not necessarily well-liked fixture. Lord and Lady Walter's dislike of Mr. Page's presence would have been typical of members of their class. Jack's distrust would not have been uncommon for members of the military, who were used to maintaining their own system of justice. Readers may also remember that Isobel Harper mentions her brother paying an "incentive" to encourage the Bow Street investigators to work quickly; this was a common way that members of all classes ensured that their cases received prompt attention. *Tales from Bow Street*, by Joan Lock, is an excellent resource for learning more about the Bow Street Runners.

There was no formal census in nineteenth-century England, so it's impossible to know exactly how many people of color lived alongside their paler counterparts in the British Isles. However, personal accounts and legal records indicate that there were many of them.

This isn't really surprising. Britain traded with, and colonized, countries in East Asia, South Asia, and the Middle East, and men and women from all parts of the world found their way into the cities and ports of England. Many came to England as interpreters, ambassadors, and for business, and there are records of upper-class members of African and Asian nations visiting the British court back into the sixteenth century. Indian sailors, at the time known as lascars, also served in the British navy.

England did participate in the African slave trade, and many members of the English upper classes held slaves in bondage until 1772, when the case of *Somerset v Stewart* was generally understood to abolish slavery in England and Wales, though slaves were still illegally bought and sold in the country. In Scotland, the case of *Knight v Wedderburn* ruled in 1778 that slavery had no basis in Scottish common law. (Slavery in most of the British Empire was suppressed after the Slave Trade Act of 1807 and formally ended by the Slavery Abolition Act of 1833, with the final holdouts of the East India Company, Ceylon, and Helena ending slavery in 1843.) Many former slaves stayed in England after the 1772 case, becoming servants, joining the military, starting businesses, and registering as members of local parishes.

Though people of color could and did live solidly middle-class lives (the middle class itself being a relatively new invention), it would have been more difficult for them to become part of the upper class. However, as Allison Blakely of Boston University has written, there were many children of mixed racial heritage born in Europe in the eighteenth and nineteenth centuries, and many of them went on to become members of the middle and sometimes even upper classes. For this reason, Ofelia and Jack are both mixed-race, with their English families facilitating their entry into Mayfair society. Ofelia herself is inspired partly by Miss Lambe, a mixed-race heiress from the West Indies who appears briefly and tantalizingly in Jane Austen's unfinished novel *Sanditon*. To learn more about people of color living in England in the nineteenth century, I recommend reading *Black London: Life Before Emancipation*, by Gretchen Holbrook Gerzina, and *Representing Mixed Race in Jamaica and England From the Abolition Era to the Present*, by Sara Salih, as well as Hakim Adi's writing on the West African diaspora. The websites Black Past: Remembered and Reclaimed (www.blackpast.org) and People of Color in European Art History (medievalpoc.tumblr.com) are also invaluable resources.

The East India Company is often portrayed as a villain in contemporary media, and with good reason: it was a cultural bulldozer that did immense harm to the people of India. However, there were eras when its members were as interested in integrating themselves with Indian society as they were in asserting British dominance.

Before the Regency era, many British men in India adopted Indian dress, spoke the local languages, and in general tried to blend in with the ruling Mughal class. Many men in the East India Company married Indian wives in legally sanctioned unions. These families would either remain in India or move back to England, where they would mostly integrate into British society. By the 1780s, the wills of more than a third of British men in India left their property and money to Indian wives or children of mixed Anglo-Indian heritage. Colonel James Kirkpatrick, the officer Jack mentions, was the British ambassador at the Court of Hyderabad in 1801 when he married a young Muslim woman named Khair un-Nissa.

By the time Lily is in London, though, the practice of marrying Indian wives was less common than it had been in previous centuries, and mixed families often attempted to integrate themselves fully into British culture while their relatives worked to hide the fact that a mixed marriage had taken place at all. The ability of these children to integrate themselves into British society was, unsurprisingly, largely dependent on skin color, a fact that both Lily and Jack comment on. To learn more about Anglo-Indian families, I recommend William Dalrymple's book *White Mughals: Love and Betrayal in Eighteenth-Century India*.

I tried not to fiddle too much with the facts of race and policing in Lily's London, but the same can't be said for the architecture. Visitors to Half Moon Street will likely notice that there is, in fact, no alley next to number thirteen. Though I could argue that we don't know for sure there *wasn't* an alley in 1815, I don't actually know one way or another what the street looked like. Readers may also wonder if it was common for members of the upper class to have purchased property so close to the site of Regent's Park, as Lord Walter's father did. The answer is that it would have been strange for the Walters not to live in Mayfair or an adjacent neighborhood. But they wouldn't have had room for large gardens there, and if you've come this far, I'm sure you will understand why they needed to have a garden. I promise to make it up to Serena in the future with a new house.

Angelica Catalani was an Italian opera singer who is often called one of the greatest bravura singers of all time. She was incredibly popular in London, but I have played fast and loose with the time she spent there. Madame Catalani made her London debut in 1806 at the King's Theatre in Haymarket and had left London by 1813. She did leave Paris in 1815 after the return of Napoleon, but from there she traveled through Continental Europe, not back to London. I hope she would not mind that I had her give a private performance for Lady Jersey's friends, especially as the audience was so appreciative of her talent.

If you want to learn more about Regency England, there are few books more entertaining than *Georgette Heyer's Regency World*, by Jennifer Kloester. I also recommend *Our Tempestuous Day: A History of Regency England*, by Carolly Erickson.

Finally, I owe one character an apology. Mr. Neve was really a magistrate at the Marlborough Street Magistrates Court, located at 19–21 Great Marlborough Street, in 1815. And I never found any record of him taking bribes relating to his cases. I can only ask his forgiveness and say that if he did, very few of his contemporaries would have judged him for it, as more than one of them did the same.

ACKNOWLEDGMENTS

Though writing often looks like a solitary endeavor, I owe many people a great deal of gratitude for helping this book make its way into your hands:

To my agent Whitney Ross, for her tireless enthusiasm, encouragement, and insight. Having a partner and guide like you is an absolute gift. And to everyone at Irene Goodman Literary Agency for the endless hours of work they do behind the scenes.

To Faith Black Ross, who knew what needed to change even when I wasn't sure. Every book needs a great editor, and I really hit the jackpot with mine.

To the entire team at Crooked Lane Books, especially Chelsey Emmelhainz, Ashley Di Dio, Jenny Chen, Rachel Keith, Melissa Rechter, and Sophie Green. And to Nicole Lecht, who designed the beautiful cover.

To the generous readers who gave their time and insight, particularly Alexander Gillies and Abigail Fine. And especially to Neena Narayanan, the first person other than me to read it cover to cover, long before there was any cover to be seen. Thanks for reading it again before it went out into the world.

To the entire beach crew. You've spent many years watching me write while we're supposed to be on vacation, and your enthusiasm and encouragement (not to mention your ideas for the next one) have meant more to me than you know.

To my parents, Jim and Andrea Schellman, who raised three kids and turned them all into readers, and who believed me when I told them I would write a book one day, even though I was only six years old.

Finally, and with all my heart, to Brian and Oliver.

One of you is the best husband I could ask for and a source of endless support. You were there every time I needed a listening ear, an extra hour to write, a critical eye, or another cup of tea. This book would not have happened without you.

And one of you was absolutely no help at all, but I'm glad you were there for it anyway.